How
    Firm
      a
Foundation

♣ ♣ ♣ ♣ ♣ ♣ ♣ ♣ ♣ ♣ ♣ ♣ ♣ ♣

Books by Patrick Dennis

Auntie Mame
Guestward Ho (*with Barbara Hooton*)
Around the World With Auntie Mame
The Pink Hotel (*with Dorothy Erskine*)
Little Me
Genius
First Lady
The Joyous Season
Tony
How Firm a Foundation

How Firm a Foundation

BY

Patrick Dennis

William Morrow & Company, Inc.

New York 1968

Published simultaneously in Canada by George J. McLeod Limited, Toronto.

Printed in the United States of America.

Library of Congress Catalog Card Number 68–8363

FOR W. McP.

Contents

Part One

♣ ♧ ♣ ♧ ♣ ♧ ♣ ♧ ♣ ♧ ♣ ♧ ♣ ♧ ♣

Part Two

♣ ♧ ♣ ♧ ♣ ♧ ♣ ♧ ♣ ♧ ♣ ♧ ♣ ♧ ♣

Part Three

Part One

♣ ♧ ♣ ♧ ♣ ♧ ♣ ♧ ♣ ♧ ♣ ♧ ♣ ♧ ♣ ♧ ♣

Arrival

♣ ♧ ♣ ♧ ♣ ♧ ♣ ♧ ♣ ♧ ♣ ♧ ♣ ♧ ♣

It was a horrible taxicab. Was it a Kaiser? A Frazer? A Tucker? Young Mr. Smith was not entirely certain, but he knew that it was one of the post-World War II Brave New Brands that had come hopefully and gone ignominiously during his early childhood. Nor had the driver's attempts at interior decoration—leopard plush seat covers, a pair of dirty white baby shoes dangling from the rear-view mirror, a hula doll writhing her pelvis at the back window, a spray of grimy paper roses where the ashtray should have been, and a plastic Jesus wobbling on the dashboard—done much to improve the car. It shuddered and heaved as it crept up the slight incline leading from the village's main street to the highway.

The highway, too, was a disappointment. Nowhere to be seen were the clover leaves, underpasses, and viaducts; the artistic clumps of trees and shrubbery; the discreet signs threatening drastic treatment and severe fines for drivers who sped, drank, or littered, signs which, back home in the Middle West, Mr. Smith had come to accept as the norm. This was a very bleak highway—gray, pitted, and splotched with gooey patches of tar.

The entire trip—a matter, now, of some three hours—had been depressing. The train out of Grand Central Station had smelled like a locker room, had been late, and had had its air conditioning stop dead at 125th Street. In a vast railroad yard at a place called Harmon, Mr. Smith had been forced to change trains and, quite unaided by any employee of the Penn Central System, to wallop everything he possessed from the large express train to a little sort of trolley car, painted red, white, and blue, that stood throbbing impatiently some distance away. Mr. Smith's worldly goods—two suitcases, a foot locker, a portable typewriter, an attaché case, and two heavy cartons of books—had taken up more than their fair share of space and he had been scolded for his lack of consideration even though the train contained no other passenger to be discommoded. From then on the little trolley had stopped at every station along the Hudson River—each drearier, dirtier, and more deserted than the last. When he had finally dismounted, in an avalanche of luggage, at the dreariest, dirtiest, and most deserted station of them all, he could hardly believe that he had traveled less than fifty miles.

In all of Mr. Smith's twenty-five years his contact with the rich had been limited to sharing a room at college with the son of a Michigan motor magnate until the boy had flunked freshman English and been drafted. He hadn't been sure of what to expect from the Fennessey family and their fabulous country estate, but surely something more along the lines of Xanadu than this pokey Hudson Valley village with its gritty railroad station. In vain had he looked for one of the Fennessey limousines to be purring at the curb. No. There had been nothing but this antique taxicab with its driver who had sat at the wheel philosophically picking his teeth while young Mr. Smith loaded his luggage into the cab.

The taxi came now to a crossroads—a liquor store, a dilap-
idated grocery advertising itself as a supermarket, a scaley
old shed that called itself the "Slipper Inn—Dine and
Dance," and a depressing compound of a dozen little lean-tos
known as "Cozy Courts—Showers—TV—Vacancy." It was
the sort of place which Mr. Smith, who had little firsthand
knowledge of such matters, suspected would fill, vacate, and
refill at two-hour intervals every Saturday night and at almost
no other time.

The taxi stalled. "Motherin' heap!" the driver growled.
With a phthisic wheezing and retching the car was coaxed
back to life; a terrible scraping of gears and the taxi darted
forward again. The driver turned at the Cozy Courts onto a
gravel road. At that moment all ugliness was gone.

The hot, humid Hudson Valley temperature of June
dropped ten degrees as the taxi plunged beneath a towering
arch of elms. And then suddenly, set high on a hill, loomed
a vast, crenelated building with a glimpse of the Hudson glit-
tering beyond it. "Why, it looks like a castle on the Rhine,"
Mr. Smith noted with surprise. (He had traveled very little.)

"What's that, Jack?" the driver said.

Like thousands of other young Methodist men named John
Wesley Smith, Mr. Smith had never been called Jack in his
life.

"I said, is that the Fennessey place, Mack?"

"Naw. Yoosta belong to this big railroad president. Dead
now. Kids sold it off to some garmentworkers' union. Nothin'
but a pack of Commies there now, fyask me."

"I . . . did . . . not . . . ask . . . you," John Wesley
Smith said with remarkable control. Not for nothing was he
the only child of the woman who had singlehandedly organ-
ized branches of the League of Women Voters, Planned Par-
enthood, the Anti-Defamation League, a Foreign Affairs dis-
cussion group, a Hundred Great Books Reading Circle, and

a powerful little-theater group in a pokey Midwestern town heretofore interested in nothing beyond bridge, gossip, the Epworth League, and recipes from the *Woman's Home Companion.*

The car raced on and so now did the driver. John Wesley applied his imaginary earplugs. Four years in a college dormitory, two in army barracks, a dozen summers as counselor in various boys' camps, and a year as paying guest of the musical and prolific Haskell family when he taught at Ponsonby had given him plenty of practice at not hearing what he did not wish to hear.

"An' we call that Nigger Heaven," the driver shouted, as they passed an endless stretch of white rail fencing with horses gamboling over an emerald pasture and, at the summit of a rise, a white Greek revival temple, its porticoes, pillars, and pediments gleaming. "Some smart-assed bastard got all these coons convinced he's God and lemme tell ya, Jack, they live high on the hog. Christ, the classa people we got livin' out here now." He leaned out the window and spat. But he did not lean out far enough. John Wesley was caught square in the eye.

The earplug trick broke down completely. John Wesley clenched his fists until his knuckles were white. "Listen, you stupid slob—" But the driver had already launched into a diatribe against a psychiatric group established in the neighboring pink Palladian villa. John Wesley tried to soothe himself by counting the carbuncles on the back of the driver's neck.

Finally there loomed the biggest place of all, surrounded by an undulating wall of brick stretching for miles on either side of the road. Far away at the end of a blue gravel drive far wider and better kept than the public road, John Wesley could see a gloriously sprawling Georgian house.

"And this here's the worst one of the lot. A foundation they call it. Family the name of Fennessey—Irish as Paddy's pig an' richer'n God. Solid-gold faucets in the bathrooms. I know. My cousin Ernie's a plumber in Peekskill an' he told me."

"Then *this* is the Fennessey Foundation?"

"That's what I'm tellin' yuh, Jack. Marble bathtubs. Even the hinges on the terlet seats is gold." The gears shrieked in protest and with a great shuddering and knocking the car lurched up the drive, eventually stopping with a sob, a gasp and a final paroxysm at the massive portico of the Fennessey Foundation.

"I sure hope you ain't comin' for a loan—grant, they call it. There hasn't been a Fennessey livin' here since Chrissmus. They're all in Florida and Europe and their fancy finishing schools while you and me is workin' our asses off to pay for it. . . . Want I should wait?"

"No, thanks. What do I owe you?"

"Eight bucks."

"Eight *dollars?* That's more than the train fare here from New York."

"Just look at all the stuff you got for me to haul. This is a very valuable car."

"It's been ready for the junk heap for the last fifteen years. Now unload my things and be quick about it."

"Hey, who the hell you think you are?"

"I think that I am John Wesley Smith, Director of Projects at the Fennessey Foundation."

The magnificence, the munificence, the beneficence of the Fennesseys and their foundation had been made known to John Wesley and the public some time between his graduating from college and being shipped overseas. In some dusty army training camp, he had come across on page two of *The New York Times* education section a discreet story revealing that a splendid new nonprofit foundation amounting to the not unimpressive sum of one billion dollars had sprung full blown from the brow of Justin Fennessey, nominal head of the Fennessey family. For *The New York Times,* as well as for the amount of money involved, the article had been surprisingly brief—somewhere between six and seven inches in length; too long to be classified as filler but *much* too short to rank with the banner headline whoopdedoo attendant upon, say, the forming of the Ford Foundation. In a style almost academic in its dreariness, the *Times* piece stated that Mr. Justin Fennessey, president and chairman of the board of etc., etc., etc., had announced at a small press conference the transfer of a fund of one billion dollars by the Fennessey family to the Fennessey Foundation for the Furtherance of the Arts and Sciences. A short history of the immense Fennessey fortune had followed as well as the information that details would be released at a later date.

If further details had been announced, John Wesley had not heard them. But he rather liked that. Mother had always told him that truly good deeds were done quietly, almost surreptitiously. Unlike, say, again, the Ford Foundation, the Fennessey Foundation had been most reticent—downright coy—about telling an indifferent world just how and when it went about furthering the arts and sciences. There were no overblown press releases to hog up front pages across the nation, no self-aggrandizing television programs and certainly no breath of scandal. Aside from a fairly obvious fifty-story building constructed on the site of the old Fennessey house on Fifth Avenue and Sixtieth Street, the Fennessey Foundation moved in a mysterious way its wonders to perform. In fact, John Wesley had completely forgotten the existence of a Fennessey Foundation until he was safely back in civilian life.

Armed with an honorable discharge and his M.A. in English, he registered with a number of teachers' agencies to find the first job of his academic career. The pickings were not

exactly lush nor the salaries offered, during a critical short-
age of qualified teachers, impressive. John Wesley narrowed
the field down to three choices: a public high school in Pitts-
burgh, a boarding establishment for semiretarded boys in
Vermont, and Ponsonby College (until quite recently known
as the Misses Ponsonbys' Academy for Young Gentlewomen)
thirty minutes above Manhattan Island. The salary at Ponsonby was appreciably lower than the others, but John Wesley chose it because of a.) the amazing scope offered to a
beginning instructor; b.) the school's proximity to New York
and the theater; and c.) the snow job performed on him by
Ponsonby's president, a carefully vivacious lady recently
emergent from a difficult climacteric.

Ponsonby College was rather reverently spoken of—by
anyone who spoke of it at all—as "excellent . . . excellent
and exclusive." John Wesley soon learned that it was no such
thing. Ponsonby was an old-fashioned finishing school that
had had the *chutzpah* eventually to call itself a "junior college" and then to expand into a four-year liberal arts institution concentrating on flower arranging in "Applied Botany
I" and other basic nonsense. Inclusion in the student body of
a pale, Haitian Negress of undeniable *chicté* had effectively
removed the stigma of "segregated snob school" and all
stumbling blocks toward receiving a cushy federal grant.

In academic circles Ponsonby was known as an idiots' retreat where social butterflies could rest between parties in
town and weekends at Princeton or Yale. With parental consent the girls could—and usually did—flutter off to places
like Palm Beach and Nassau during the inclement winter
months. During his year as an instructor John Wesley arrived
at his seminar in Contemporary Drama (very popular because it involved a field trip to a matinee in New York every
Wednesday and because John Wesley was young, nice-
looking, and single) one cold January day to find the class-

room populated by six girls instead of thirty. And so it remained for the next three weeks until the rest of his students drifted back, garrulously comparing suntans and conquests. When John Wesley righteously suggested flunking the whole class, the president flapped her silvered eyelids in amazement. "Re-ally, Mr. Smith, education is for living and living *is* education." No girl whose tuition was paid had ever been kicked out of Ponsonby for any reason short of pregnancy, and the availability of The Pill had put an end to any such embarrassment as that. With science on her side, the president could—and often did—say that a Ponsonby girl was A Lady.

Ladies or not, John Wesley found them spoiled, empty-headed little baggages with rich fathers and a sort of superficial worldliness that began with knowing the In places to lunch and ended with an inventory of the Way Out places to dance. He grew to dislike and disapprove the Ponsonby girls almost as much as he grew to dislike and disapprove the school itself.

Of all the girls he encountered during his year on the Ponsonby faculty, Deirdre Fennessey irritated him the most. Her father, naturally, was the richest of all the rich fathers and Deirdre was the most spoiled and emptiest-headed of all the little baggages enrolled. She was also the prettiest, in her endless array of cashmere sweaters, provocatively snug; in her countless furs—odd and unlikely things like lynx and leopard and tiger and zebra; beaver, badger, otter, and guanaco. (The various forms of mink appeared later in the year, after Deirdre made her debut and could be considered, at least chronologically, "adult.") The clatter of her gold bracelets, the incessant drone of her conversation in the rear of the classroom drove John Wesley nearly to distraction. When there was silence, he always knew, without bothering to look, that Miss Fennessey was either absent or asleep. On the rare occasions when she turned in a paper, it was a disaster. Her penmanship was so determinedly smart as to be almost entirely illegible—bristling with Greek E's and D's, N's and M's indistinguishable from U's and W's, the F's, G's, J's, Q's, T's, Y's, and Z's slashed with huge diagonal crossings, the I's and J's dotted with O's. And what could be deciphered was unreadable. Miss Fennessey's spelling was abominable and her punctuation nonexistent. But her opinions! After a field trip to a matinee performance of *The Persecution and Assassination of Marat as Performed by the Inmates of the Asylum of Charenton Under the Direction of the Marquis de Sade* Deirdre's report read, "When I tried to go up the isle [*sic*] for an orange aide [sic] a lot of crazy actors bumped into me so I went to Sardi's instead and met Jane Fonda at the next table. It was very interesting."

Too outraged to be amused, he requested that Miss Fennessey be dropped from his classes, if not the entire college. This suggestion was greeted by a goatish glare from the president, the icy reminder that the Fennesseys were a very important family and that Ponsonby College could well use an endowment of any number of millions of dollars which Justin Fennessey might be persuaded to part with. Deirdre stayed on.

When John Wesley, as *the* drama authority of Ponsonby, held tryouts for *Pygmalion,* Miss Fennessey appeared—quite late—in full-length mink, as though she might have been Tallulah Bankhead, to read for the role of Eliza. Out of rancor, John Wesley made her wait until the last, gave her the most difficult scene in the play to read, and sat in the back of the darkened school auditorium ready to cut her off with a terse, "Thank you, Miss Fennessey." Instead he was surprised, even astounded. The girl was good, not that the competition had been overpowering. Presumably unable to read the printed word, Deirdre put the script down and improvised in quite credible Cockney for the better part of ten minutes. There was no question about it. Miss Fennessey won the role hands down. It was only when rehearsals began that she asked, to John Wesley's fury, when they were going to sing the music. The ignorant little trollop assumed she was to be in *My Fair Lady*. She had never even heard of *Pygmalion*, much less George Bernard Shaw.

But once Deirdre discovered just what play she was performing, once she learned the lines as created by G.B.S. and not D.F., she proved to be a hard and willing worker, punctual for rehearsals, amenable to direction, and, in a strangely intuitive way, intelligent. Even so, he failed her in English.

John Wesley was about to sign on at Ponsonby for another year—no better offer having come along—when the letter from the Fennessey Foundation appeared in his mailbox. It offered him what seemed like the earth, the sun, the moon, and the stars. Would John Wesley be at all interested in becoming Director of Projects at the Fennessey Foundation commencing immediately after the school year? Would he be *interested?* What idealistic young man of twenty-five wouldn't be overjoyed to have a fund of one billion dollars to spread around to worthy causes? But there was the rub. Who, in his right mind, would select an undistinguished young instructor from an inane finishing school for such a job? He almost suspected Miss Fennessey of having written the letter herself as retaliation for flunking English. But then the spelling, the punctuation, the grammar of the letter were far beyond her talents in composition. Risking a couple of hard-come-by dollars on a person-to-person call to New York, John Wesley telephoned Justin Fennessey. At least the magic words "Ponsonby College" might get him through to the great man himself. In a surprisingly short time a series of operators, receptionists, secretaries of secretaries, and Mr. Fennessey's secretary were penetrated and Justin Fennessey's voice came chuckling and chortling over the wire. It was no joke. Could John Wesley come in for an interview?

Earnest in blue serge, John Wesley guiltily took a day's sick leave and went to New York for his interview with Justin Fennessey. The interview was almost too easy. He was kept waiting, beneath a Braque, for less than three minutes. Justin Fennessey was most democratic although rather vague as to what John Wesley's exact duties were to be. In the course of the conversation, John Wesley volunteered to help the Fennessey children with a little summer tutoring. The salary offered was rather disappointing—only a hundred dollars more than the inadequate pay offered by Ponsonby—but, as Justin pointed out, it was only for a three-month trial period. After that, a new contract would be forthcoming with an adjusted salary. And what's more, all living expenses—even laundry—were included. Perhaps it was the laundry that won over John Wesley. Anyhow, it was better than pushing a book cart all summer in the library back home or teaching swimming at an insect-infested boys' camp. Loading John Wesley down with a thick packet of exquisitely printed brochures describing the aims of the Fennessey Foundation, Justin Fennessey democratically suggested lunch and even more democratically took him to Horn & Hardart's to eat it. "My favorite spot, Mr. Smith," Justin said more than once. "You get to see the *real* people here." John Wesley rather expected something more along the lines of the Knickerbocker Club, but his admiration for Justin Fennessey's liberal spirit almost made up for his disappointment in the chilly chicken-pot pie.

And so John Wesley Smith, trustworthy, loyal, helpful, friendly, courteous, kind, obedient, cheerful, thrifty, brave, clean, and reverent, signed his ninety-day trial contract and arrived at this opulent manor house to Do Good.

Travis, the butler, let him in, assisted in the task by two

footmen and a feisty little Irish woman named Miss Bridget Rafferty—longish black dress, white hair, blue eyes, and somewhere between sixty and one thousand years old—who greeted him with a speechless bob of the head.

A splendid procession formed in the marble and malachite rotunda to march the length of what was a gallery in every sense of the word. John Wesley had, of course, heard of the Fennessey Collection. Who had not? Now he was to see a fraction of it, a privilege granted to precious few others.

The gallery on the main floor of the Fennessey Foundation was better than a hundred feet long and twenty feet wide, its porphyry floor casually strewn with three Aubusson palace carpets, its walls hung with the larger and older canvases of the collection—Rubens, Velazquez, Reynolds, Titian, Rembrandt, and others who had made the grade before the nineteenth century. The floor above could be reached by a horseshoe staircase, its walls hung with Beauvais tapestries, or an elevator containing a medium-sized Goya. Travis chose the staircase.

The gallery on the bedroom floor was identical to the one below, except that it was devoted to painters of the last hundred years and it was, John Wesley soon learned, in a state of perpetual flux. True, the giants of the age—Sargent, Whistler, Homer, Renoir, Cézanne, Picasso, Van Gogh, Modigliani, Matisse, even Salvador Dali—had achieved a serene security there in their old age. But Justin Fennessey, who had been largely responsible for putting the collection together, had qualms, fits, and starts about the lesser names and the painters likely to go in and out of fashion. No issue of *Apollo*, *Art News*, or *The Connoisseur* arrived without causing an agonized reshuffling of the upper gallery. The merest mention in one of these august journals of the Pre-Raphaelite Brotherhood would cause the uncrating of the most languorous works of Burne-Jones, Millais, and William Holman Hunt. A

critical reappraisal of Sir Edwin Landseer could bring a menagerie of noble watchdogs, virile rams, and stags at bay into
the upper gallery to stare limpidly from their massive frames
until all the fuss was forgotten and another critic had written
a kind word about Marie Laurencin, Orozco, Rivera, Florine
Stettheimer, or any of the other in-and-out-of-fashion painters of recent history. Even the stickiest nudes of Bouguereau
(they had cost practically nothing bought *en bloc* by Justin's
agent in Paris) waited, veiled, in the wings on the off chance
that *some* authority might cast them a friendly nod.

As for the *very* modern—the Pops, the Ops, and the
Blobs—Justin Fennessey was in a perpetual sweat of in-
decision. The sound effects in the Marina Stern canvas made
his blood run cold. But then *Mrs. Kennedy* owned a Stern
and Mrs. Kennedy ought to know. Justin considered Pedro
Friedeberg's meticulous painting entitled *The Immaculate
Conception of the Fennessey Foundation on a Peat Bog in
County Kilkenny* a direct slap in the face. He had bought the
Friedeberg to get it off the market. What if the Hartford or
the Modern or some really *public* museum were to buy it
and, worse, hang it? Still, Justin had been widely congratulated for acquiring the Friedeberg—and so inexpensively.
Andy Warhol's painting of two cans of Fennessey's Kilkenny
Ale was another sore point. No Fennessey really enjoyed recalling the cornerstone of the family's fortune. Still, a Warhol
was a Warhol and no well-rounded collection could afford to
be without one. It hung, next to the Friedeberg, in the most
ill-lit corner of the upper gallery until it could be retired
gracefully to the warehouse with the Pre-Raphaelites and
Barbizons, to be replaced by someone due for reappraisal—a
Bérard, a Vertès, even a Cocteau.

Ducking under a Calder mobile, the parade turned
smartly to the right and continued down another, narrower
corridor, less dramatically lighted and hung with the lesser

works of the lesser moderns and with what Justin Fennessey had been assured was a Miró forgery by Miró himself.

After so much grandeur, the room assigned to John Wesley was something of a letdown. Nothing wrong with it, to be sure, but disappointing withal. It had actually been designated on the building plans as a room for a sort of upper underling—a secretary, a valet, a personal maid, a governess or a nurse; any kind of glorified servant who had to be at his employer's constant beck and call rather than tucked away under the eaves with the rank and file. The room reminded John Wesley of the only hotels he had ever stayed in—clean, comfortable, and inexpensive, but little more. All that distinguished it from the single-and-bath he had occupied in New York the night before was a *very* unfashionable gynecological view of the inside of a gladiolus painted in the thirties by Georgia O'Keeffe.

Averting her gaze from the O'Keeffe, Miss Rafferty said, "There's towels in the bathroom. If there's anything more you're wanting, ring."

John Wesley wondered if he should tip the procession that had convoyed him to his room. He decided against it largely because he had no change. "Thank you," he said.

The butler said, "The others are having tea in the library, sir—too hot on the terrace. It's the first door to the left at the foot of the stairs—between the El Greco and the small Rubens."

"Thank you," John Wesley said again.

"If you're hungry after your trip, I could ask Cook to—"

"Thank you. I have lunched." John Wesley hoped that the statement lent dignity to the tuna fish on toast and milk shake gulped down in Grand Central Station.

"Very well, sir."

The bathroom, while adequate in every way, was not marble, as promised by the taxi driver, but of plain white tile and porcelain, and John Wesley noticed, with only a little twinge of disappointment, that the hinges on the toilet seat were chromium.

Washing his hands and mopping his face with the damp end of an Irish linen towel, John Wesley gave himself a pat and a shake, and resolved to unpack and put his books away right after meeting the rest of the Fennessey Foundation staff and being shown his office. He took a deep breath and made his way down to the library.

Finding it was not easy. Naturally John Wesley had long known the differences between Rubens (fat) and El Greco (thin), but on descending the staircase, his none-too-secure composure was shattered by a maniacal bellow and a smashing of glass from the floor above his own. Taking the wrong turning on the ground floor, he stumbled first into a music room (Regency), then into the stained-glass gloom of a chapel (Gothic), then into a dim, narrow room (early YMCA) occupied by a man in vestments snoring on a cot, and finally into a conservatory (Edwardian) where a footman filling a silver bowl with blooms directed him to the library (late Georgian).

Tea

In the library Peggy O'Neil, secretary to the Executive Director, was knitting—as always—her Siamese-cat eyes cast downward as she rounded off the heel of an Argyle sock. In her three years with the Fennessey Foundation, Peggy had knitted five dresses, three suits, six coats, twelve sweaters, and God only knew how many mufflers and pairs of socks. She gave them away the minute they were finished. Everyone ever connected with the Fennessey Foundation had at least one specimen of Peggy's work.

Mr. Nelson, the male nurse, was, as always, doing needlepoint seats for his dozen nonexistent Chippendale dining chairs. He was on the twelfth now, with only inches to go, and a trifle worried about what to turn to next—a *gros point* carpet to lay under his imaginary dining table, or crewelwork curtains to hang at equally imaginary diningroom windows. And, if so, how many windows and how long and how wide? It was so difficult to decorate a dining room that did not yet exist. Of course old Mr. Fennessey might die, and then . . . But Mr. Nelson knew what would happen then: Another cantankerous old man with his bedpans and catheters and alcohol rubs; another series of boring trips to salubrious places like Florida, Arizona, California, and Maine; another circle of predatory relatives asking how the dear old soul was doing while groaning over the cost of every aspirin tablet required to keep the moribund body alive another day. "A little more tea, please, Travis, and just one more of those de-li-ci-ous water-crest sandwiches. Then I really must run up and see how my poor gentleman is doing. Excuse me, Mr. Earnshaw, I truly didn't mean to interrupt."

If Mr. Nelson, or anyone else with the exception of Justin Fennessey, were ever to speak it would be almost impossible to do so *without* interrupting J. Winstanley Earnshaw, Executive Director of the Fennessey Foundation. Mr. Earnshaw could eat and talk his way through a turkey dinner without ever spilling a morsel or missing a word. Today he was telling the assembled tea party for the hundredth time what a magnificent job J. Winstanley Earnshaw had done of raising funds for a youth group in Wauwatosa, Wisconsin. The story was always the same, only the amount of money acquired changed with each retelling—and it never grew smaller. "Up and coming little city, Wauwatosa, but not accustomed to thinking in really *big* money. So you can imagine what the board said when I dragged in six millions."

"I thought it was five million, Stan," Peggy said. "Nothing more, thank you, Travis, except your foot. I want to be sure that *this* pair is big enough."

"Thank you, Peg, perhaps you're right." Mr. Earnshaw grinned winningly, the laugh lines racing from the corners of his gray eyes up into his gray—*prematurely* gray—crew cut. "But give or take a million, six. I remember at the testimonial banquet they gave for me after the whole campaign was over and the results were in, the mayor of Wauwatosa said, 'Without Stan Earnshaw—' "

"Now you really must excuse me, Mr. Earnshaw," Mr. Nelson said, thrusting his needlework into a baize bag and brushing bits of bright wool from his white trousers. "I must see how our patient is doing. Coming, Father Alonzo?"

"*Mande usted?*" Father Alonzo said. And then he translated: "Wot?" Father Alonzo, a Mexican, had been resident priest in the Fennessey household ever since Miss Genevieve Fennessey had shucked her first husband to become the Marquesa de Mondragon. Father Alonzo, a distant cousin of Chuchu Mondragon, had been especially helpful in arranging Genevieve's papal annulment and second marriage, as well as the purchase of the papal title. Those onerous tasks performed, Father Alonzo felt that he had done enough. For the next twenty years, as spiritual attaché to the Fennessey family, he was more than willing to say mass every day (even if no one attended), to christen various Fennessey grandchildren, and to catechize them—in Spanish. Father Alonzo saw no need to learn English. Spanish and Latin were enough. God was an accomplished linguist and could readily understand what His poor sinners were saying, even if Father Alonzo could not. Just look at the thousands of happy converts in Africa and Asia! Anyhow, it made the semiannual Fennessey confessions—both given and received—much easier for all concerned. A rose window here, an orphanage there made absolution more meaningful. Father Alonzo purred with pride when he considered what good works Genevieve Fennessey's annulment, remarriage, and title had made possible.

"I say," Mr. Nelson said, raising his voice as though he were speaking to someone quite deaf or not entirely bright, "do you wish to visit old Mr. Fennessey?"

"When ee osk for me," Father Alonzo said pointedly. Visit the Sick, Bury the Dead were good enough in their own way. But he had been made only too vividly aware last week, when an emesis basin and a glass of barley water were flung at his retreating back, that old Mr. Fennessey would be easier to handle either comatose or cooled. *"Pobre viejo,"* Father Alonzo added. "Poooor ole monn," he translated. "Ai ouil be in cha-pel."

"Sound asleep," Peggy said without looking up from her knitting.

"Permiso?"

"Sure, pleasant dreams," Peggy said.

"Muchas gracias. Hasta la cena."

Miss O'Neil and Mr. Earnshaw were alone together in the library. It was the hour of the day that Peggy dreaded most. Sometimes she wished for proficiency with harpoon or hatpin instead of the knitting needle.

"Peggy baby," Mr. Earnshaw began, as always, with a low, husky rumble, as though what was to follow concerned peristalsis rather than passion. "I've been doing some tall thinking about *us*—about you and me." Plop! He landed beside her on the tufted leather sofa. Tea on the terrace was much more relaxing, Peggy reflected, because Stan couldn't make quite such a lunge on the wrought-iron furniture—not without breaking every bone in his body.

"Oh, Stan, *will* you come off it! Act your age—or at least half of it."

"I'm not so damned old, Peg."

"Only forty-five, Stan. Easily old enough to be my father."

"Just because my hair is gray doesn't mean that I haven't got plenty of good years ahead of me."

"And plenty of better ones behind you. Don't tell me—I just mailed off the alimony checks to the last two Mrs. Earnshaws. By the way, Stan, I think you're almost overdrawn. Then there are the camp fees for the children and . . ."

"Oh, Peggy, Peggy, P . . ." Mr. Earnshaw's voice became muffled in Peggy's neck.

"Will you please get out of my hair, Stan? I just washed it."

"Ahem!" It was Travis at the library door. Mr. Earnshaw

leapt to attention. He had done two years at West Point—the subject of several dozen often-repeated anecdotes—before flunking out. Peggy could almost hear his shoulder blades snap together, his buttocks compress, the gasp of his diaphragm contracting. A fine figure of a man, she had to admit. He was able to strike this attitude, on and off, for sometimes as long as five minutes a day.

"What is it, Travis?" Mr. Earnshaw said, with just the hint of tolerant annoyance the late Erich von Stroheim might have given a stock Prussian general.

"Mr. Smith is here, sir."

"Mr. Smith? *Smith?*" J. Winstanley Earnshaw gave the name Smith the delivery that might have been expected of Anthony Comstock mouthing words such as sperm, sputum, or spirochete.

"He's our new—uh—Director of Projects, Stan," Peggy said, still counting the stitches in the heel of the sock she was knitting. "Justin Fennessey hired him last week. He was Miss Deidre's English teacher at Ponsonby."

"But . . . but why, why wasn't I told?" Mr. Earnshaw said, his voice a querulous whimper. It made Peggy think of Judith Anderson's thousandth performance of *Medea*.

"It's on your calendar, Stan. I wrote it there myself. In red."

"Impossible!" Mr. Earnshaw stormed. (Who was it now, Basil Rathbone, Maurice Evans, Laurence Olivier?) With a dramatic swirl—the West Point posture was still held and Peggy could almost hear the clank of a sword, the swish of a cape—Mr. Earnshaw marched out of the room to return with his thick, morocco-bound calendar. "You see, Miss O'Neil, there is nothing written down on my agenda for today. *Nothing!*"

Raising her turquoise eyes from her knitting, Peggy took the calendar, blew the dust from its exposed surface, and riffled through it. "You might at least turn the pages once a week, Stan. Here it is. 'John Wesley Smith. Three-fifteen train.' You *could* have sent a car for him. He's here to direct projects—also to get Miss Deirdre and the twins through school."

"Oh, my God, Peg. Why didn't you tell me?"

"I did. You've got it there in writing. In red."

"I would have met his train."

"Quel treat, as the French say."

"Do I look all right?"

"Exquisite as always, Stan. Suck in your gut."

"Really, Peg! *Pas devant les domestiques.*"

"*Merci bien,* Molière. Travis, please ask Mr. Smith to come in. Or would General Earnshaw rather review him on the parade ground?"

J. Winstanley Earnshaw shot out of the room and shot right back in, brandishing a baton of rolled papers. He rattled them portentously, folded them up, and tucked them into the breast pocket of his sport jacket. Their bulk gave him still more chest, if a bit lopsided.

"Well, where *is* this John Wesley Smith?" he asked.

"Perhaps on the toilet, Stan. I really don't know."

The library doors opened.

"How do you do? I'm John Wesley Smith."

Peggy put down her knitting, looked up, smiled, and opened her mouth to speak. A conditioned reflex, she supposed, because before her lips were parted J. Winstanley Earnshaw was into his best West Point stance, pumping John Wesley's hand *and* talking. Peg really should have remembered that Stan always had the first, as well as the last, word.

"Welcome aboard! Trip not too uncomfortable, I hope? Would have been at the station, but a rather important meeting—kept me longer than I'd expected. Room all right?" J. Winstanley Earnshaw had the knack of thinking fast if not profoundly. Peg had to admire that. In the less-than-five minutes that had elapsed between the announcement of John Wesley's arrival and his appearance in the library, Stan had been able to trot (buttocks flabby, shoulders hunched) to his desk, dig out Justin Fennessey's letter concerning the new Director of Projects with its attached résumé, skim over the high points, and speak now with the authority of one who had written a doctoral thesis on the subject of John Wesley Smith.

"Justin—Mr. Fennessey, that is—has spoken to me at some length about you, Mr. Smith. Seems to think very highly of you."

"Thank you."

Peggy looked up round-eyed. "This boy's got guts," she thought, "he was able to get two words in." She resumed her knitting, neatly rounding the bend of a heel, and listened to Mr. Earnshaw rumble on.

"I understand that you were associated with Miss Deirdre Fennessey at Ponsonby. Excellent school—excellent *and* exclusive—and a remarkable girl. Very talented, I believe."

"Very," John Wesley said.

Peggy sighed as Mr. Earnshaw droned on, dropping the names of famous philanthropists, educators and do-gooders whom he might or might not have met. "Rockefeller Foundation . . . Boys' Town . . . Ford Foundation . . . Lady Baden-Powell . . . adult education . . . youth movement . . . advisory capacity to the Peace Corps . . . Sargent and I . . . John McCloy . . . seven million singlehanded in Wauwatosa . . . U.S.O. . . . as I said to Ike . . . American Field Service International Scholarships . . . when the Junior League called me in . . ." Stan's monologues had the hypnotic effect of a record played over and over. Peggy had timed him once. He could speak for exactly four hours and twenty minutes without stopping and without repeating himself, while his glazed auditors bobbed and swayed helplessly, like poplar trees in the monsoon of his eloquence. Peggy had once made the mistake of saying that she envied the deaf, only to have Stan do a half-hour soliloquy on his work with the Lexington School and the wonders of lip reading. But today Stan was not in top fighting form. A cucumber mousse had been served for luncheon. As Stan had said—and often—"I like cucumbers, but cucumbers don't like me. Hahahaha." In the midst of an enlightening anecdote about his work with Mary Pickford and the George Junior Republic, his hand flew to his Adam's apple, his eyes bulged dangerously, his cheeks puffed out like spinnaker sails, his whole body heaved and shuddered. There could be no question about it; Mr. Earnshaw's energies were suddenly engaged in muffling what should have been a thunderous belch. "Excuse me," he gasped. He was too late. His timing seriously off, John Wesley had got the bit between his own teeth.

"Now about my office?"

"Y-your what?"

"My office. I have a lot of books, papers, plans for new projects for the foundation, and there's no place in my room to keep them, so I may just as well get settled in tonight. Then tomorrow . . ."

For once, Mr. Earnshaw was taken aback. "Office? Well now, Smi . . . *John*. And you must call *me* Stan. It's—uh—after five and there's no need—uh—*killing* ourselves today, *is* there, Peggy?"

"I don't know why not, Stan."

"It won't be any trouble," John Wesley said. He did not use first names until he knew people quite well. Up to that point he avoided any form of address. "I can bring the things down from upstairs. I like arranging them myself."

"Well, Justin didn't say just *which* office was, uh—"

"I suppose the office that the last Director of Projects had," John Wesley said.

"*Last* Director of Projects?" Stan gulped.

"Yes. Wherever *he* did his work—interviews, research, study."

"Mr. Smith," Peggy said, "there *wasn't* a Director of Projects before you."

"*Exactly!* That's perfectly correct, Peg. It's a sort of . . . uh . . . new post I created in the interests of— Great Scott! Would you look at the time! Some very important *things* I have to go over before Justin—Mr. Fennessey, that is—and the rest of the family arrive tomorrow. Board meeting, you know." Mr. Earnshaw rose to his feet, told the top of his head to go up, his blades and buttocks to compress. "Don't knock yourself out the first day. Take any questions up with Miss O'Neil. Peggy, uh, you've met Mr. Smith?"

"You haven't given us a chance yet, Stan."

"So sorry. I got carried away showing the ropes to a new—"

"How do you do, Miss O'Neil?"

"Peggy here is our girl Friday. Well, until dinner." J. Winstanley Earnshaw, officer and gentleman, beat a hasty retreat to his bedroom, the Pepto-Bismol and perhaps a shot of Scotch. Oh, *definitely* a shot of Scotch!

John Wesley was accustomed to the vagaries of people in authority—the dean at college, his commanding officer in the army, the president of Ponsonby. He accepted them stoically and with faith in God's Infinite Wisdom. But today he found himself questioning God's Infinite Wisdom in placing a pompous windbag like J. Winstanley Earnshaw at the head of a billion-dollar foundation. "Maybe it's the heat—or the trip," he muttered.

"I'm sorry?" Peggy asked.

"Uh, nothing. Well, as long as there's no office to move into yet, I may as well go upstairs and unpack."

"Yes. Mr. Smith, why don't you? Cocktails at seven-thirty, dinner at eight. And we don't dress."

"Thank you, Miss O'Neil."

"Not at all, Mr. Smith." Watching him march up the gallery, Peggy thought, The poor darling! The poor, innocent baby!

Gramps

♣ ♧ ♣ ♧ ♣ ♧ ♣ ♧ ♣ ♧ ♣ ♧ ♣ ♧ ♣

Dinner was more confusing for John Wesley Smith than any ordeal of the day. Miss O'Neil, crisp, cool and efficient, summoned him to the "small sitting room," as she called it. Could there have been a larger one? He counted two sofas and sixteen chairs. There she introduced him to Father Somebody who was dressed all in black and to a Mr. Someone Else, dressed all in white. Father Whoever spoke no English between "Pliss to mate you" and "Goo' night." The other man barely did, or at least whatever he was talking about made no sense to John Wesley. His entire conversation consisted of mystifying terms like "Aubusson stitch," "*moquette*," "crewel," "Axminster," and, weirdest of all, something about how he'd used some strands of his own hair for "floral shadings," whatever *that* meant. Mr. Earnshaw had carried the whole conversation singlehanded.

The meal itself was good but not hearty. Like many of the very rich, the Fennesseys were not prodigal with food. There was one of everything: one cup of jellied consommé, one slice of chicken, one potato, one perfectly fluted mushroom, one leaf of lettuce, one dollop of lemon ice. Second helpings were not proffered. It required six people to prepare and five people to serve. The silver, the porcelain, the crystal, linen and flowers were exquisite, but hardly nourishing. A family of Sicilian immigrants, improbably invited to the Fennessey dinner table, would have considered the entire meal a sort of unusual antipasto, piled into their car and driven to the nearest pizzeria for the main course.

At ten, when John Wesley rose to say good night, Miss O'Neil said quickly, "Wait. I'll come with you."

Then Mr. Earnshaw—or Stan, as one was supposed to call him—halted in the middle of a long story about establishing a community center somewhere in Texas and said, "Oh, don't go to bed now, Peg o' my heart. Stay and have a nightcap with Stan."

"No thanks, Stan," Miss O'Neil said briskly. "And you'd better not, either. Big day tomorrow. The Fennesseys are coming—*all* of them."

"Then a little moonlight stroll?"

"No thanks. See you in the morning, Stan. Coming, Mr. Smith?"

They walked silently through the upper gallery until they arrived at a door down the corridor from his own. "Here's where I get off," Miss O'Neil said. "Thanks for the protection." Now what did she mean by that, John Wesley wondered.

The day had been stifling and tiring and frustrating and confusing. He didn't know quite what he had expected of the summer quarters of the Fennessey Foundation, but certainly not this. Now he was too tired to sleep. He almost wished that he had taken a cocktail before dinner and a glass of wine at table—even that gentleman of the cloth had put away three glasses of wine and two cognacs. But then he was a Papist.

John Wesley lay beneath his sheet in a small pool of sweat,

wishing that he were uninhibited enough to sleep without pajamas. For some reason he had always imagined that the Hudson River Valley would be delightfully cool. In the winter it was—usually below zero—in the summer temperatures soared into the nineties. In the interest of economy, this bedroom wing had not been air conditioned. It did not, after all, house any of the Fennesseys—only those who served them.

The clock in the stable struck three high chimes and then eleven deep ones. Quarter of twelve. It had been going on like that every fifteen minutes. John Wesley got out of bed, straightened his pajama jacket, and retied the drawstring of his trousers. Perhaps if he stayed out of the bed long enough it would cool down and dry off. He went to the window and sat down in the little chintz-covered easy chair. One leg was shorter than the others and it teetered ominously. A stray puff of air stirred the blinds at the window. John Wesley lifted his nose, like a birdling about to be fed. The breeze was hotter than he was. He tried to force out a yawn, but a ravenous little rattle from deep inside was all that emerged. For the first time since his arrival, he raised the Venetian blinds at his window and looked out and gasped. Below him, the biggest, most beautiful swimming pool he had ever seen glimmered whitely in the moonlight. It looked like the setting for a Roman orgy. Just gazing down at it made him feel cooler. The clock in the stable struck four high notes, twelve low ones.

"Well, why not?" John Wesley asked himself. In the darkness, he stepped out of his pajamas, folded them neatly and laid them at the foot of his bed. Then he wriggled into his bathing trunks, collected a towel and his slightly threadbare dressing gown from the bathroom, and quietly opened the door.

The house was enormous and quite confusing enough by daylight. *Somewhere* he took a wrong turning and found himself at the head of a flight of stairs—not the horseshoe staircase that connected the upper and lower galleries, but a straight, narrow one. Through a glass door at the bottom he saw the swimming pool. Touching the knob he vaguely considered the possibility of watchdogs—ferocious mastiffs, bloodthirsty Doberman pinschers, trained to leap for the throat. Nonsense, he would have heard them earlier.

The pool was even better than it had looked: the water soft, cool and delicious. He emerged, noiseless, as the stable clock struck half past twelve, and patted himself dry with the towel, very gently so as not to destroy the wonderful chill he felt. Then he put on his robe and tiptoed quietly back to the house. But now where were the stairs? He stood in a small, square sort of vestibule with a door in each of its four walls. They were all closed. John Wesley opened one of them, raised his bare foot, and groped for the first step. Nothing. With his hand he felt along the wall for a light switch. He snapped it on and saw that he was standing in a white-tiled kitchen. A place about the size of the kitchen at Ponsonby College. A huge stove gleamed dully from beneath a soaring hood of stainless steel. Near it stood a pair of steel doors which made John Wesley think of the walk-in refrigerator at the Thrif-Tee Meat Market back home, or even the vault at the Prairie National Bank. John Wesley blinked and then blinked again. He was aware of a slight movement. Looking to his right he saw a white-haired man seated at a chopping block, a bottle of beer in one hand, a meat cleaver in the other.

John Wesley opened his mouth to gasp, to yell, to shout the house down. No sound came out.

"Sit down, sonny," the old man said. A flick of the wrist and he had half buried the cleaver in the maple chopping block. "I said, *sit down*." His blunt, bony fingers drummed on the handle of the cleaver. Under the circumstances, John Wesley could think of little to do but obey.

"And why are you shiverin' that way?"

"I-I-I-I'm c-c-c-c-co-o-o-old."

"Cold fer the lova God? On a night like this?"

"I-I've b-been swimming."

The old man considered the answer silently. As he did so, John Wesley—terrified though he was—could not help observing his tablemate. The old man—he must have been sixty, possibly even sixty-five—made him think of the national colors. He had the reddest face, the whitest hair, and the bluest eyes John Wesley had ever seen. He was a burglar, that was it! An alcoholic burglar. But a burglar would hardly go about his nightly business in baby blue pajamas. John Wesley concluded that he was sitting nose-to-nose with an escaped lunatic from one of the Hudson Valley institutions—and a homicidal one at that.

"Good," the old man said, emptying the bottle in a single gulp. "Fennessey's Kilkenny Ale. They don't make nothing near so good in this country, or on the other side nayther. Sonny, run to the cold chest and get us out two bottles."

Gathering his robe around him, John Wesley opened the doors of the cavernous refrigerator and looked inside. It was considerably larger than his bedroom upstairs, which he fervently wished he had never left. Was the crafty old maniac going to lock him inside to freeze to death, or would he simply do him in with one merciful blow of the meat cleaver?

"And be quick about it!"

"Y-yes, sir." Keeping one bare foot against the open door, John Wesley flicked out a trembling hand, grabbed up two bottles of Fennessey's Ale, and leapt awkwardly backward into the dubious safety of the kitchen. With a sigh of relief he slammed the refrigerator doors.

"Clumsy, ain't you?" the old man said dispassionately. "Here, gimme them!" Lifting each bottle to his mouth, he uncapped them with the whitest teeth John Wesley had ever seen. "Never been to dintist in me life. Have you?"

"Several times."

"No true child o' mine. Say, which one are you, anyways? Sure, you're not Desmond. You're not Jenny's Spaniard, and that's a fact. You couldn't be the Christ-killer Martha married. Although, between you an' I an' the gatepost, sonny, Martha was lucky to get even him."

John Wesley hadn't the faintest idea of what he was talking about, but he was in no position to complain. "M-my name is—"

The old man no longer seemed to care. "Here's mud in yer eye, sonny," he said, lifting his bottle. John Wesley had little choice. The icy bottle clinked against his chattering teeth. "The condemned," he thought, "drank a hearty ale. We who are about to die salute you."

"And so now what d'ye think of all this?"

"All . . . this . . . what—uh—sir?"

"All this falderal," the old man said, gesturing around the mammoth kitchen with his bottle. "Fifty thousand dollars it cost. And not a morsel comes out of it that's fit to throw to swine. When I first got married Noreen and me we *lived* in the kitchen—sat in it, ate in it, did the wash in it, scrubbed the kid in it, brewed the beer in it, even cooked in it. Poor as Job's turkey we were then, but there wasn't a meal Noreen ever served—may God rest her pure, sweet soul—that wasn't a banquet compared to the muck they dish out of here. Fennessey Foundation, they call it. I call it Fennessey Damnation." He chortled immoderately at his jest. John Wesley joined in tepidly.

"And have ye seen them pictures? Especially the ones upstairs, sonny. Millions and millions spent on them. And who earned the money, mind you? Millions, sonny, and there ain't a one I couldn't paint better meself with a load on." He chuckled again. The bright blue eyes clouded and took on a dreamy look. "Will I ever forget the time Noreen and me moved to this flat in Brooklyn. Oh, we thought we were up

with all the swells. 'Swills,' *I* called 'em. Well, sonny, nothin'
would do but Noreen—may God rest her pure, sweet soul—
wanted the new kitchen painted, and pink, if ye please. Well,
I'd had a few with the boys at Paddy O'Rourke's—Paddy
was a grand one. So I come totterin' home, three sheets to the
wind, and I says, 'Noreen, me love, *I'll* paint yer kitchen fer
ye. Just you 'tend to the brew.' Oh, she had a temper, Noreen
had—like a Kilkenny cat! Next thing I knew she'd emptied
the whole paint bucket over me head, gave me a shove
ag'inst the wall, and marched off to spend the night with her
sister. Well, sonny, whin I come to I looked at the wall where
she'd pushed me. There it was, a big round pink blob where
me head had struck; and a bigger pinker one where me rump
hit; and down at the bottom a big pink smear where the
bucket landed. And, sonny, there's a big thing upstairs with
three pink daubs on it that don't look near as professional."

John Wesley had to laugh. It sounded exactly like the
heroic Adolph Gottlieb canvas that hung between a Derain
and a Rouault in the upper gallery.

"Those were happy days, son. Happy days long gone,
more's the pity. When I think back to 'em, sometimes I wonder if . . ."

"*Sir!* Whatever are you doing down here . . . ?"

John Wesley spun around in his chair. There stood the
man who had worn white at dinner, now wearing an orange
kimono and a frantic expression.

"Oh, it's you is it, Miss Nelly? Back to your tattin'. Be gone
with you." He raised his arm and John Wesley heard a whiz-
zing sound and a ghastly crash.

"He's killed him," John Wesley thought. "The meat
cleaver!"

"Why, *Mis*-ter . . ."

"Off with ye, Nelly, or next time I'll use *this*."

John Wesley opened his eyes. The crazy old man was

brandishing the cleaver. Dark brown ale and amber foam cascaded down the white tile wall—very much like the Jackson Pollack that hung upstairs, John Wesley thought—a scant inch from where Mr. Nelson stood.

The door flew open and Miss Rafferty burst in, clad in a black wrapper like a monk's robe, with her sparse white hair hanging down her back in a tight little rat's tail of a braid.

"Uncle Frankie! What in the name of our Holy Mother are you doing up at this hour?"

"Out! Out the lot of yez! As for you, Bridget Rafferty—"

"Gramps!" It was Peggy O'Neil standing in the kitchen doorway in a long white robe and looking just a little like a loving mother who has caught her only child in the jam jar.

"Pegeen, darling!"

"Gramps, you promised!"

"Oh, Pegeen love, it was so lonely up there with nobody to talk to but Nelly and her fancy sewin' . . ."

"Mr. Nelson does lovely needlework, Gramps. And you can always come to my room. You know that. So instead, what do you do but—"

"I'll tell you what he does, Miss Peggy," Miss Rafferty said, twitching her thin shoulders indignantly. "He upsets the whole household. That's what he does! No wonder we can't keep help. And would you please look at what himself has been doing: drinking that filthy stuff when Doctor *told* him—"

"Filthy stuff, is it?" the old man roared. "I'd like to know where *you'd* be, Briddy Rafferty—and all the rest of yer meachin' relations—without it. Why, if it wasn't for—"

"You're absolutely right, Gramps, as always," Peggy said. "Now it's very late and I want you to go upstairs with Mr. Nelson and go back to bed. No back talk, just kiss me good night and off you go!"

The old man got to his feet, standing straight as a ramrod.

"There's a dear," Peggy said. "Nighty-night."

"Oh, please do let me help you, Mr.—"

"Take your lily-white hands off me, Nelly, or I'll break you in two." With Mr. Nelson and Miss Rafferty following, the old man left the kitchen.

"Thus the happy hours fly," Peggy said, sitting down at the chopping block.

"Your grandfather?" John Wesley said.

"*My* grandfather? He's been under the sod since I was two years old—and that wasn't yesterday."

"But who was it?"

"Don't you know? You are new around here. That was John Francis Xavier Fennessey, father of the late Terrence, grandfather of Justin, Genevieve, and Desmond, and great-grandfather of—"

"Impossible!" John Wesley gasped. "He's dead."

"Were you at the funeral?"

"W-well no, b-but . . . Why, he'd have to be a hundred years old!"

"How old do you think this specimen is?"

"Sixty. Seventy?"

"He'll be ninety-five in September."

"But he can't be. He's strong as an ox."

"And twice as stubborn. He amazes medical science. He amazes everyone. They used to trot him out for television interviews every birthday. But they stopped at ninety-two when he was cut off the air."

"Why?"

"Well, the poor old darling was having a little prostate trouble at the time—long since repaired—and when they said, 'What have you been doing since your last birthday?' Gramps said, 'Pissing cinders.' " John Wesley blushed purple. "Forgive me, Mr. Smith. I merely quote. But you've got to admit that old Mr. Rockefeller, Henry Ford, Jesse Jones,

George Washington Hill—none of them—ever had half the style that Gramps has. Anyhow, he's much richer."

"And Miss Rafferty?"

"Cousin Briddy? She's his niece, the official poor relation. Uncle Frankie only settled a million dollars on her so she has to watch every penny. And the first one is still in the bank. She's employed by the Fennessey Foundation as house-keeper. 'Custodian' is her actual title."

"And the old man lives here?"

"Up in the Geriatrics Research Clinic on the top floor, bless his heart."

"Why, it's like *Jane Eyre!* And he's stark, staring mad."

"Mr. Smith, we should all be crazy enough to parlay home-brew and hod carrying into a fortune." Peggy picked up John Wesley's bottle. "It's still pretty good ale. My father was devoted to it. In fact, you might say that the Fennesseys brought about the O'Neils' ruin in more ways than one. Frankly, I preferred the *old* label."

"This one is very neat and modern. Smart."

"It's Justin Fennessey's doing. Our art expert. He commissioned Frank Lloyd Wright to design it. Gutenberg wasn't available. The first label was a real gas—all harps and shamrocks with the name printed in Gaelic and a full color picture of the *original* Mrs. Fennessey done up as Kathleen Mavourneen. The young Fennesseys found it infra-dig. Oh, forgive me! *Do* have another."

"Miss O'Neil, I don't drink."

"Around here you'd better learn to—and fast. In fact, there's a lot you've got to learn. Big day tomorrow. The Fennesseys are coming, hurrah, hurrah! Well, good night, Mr. Smith." A swish of her long, white robe and she was gone.

John Wesley got to his feet, went to the enormous refrigerator, and took out another bottle of Fennessey's Kilkenny Ale.

Preparations

♣ ♧ ♣ ♧ ♣ ♧ ♣ ♧ ♣ ♧ ♣ ♧ ♣ ♧ ♣

Shortly after seven o'clock the fountains that fed the swimming pool had been turned on and clear, sparkling water cascaded down a series of white marble plateaus to foam playfully at the deep end. To John Wesley, looking from his bedroom window, the pool seemed mightily tempting, but business was business and besides his stomach was one solid Gordian knot of hunger. A few peafowl—silent because their vocal cords had been scientifically severed in the interests of peace and quiet—strutted about the lawn, pecking irascibly at some equally decorative birds of paradise. John Wesley considered the possibility of catching one, wringing its neck, and devouring it raw.

By eight o'clock, when he ventured out in search of food, the upper corridors seethed with activity. Footmen were dashing everywhere with vases of flowers. Father Alonzo, looking like a mournful crow in his vestments, nodded lugubriously, made the sign of the cross, and passed on. More footmen appeared with more bouquets—not the usual peonies, snapdragons, and gladioli of summer, but rare, exotic, slightly ugly specimens that John Wesley had always associated with the orchid family and sin. Then a terrible thought occurred to him. Old Mr. Fennessey was dead.

Muffling his footsteps, John Wesley descended the horse-shoe stairs. The ground floor was also a turmoil of activity. Men with great, roaring machines were scouring, then drying, then buffing the floors. Big throbbing hoses, coiled like pythons on the rugs, attacked any stray speck of dust, sucking it downward into a vast central vacuum plant. More footmen appeared with more flowers—this time urns with towering clumps of nodding lilies. Preparing for the wake, he supposed.

Approaching the dining room, he tried to look suitably grave. Hunger helped enormously to achieve the effect. But the dining room was empty. The gleaming table was expanded to four times the length it had been the night before. In the exact center stood a mammoth epergne heaped with apples, pears, and grapes. There was no other sign of nourishment. In desperation John Wesley reached out to pluck just one grape, but the fruit was tinted alabaster. He wished then that he had retained more of his college course in comparative religions. Was there to be some sort of elaborate ritual of fasting until such time as the body would be laid to rest?

Travis appeared looking distracted. "Good morning, sir. Enjoy your breakfast, sir?"

"What breakfast?"

"Wasn't it sent to your room, sir?"

John Wesley was shocked. Only illness—and a very grave one—could excuse breakfast in bed.

"You need only telephone the kitchen any time after seven, sir. I'll have something sent up to you immediately."

"And old Mr. Fennessey?"

"The usual; grapefruit, porridge, two three-minute eggs, rolls, orange marmalade, and tea."

"I—I see. Well, if you'll please have the same sent to me."

"Very well, sir. And now if you'll forgive me. The Fennesseys are coming."

Fed, he went downstairs again on the stroke of nine ready to do his first day's work. The house was now still and immaculate, a monument to formal elegance, each petal of each flower as permanent as the alabaster fruit in the dining room. In the library, Miss Rafferty, wearing one white glove, was checking for dust. She gave him a quick, wordless automaton's bob of the head and bustled off, presumably to yet another room. He read *The New York Times*—all of it—glancing often at his watch. Shortly after ten he heard the voices of Miss O'Neil and Mr. Earnshaw echoing in the rotunda and he straightened his tie and hurried, almost running, to report for work.

"Don't ever sneak up behind me like that again, Stan," Miss O'Neil was saying. "I've told you before and I meant it. One word to Justin Fennessey and—"

"Aw, Peggy, I only—"

"G-good morning. I've been waiting in the library."

"Ah! Smith! Good morning! Sleep well, I trust?"

"I was wondering just where to start and on what?"

"Yes. Well, Miss O'Neil will undoubtedly be able to help you. I've got to get into the village. Haircut. The Fennesseys are coming, you know. Big day. Well, *au revoir!*"

He was alone with Miss O'Neil.

"Well now, Miss O'Neil, what do you think I should do first?"

"Do?"

"Yes, *do.*"

"Well, I really don't know, Mr. Smith. The children aren't here yet."

"What children?"

"Why, Miss Deirdre and the twins. Do you ride? Swim? Or perhaps a nice walk?"

"Miss O'Neil, I have been hired as Director of Projects."

She gave him a curious, blue stare. "Uh, Mr. Smith, just what did Justin—Mr. Fennessey, that is—*tell* you that your, uh, duties here would be?"

"Why, looking into new projects for the foundation to sponsor; investigating them; developing new activities for the foundation—that sort of thing."

"And—and the children?"

"Why, naturally, I told Mr. Fennessey that I'd be delighted to help them through the subjects they were failing during the summer. Miss Deirdre Fennessey needs work in English. The boy—Sean, is it?—is failing math and the younger daughter, Shelagh, needs work in French. What I suspect is that they all could use a course in remedial reading."

"I . . . see," Miss O'Neil said in a tone of voice implying that she did not. "Well, the mail is in. You could start with that, maybe. But be careful not to mess up the library. The Fennesseys are coming."

"I know."

Seated at the vast partners' desk in the library, he was confronted with a neat stack of opened letters. "These are all applications for handouts," Peggy said. "I suppose you'd call them grants. You might be interested to read some of them. All the nuts in this world don't live here."

"And what do I do with them?"

"Just read them, if you want to, and give them back to me."

"B-but shouldn't I dictate answers?"

"The answers are all the same. Here. This is it," she said, handing him a sheet of paper.

The paper was like velvet and nearly as thick, the engraving deep and smartly incised.

THE FENNESSEY FOUNDATION
For the Furtherance of the Arts and Sciences
THE FENNESSEY BUILDING
Fifth Avenue at 60th Street
New York   10021
Cable Address: Fennefou

Dear   (name)   :

We have read with interest your letter of (date) .

Your application will be reviewed at the next meeting of the Board of Directors of the Fennessey Foundation. If it receives the approval of the Board, you will hear from us at some future date.

Sincerely yours,

Margaret O'Neil
Assistant to Justin Fennessey

"This letter goes to everyone?"

"It seems to cover almost any exigency. It says nothing very politely. I simply fill in the vital statistics on the electric typewriter."

John Wesley glanced at the letter on the top of the pile. It was an application to view the Fennessey Collection. "But what about a letter like this, asking to see the pictures? Wouldn't it be easier to send a card stating what days the gallery is open to the public?"

"What do you mean 'open to the public'?"

"Well, isn't it like the Frick or the Guggenheim? I mean aren't there days when the public is admitted?"

For once Miss O'Neil's composure seemed to desert her. "Uh—er—Mr. Smith, I have a great deal to do today. The Fennesseys—"

"I know: The Fennesseys are coming. But just one thing: Suppose that I should find in this pile of letters something that seems worthwhile and interesting—worth considering for a grant. What then?"

"It gets the same letter. They all do. Anyway, you probably won't. They're mostly crank letters."

"But *if* I should find something that *isn't* a crank letter?"

"W-well, I guess you'd just mark it for Justin Fennessey's attention and put it on top of the pile. But most of the letters are applications to visit the gallery."

"Do you mean a simple request to look at the pictures has to go before a board of directors? Couldn't we at least send a catalogue?"

"Mr. Smith, the catalogue of the Fennessey Collection retails at two hundred dollars. It was a big Christmas item last year. You'll find it on some of the very best coffee tables. In fact, there's one on *that* coffee table." Sure enough, there it lay, bound in white calf and measuring roughly two feet by three feet. "Full-color plates, text by Justin Fennessey—what there is of it—introduction by the Marqués Jesús de Mondragon y Alonzo. Well, it makes a hell of a doorstop. And now, Mr. Smith, you must excuse me. I'm really very busy. The—"

"Yes, the Fennessey's are coming."

There were seventy letters in all, more than half of them requesting admission to the Fennessey Collection. About the others, Miss O'Neil had been largely correct. Crank letters prevailed. Three different crackpot schemes, laboriously outlined, guaranteed eternal world peace in exchange for grants ranging from one hundred to five million dollars. Four widely diverse religious cults were heard from. A vegetarian, quite overlooking the Fennessey packing interests, put forth the theory that the consumption of meat was the direct cause of blindness, insanity, cancer, syphilis, and war, and requested an annual grant of ten thousand dollars over the next ten years to outlaw the slaughter of animals. There were communications from the intensely erudite as well: someone asking for a grant to finish a thesis on Atonal Music as Originated in Tribal Chants of the Ute Indians. John Wesley wondered if as many as three people, including Ute Indians, could possibly care. An unknown modern-dance group wanted money for choreographing and mounting a ballet which was to take place, as John Wesley interpreted the letter, within the womb of Eve. Etc., etc., etc.

Out of the whole stack, two letters showed indications of real and worthy causes. One came from a priest in Nebraska asking money only for building materials, which had been figured down to the last nail, to add a small library onto an orphanage. Labor, the priest explained, would be forthcoming from the orphanage itself; books could be acquired gradually from other sources. The second letter came from a small, educational television station not a dozen miles from John Wesley's home town. He knew it well. It stood as a sort of torch of culture in a vast, arid prairie. The station needed fifteen hundred dollars to keep going until the end of the year.

Earmarking them for Justin Fennessey's attention, John Wesley commenced writing earnest recommendations in his rather bookkeeperish hand. Only commenced, that is, before he heard footsteps, looked up, and gulped. Here was Miss Fennessey—his students were always "Miss" to him—standing over him in a sort of tight white diaper and two cups that barely contained her breasts. It was worse than naked, really. He felt himself blushing and hoped that it might pass as sunburn.

"So you're the one who's going to bone me up on English this summer?" Deirdre began.

"Among other duties, Miss Fennessey."

"You'll be sorry you ever flunked me." Deirdre knew when she had driven here with the twins this morning that there was to be some sort of tutor this summer. There always was, usually covered with pimples and religious medals. But she had never been told—nor, indeed, ever bothered to ask—the name of this summer's victim. And Deirdre was delighted to see that it was none other than old Smitty. Maybe this summer wouldn't be *quite* so deadly. She had hated every minute of school starting with kindergarten right up through her second year at Ponsonby, if you could count that as a school; had been so indifferent about college that she barely remembered the names of her teachers—not that Smith was so difficult to grasp. But this one she'd really *liked*. And he wasn't exactly decrepit, either.

"Whatcha hanging around this dark hole for?" Deirdre asked, summarily dismissing the certified Georgian grandeur of the room. "Come out and get some sun. Take a swim."

"I'm afraid I can't, Miss Fennessey," John Wesley answered primly. "I'm working."

"On what, for God's sweet sake?" Deirdre bent over the desk to look, her breasts all but escaping their skimpy moorings. John Wesley blushed scarlet.

"On some grants I'm recommending."

"*Grants?* Oh, balls to that! Come on." She gave her bikini a hitch, and titruped out to the pool.

Mr. and Mrs. Justin Fennessey

♣ ♧ ♣ ♧ ♣ ♧ ♣ ♧ ♣ ♧ ♣ ♧ ♣ ♧ ♣

"Justin, do be careful," Lydia Fennessey said to her husband. Honestly, when a man handled a car as badly as Justin did, why did he insist on taking the wheel at all? Lydia knew, all right. It was this democracy bit he was going through, as though the male climacteric weren't enough. Justin wanted to be an ordinary man—and he *was* that, God knew—he just wanted to be one of the gang.

Well, Lydia didn't, thank you. She'd *been* one of the gang for nineteen long, cold years before she'd hooked Justin. And that was more than enough. The next nineteen had been *somewhat* better. Lydia Leach of the regal bearing, the husky voice, and the slightly hawkish profile had played enough great ladies in summer stock to know exactly how it was done. As Mrs. Justin Fennessey she had eagerly contemplated a long, long run in her favorite role—and at considerably more than Equity minimum.

"Justin, the window, please. My hair," Lydia said, raising a Gainsborough hand to her classic Pysche knot.

"You bet, pussykins!" The window slid closed.

"Oh, really, Justin!" You bet, pussykins, indeed! Who did he think he was kidding? Justin was just about as democratic as Queen Victoria and not nearly so amusing. And he never had been. Some people are just *better* being rich and stodgy. Justin was a prime example. During their courtship Lydia always had the discomforting suspicion that Justin might actually be trying to sell her a cemetery plot. Sometimes she wished he had. Crazy Kitty, who'd shared a dressing room at the Winter Garden with Lydia, had probably been right. "Lyd, kid," Kitty had said, gazing philosophically into the cold-cream jar, "if you marry for money you work for it later."

"Justin! Didn't you *see* that blue car?"

"Sorry, pussykins."

"Justin, dear," Lydia began in rich, measured, patient tones as though she were trying to explain to a child how dangerous it can be to play with matches. "With a perfectly good Rolls-Royce sitting up on blocks in New York and Adamson to drive it, why are we risking life and limb jouncing around in this mothering station wagon with 'Fennessey-Oh' painted on the side of it like a Good Humor truck?"

"Aw, honey, you think I want to ride around in the back of some hearse . . ."

"That may be sooner than you think, Justin. *Please* keep your eye on the road."

"Come on, Lyd, let's live a little while there's still time."

"I give it about five minutes at this rate, Justin, and then we'll both be beside the common people—on the next slab in the morgue."

"Relax, honey—'And Leave the Driving to Us!'" Justin Fennessey laughed immoderately, switched on the radio, and bleated along with a rock 'n' roll number.

Lydia could barely contain her irritation. She had trained

long and carefully for her short-lived career in the theater—
voice, diction, mime, movement, ballet (both classical and
jazz), even fencing. Lydia had the pitch of a tuning fork and
here she was sitting next to Justin who at forty-seven, going
on seventy-four, was singing away like a tone-deaf juvenile
delinquent. Up until this democracy thing, Justin wouldn't
have listened to anything newer than Vivaldi. And now here
he was in bright madras singing "Yeh, yeh, yeh!" one quarter
tone off. She wondered if she might not just slap him.

More than once in their life together Lydia had actually
suggested to Justin that she had given up a great career to
marry him, just as she sometimes reminded him that she had
taken Catholic instruction to please him. Her career had
amounted to considerably less than Lydia now believed:
three summers on the straw-hat circuit; two winters seeking
—but not finding—work on Broadway; and her final winter
in a frightful musical comedy in which she did nothing but
stand around looking stately until the middle of the second
act, when she slithered down a flight of stairs to deliver her
one line: "The prince is having a party tonight and you're all
invited!"

Justin Fennessey, fresh from World War II and Georgetown Law School, thought that Lydia Leach slithered down
stairs like nothing on earth. So did Lydia. And she was more
than willing to give up the painted staircase at the Winter
Garden for the more substantial marble one in Justin's mother's house on Fifth Avenue. Time and patience were all that
were necessary before Father Alonzo would grant extreme
unction to Mrs. Fennessey and the house and staircase would
be Lydia's permanent setting. It took more time and patience
than Lydia could have imagined in her wildest dreams.
Meanwhile, not too uncomfortable in the role of a little Park
Avenue bride, she produced Deirdre, to clinch the will, and
—to her horror—the twins three years later as a sort of codi-
cil. While waiting to take her rightful place as *the* Mrs. Fen-

nessey, Lydia contented herself, more or less, with watching Justin acquire dozens of French Impressionist and post-Impressionist paintings and giving boring dinner parties for the boring art critics and curators Justin kept dragging home. All this time Lydia dreamed of her grand entrance down the Fennessey staircase. All of her mother-in-law's murky paintings could be given to some worthy charity. A really sensational stage designer along the lines of Oliver Messel could do over the old Fifth Avenue house to show off Justin's collection. The housewarming would include some amusing people like the Lunts, the Gilbert Millers, and Noël Coward to jazz up Justin's lugubrious herd of art experts. And Lydia would sweep down the staircase wearing . . . wearing . . .

And then what had happened? Lydia had hardly got home from the funeral when the iron ball hit the house on Fifth Avenue to make way for the Fennessey Building and, subsequently, for the Fennessey Foundation. Before Lydia quite knew what was going on, Justin and that wily Irish lawyer, Cornelius Slattery, were talking about tax exemptions, membership corporations, benevolent purposes—words she didn't even understand. It hit Lydia like the iron ball that destroyed the old Fennessey mansion. Before she could marshal her forces and after a lot of mumbo jumbo about New York State income taxes, Lydia found herself living at Fennessey-Oh, a farm, thank you, in Connecticut, surrounded by her late mother-in-law's gloomy paintings and two lousy Utrillos. (Everything chic had gone to the Fennessey Foundation!)

Lydia gave a sharp shriek.

"What's the matter, puss?" Justin said.

"Justin, it's that effing dog!" The Weimaraner bitch on the seat behind her had licked Lydia's neck from nape to Psyche knot with her long, cold pink tongue.

"Poor old Gretchen. She's in heat," Justin said.

"Well, *I'm not*, thank you," Lydia said. "Couldn't you have her spayed or something? She's a sight! All she needs is Romulus and Remus."

"But, pussykins, Gretchen's a prize bitch."

"Don't tell *me*."

Moving out of town was one thing. Settling into Fennessey-Oh with Mrs. Fennessey's grim canvases and, oh yes, Justin's two rotten Utrillos, was another. But the Weimaraners came under the heading of Just Too Much. There was a staircase at Fennessey-Oh, all right: seventeenth century and so steep you could hardly get up it with an alpenstock. But just try to come *down* it without tripping over a dozen stinking Weimaraners all called krautish names like Klaus and Karl and Kunegunde. Lydia didn't know one Weimaraner from another and didn't *want* to. All Lydia knew was that whenever she turned around another litter—and always litters of ten, twelve, fourteen—had arrived. The world had seemed overcrowded enough without Justin's turning into a dog gynecologist and midwife.

"Would you mind, Justin, turning that mothering radio down—or even *off?* I have a splitting headache." Lydia had drunk three gibsons before lunch: one alone while Justin was out in the kennels pimping a wild, sweet coupling between Fritz and Trudi, or whichever; another with Justin in the study, ass-deep in Weimaraners; and a third all by herself while Justin was midwifing Lotte or Lisl or Lydia (Yes, he had even named one of the bitches Lydia, thank you!) through a breech delivery. He had been able to save the whole litter—*just eight!* Now Lydia wished that she had drunk only two gibsons before lunch and had the other one right now. She sighed, the car swerved wildly. One of Justin's fellow men called him a short and very unattractive word.

"Wouldn't you like *me* to take the wheel?"

"I think Gretchen wants to wet, puss."

"I *know* I do."

"Shall we stop?"

"Unless you think Gretchen and I can manage through an open window."

"How about the next Howard Johnson's?"

"No, Justin, *not* the next Howard Johnson's or any other Howard Johnson's. We have *pâté* sandwiches and two splits of cold champagne in the hamper."

"Aw, pussykins, you know how I hate all that fancy stuff. Just a hamburger and—"

"You must force yourself, Justin." For God's sake, Lydia thought, if I'd told him it was liverwurst and beer he'd wolf it down like a—well, like a Weimaraner, and then give me an hour sermon on the joys of the Common Man. "Here's a pretty place, right— *Justin!* Signal when you stop!"

"Sure you want to stop here, puss? There could be bulls. Snakes."

"We'll be a lot safer out of the car than in it. Come, Justin!"

Lydia felt a little better. She'd drunk her own split of champagne and half of Justin's while he'd been raving about the delights of Dr. Pepper, whoever that was. She was back in the station wagon now, behind the wheel, where she intended to remain for the rest of the trip. Justin was loping over the meadow trying to lure Gretchen to his side. So obedient, Weimaraners! Lydia wondered why Justin hadn't thought of raising horses instead. They weren't much larger, they had only one baby at a time and not nearly as often and they'd probably stay out of the house! If she had to live in the country at all, Lydia rather fancied herself striding about in jodhpurs. She'd played a whole act in riding clothes at the summer theater at Ogunquit and looked divine. Or if Justin wanted a *real* tax loss, what about race horses? Lydia could almost see the Fennessey silks—something really chic, emerald and aqua, say.

"Here we are, puss," Justin said, with just a touch of southwestern drawl. "In you get, old girl!" The station wagon rocked dangerously as seventy-five pounds of passionate Weimaraner lumbered into the back seat. Saying something absolutely repulsive about how *pâté de fois gras* smelled like a puppy's breath, Justin got in beside Lydia and she started off.

Lydia thought about her children. She was not a bad mother. She simply would have preferred her offspring to have been born grown-up. She was even beginning to be fond of Deirdre, the eldest. Lydia had always found good nurses, got her children into the best schools, within the bounds of the Fennessey Catholicism (St. David's and the Portsmouth Priory for Sean; various Convents of the Sacred Heart for Shelagh and Deirdre), and had even dared to expose Deirdre to two years at Ponsonby, which was interdenominational, very smart, and not too likely to interfere with a girl's social life. Every summer she had broken her neck to find clean-cut young men from Georgetown and Fordham to tutor the children through whatever subjects they were failing. Lydia had done her damnedest. What more could any mother do?

"Justin," she said, "about the children's tutor . . ."

"Oh, yes, pussykins. Very nice guy. A Protestant," Justin added pregnantly.

"Poor lost soul," Lydia said with an edge to her rich contralto. Really, how could he be such an idiot? What did he think Lydia had been in the days when he was awkwardly trying to get her into the hay—a Druid?

"Name of Smith. He taught Deirdre English at Ponsonby."

Lydia brightened. "Oh! You mean that sort of blondish young man who directed her in the play?" Lydia had given

up the theater permanently and gladly to become Mrs. Justin
Fennessey. She didn't even like to *go* to it very much, attended rarely, and then only to criticize the work of established performers. It had been with the greatest reluctance
last winter that Lydia had climbed into one of her many
good country beiges (mink on the *inside*) and ridden up to
Ponsonby (Justin driving) to see her daughter Deirdre cavorting about in *Pygmalion*. The play, of course, had been
appalling—lots of giggling college girls and the male parts
played by some minty boys from Bard. But Deirdre had been
the most delightful surprise. The girl was actually good, and
Lydia had been even more analytical than usual. Was it maternal pride? No. Lydia had none. Then it had to be Talent;
Quicksilver; the *Spark*—inherited, of course, from Lydia
herself.

"That's the one, puss. He says Dee Dee's a born little
trouper. Now if she can just get through English this summer
and the twins . . ."

Lydia's nostrils quivered. It was the old fire horse smelling
smoke. True, she had forsaken her own career for marriage
and motherhood—the Real Values. But if she had produced
a daughter with the divine gift, would it be *right* not to en-
courage the girl, give her the benefit of her own experience,
ease the way on the rocky road to stardom?

"Mr. What's-his-name . . ."

"Smith. John Wesley Smith, puss."

"Then this Mr. Smith really thinks that Deirdre is more
than just a gifted—uh—amateur?" Lydia loathed amateurs.

"That's what he said to me when I interviewed him. By the
way, we're calling him Director of Projects. Now, about Sean
and Shelagh—"

"Shut up for a minute, Justin, I'm thinking." Thinking, indeed! Lydia's mind had already raced ahead to the most brilliant opening night in theatrical history. Lydia would be

standing beside her daughter on the stage, the bouquets! The
standing ovation! A star is born!

"Dear," Lydia said with husky tenderness, "don't you think
that Deirdre's had about enough of Ponsonby? I mean, it's a
rather sil-ly college and she's no student."

"Puss! Education is—"

"Just a minute, Justin. I was wondering why the Fennessey
Foundation might not just branch out into the *performing*
arts; inject new vitality into the theater or the cinema—even
produce a few worthwhile new works."

Justin Fennessey paled. "Pussykins! Have you any idea
what that would cost? We'd have to pour a perfect fortune
into . . ."

"Isn't that what the Fennessey Foundation is *for,* Justin?"

"W-well, yes, in a manner of speaking . . ."

"Then, darling, don't you feel that when we have an actress of unusual talent right in the family, it would be *wrong*
not to—"

"A Fennessey would have no business being on the stage,
Lydia."

"Justin, that was a very old-fashioned remark." Christ, how
stuffy Justin really was! Lydia drew a deep breath and
paused for one beat. "*Undemocratic!*" Justin leapt like a
trout. Lydia knew that she had struck home. Perhaps this
democracy nonsense would be a bit of a good thing—for the
time being, at least.

"W-well, pussykins, I—I only meant . . ."

"It's too early to decide anything now, Justin," Lydia said
soothingly. "We can discuss it much better in the morning."
She reached out and patted her husband's hairless white
hand.

Jenny

Sra. la Marquesa Genevieve Fennessey de Mondragon y Alonzo drummed her glossy coral nails on her alligator bag and tried not to look out at the ugliness of the highway. If there was anything that Jenny hated it was ugliness. And if there was anything else she hated, it was being called Jenny. Jenny tried to bear in mind that, depending on the language being spoken, she was either Zhan-vyév or Heno-váy-va.

The car had already passed Cold Spring and if that idiot didn't look sharp they'd end up in Wappinger's Falls or worse. The marquesa arranged her coral lips into the position she felt essential for speaking Spanish and touched the lever that would send the glass between her and chauffeur sliding downward. *"A la derecha en la esquina próxima, por favor, Eulalio."*

"Sí, como no, señora," the chauffeur began. It was Eulalio's custom to add a few more totally unnecessary niceties before doing exactly opposite what he had been asked to do. But he was drowned out by a shrill giggle.

"What do you find so amusing, Consuelo?" the marquesa asked.

"Oh, Mummy, when you try to speak Spanish it's so fun-ny."

"Really, dear? In the convent I was considered to have a pure Castilian accent." Thirty years ago Miss Jenny Fennessey had been sent to a very expensive nunnery catering exclusively to the daughters of successful politicians and the granddaughters of wealthy contractors, who formed the Old Guard. Jenny had learned sewing and genuflection and she had abandoned both some time ago. Even so, Jenny felt that she had been a lot better prepared for Real Life than her daughter, Consuelo, the dismaying product of Mexico's most exclusive school for girls.

"Consuelo, darling, Mummy has *asked* you not to fiddle with your lenses."

"But they itch, Mummy."

"Of course they do, darling," said Jenny, adjusting her windowpane sunglasses with the amusing frames. "Dr. Obregon *told* you they would. You just keep them in an hour longer each day until your eyes get accustomed to them. It's as simple as that." My God, how could she, with the vision of a vulture, have given birth to a *mole?*

"And do leave your nose alone, Consuelo. You can't expect the swelling to go down if you continually—"

"But, Mummy, when I wear the contact lenses it makes my nose run and—"

"Well, darling, haven't you a hankie in your bag? Hasn't Mummy told you that a *lady* always carries a fresh *mouchoir?* Here!" The marquesa plunged into her handbag and finding no handkerchief, fresh or otherwise, thrust a wad of Kleenex at her daughter. "Now *gently*, Consuelo. You've just had a very delicate and, I hope, ve-ry successful operation. But you can't expect your nose to take its new shape if you go grabbing at it like a doorknob." Consuelo giggled violently.

"And, darling, *don't* giggle." The marquesa cast a despairing glance at her daughter and tried to draw some consolation from realizing that at least the two black eyes subsequent to Consuelo's recent rhinoplasty had faded away. It didn't help very much. The marquesa made a mental note: "Mustache to be removed."

The marquesa gave a little snort of despair through her own delicate and God-given nostrils. The car hit a bump in the pavement and Luis Fernando stirred from his slumber. The marquesa gazed at her son and felt a little better—the mass of blue-black ringlets, the deeply carved widow's peak, the raven's-wing brows, the apricot flesh, the velvet eyes behind the tangle of glossy lashes. Wouldn't you think that after having had a perfectly beautiful son like Luis Fernando a daughter coming along two years afterward would look at least human?

"Pleasant dreams, my darling?" she said, stroking Luis Fernando's long, thin hand.

Luis Fernando smiled, displaying his two even rows of blue-white teeth, the thrilling parentheses of his dimples. "Sí, *Mamacita*."

"*Mi tesoro!*"

Luis Fernando undid the silver Jockey Club button that held his blazer snugly about his wasp waist and stretched voluptuously. The marquesa felt a little thrill race through her. "Go back to sleep, darling. You must be exhausted. . . . Consuelo, will you *stop* gnawing at your nails!"

Some of us are just born beautiful, she thought. Look at Luis Fernando; look at me; even that slob Chuchu, if he'd do something about his weight. And then the marquesa thought distastefully of her daughters. There were two of them. First —longer ago than the marquesa cared to think—had come

Martha, the only issue of her disastrous first marriage. Martha's father had been the white hope of the Notre Dame backfield, massive, big-boned, florid, and covered with red hair. Divine in a man, the marquesa quite conceded that, but does his *daughter* have to be built like a Mack truck and covered with red hair, too? The idea! How could any girl be Jenny Fennessey's child and then never take her slightly bulbous nose out of a book; go to Radcliffe, of all places; and then run off with a pimply pinko from Harvard? Well, Martha was a lost cause—and so were her children!

The marquesa, touching the firm perfection of her own blonde coiffure, considered once again her youngest. "Consuelo, darling, I wonder how you'd look as a redhead? Mmmmm. No."

"Oh, Mummy!" Consuelo giggled inanely. The marquesa shuddered slightly. Well, unlike her half-sister Martha, Consuelo was no headstrong intellectual. Far from it. Consuelo was probably the only girl in the long history of Mexico sufficiently stupid to flunk out of the Instituto Familiar y Social. But Consuelo would do what she was told to do; not well, perhaps, but at least without a lot of arguing. And if Consuelo couldn't be beautiful, she might be interesting—but not *very* interesting, the marquesa concluded dismally.

The marquesa tried to face the problem of Consuelo realistically and objectively. The nose job, after the swelling subsided, would be a help. At least Consuelo wouldn't look as though she'd been blasted out of the side of Mount Rushmore. Her skin, while swarthy, was rather good. If Consuelo would never have Jenny's magnolia-white complexion, why not go the other way? Throw her into the sun and let her burn to a good Indian brown. Look at Lena Horne! Very effective with all the white debut dresses the marquesa had ordered in New York last week. As for Consuelo's figure, it would be much better after a summer of dieting. And long ball gowns would cover her legs nicely. Consuelo might never be another Brenda Frazier—Jenny's own contemporary—or even another Jenny Fennessey, but she could have a very successful season *if she'd just listen!*

The title would help, too. There were, of course, purists who said that the name Mondragon was as common as pig tracks and the title, a papal one, bought and paid for with the Fennessey money. But these detractors became fewer and farther between each year as Jenny had more and more of her personal possessions embellished with a marquisal coronet. The marquesa was even vaguely aware of certain irreverent young people who spoke of her as "Mom Dragon." But there was nothing she could do about that except ignore it. *Noblesse oblige!* Luis Fernando, as the tall, handsome, older brother, was a decided asset. He could always be used as bait to have Consuelo invited to the better dances. Even Don Jesús, the first Marqués de Mondragon and second Mr. Jenny Fennessey, could be dealt with. The slightest tightening of the purse strings . . .

Twenty years ago, mere hours after her Mexican divorce from Tom Muldoon, Jenny had come across Chuchu Mondragon singing in the seedy Juárez night club she had chosen for an evening of slumming. A certain feral quality in Chuchu had struck a response deep down in Jenny and it was not long before the Fennessey lawyers were boning up on canon law and probing the possibilities of a papal annulment and remarriage beneath the pontifical umbrella, while Jenny, just slightly pregnant with Luis Fernando, shrieked encouragement over the long-distance lines from a little villa for two in Acapulco. Everything had been accomplished in the nick of time and today Jenny wondered why. If it weren't for the title and gorgeous Luis Fernando, she wouldn't have bothered at all. In the two decades following their hasty vows in the lobby of the maternity clinic, Chuchu—Don

Jesús, that is—had gained an average of three pounds a year, so that what had appealed to Jenny most was all but invisible beneath the blubber. And he had cost Jenny a packet, too. In addition to his allowance and two expensive bastardy suits, there had been a couple of dozen ruinous projects; Chez Chuchu, the night club in Mexico City; raising Black Angus cattle in the state of Morelos; importing olive trees from Spain; breeding Eskimo huskies in the sweltering heat of Guerrero—just to mention a few. Jenny could forgive those. They only involved money. But for siring this lump of a Consuelo on her. Never!

Jenny fixed her daughter with a tight little V-shaped smile, intended to be maternal. "It's going to be such a lovely year for you, darling. Gay! I thought a little dance for you out here in the country—sort of a dry run—just before Labor Day. Then into town for the Cotillion, the Cardinal's Ball, the assemblies, and some of the better private parties. Then, of course, your own dance—the big one in town. Consuelo, are you listening?"

"Yes, Mummy." Again the giggle.

"Then back home to Mexico for Epiphany—*la Noche de los Tres Reyes*," she translated considerately, "and your *Mexican* party. Then right after *Semana Santa* we *might* try London," the marquesa added dubiously. Never having cut much ice in London herself, she couldn't quite see Consuelo being the toast of it. "Consuelo, *don't* pick the polish off your nails!"

"Yes, Mummy."

"Mummy wants you to meet some nice boys—girls, too, of course—and—oh, my God!" Jenny leaned forward and rapped furiously on the glass with her big diamond ring. "Eulalio! No! No! No! For God's sake, Consuelo, don't just sit there. *Tell* him! He's gone right past the gate. Tell him to turn around this minute!"

While Consuelo instructed the chauffeur in her slightly silly, singsong Spanish, the marquesa gently stroked Luis Fernando's arm. "Wake up, my darling," she crooned. "We're almost there."

The Playboy of the Western World

♣ ⚜ ♣ ⚜ ♣ ⚜ ♣ ⚜ ♣ ⚜ ♣ ⚜ ♣ ⚜ ♣

It had all been too confusing, the arrivals of various Fennesseys in their various cars with their mountains of luggage.

"Don't let me try to influence you," Peggy had said to John Wesley, "but it may be easier for you if you just lie low somewhere until dinnertime. There'll be all kinds of confusion—kissing, embracing, bullying poor Gramps; all the rest of it. There's nothing for you to do down here anyhow."

Almost sullenly John Wesley had gone to his little bedroom and tried to read. He had not been terribly successful. At five o'clock there was the sound of a small jet. John Wesley thought nothing of it. It came closer and closer and closer and suddenly John Wesley heard it dive. From force of habit John Wesley dived too. The plane flew off and then it dived again. The Fennessey Foundation was being buzzed! Who could be doing it—a jealous Ford, a rancorous Rockefeller? It hardly seemed probable.

Once more the plane dived over the great Georgian house, almost clipping off a chimney pot. This time John Wesley craned his neck and looked out of the window. It was a small, private plane—not so small, really; a Lear jet built for about ten passengers. Several windows away, he could see Miss Rafferty shaking her fist in the general direction of heaven and screaming incoherent curses at "that-black-devil-of-a-Desmond-Fennessey." And then John Wesley heard the jet land a short distance away.

There was a rapping at John Wesley's door. It was Peggy O'Neil.

"Oh, Lord," she said, "it's himself—the Playboy of the Western World, Desmond Adair Fennessey. Look, I suppose this is a silly question, but would you possibly know anything about how to drive a pickup truck?"

"As a matter of fact, yes."

"Then would you be a real prince and give me a lift out to the landing strip? Mrs. Justin and the marquesa have the whole house in such an uproar that there isn't one single available man to drive out and collect Desmond *and* his things."

"Things?"

"Portable bar, folding massage table, cases of liquor, trunks of clothes, golf clubs, polo sticks, perhaps a pony or two. You know, simple things like that. How else would an unencumbered bachelor travel?"

Hidden behind a forest of majestic oaks and a remarkably short distance from the house lay the landing strip. Landing strip, indeed! It was practically an airdrome and nearly as big as the municipal airport in John Wesley's home town. The words "Fennessey Foundation" were spelled out in whitewashed rocks.

"Uh, excuse me," John Wesley said, "but exactly why does the Fennessey Foundation need its own airport—or whatever you call this?"

"For Desmond."

"Desmond?"

"For Desmond Fennessey. He's always in something of a hurry and gets impatient with pokey means of transportation such as cars and trains and commercial airlines. And here comes our boy now."

For some ridiculous reason John Wesley had expected something along the lines of Charles Augustus Lindbergh or Wiley Post to descend from the plane—leather helmet, goggles, puttees and glamour. Instead, a tall, wasp-waisted man dressed, perhaps, for a stroll in St. James's Street, was assisted off the plane by a little brown Filipino who, in his black sack suit and bowler, looked as British as possible under the circumstances.

"Peggy, love," Desmond Fennessey called. "How splendid to see you. I was afraid it might be brother Justin and I am simply not up to facing that before I've had just everything —bath, shave, massage, high colonic, and lots to drink."

"I'd say that you'd already had plenty to drink," Peggy said. "Excuse me. Mr. Desmond Fennessey, this is Mr. Smith."

"*Enchanté*," Desmond said, stretching out his hand. "I was lunching with some frightfully amusing people in Detroit. Remarkably smooth trip." He swayed alarmingly.

"It must have been a remarkably smooth lunch, too," Peggy said. "Really, Desmond, do you have to get yourself into this condition *every* day?"

"Not every day, Peggy love. But on those rare days when one must reconvene with Justin, Lydia, Jenny, *Grandpère*, Cousin Briddy—the Fennesseys in general—a certain amount of anesthesia is advisable. What a chic car! Is Justin the Man of the People, Justin the Rail Splitter, now driving a truck?" Desmond lurched against John Wesley. "So sorry, old man. I was lunching with some frightfully amusing people in Detroit and . . ." And Desmond said no more.

At the house Desmond Fennessey was assisted out of the pickup truck by Travis, two footmen, and his valet. "Thanks," Peggy said to John Wesley. "Don't worry about all of his gear in back. The men can take care of that."

"I'm more worried about Mr. Fennessey. Does he drink like this every day?"

"Yes. But don't be. Two Alka-Seltzers in vodka and he'll be his dear, sweet self again."

"I can't believe it."

"It's a big cure in Desmond's set. The Alka-Seltzer is to take care of what he's drunk already and the vodka is to give him a start on what's ahead."

"But he can barely walk now."

"Just wait. Just wait until dinner."

Reunion

If his first night at the summer quarters of the Fennessey Foundation had seemed confusing to John Wesley, it was nothing as compared to the second. The Fennesseys—or most of them—had, indeed, arrived.

John Wesley appeared in the large drawing room (French; four sofas, thirty chairs) at the cocktail hour to find it empty, save for the aristocratic Mrs. Justin Fennessey. Lydia would have preferred to have made an entrance—if possible, by descending the stairs—but, on the whole, she was not displeased. Lydia's downward entrances really called for an audience of more than one and just now everyone else was at some sort of mass of thanksgiving which Justin had arranged with Father Alonzo. Whenever the Fennesseys congregated prayers at first fell hot and heavy in the hotter and heavier little chapel. After a day or two, more amusing diversions, such as violent quarrels, occupied their attention. Lydia had been in her bath when Justin had announced this big revival meeting, or whatever it was. Naturally it would have been rude—sacrilegious—to have arrived in the chapel late. Better not to go at all. Much better. And now this not unattractive young man had discovered her seated alone in the drawing room; yards of *café au lait* chiffon spilling over the sides of a putty-colored *fauteuil*, a calf-bound copy of *The Prophet* lying on her lap and Gretchen dozing at her feet. The color scheme was divine. Subtle. And Lydia might just get a few ladylike licks in before that garish Jenny clattered in wearing one of her shrieking Acapulco prints.

"Mr. Smith," Lydia said, in her Great Lady Voice, "how frightfully nice to see you agayne."

"G-good evening," John Wesley said. In the wilderness of French furniture he looked for a place to sit—not too near and yet not too pointedly far away from the terrifying grandeur of Lydia.

"Right here beside me," Lydia said, "and we'll have a nice little chin. Get to know each other. Really well, I hope." That line, Lydia believed, came from an old Philip Barry play she had done one summer at Woonsocket. Or had it been something by Rachel Crothers at Canal Fulton? "You're interested in the theatah, I believe?"

"Very."

"How nice. So am I. I even have a little confession to make." A tinkling, Baccarat laugh. "*I* had a brief fling on the stage myself when I was just a girl."

"Really, Mrs. Fennessey?" Society, John Wesley had always believed, rarely performed.

"Yes. Really. Of course Mummy was furious." Mummy—she was called Mom in those days, just as Lydia was known as Lena—had, indeed, been as sore as a crab. What was the big idea of Lena's play-acting around the East when she should have been back home in Michigan helping around the lunchroom at the height of the tourist season? "But it was such a lark!" And now Lydia began to drop, one by one, some of the biggest theatrical names who had played with her. As there had been at least one visiting star each week, it made an impressive catalogue. Lydia was merely careful not to mention any star who was dead or past the age of sixty. She was on the sunny side of forty—just—and not anxious to place herself in a category with, say, Sarah Bernhardt.

John Wesley leaned forward attentively. "It must have been fascinating to have known all those famous stars," he said. Lydia sensed that he had been about to add " 'way back then." She did not so much change as *shift* the subject.

"Oh, nonsense. They had no time for silly little me." That had been true. None of them had been more than civil to an importunate little summer apprentice twenty years ago. Today even the biggest of them had all the time in the world for Mrs. Justin Fennessey if Lydia would even bother to bother. On the whole, Lydia now found them more interesting to talk about than to talk to. "Yes. Just an eager little amateur. Like Deirdre."

"Deirdre—Miss Fennessey, that is—is a good deal more than just an eager little amateur, Mrs. Fennessey."

"Truly, Mr. Smith?" Now things were taking a turn for the better. In less than ten minutes she had got the conversation right around to where she wanted it. She tried on an expression of puzzled concern. "Then you think that Deirdre might be . . . serious . . . about a career in the theater; that this is more than just a passing phase?"

"She has a lot of power, a lot of talent. Although she lacks discipline," John Wesley added with a certain air of disapproval.

"Hmmmmmm."

"Of course it's possible that you and Mr. Fennessey might not want her to go on the stage. It's no life for a girl who's used to . . . well, to all this. I mean a girl with wealth and social position . . ."

Lydia smiled charmingly. "I don't agree at all, Mr. Smith." Twenty years ago Lydia had been in perfect accord. As an unemployed young hopeful, with one good black suit and two pairs of nylons, she had feared and hated those confident, comfortable, well-dressed girls from the faraway world of Wealth and Society who were competing with her. It just wasn't *fair!* Today Lydia could be more liberal. As a landmark in that World of Wealth and Society, Lydia saw nothing wrong with a girl who had had the Advantages going out and landing a job on the stage—especially if that girl happened to be her own daughter. "No. I truly don't. I want my children to know what life is like. I mean *real* life. Not just the silly little debutante's existence that I led as a girl."

John Wesley beamed with approval. From the floor at Lydia's feet, Gretchen broke wind eloquently. John Wesley blushed crimson. Lydia touched her pearls and tried to continue. For Christ's sake, hadn't she once played the whole last act of *Easy Virtue* in a tent with Connie Bennett during a hurricane? But somehow the magic was gone. Really, that effing dog! And now Lydia heard the rest of them charging from the chapel as though it were on fire!

"We must talk about this agayne, Mr. Smith. I think we shan't mention it to Justin just yet, but I have plans, Mr. Smith. Plans for Deirdre and for the theatah *and for you.*"

And now the room rang with the voices of more Fennesseys. The Marquesa de Mondragon y Alonzo, wearing persimmon pajamas, appeared first on the arm of her brother Desmond. If any two Fennesseys could be said to like one another, the closest were Jenny and Desmond, who formed a sort of armed alliance against the dreariness of Justin.

"Lydia!" Jenny cried.

"Jenny! Darling! And Desmond!"

Kisses.

Then Lydia decided to take over. Jenny—really, those pajamas!—might have been born a Fennessey and bought a marquisate, but Lydia had married Justin and could rightfully be known as First Lady of the Fennessey Family. God knew she'd earned it. "Mr. Smith," Lydia said, "I wonder if you've met my sister-in-law Je . . ."

"The Marquesa de Mondragon," Jenny said, stretching out a limp hand. That ex-chorus girl had already called her Jenny once tonight and that was enough.

"H-how do you do?" John Wesley said. It was his custom to give any female's outstretched hand a firm but gentle squeeze. Yet here was the marquesa's held at shoulder height, as though she were about to dance a minuet. He wondered if he ought to kiss it, as he had seen J. Winstanley Earnshaw do in the driveway this evening. John Wesley had had no past experience with the hands of nobility. He decided instead to compromise and bow very low over the marquesa's wrist. The gesture would probably have gone smoothly had not Gretchen, thoroughly awakened by Jenny's clangorous arrival, decided to get to her feet and investigate him. John Wesley, feeling a sudden prod at his rear end, leapt like a trout, all but diving into the marquesa's décolletage.

"Oooof!" John Wesley heard himself saying.

"Honestly, Lydia," Jenny said, "does Justin still keep those obscene German dogs?"

"What's this about your big brother?" It was Justin Fennessey at the drawing-room door with J. Stanley Earnshaw hot on his heels. "Well! John Wesley Smith, as I live and breathe!" He strode boyishly across the room, his right hand outstretched. There was a sharp yelp from Gretchen. "Aw! Did Daddy step on his little mommy-dog's paw?"

"Justin," Lydia said, "will you please get that bitch out of here?"

Both John Wesley and Jenny wheeled. And then both realized what Lydia was talking about.

"But, pussykins, Gretchen's in heat."

"And she's also in the way. Sean! Shelagh!" Lydia called.

Two adolescents appeared at the doorway. John Wesley recognized them immediately as Justin Fennessey's twin children. They had the misfortune to resemble their father. "Darlings," Lydia said smoothly. "Will you please take Gretchen out and give her to somebody?"

"Give her to somebody?" Shelagh said.

"To one of the servants, dear. And ask him to lock her up in the stable."

"Oh, poor old Gretchen," Justin said.

"*Right now*," Lydia said. "And then come back in and meet your . . . meet Mr. Smith."

My God, Jenny thought, the airs and graces that two-bit hoofer gives herself! She's really mother superior. And of all the blah little getups! Almost as dreary as that gray quaker costume she wore when Jus brought her home to meet Mamma. She'll never have any flair if she tries for a million years. Aloud Jenny said, "That's a divine outfit, Lydia."

"Thank you, darling," Lydia said. Thank you and that's all. Torture couldn't get Lydia to compromise her principles enough to make any comment—other than adverse—on Jenny's pajamas. Jenny was five—no, *six*—years older than Lydia. Lydia could remember back to Mackinaw City when she was a scrawny twelve-year-old looking at magazine pictures of the high life in New York. There had been Miss Genevieve Fennessey lunching at Armando's, page-boy bob hanging to her rump, a silver fox chubby with Superman shoulders, and a spray of orchids. Tacky, tacky, tacky! And would you please look at her now—more like a retired madam every day, right down to the Jungle Gardenia perfume. And the hair! Oh, dear God, Jenny's hair! Does she or doesn't she? Well, you'd have to be groping around town with a tin cup and a white cane not to know for sure. "And how is Chuchu, Jenny?"

"Do you mean Don Jesús, Lydia?"

"Yes, Jenny. I mean Chuchu."

"Well, de-ar, Don Jesús is ra-ther worried. It's Luis Fernando. You know he's only twenty and he's taken to running around with this little actress and—"

"Is anyone for a drink?" Desmond asked. Desmond enjoyed watching the two sisters-in-law going at one another—for a short time. After the first thousand dagger thrusts it got boring, just like anything else.

"Say, Dez," Justin roared, as though his brother had just stumbled upon the law of gravity, "that's a *great* idea! What do you think, Stan?"

"Oh, I've never said no to a drop of the creature, Justin. Heheheh. I'll just ring for one of the men." Stan all but sprinted to the bell.

"I think a claret lemonade sounds good. How does that strike everyone?"

"Right in the solar plexus, thank you, Justin," Lydia said. "I'd like a double gibson made with Tanqueray gin."

"And so would I," Jenny said, for once seeing eye to eye with her sister-in-law. As John Wesley really didn't know the difference, he said that that sounded good.

Before the drinks arrived, so did some more Fennesseys. Luis Fernando, in a silvery silk suit reminiscent of both race track and bull ring, slithered in like a clothes-conscious cobra and gave John Wesley lessons in how women's hands *ought* to be kissed. "*Mon image,*" he groaned over his mother's wrist, "*ma tante,*" over Lydia's cluster of diamonds. Miss Peggy O'Neil, unmarried, received only a respectful bow with an audible clicking of the heels, Miss Bridget Rafferty an unconnected kiss on each cheek. Consuelo's entrance was less polished but more noteworthy. She wore, like her mother, pajamas, but cut almost to the waist in front. She giggled at

the doorway, tripped over the edge of the rug and fell head-
long into John Wesley's arms. She giggled again.

Miss Rafferty crossed herself. Peggy O'Neil emitted "Oi
veh!" under her breath.

"Poor Consuelo," Lydia said. "I don't blame you, dear.
Those heels are impractical for such a big girl."

"Consuelo, darling," Jenny said levelly. "Those pajamas."

"You told me to put them on, Mummy."

"But I didn't tell you to put them on backward, did I?
Why don't you just slip up to your room and change into
something else?"

"Yes, I think you should, Consuelo," Lydia said sweetly.
"The color is a little . . . uh . . . dominating." Deirdre, on
the other hand, looked divine, Lydia thought. Even if her
skirt was too short.

Consuelo hobbled out as Travis appeared, followed by a
footman pushing what amounted to a chuck wagon covered
with decanters. Justin bolted across the room. He grasped
the footman's right hand and pumped it violently. "Winston!
Good to see you again! How's your mother?" The footman
looked confused and tried to break free. No success. "These
men have been with us for so long," Justin explained to John
Wesley, "that they're just like my own children."

"Well, Dad," Deirdre said, "I think you ought to know that
Winston left two years ago."

"Yes, Mr. Fennessey," Peggy O'Neil said. "This one is
named Charles. He started last week."

"Oh," Justin said. "Well, welcome aboard anyhow. *Now!*
Who's having what?"

After an almost impossible amount of time and confusion,
the right drinks reached the right hands. Desmond, Jenny,
Lydia, and Stan had each finished theirs before Justin had
bumbled his way through the orders. One sip and John Wesley thought that he had been anesthetized. Eventually every-

one had a more or less full glass at more or less the same time. Justin Fennessey rose, stepped to the center of the room, and smiled, he hoped boyishly. "Folks," Justin said. Lydia and Desmond exchanged a glance of despair. The word sounded so democratic, so folksy, that Justin tried it on again. "Folks, it's been six long months since this big happy family has been together . . ."

"Not long enough," Jenny sighed. Desmond snickered.

"We've just had a little powwow of thanks to the Boss Man Upstairs . . ."

"Justin, really," Lydia said. A few homely, wholesome words from Justin could often serve to unite the most antipathetic of the Fennesseys as effectively as some impending disaster such as an earthquake or financial ruin.

"Begging your pardons, Padre, Cousin Briddy." Miss Rafferty had not been listening. Father Alonzo had, most attentively. But he hadn't understood Justin's first word.

"And now, folks, I think it's high time to hoist our glasses to *another* wonderful Man Upstairs—dear old Gramps."

"Hear! Hear!" Mr. Earnshaw said, hopefully lifting his glass. But Justin was far from finished.

"Grandpa wanted so much to be down here with all his kids tonight. But I'm afraid it just wasn't possible. He—" The great house shook with a terrible crash from above. Peggy O'Neil wondered just which Man Upstairs could have caused it. She was pretty sure that she knew.

Undaunted, Justin plunged on. "First thing I always do when I get here is rush up to the top floor to see if that wonderful old guy is still with his kids' kids and *their* kids. I guess we all do."

"We all damned well have to," Desmond muttered. Deirdre went off into a small storm of sniggers.

"And this evening when I said to him, 'Gramps, howsabout putting on the feed bag with your folks tonight?' well, let me tell you: Tears came to those fine old blue eyes of his and he said, 'Sonny,'—he always calls me 'sonny'—" (It occurred to John Wesley that old Mr. Fennessey always called *everyone* "sonny.") "—he said, 'Sonny, I'd love to. But the old ticker just won't allow me to come downstairs and sit at the head of the table with my happy family. But tell 'em that their grandpa said "Bless you all." ' "

A four-letter word formed on Peggy's lips. Another fearful crash from the top floor quite put it out of her mind.

A little louder than before, Justin continued: "We've all got to bear in mind that dear old Gramps is in his ninety-fifth summer and I'm afraid that he's not going to be with us very much longer." He paused dramatically, swallowed, and paused again.

But Justin had by no means cornered the dramatics market, not in that room full of star performers. Lydia, recalling her brilliant work as a walk-on in some far distant revival of *La dame aux camélias,* clutched the wire and foam rubber of her left breast, drew her fine, full brows into a *circonflexe* of anguish over her imperious beak of a nose. Not to be outdone, Jenny forced her own hairline eyebrows into two Spanish *tildes,* as though her forehead were spelling out *ñoño.* J. Winstanley Earnshaw tried, with moderate success, the old West Point trick of sitting so erect that he could turn his head all the way to the right without wrinkling his jacket. The final effect fell somewhere between his intended look of noble suffering and that of a slipped disc. Desmond sighed, deeply and profoundly, whether from emotion or boredom no one could tell. Luis Fernando allowed his feathery lashes to lower to his cheekbones, pausing briefly to take in his cousin Deirdre's feet and ankles. He wondered if she slept around, as all gringas did, except for his sainted mother. Father Alonzo, who hadn't the faintest idea what Señor Hoosteen was going on so about, also closed his eyes. Owing to the onslaught of Fennesseys, he had missed his siesta. Deirdre cast a veiled glance at John Wesley and speculated on what romantic possibilities, if any, might present themselves here in Drearsville. John Wesley blushed—not because of what Deirdre was thinking but because Justin's ranting was really less embarrassing to endure than this moment of deathly silence. The twins looked at John Wesley and then at one another. A push-over, they agreed. Miss Rafferty moaned, nothing more. Peggy, ever so softly, said the four-letter word.

The reverent hush was shattered by Consuelo, who entered, tripping, with Mr. Nelson at her heels, and spouting Spanish. "*Mamá! Mamacita! El viejo loco arriba—*"

"*Consuelo, amor, habla usted en el inglés, por favor,*" Jenny said in her mangled Spanish. (Even in bed she had never mastered the familiar form.)

"I've come to say—" Mr. Nelson burst out indignantly, brandishing one of his needle-point seat covers.

"Mummy, there's this crazy old man upstairs throwing things all over the place—"

"Can you be speaking of your great-grandfather, Consuelo?" Lydia asked in a tone implying hurt, shock, and disapproval.

"He says the house is full of bead-fumbling vu-vultures and he'd rather eat with pigs," Consuelo shrieked.

"Mr. Nelson," Justin said, thrusting out a democratic hand, "tell me, is there anything wrong with Grandpa?"

"Nothing," Mr. Nelson snapped, ignoring the outstretched hand and holding up the needle point, "except that he's the meanest old mick ever to draw the breath of life. The old bastard just peed all over my needle point. On purpose, too."

The twins collapsed into giggles, Consuelo into a fit of hysterical weeping.

"Mr. Nelson," Justin began, in a tone that managed to be

at one and the same time kindly yet firm, "you are speaking
of our grandfather—"

"That's your hard luck, dearie, not mine!"

"—a nonagenarian. A poor old man with only weeks, days,
perhaps hours to live—"

"That's what I've been hoping, too. No such luck, Mr. Fennessey. That old devil will outlast me and all the rest of—"

Another roar and a crash from above.

"Mother o' God," gasped Miss Rafferty, blessing herself.
"I'd best go up and see to Uncle Frankie."

"Maybe I'd better do it," Peggy said. "Don't hold dinner
for me, please. And, Mr. Nelson, why don't you take the
night off?"

The conversation after that was somewhat strained.

Office Hours

♣ ⚘ ♣ ⚘ ♣ ⚘ ♣ ⚘ ♣ ⚘ ♣ ⚘ ♣ ⚘ ♣ ⚘ ♣

Even with so many Fennesseys in residence, the night had been quiet. John Wesley was conscious of the striking of the stable clock only three or four times, and with it the howling of a dog. That large, silver creature with the ghostly eyes, he supposed. He rose at seven, shaved, showered, and went uninhibitedly down to the pool to swim the equivalent of a mile as violently as possible. Then he ordered a lumberjack's breakfast, surreptitiously buttering all the left-over rolls, wrapping them in Kleenex, and filing them away with his shirts to soothe the pangs of hunger which he had already learned would strike shortly after luncheon and again during the night. (The maids grumbled a great deal about crumbs in the dresser drawers, but all Fennessey guests did it—or went hungry.)

At nine, in the still, flawless library, John Wesley sat waiting to go to work. And waiting is just what he did. Save for the company of *The New York Times* and an occasional passing servant, he was quite alone for the next hour. At ten-fifteen Miss Rafferty, without so much as a nod in his direction, marched through the room on her endless quest for a mote of dust and out again, her single glove still virginally white.

A few seconds later John Wesley's ear was pierced by one of Miss Rafferty's shrillest screams followed by the sounds of scuffling. "Oh! Oh, get off of me! Oh, stop it, you filthy thing!"

He rushed into the gallery and found Miss Rafferty, not in the embrace of a Jack the Ripper but of Gretchen, the passionate Weimaraner, paws on Miss Rafferty's shoulders and tongue hungrily lapping at her face. A vision of Leda and the Swan flashed through John Wesley's mind.

"Justin!" she shrieked. "Where are you? Get that dirty dog outta here! The help's just cleaned. Oh. Oh! *Oh!*"

"She's just affectionate, Cousin Briddy." Justin's voice, full of chuckles, came from around the corner. "Aren't you, Gretchen? Here, girl."

Gretchen responded only to the extent that she jumped off Miss Rafferty, who instantly fled, and raced, slipping and sliding on the porphyry floors, the length of the gallery to bury her snout ecstatically between John Wesley's legs. Prying her loose, he gave her silver coat a tentative distasteful pat and quickly withdrew his hand. It smelled very bad. Gretchen had obviously been rolling in something awful.

"Here, Gretchen! Heel, baby!" Justin Fennessey appeared in country costume—Bermuda shorts, a pink button-down shirt, and a jaunty pink linen cap. The total effect was one of a very large child all dressed up for a Beautiful Baby Contest. (There was no reason to hope that he would win.) Try as he would, John Wesley could not tear his eyes from Justin's white, hairless, old-lady legs; the dimpled knees; the plump calves; the ankles swelling slightly over tasseled moccasins. No question about it—that generation's looks had gone to Desmond and the marquesa.

"Well! John Wesley Smith! Top o' the mornin'," Justin said, conscientiously dropping the final consonants. "Beautiful out here, isn't it? Up with the birds. An icy plunge in the pool at seven o'clock. A good tromp with Gretchen here—down, girl!"

The pool was very large but not so big that John Wesley could have missed Justin Fennessey had he been in it at seven this morning.

"Well, that must be very nice, sir," John Wesley said.

"Just get out here away from the pressures of town and unwind. Had a long talk with this old Yankee farmer—the one who runs the motel down the road. Fascinating. Get the viewpoint of the other fellah. Well, I'll be—"

"Uh, Mr. Fennessey, I, uh, wondered just where you wanted me to set up my office and—"

"Your what?"

"Office. My office. You know, a place where I can start to do my work."

"Oh. Yes. Yes, of course. Splendid idea. Swell. You must ask Stan about that."

"I already have. He told me to ask you."

"Oh. Oh, did he? Well, yes. We must see about that. Lots to do today. First day out here and all. Well, we'll talk about the office a little later. Come on, Gretchen, upstairs and see Mommy." Buttocks bouncing, Justin made a game attempt at taking the stairs two at a time, gave up on the sixth. Gretchen, on the other hand, bounded upward, loosening two carpet rods on the way.

From the floor above John Wesley heard Lydia Fennessey's voice saying, "Oh, really Justin, will you take that effing dog *out* of here! Get off my bed, damn you!" Then the door closed.

Alone once again, John Wesley decided to take in *very slowly* the Fennessey Collection of old masters. It was an opportunity apparently afforded to so few. At the Van Dyck he was interrupted by Peggy O'Neil emerging from the elevator.

"Good morning, Miss O'Neil. Everything all right up above?"

"Fine. So far."

"Did—did he have another—uh—seizure last night?"

"Who, Gramps? Certainly not. I gave him two Kilkenny Ales and he slept like a log. He's now having an invalid's tray of grapefruit, flannel cakes, sausages, potato bread, and Irish tea."

"Well, just what *is* the matter with old Mr. Fennessey?"

"Nothing, really, except that he's so very old. The machine's running down. The poor old boy has lapses of memory. Time means very little to him. He has his odd moments, as you know. But he's still strong and healthy and he's got most of his marbles, which is more than I can say for his— The real trouble is that he's bored and lonely and has nothing to do around here."

"I can understand that—perfectly," John Wesley said. "But with all this money and all this family, couldn't he more or less putter around the house and—"

"He could. But it wouldn't work. You see, he really doesn't like this house or his family. And as far as they're concerned . . . well, he's an embarrassment. Having him up on the top floor being waited on hand and foot is one thing. But on days like his birthday and Christmas and Thanksgiving when he's all gussied up in a Charvet robe and comes down to join in the fun, he's a living reminder that if it weren't for the second potato famine, there wouldn't be a Fennessey Foundation. It's not easy to be a connoisseur of the arts or an international playboy or a very grand marquesa when the old darling is talking about carrying hods and brewing beer in a tenement kitchen. But he's happy enough. Happier away from them than he is with them. He's—" A roar and a crash echoed through the house.

"He's at it again," John Wesley said.

"I'd better run."

"Miss O'Neil, before you go—I, uh, feel that I know you better than anyone in the house and I want to ask you about my work . . ."

But Peggy was already into the elevator. It was eleven-fifteen. Another long day stretched out ahead of him.

Determined to waylay Justin Fennessey, to discover what his exact duties were to be and when he could begin performing them, John Wesley posted himself in the music room, which afforded a better view of the traffic than the library. At half-past eleven he saw the elevator door open and the marquesa and her daughter emerge—summer dresses, hats, gloves—and head toward the main door.

"But Mum-my, will it hurt?"

"Certainly it won't hurt, Consuelo. She's a very good woman, Budapest-trained. God knows what she's doing out here in this wilderness. You just feel a little electric shock and then—"

"Ooooooh!"

"Do you want to spend the rest of your life having that smelly wax put on your upper lip every month?"

"No, but . . ."

"Then do as Mummy says, Consuelo. And *stop* rubbing your *eyes!*"

John Wesley heard the sound of a car door opening and closing, the purr of an expensive motor, and a slight hissing of gravel; then there was silence.

Luis Fernando appeared next, slinking down the stairs in a skin-tight jump suit open to the navel. In a gallery filled with art treasures, he went directly to his favorite picture—a mammoth Chippendale mirror. John Wesley watched him smooth his glossy eyebrows, pat the sweeping sides of his—yes, it could only be called that—coiffure, and run his hands down his narrow hips. A prettyish maid appeared, languidly trailing a feather duster. Luis Fernando wet his lips, puffed out his chest and cast a bewitching smile. The maid simpered, giggled, and ran. Luis Fernando pouted and returned to the mirror.

John Wesley could hear Deirdre Fennessey's voice long before he saw her. "No, no, no! It's my car and I'm going out in it *alone*."

"But where, Dee Dee?" This voice belonged to Shelagh.

"Out. Just out. Away from here and away from the two of you."

"But what are we supposed to do?" It was Sean, the other Fennessey twin.

"Why don't you put on your bathing suits and drown yourselves in the pool?"

Miss Fennessey clattered down the staircase. Luis Fernando spun around and preened again. "Deirdre?" he said in a mellifluous voice.

"What?"

"Did you hear me last night—beneath your window?"

"Yeah, I heard you." The tone was bored.

"Do you know what I wanted?"

"Yes. And do you know what *I* wanted?"

"What? Tell me."

"A bucket of water."

"Deirdre!" Luis Fernando darted forward and grabbed for her wrist.

"Oh, climb off, Louie. Anyhow, I'm late."

"Where are you going?"

"Out."

"Take me with you."

"Take you with me? The reason I'm going is to get away from you."

"In my country no woman would dare to speak to a man like that."

"Then why don't you go back there?"

Deirdre banged off in one direction, Luis Fernando in another. He kicked out at a table, setting a malachite urn filled with lilies to teetering dangerously. A few moments later John Wesley looked out the window and saw him at the pool wearing little more than a jock strap and rubbing sun-tan lotion into his amber flesh as though he were caressing his bride.

There was a long, long wait before anyone else appeared—least of all Justin Fennessey. John Wesley was conscious of telephones ringing in far distant parts of the house. In time, Desmond Fennessey's Filipino servant skipped down the staircase, carrying a small overnight bag. At the foot of the stairs he was apprehended by Miss Rafferty.

"And what is it you think you're doing on the front stairs?"

"Mr. Fennessey say, 'Get out quickest way.' I go now." With that he danced down the gallery and out the front door.

"And using the front door. Filthy heathen."

"Cousin Briddy. More radiant than ever!" Desmond Fennessey, pink, polished, and glistening, came athletically down the stairs.

"Desmond Fennessey, I'll thank you to keep that dirty little brown monkey on the service stairs and not using the front door of *this* house. The class of servant we get today!"

"We're all the servants of the Lord, Briddy. Oh, and Briddy?" Desmond lowered his voice.

"Yes?"

"Come to my room at eleven tonight and please wear that bewitching black lace nightgown."

"Oh!" Miss Rafferty bustled indignantly away.

"Desmond! Desmond!" It was Lydia Fennessey, looking less pulled-together than usual.

"What is it, Lyd?"

"Where are you going?"

"I'm flying into New York for the day—or maybe Boston. *I* don't know. Anyplace that isn't here."

"For God's sake take me with you!"

"Why, Lydia!"

"Oh, Desmond, don't camp so. It's Justin."

"What's the matter with Our Leader?"

"He's getting ardent."

"Getting what?"

"You heard me. He's in the shower singing '*L'Amour Toujours L'Amour.*' That's always a sign."

Desmond laughed. "Justin as the beast aroused is a picture I'd like to see."

"No you wouldn't. Oh, do hurry, Desmond!"

"All right, Lydia. The plane's all ready. Your virtue is safe once more." Together they fled.

John Wesley was horrified, but slightly encouraged. With no one left in the house, he might possibly—just possibly—have a moment alone with Justin Fennessey. He stepped out of the music room just in time to encounter Travis.

"Mr. Smith," the butler said, "there's a gentleman at the front door with some questions concerning the foundation. I wonder if you might not be able to help him. I can't find Mr. Earnshaw and Mr. Fennessey left instructions that he was not to be disturbed before luncheon."

John Wesley knew nothing about the Fennessey Foundation, but at least talking to some idle passer-by might feel like work. "I'll try."

"In the library, sir?"

"Well, yes. I suppose so."

Except for failing college girls, either tearful or defiant, John Wesley had never interviewed anyone before. Seated at the desk in the library, he wished for a little more advance notice so that he could muster up a few of the pompous banalities which had been used on him by headmasters, school

principals, deans of men, and chairmen of English depart-
ments. Failing that, he wished at least for a few standard
barriers to place between him and his interviewee—the
fountain pen impaling an onyx slab, telephones and a
squawk box, at least a silver-framed photograph of wife and
children. There were not even any papers on the desk more
businesslike than *The New York Times.*

Travis appeared at the door but before he could announce
the visitor's name the man was in the room, had flashed a
wallet, shaken hands, and seated himself opposite John Wesley. His name was Bertram and John Wesley had the vague,
uneasy feeling that he was somehow connected with the federal government. Mr. Bertram did everything—walking,
talking, standing, sitting—on the double. His speech was so
rapid-fire that his sentences seemed to have no beginnings;
just a middle and end.

". . . little run-down on the activities of the Fennessey
Foundation . . . incorporated April 1965 . . . form 1023
. . . application exemption federal income taxes . . ."

"W-well, I—"

"What is your exact position with the foundation?"

"Uh, Director of Projects."

"Just the man I need to see . . . major projects of foundation over last two, three years . . ."

"Well, I . . . well, of course there's the Fennessey Collection."

"Pictures?"

"Yes. It's very famous. The catalogue is right there on that
table if you'd like to—"

"Won't be necessary. How often is it open to public?"

"Well . . . well, you see, Mr. . . . Is it Bertram? Well,
you see I just started here a couple of days ago. I'm a little
new at all this myself. Just learning the ropes."

Peggy O'Neil came in with a stack of envelopes. "Mr.

Smith, the mail's here. Nothing much. But if you're bored and want something to— Oh!"

"Oh, Miss O'Neil. This is Mr.—uh—Bertram."

Mr. Bertram rose to his feet, darted across the carpet, flicked his wallet in front of Peggy's nose. "Right. Bertram. Internal Revenue Service. Routine check-up. Nonprofit foundations. Pleased to meet you."

"How do you do, Mr. Bertram," Peggy said smoothly. "I'm afraid you find us at a rather bad time. We've just moved out to the summer quarters. Most of the staff isn't here yet—particularly the accountant, who is the man you probably want most to see. Mr. Smith has just started with the Fennessey Foundation and I'm afraid he won't be able to tell you as much as—"

"Peggy? Have you seen my tennis shorts anywhere?" It was Stan Earnshaw. "Oh. Excuse me."

A sly look came across Peggy's face. "But *here* is the man who can undoubtedly tell you everything you want to know. This is our Executive Director, Mr. Earnshaw. Mr. Earnshaw, this is Mr. Bertram, *from the government.*"

Stan blanched for a moment and then snapped into his old West Point posture. "Mr. Bertram! J. Winstanley Earnshaw. A pleasure! How good of you to take the trouble to come all the way out here to look over our little operation."

"Looks pretty big to me."

"Oh, no. Just a skeleton staff at the moment. Takes a while to get the show on the road. Just opening the summer quarters. Hardly anyone here—just the family, so to speak. Heheheheh!"

"That?" Mr. Bertram said, jerking his head in the direction of Luis Fernando, who lay supine in the sun at the edge of the pool.

As it was about the only question so far that John Wesley

could answer, he opened his mouth to speak. Pitted against J. Winstanley Earnshaw, he should have known better.

"Oh, *that?* Heheheheh. Yes. That's, uh, Louie. Louie the lifeguard."

"*Lifeguard?*"

"Uh, yes. Mr. Fennessey—Mr. *Justin* Fennessey that is—decided that as long as it was so warm out here in the Hudson Valley, and as long as we had that big pool and as long as there were so many underprivileged kiddies out here, he'd open it as a community swimming pool. Just a part of the Fennessey Foundation's many, uh, public services."

"But where are the kids?"

As though to answer his question, Sean and Shelagh, amiably striking out at one another, gamboled into view.

"Well, sir," Stan said with almost audible relief, "there are two of them right now. Of course it's still early. You should see this place in the afternoons—little tykes splashing around out there. Do your heart good."

Even more phrenetically than he spoke, Mr. Bertram jotted in a little notebook and snapped it closed. "Picture collection?"

"Oh, uh, yes."

"Yes, what?"

"The collection. One of the finest—if not *the* finest—in the country."

"How does the public get to see it? And when?"

"Pussykins! Pussykins? Kitty, kitty, kitty!" John Wesley heard the voice of Justin Fennessey. He was not aware that Justin kept cats on the premises, too, but by now nothing would have surprised him.

Justin entered the library wearing a black mandarin robe, his sparse hair glistening with brilliantine. Seeing the room filled with people, he pinkened becomingly.

"Oh, excuse me," Justin said. "I was looking for Mrs. Fennessey."

"And here's someone who's been looking for you, Mr. Fennessey. This is Mr. Bertram," Peggy said. Then she added pointedly, "Mr. Smith, I have the mail ready for you. Shall I bring it to your office?"

"Office?"

"Yes. Or would you rather come with me, *now?*"

John Wesley was only too happy to leave. As he followed Peggy out, Mr. Bertram was saying, "Now for a few facts about the foundation's activities."

John Wesley felt his anger mounting. He was not a demanding person, but he was sick of being shunted around from person to person from room to room from day to day in order to discover what his job was to be and when it was to begin. "Listen, Miss O'Neil," he said as they walked down the gallery, "I wish you'd tell me exactly what's going on in this . . . this madhouse."

Peggy laughed. "It seems to be a routine investigation of tax-exempt foundations—such as this one. I suppose Mr. Bertram or Bertrand or whatever his name is *could* have picked a wilder moment, but on short notice this one wasn't bad: Justin caught with his pants down; Luis Fernando, ditto. I almost wish that Stan had found those tennis shorts. You've got to admit that it was kind of funny."

"I don't admit anything of the sort. I was hired to work in an important capacity for an important foundation. I gave up my job to do it."

"But it wasn't a very good job, was it, Mr. Smith?"

"No, but at least it *was* a job. I knew what I was supposed to do and where. What's more, I did it."

"I'm sorry that things seem a bit confused here, Mr. Smith."

"*Seem* a bit confused?"

"*Are* a bit confused. You'll grow accustomed to it," she said, ringing for the elevator.

"No, I won't. It shouldn't be asking too much just to find out what I'm supposed to do and where and when."

"There's an enormous library here. You could always read."

"I tried that, Miss O'Neil. They've got the complete works of everybody bound in green morocco. The pages haven't been cut in any of them. The *Complete Works of Swift* turn out to be the doors to a television set. Marcel Proust covers a liquor cabinet. And the *Congressional Record* leads to a . . . a—"

"I know, Mr. Smith. A toilet." She entered the elevator. "Mr. Smith, it's not my place to say this. I will anyhow. You strike me as a very bright, very honest, very conscientious young man. If you're half as bright as I think you are, you'll . . . you'll go to your room with a bottle or two of Fennessey's Kilkenny Ale. To prepare yourself for lunch. Which is just what I am about to do." The elevator doors closed with quiet finality.

When John Wesley finally cornered him, Justin was in a rage. But in his banker's-gray summer suit, with his bland white face, his neutral hair, his oyster eyes expressionless behind rimless glasses, it took someone with more experience of Justin to know it. Lydia could have told John Wesley in a second, but Lydia was not there, which was the first of many reasons for Justin's anger.

The second reason concerned the surprise visit of Mr. Bertram. Uneventful as his call had been, Justin did not like to be surprised.

The third reason dealt exclusively with J. Winstanley Earnshaw and his needless torrent of glib conversation with the government man. The idea, pointing out Justin's own children as penniless waifs enjoying the bounty of the Fennessey Foundation! Now Justin would probably be *forced* to open the pool to the public, who would run in the flower beds and do heaven only knew what in the pool itself. And then, after that annoying Mr. Bertram had written a lot of things in his notebook and gone, Stan's nudging, winking, "that-was-a-close-one-eh-chum" mateyness was infuriating. From Stan's loquacious intimacy, anyone would think that the Fennessey Foundation were, well, not quite honest.

And the fourth reason was that he had finally been cornered by John Wesley Smith. Justin had, at last, been pinned down. He hated being pinned down, making any firm decision, committing himself in any way. Justin was a past master at geniality. He had always prided himself on his monthly visits (plus the day before Christmas and the morning of Good Friday) to each of the top ten floors of the Fennessey Building, wherein worked all of the employees of all of the Fennessey enterprises. Fast on his feet, lenses gleaming cordiality, cheeks dimpling with paternal pride, Justin could ricochet from office to office, desk to desk like a cue ball on a billiard table, shaking hands, patting shoulders, remembering first names, inquiring solicitously about mothers with strokes, fathers with prostate problems, pregnant wives, unemployed husbands, ailing children, yet never stopping long enough in any one spot to be confronted with painful questions about raises or promotions. Par for the course—one hundred thousand square feet—was an hour and ten minutes, including waiting for the elevators. The Fennessey employees, touched and flattered, thought that Mr. Justin was the greatest guy ever, as did Mr. Justin. It was only later, going drearily home to their moribund mothers, catheterized fathers, swollen wives, disgruntled husbands, and whimpering children that they remember that important question they had been meaning to ask Mr. Fennessey personally.

Justin felt now that he had misjudged John Wesley and because of it he felt somehow cheated. The young man was intelligent, certainly, and a good teacher. (Justin liked to be surrounded by intelligent people and to get quality for his money.) But Justin had counted rather too heavily on John Wesley's being useful, ornamental, and silent, like the pair of Ming Dynasty lamps in the morning room, the scene of their encounter. And now he found that the young man was not only vocal but absolutely—well, there was no other word for it—importunate.

"Mr. Fennessey," John Wesley had said, as Justin rose from the luncheon table, "I would like a word with you."

"Well, that's, uh, haha, splendid, Smith. But could it wait a bit? Rather busy day today."

"It won't take a minute, Mr. Fennessey. So if we could just do it now, I could be busy, too."

"Well, I'm really awfully . . ." Justin had been able to say no more. He had felt a firm hand on his elbow, felt himself being steered into the empty morning room.

"Well, Mr. Smith?"

"Well, Mr. Fennessey. Here I am—with nothing to do and no place to do it. I've got a lot of ideas and I'd like to get started."

"Well, yes. Yes, certainly. Of course. Naturally it's rather quiet during the summers. I suppose every business is—haha —except the ice cream business. Haha."

"Still, Mr. Fennessey there must be something for me to do or you wouldn't have hired me in the first place. If you'll just tell me what, when, and where, I can get started and I won't be in your way any longer."

Really, of all the goddam pains! "Well, Mr. Smith, of course there are the children. They all need a little help in their studies."

"Yes, I understand that, Mr. Fennessey. We agreed that I'd bring them up in their schoolwork during the summer. There's Miss Fennessey's English, the twins' French and algebra . . ."

"Oh, yes, Smith. And my sister, the marquesa, was wondering if you might not just brush up her daughter's French—but on a different level, of course. Purely social conversation."

"W-why, yes. I'd be glad to. Now about my work, Mr. Fennessey—"

That had done it. Thoroughly annoyed and sick of being pushed around by this little schoolteacher, Justin had finally got the bit between his teeth and asserted himself. "Your work will be very simple, Mr. Smith. You can start with Sean at nine every morning. Two hours of math. Then two hours of French with Shelagh—very weak on verbs, haha. Deirdre likes to sleep late, so you could tackle her English right after lunch. Say two or two-thirty. And then another two hours with Consuelo, just speaking French."

"But that's eight hours a day, Mr. Fennessey."

Tipping his head back and concentrating on the chandelier, Justin considered the problem as though it were one in advanced calculus. "Mmmm. Yes, that's right, Smith. Four children. Two hours apiece. That's eight hours."

"But, Mr. Fennessey, my work for the foundation?"

"Well, haha, that can be sort of tucked in. As I say, we're not very busy during the summer."

"There's still a good deal of mail every day, Mr. Fennessey."

"Miss O'Neil can handle all that, Smith. She's very capable."

"I'm sure she is. But sometimes there are new projects suggested that strike me as quite worthwhile. I marked two of them for your attention yesterday—"

"Oh, did you? Swell! However, you mustn't take all those letters too seriously. Most of them come to nothing."

"But some of them—only a few—seem worthy of—"

"Yes, yes, Smith." Justin had risen and in his best, light-foot, cue-ball fashion, had sidled toward the door of the morning room only to find that this neat, compact young man had been even faster on his feet and was unobtrusively but most decidedly blocking the way. "Keep marking them. Good idea for us to know what's going on in the world. Oh, and by the way, you swim, don't you?"

"Certainly."

"Well, I wish you'd find just a little time to work on Sean's diving. The boy will *not* keep his head down."

"And just where am I to do all of this, Mr. Fennessey?"

"Why, in the swimming pool, naturally."

"I meant the tutoring and my work as Director of Projects."

"Oh. Oh, that. Well, don't worry. We'll find some place."

"Yes, but when? I would like to get started."

"Oh, yes. Of course you would. Haha. Well, remind me to speak to Travis about finding a place for you."

Travis appeared at the door. "A long-distance call for you, Mr. Fennessey. It's from your kennels."

"Oh, dear!"

"Couldn't we settle with Travis now, Mr. Fennessey? Where I'm to—"

"Excuse me, Mr. Smith." The cue ball and Travis shot out of the morning room and John Wesley had been left, as usual, all alone.

Servants'
Quarters

♣ ♧ ♣ ♧ ♣ ♧ ♣ ♧ ♣ ♧ ♣ ♧ ♣ ♧ ♣

Travis entered what was called, with apparent seriousness, his "sitting room," one of two cubicles that made up the "butler's suite." Butler's suite, indeed! A dirty little rabbit warren up under the eaves, that's what it was! And *hot?* The only reminder of air conditioning was the constant roar of the mammoth motors chilling the rest of the house. Nevertheless, he shut and locked the door, cutting off any hope of a vagrant breeze but insuring absolute privacy. With Justin lathered up over his dim-witted dogs and all the rest of the Fennesseys away from the house, he could spend an hour or two safely poring over the accounts. Not the household accounts. They had already been done, with Miss Rafferty breathing down his neck. (The way that old bitch and her crock of lard of a nephew, Justin, fussed about the electric bill you'd think that the two of them spent their lives on a treadmill supplying the power!)

No, these were the personal accounts of Elbert L. Travis—ten per cent from the butcher, ten per cent from the greengrocer, ten per cent from the hardware, ten per cent from the fishmonger. . . . Then there was the ten per cent from each of the two footmen, one of whom was probably at this very moment plowing into Kathleen, the prettiest of the maids and in perpetual heat, and the other tippling from the well-stocked Fennessey cellar. One word to Miss Rafferty and all three of them would be sent packing without severance pay or references. So naturally his silence was worth money from all of them each and every payday, just as his knowledge that the cook was a reformed paregoric addict and one of the gardeners had done time for armed robbery was cash in the bank. Actually, quite a number of banks by now, where it was growing steadily, safely at compound interest.

Travis slipped out of his morning suit and hung it up with great care. His morning and evening suits were made, at considerable Fennessey expense, in London by Kilgour, French & Stanbury—the same place where Desmond Fennessey's clothes were made. They were of the best quality and Travis wore them out with amazing speed. Two sets of everything twice a year. When the new clothes were delivered, Travis had a ready market for the old ones—morning suits to an undertaker in Poughkeepsie, evening suits to a waiter in New York at fifty bucks each. It was a shame, really, when they had cost hundreds. But still it was money in the bank.

Travis put on the dressing gown that Desmond thought he had left in Las Vegas and sat down to work at the rickety little table known as "Travis' desk" with more eager anticipation than usual. The ten per cents, while nothing to sneer at, had not been adding up to as much as in former years, but today Travis had a scheme that would make all that seem piddling. He would save it for the last.

Until today, Travis had rather missed the good old days in the vast Fennessey house on Fifth Avenue when there were considerable florists' bills to share. Oh, one or two of them had balked at paying Travis a commission. Idiots! Just an hour on a hot radiator and a hundred-dollar box of roses looked like last week's tossed salad.

"Mrs. Fennessey, madam, I don't like to give trouble, but the flowers for the table—especially with the cardinal coming to dine. It's a disgrace, if I may say so, Mrs. Fennessey. And so expensive, too."

"Oh, Travis," the late Mrs. Fennessey would say, staring aghast into the box of dead American beauties as though it were the coffin of her lover, "how horrible!" (Of course she pronounced it "hawwrubble," poor dumb bitch!) "Surely in a city this size there must be a more reliable florist?"

"If I might make a suggestion, madam . . ."

Now out here in the country with that bloody damned greenhouse . . . Oh, well. You make a little, you lose a little.

There was no such thing as a poor butler and Travis was one of the richest. He was an old family retainer. He looked forty and he had been with Fennesseys for forty years. He had also looked forty forty years ago when, as a second-class cabin steward of twenty, he had jumped ship in New York and appeared at the Fennessey mansion on Fifth Avenue, in a stolen bowler, as a full-fledged English butler armed with forged letters of reference.

Those letters! Travis had always thought that Americans were dumb and Irish even dumber. But the combination of the two! That was the Fennessey family for you.

Those letters! They had been so bad that Travis was still ashamed of them. Written on samples of paper pinched from Cartier and signed with the names of London stores—Lady Lillywhite, the Countess of Selfridge, the Honorable Mrs. Debenham-Freebody, Colonel Asprey, O.B.E.—they hadn't even been spelled correctly. And the grammar! Still, what had the Fennesseys known about real aristocracy? Travis could have signed one Queen Mary and it wouldn't have made any difference.

The arrival of Elbert L. Travis at the Fennessey service

door had been the crossing of two trajectories. Travis had stolen off the Cunard liner at a time when the climate of England was most decidedly unhealthy—whining, pregnant Beryl expecting him to come back home and marry her, and there was that matter of a pearl necklace missing from a stateroom on A Deck. At that time, Mrs. Terrence Fennessey, recently photographed by *Town & Country* with Desmond on her lap, Justin and Genevieve at her feet, was looking with dismay upon the fresh-faced but untrained Katies and Norahs and Moiras who supervised her household. After all, if the Fennesseys had arrived at a point where the cardinal came to dine, an acolyte of sorts would be needed to see to the candles. A hesitant advertisement in *The New York Times* brought Elbert L. Travis. The rest was history.

Travis had sized up the situation perfectly and given the lady what she wanted—a parody of a parody of a stage butler, full of "Yes, modom" and "If it pleases milady." Quickly and efficiently young Travis had rid the house of its Katies and Norahs and Moiras, of the cantankerous old biddy of a cook, of the ancient Jiggs of a chauffeur who talked over his shoulder to Mrs. Fennessey as he drove the Pierce-Arrow limousine. They were replaced by a crew of Travis' own discoveries—loyal, subservient, and financially responsible only to Travis. Oh, he'd pulled some clangers at first—white wigs, breeches, and gloves for the footmen, pink silk shades on the candles, calling the napkins "serviettes." But he had learned fast and, anyhow, forty years ago no one who knew any better would have set foot in the Fennessey house. As for the Fennesseys themselves, well!

One look at them and Travis had realized that he had the upper hand. Master Justin had been seven and as mealy-mouthed a little prig as you could hope to find. Miss Genevieve, at six, was even then a slut. And young Master Desmond a supercilious little smart-ass from birth. They had not changed. As for their father, Mr. Terrence Fennessey, he was rarely seen. He was a quiet, colorless man completely absorbed in doubling and trebling the family's millions. Travis hadn't disliked Mrs. Fennessey; he had simply despised her. Pitiful, that's what she had been. Niece of a bishop, sister of a monsignor, she was, socially speaking, a step up for the Fennesseys. "A pig would have been!" Travis spat. Shy and rather pallid, she had spent most of her time at prayer—R.C. of course!—yearning only tepidly for social triumphs beyond the ladies' sodality and the Auxiliary of the Sisters of the Precious Blood. Oh, with the Fifth Avenue Fennesseys it had been like taking candy from a baby!

The only Fennessey whom Travis had ever respected— feared—was the old man himself, John Francis Xavier Fennessey, "Gramps," founder of the whole empire in the Promised Land. Not only had he made fun of his sickly son and daughter-in-law in their terrible splendor, he had even dared to make fun of *Travis!* But the old devil's visits to the Terrence Fennessey mansion had been confined, to the satisfaction of all concerned, to Christmas and Easter. Otherwise he had stayed away in his widower's hotel suite leaving the patronage and the pickings to Travis.

Travis had seen the children through their first holy communions (heathenish, papist mumbo jumbo!); packed young Justin and Desmond off to boarding schools and colleges (popish, needless to say); set out the place cards for Miss Genevieve's debut dinner dance (by that time, the Fennesseys were so rich and *nice* people so poor that the turnout was amazing); and, a season later, even arranged for the debutante an unmentioned and unmentionable operation (full details of which lay in Travis' safe-deposit box). Travis had supervised the christening luncheons for the grandchildren, had summoned that bad-smelling, Spanish-talking Father Alonzo to administer the last rites to Mr. Terrence Fennessey, when the last of a ten-year series of heart attacks carried him off, and to his patroness Mrs. Fennessey, who followed her husband punctually. Travis had arranged their funerals, the wakes preceding them and the buffets following (Travis did a lovely funeral, he had to admit it), and banked the bequests they left him in their wills. For forty years Travis had been the Fennesseys' trusted servitor, friend, social mentor—and every day, for forty years, Travis hated them a little more.

Muttering, he endorsed the last of the checks made out to "Bearer" and totted up their impressive total on his deposit slip. But not impressive enough when he thought of the one bloody billion dollars the Fennesseys were worth today. One billion bucks, if you please, when Travis had had to teach them the difference between an oyster fork and a pastry fork! Forty bleeding years of servitude and today they had a billion dollars. And what did poor Travis have? Plenty!

"Clara!" Travis said aloud. It was time to tell Justin the sad news that poor Clara was due for another operation. Poor Clara—Mrs. Travis, that is—had been moribund for forty years, hidden away in a nursing home that was located sometimes in England, sometimes in Canada, but always well out of reach. None of the Fennesseys had ever known exactly what ailed Clara and Travis never exactly said. Justin thought that it was her lungs; Desmond felt that she was a mental case; Genevieve hinted darkly at cancer. The late Mrs. Fennessey had prayed long hours for Clara's recovery or, failing that, at least a blessed release. But every six months Clara Travis was forced to undergo another operation and each trip to surgery called for a pat on the shoulder and a check for at least five hundred dollars—sometimes more. Had any of the Fennesseys ever stopped to think about it, Clara's frail body would have looked like corduroy after forty years of semiannual surgery. But no one ever did. They all thought of Travis as especially noble to carry the cross of an invalid wife on his modest earnings.

Travis supposed that he ought to announce Clara's demise. God knew she was eviscerated after eighty critical openings —there couldn't possibly be another organ to remove or another place to carve. If Travis were suddenly to pull an even longer face and announce that his beloved wife had died . . . No. Passed away? No. Passed over? No, that sounded like a Jewish holiday. Passed on? Gone to a happier place? Been taken? Hmmmm. Well, if Travis did that, there would surely be an easy touch of, say, two thousand for funeral expenses. But then it would be literally killing the goose that laid the golden egg. No, Clara's battered body could go under the knife at least two or three more times. Then kill her off.

Travis flipped the pages of his calendar to December and jotted "Clara" down on the eighth—something to do with the Immaculate Conception, he noticed. That was a good omen. No living person had ever been conceived as immaculately as his fictitious wife and, anyhow, operations around Christmas time paid much better than the summer ones.

But after that visitor today—that Mr. Bertram from the Internal Revenue Service—Travis saw something far more lucrative than Clara's imminent funeral, than the paltry fives and tens he received from the other servants. In his pocket was Mr. Bertram's business card and *almost* in his pocket was a sum that might amount to millions.

When he was showing Mr. Bertram out, hadn't the man as much as said that the Department of Internal Revenue was willing to pay a commission on any information that might lead to a conviction on tax evasion?

Travis had always known that the Customs Department was happy to pay informers for tip-offs. He had been modestly rewarded some years ago for warning them that Miss

Genevieve Fennessey would be returning on the *Normandie* with a new diamond and ruby necklace pinned inside her garter belt, just where she had written Mamma that it would be. And hadn't that lady customs official gone straight for the garter belt—as well as some of the outraged debutante's other nooks and crannies? It had really been the only patriotic thing for Travis to do. But he had never dreamed that the Internal Revenue boys were willing to play—and pay.

Think of it! The Fennessey Foundation! One billion dollars tucked away and the whole thing as crooked as a dog's hind leg. Travis had no idea how many millions in taxes were being avoided or evaded every year, but whatever the sum was it was plenty. Travis felt that it was only his duty . . .

He took up his pen and began to write:

"Dear Mr. Bertram . . ."

Dine and
Dance

♣ ⚛ ♣ ⚛ ♣ ⚛ ♣ ⚛ ♣ ⚛ ♣ ⚛ ♣ ⚛ ♣

Shortly after Justin rushed to his dogs and Travis stole quietly off to plot his fleecing of the Fennesseys, John Wesley stormed out of the morning room. Temper, he knew, was a sign of weakness, of stupidity and savagery, but at the moment John Wesley was both conscious of and indifferent to his shortcomings. He pounded up the staircase, slammed the door of his room with a violence that set the O'Keeffe awry, and kicked the rickety little chintz chair. As this last manifestation of rage hurt his foot quite badly, he quieted down a bit. With something more like calm, he fished the contract he had signed with the Fennessey Foundation out from his few papers and read it through for the first time.

True, he had glanced at the contract before signing it, but little more. The first sentence of each resounding clause had seemed so comfortingly simple that he could hardly have whipped out his pen fast enough. Recalling the demo-aristocratic Justin Fennessey, his lenses glinting sincerity like some sort of myopic Thomas Jefferson, considering the high-flown aims of the Fennessey Foundation as outlined in their exquisite brochures, and bearing in mind that he was a raw young instructor wasting his breath in a half-filled classroom at a pseudoacademic institution, John Wesley had been only too eager to sign. What idealistic young man would not have been?

Now, hands trembling with anger, he read and reread the contract. True, he was employed by the Fennessey Foundation under the nominal title of "Director of Projects." True, he had agreed to "further the academic pursuits of the minor issue, heirs and wards of the Founder." Equally true, it was a short-term contract, running from the middle of June until the middle of September—or until it would be just too late to find a decent teaching job for the following year. Nor would it be possible to walk out now. Every sentence of the contract contained a sort of escape hatch in case the Fennessey Foundation wished to rid itself of John Wesley Smith, but there appeared to be no way for John Wesley Smith to leave the Fennessey Foundation outside of a hearse.

He read the contract once more and put it down. Words like "duped," "hoodwinked," "cheated," "gullible," "naïve," and "stupid" gushed through his mind. "No," John Wesley said aloud, and stood up. No, it simply could not be. This was real life *today* and not a leftist novel of the middle thirties. No matter how things looked, Justin Fennessey was not a paunchy, evil old Mr. Moneybags trying to grind the face of the proletariat (in this case John Wesley Smith) into the dust. The Fennesseys were famous. The Fennesseys had millions—a *billion* dollars—which they were trying to give away.

Walk. Not very far, perhaps, but at least elsewhere. That was the solution. John Wesley went into the bathroom, washed his face and hands, and combed his hair. Already he felt a little better. He didn't know exactly where he was going, but he was going somewhere and right now.

In a matter of seconds, he found out. As he passed the door

marked "Miss O'Neil" it opened and Peggy stepped out. They almost collided in the corridor.

"Excuse me," John Wesley said.

"Not at all. My fault. Why the hurry?"

"Pardon me, Miss O'Neil, but is there any law that says we have to eat every meal here in the Fennessey Foundation?"

"Why, of course not. Miss Bridget would be delighted if everyone ate out. Just think what it would do for her food costs. Miss Bridget cares about food costs. Tonight, for example, she's planned melon balls in champagne. Domestic. *Blanquette de veau.* Peas . . ."

"And is there any place else to eat in this . . . this—"

"In this godforsaken countryside?"

"Yes."

"There's the Slipper Inn—Dine and Dance. You may have noticed it driving out from the village."

"Is that all?"

"That's all."

"What's it like?"

"Pretty bad."

"But at least it's . . ."

"At least it's not here. Is that what you were about to say?"

"Yes. Listen, you wouldn't like to come with me, would you?"

"Why, Mr. Smith. I—I'd love to. But I'm hardly dressed for—"

"For the Slipper Inn? You look just fine. I'll call a taxi."

"No need for that. I have a car of sorts. Or we could even walk. I hate that cab driver."

"So do I."

"But I will call Travis and tell him to take off two places. There'll be dancing in the pantry tonight. With two people out of the way they'll be saving at least three dollars. It's that domestic champagne."

The Slipper Inn—Dine and Dance was a treasure trove of

horrors. It was, however, too far off the beaten track to come to the attention of those gushing connoisseurs of the hideous who were busy admiring Thonet chairs and Tiffany lamps in more populous places. As for the locals, they had too long been accustomed to the Slipper Inn's tubular chromium furniture, its circular blue-tinted mirrors, its mural depicting marcelled ladies and monocled gentlemen stepping regally down from the running boards of V-front town cars, its paper napkins decorated with perky scotty dogs, its peacock juke box to pay much attention to what was a true period piece. Intact, the Slipper Inn—Dine and Dance would have been the sensation of the Musée des Arts Décoratifs or even of the Smithsonian Institution, for it represented flawlessly the taste of the dead center of the American middle class between the Chicago World's Fair of 1933 and the New York World's Fair of 1939. Even the graffiti scratched on the walls of the men's room—its door marked "Pointers" as against "Setters"—had a quaint, normal, old-fashioned innocence.

Except for a local rustic haggling with the bartender over a double play that had spelled disaster for the New York Mets, the Slipper Inn—Dine and Dance was deserted when John Wesley and Peggy arrived. It was John Wesley's first visit to a place such as this and it was disappointing. If he were going to misbehave—storm out of the Fennessey house, play truant from the dinner table, assert himself—he wanted to go whole hog: noisemakers, funny hats, confetti, serpentine with the *jeunesse dorée* of the community. He wanted, in short, a bacchanal as celebrated in all those old movies.

"We'll have to sit in a booth," Peggy said. "Curly is very strict about us girls propped up at the bar."

"We'll want to have dinner anyhow, won't we?" John Wesley said.

"I'm not sure that we'll *want* to. But anyhow, we're here—for better or worse."

Seated on the red leatherette of a rump-sprung booth, John Wesley resolutely ordered a Tom Collins for himself and a Scotch and water for Peggy. In his few days of experimentation with alcohol at the Fennessey Foundation he discovered that, in the long run, something rather lemonadey like a Tom Collins was a lot pleasanter to get down. The concoction, as prepared by Curly of the Slipper Inn—Dine and Dance was not. "Miss O'Neil," John Wesley said purposefully, "I'd like to ask you a few questions. Questions about the Fennessey Foundation."

"Very well, but I think you might begin by calling me Peggy. We're in this thing together."

"Can you tell me, Peggy, just how many Directors of Projects there have been before me?"

"I did tell you. None."

"And"—John Wesley nearly choked on the words—"summer tutors?"

"There have been summer tutors ever since the Fennessey children were too big to have governesses. Last year we had Mr. Regan from Georgetown. The year before young Mr.—I forget his name; he had red hair—from Holy Cross. The year before that—"

"Do you mean that Mr. Justin Fennessey hires tutors for his children at the public's expense?"

"I . . . I think that you're the first ever to be put on the actual payroll of the Fennessey Foundation. Before you, Justin paid for his children's supplementary education out of his own pocket."

"And that great big house? All those servants? The cars? The gardens? Why, the flowers alone must cost—"

"The servants are employees of the Fennessey Foundation, Wes. Just like you and me. The house is the summer quarters of the foundation. There's another in Palm Beach—Spanish. It stretches from the ocean to Lake Worth and it may be even bigger. I've never bothered to count the rooms. You've seen the building in New York . . ."

"Do you mean that the Fennessey Foundation occupies that whole place?"

"Not quite. The foundation is only in the penthouse. It has the nicest view. The top ten floors are filled with other Fennessey enterprises—Kilkenny Ale, the Fennessey Construction Corporation, Fennessey Demolitions, the Fennessey Trust (that's real estate), the Fennessey Fund (investments, I think), and all the other family businesses. Justin felt that it was more efficient to keep them all under one roof. It saves taxi fare."

"And the rest of the building?"

"It's just like any other office building—doctors, dentists, accounting firms. A few big companies lease whole floors and sometimes two or three."

"And they all pay rent to the Fennessey Foundation?"

"Well, they'd damned well better."

"But the income must be . . . must be . . ."

"It's more than mine is."

"And all of this—all these millions and millions of dollars. You mean they don't pay taxes?"

"You'd have to ask Mr. Slattery."

"Who's Mr. Slattery?"

"Cornelius F. X. Slattery. He's Justin's lawyer. He arranged all of this. Very clever, I believe. Although you'd never guess it to meet him socially."

"And you mean that all this . . . this sort of hanky-panky is legal?"

"Not being a lawyer, I can't tell you, Wes. But I guess it must be."

"Well, can you tell me one thing that the Fennessey Foundation has ever *done?*"

"That is a matter of public record. You could read all

about the foundation's grants and good works in any newspaper."

"But I never have."

"Neither has anyone else, although Stan Earnshaw grinds
out an occasional press release—not very inspired but long. I
know. I type them."

"Miss O'Neil, I'm amazed."

"By what, *Mister* Smith?"

"Why, by what you've told me, Peggy."

"I've told you nothing, Wes. I've simply tried to answer
your questions."

"You shock me."

"Yes, I can see that. I've worked in lots of nonprofit foundations before. I know the types they attract. There are the
nest builders like Stan Earnshaw, and the swinging fund
raisers. There are the no-talents who work in foundations because the jobs are easy and because they couldn't compete in
the Real World. (Stan falls under that classification, too.)
There are the dead-tired-out old academicians—they are always called 'Doctor'—who couldn't hold down jobs teaching in a reformatory. We don't have any of those, but I've
worked in foundations where they're a dime a dozen. Then
there are the eager young things just out of Smith and Ben-
nington who want to Do Something Worthwhile that isn't
quite as uncomfortable as the Peace Corps. There are the
girls who can't do anything very well who sign on until they
can find some man to marry. There are the kooks and cranks
and nuts who couldn't fit in anywhere else. Then there are
the naïve, young do-gooders heading for disappointment.
That's you."

"And what are you?"

"Me? I'm efficient. Efficient and indifferent. I do what they
tell me to do and I do it well. I don't get involved. When
quitting time comes, I shut off my mind right along with the

dictaphone and the typewriter. I don't gossip in the girls' room or sleep with the boss. I'm all theirs from nine till five. After that I'm Peggy O'Neil and I couldn't care less if the Fennessey Foundation were blown off the face of the earth."

"Do you think that's entirely honest?"

"What's dishonest about it? I give full value. They pay me for shorthand and typing and filing and answering the telephone politely. There's nothing extra in my envelope for taking their problems to bed at night. If I did, I'd be driven to drink. And speaking of drink . . ."

John Wesley ordered another round. "When did you get started in . . . in, uh, foundation work?"

"The day I finished my commercial course at Our Lady the Picture of Health."

"What?"

"Our Lady of Perpetual Help. They have a very good business course. Anyhow, they got an emergency call from some kooky outfit to send over a part-time typist. I was the lucky girl. If Mother Superior had known what kind of a place it was, she never would have sent me."

"What kind was it?"

"It called itself religious, but not the kind Mother Superior thought. It was a spook joint—reincarnation and that sort of stuff. Poor little me. I was the only bead-fumbler there. I was also the only one who could take shorthand or type. The place was founded by a batty old dame who thought she was Nefertiti and had inherited a lot of money from a husband who had no intention of coming back in *any* incarnation. They had a three-room office on Lexington Avenue where I worked with Eleanor of Aquitaine and Jezebel."

"Who?"

"My co-workers. One dear old thing who was convinced that she was really Eleanor of Aquitaine. (She was nearly old enough to be the original.) Jezebel was just a standard society nymphomaniac who didn't believe she was anything but irresistible. Her dotty old grandfather (*he* not only traced his family tree back to Charlemagne, he *was* Charlemagne) got her the job to keep her out of trouble. It didn't work. She didn't work, either. In fact nobody worked there except sweet Peggy O'Neil. And in less than a week's time I discovered that it was perfectly possible for me to do three people's jobs, the *Times* crossword and catch up on all of my reading before my co-workers even got into the office. It was a gas, that foundation."

"How could you stand it?"

"I was fascinated. The Executive Director—there's *always* an executive director—was also fascinated with me. Before the end of the summer he got an offer from the Vandergraaft Foundation. He took me with him."

"And what did the Vandergraaft Foundation do?"

"Nothing, like most of them. It was a big brownstone pile up on Fifth Avenue, and it contained one of the world's largest collections of books and manuscripts on Persian enamels."

"Did you learn a lot about Persian enamels?"

"Well, I might have, assuming that I was any more interested in them than ninety-nine-and-forty-four-one-hundredths per cent of the population. Or if the library had ever been unlocked. You had to have written permission from old Mrs. Vandergraaft herself even to be let in. Very few applied and even fewer were admitted. It was a little like the Fennessey Collection. The *real* purpose of *that* foundation was to avoid paying taxes on one of the most expensive corners in New York, to provide a happy retirement for the old family retainers, and, most important of all, to keep the old Vandergraaft house exactly as it had always been. Mrs. Vandergraaft used to hobble in every day or so just to see that the window shades were drawn level and that the Persian enamels were all locked up where nobody could see them."

"That's incredible. What did you do to keep busy?"

"I wrote the paychecks, went over the bills, handled Mrs. Vandergraaft's social correspondence (she sometimes got as many as two invitations a year—all refused), and learned French and knitting. Oh, I also got to be very fast on my feet running from the Executive Director."

"And what did he do?"

"I just told you: chased me. When he wasn't doing that he was busy buttering up the old lady and convincing the Vandergraaft heirs that they were really saving money by spending so much on the foundation."

"But I can't believe it. Surely all the foundations aren't simply tax dodges. Look at the Fords, the Rockefellers, the Carnegies."

"I didn't say that they all were. But the nonprofit foundation has inspired many a tax lawyer. In a clinical way, it's a very interesting field. Now, would you like me to tell you about my short, happy life with the Fenster Fund? They specialized in—"

"No thanks. I think I'd rather have another drink. Then we might order."

John Wesley had gone out for dinner to get away from the Fennessey Foundation and what he suspected it might actually be. He had invited Peggy to cheer him up and to help him escape, at least momentarily, from his problems. She had done neither. She had, in fact, only made matters worse. Still he liked her. She was pretty and lively and gay and John Wesley believed that beneath her hard-boiled shell she had a heart.

Perusing the fly-blown menu, John Wesley was suddenly aware of noise and people. The Slipper Inn had filled up while he and Peggy had been talking. The crowd was made up mostly of locals—the young gyrating on the tiny dance floor, their elders out for an evening of spaghetti and meat balls washed down with quantities of draught beer. It was what one might call wholesome. John Wesley approved. He raised his glass to Peggy and said, "Well, let's not think of the Fennessey Foundation or *any* foundation or, for that matter, any Fennesseys tonight. Let's just think about—"

The air was split with a crash of glasses, the splat of a brief case as it landed on the polished floor and slid between the legs of the dancers, and the thud of a very large body landing face downward and dragging a table and two chairs with it.

"Really, Desmond," a cultivated voice said, "the riffraff you associate with."

"Salt of the earth, Lydia, my dear. Salt of the earth."

John Wesley and Peggy glanced up and saw Lydia and Desmond Fennessey swaying over the mountain of flesh that lay supine on the dance floor.

"Now see here, whatever your name is," Curly was shouting. "I run a decent place."

"You run a charming place, my good man," Desmond said. "Four stars in the *Guide Michelin*."

"*I* think it's tacky," Lydia said.

"But, my dear man, surely you can see with your own eyes that the flooring here is totally unsafe. Your negligence has caused both pain and embarrassment to my dear friend lying at your feet, Ireland's most distinguished poet and playwright, uh . . . uh . . . well his name eludes me at the moment. Lydia, my dear, you have such a profound memory for these minor details. Just what *is* the name of Ireland's most distinguished poet and playwright?"

"George Bernard Shaw?"

"No. Guess again."

"Oscar Wilde?"

"No, darling girl. They're dead. I should have said Ireland's most distinguished *contemporary* poet and playwright."

"You mean that old lush wallowing away on the floor?"

"The very one, my dear."

"Rory something. Some horrid name like that. Really, Desmond, what you can pick up on a quiet afternoon in Boston!"

"*I* picked him up? *You* were the one who picked him up. That little bar on—"

"Well, I suggest that one of you pick him up off my floor and get him outta my place before I turn all of yez out."

"Well, really!" Lydia said.

"My good man," Desmond said, "that will hardly be necessary. My friends over there will vouch for our sterling characters. Surely you know them—the Duke of Ponsonby and Lady Margaret Hooligan."

"You mean Miss O'Neil?" Curly asked incredulously.

"Oh, Lord," Peggy said. "We're in for it now. Three drunks. Count 'em—one, two, three."

"Do you mean *Mrs.* Fennessey?" John Wesley was shocked.

"That's right. Vodka. Just like brother-in-law Desmond. And the more she has the statelier she gets."

The trio made its unsteady way to their table, Lydia in the lead, Desmond half supporting an enormous man in a rumpled blue suit.

"Good evening, Miss Smith, Mr. O'Neil," Lydia said thickly. "I do hope that we're not presuming."

John Wesley leapt to his feet. In doing so, he overturned a glass of water.

"Re-ally, Mr. Smith," Lydia said, "I had hardly expected to find you in an intoxicated condition. When searching for a fit tutor for my children I had—oooops!" The enormous Irishman slipped from Desmond's grip and lurched into Lydia. Both of them more or less fell into the booth opposite John Wesley.

"Happy landings, old darling," Desmond said. "Good evening. Don't mind if we join you?"

"You already seem to have," Peggy said.

"Honestly, Desmond," Lydia said again. "The sort of person you pick up!"

"If I hadn't picked him up—or if you hadn't—who would have flown the plane back home?"

"*He* flew your plane?" John Wesley stared aghast at the enormous blob of suet slumped across the table before him. Black hair sprouted from his scalp, his cheeks, his nose, his ears. Two blood-shot blue eyes stared glassily out from a tangle of black lashes. As though to support himself, he placed two hairy hands on the table and pushed back. John Wesley had never seen bigger hands or dirtier ones.

"And whom have I the pleasure of addressin'?" he mumbled.

"Yes, Desmond, do introduce your little friend, thank you very much," Lydia said. "And you might just order some drinks. I mean really, bringing me to this common place with this common man . . ."

"Bushmill's with a beer chaser," the man said.

"Ah, yes, dear boy, but first the formalities. What did you say your name was?"

"Rory Mulcahy. *Captain* Rory Mulcahy, at your service! And a Bushmill's with a beer chaser."

"Just so. Captain Mulcahy. Miss O'Neil. Mr. Smith. Captain Mulcahy writes. He was reading some of his poetry in an amusing little bar in Boston."

"About as amusing as a requiem mass, thank you," Lydia said.

Captain Mulcahy fumbled with his brief case. It sprang open and a snowstorm of grubby papers flew out, followed by a pair of soiled socks, a half-eaten apple, and a corned-beef sandwich. "Bushmill's and a beer chaser," he said, "then I'll read somethin' for yez!"

"Lydia!" It was Justin Fennessey with Gretchen, his constant companion. Gretchen bounded forward, placed both paws on the table, consumed Rory's corned-beef sandwich with a single gulp, and belched resonantly.

"Oh, my God! Justin, will you get that effing dog out of here!" Lydia shrieked.

"Lydia! Have you been drinking?"

John Wesley watched Lydia Fennessey with fascination. The change was amazing. Before his eyes she seemed to grow taller, grander, haughtier. "Justin! Re-ally! Do I *look* as though I'd been drinking?"

"Well . . . yes. Cousin Briddy told me that you'd gone off in Desmond's plane. But I heard it land nearly an hour ago and—"

"We came here for a little bite to eat, Justin," Lydia said. "Surely you got my note. You were bathing when I left, and I didn't like to disturb you."

"Note? I saw no note."

"What a pity. As I wrote you, I've spent the day in Boston on business."

"Business?"

"Yes, Justin. Foundation business. Is that not correct, Desmond?"

"Right as rain, dear girl."

"What particular business?" Justin asked. There was something in his tone that struck John Wesley as faintly ominous.

His tone must also have had the same effect on Lydia. She seemed, for once, to have lost her lines, to be waiting for help from the prompter. That assistance came in the form of a loud hiccough from Rory Mulcahy. As cool and smooth as ice, Lydia continued. "Yes, Justin. Desmond and I have acquired an interesting new playwright for the Fennessey Foundation. Justin, de-ar, I would like you to meet Captain Rory Mulcahy."

Part Two

♣ ⚘ ♣ ⚘ ♣ ⚘ ♣ ⚘ ♣ ⚘ ♣ ⚘ ♣ ⚘ ♣ ⚘ ♣

Togetherness

For once the Fennessey household was united. Everyone detested Captain Rory Mulcahy.

Justin Fennessey felt more resentment than anger. If Lydia had stayed at home observing her wifely functions, there would have been no trip to Boston with that frivolous, irresponsible Desmond and, more than likely, no Rory Mulcahy brought back. Justin was certain that she had left no note announcing her impromptu departure, but he was too embarrassed to inquire closely of Travis or any of the servants. He was equally sure that Lydia *had* been drinking—could one be with Desmond long and *not* drink? But then Lydia was always so pulled together, so frosty and outraged when Justin so much as hinted that she might have had more than two cocktails and a glass of wine at table. As for Desmond and that unspeakable Irishman, there could be no question whatever. But what Justin hated most was having this sodden reprobate already speaking of himself as playwright in residence. Rory was in residence, all right, but there was no evidence, other than the mare's nest of waste paper in his revolting brief case, that he was writing, ever had written, or ever would write a single word. With all of those nice, clean, young men graduating from Carnegie Tech or the Yale School of Drama, surely a more decent sort could have been dug up as playwright in residence. And, more to the point, what did the Fennessey Foundation need a playwright in residence *for*? Just another mouth to feed.

Lydia was even angrier than Justin. She was angry at herself, but she conveniently shifted the blame to her brother-in-law Desmond. It was all his fault: the trip to Boston; that sordid bar; getting her drunk (not that he had exactly pried her jaws apart and poured the drinks in); and falling into conversation with that raffish, high-smelling, whisky-swilling Rory Mulcahy. A good deal of it was Justin's fault, too. If he hadn't been about to force his bumbling attentions on her, she would have been perfectly happy sitting around the pool with a laced lemonade instead of fleeing to Boston. Now he required a great deal of placating and she had been forced into his bed every night and not a few afternoons since that ill-starred evening. And if he hadn't come charging into the Slipper Inn with that revolting dog, as if he were Simon Legree and a pack of bloodhounds, she would never have been caught up in this preposterous story about this preposterous Irishman being the playwright to further Deirdre's career. (Lydia was not a person who liked, *ever*, to admit that she had been incorrect in the most minute detail.) Perfectly true, Lydia wanted her daughter's career furthered, but if there had to be a playwright in residence, couldn't it possibly be something nice-looking, well bred, and amusing, more along the lines of Edward Albee or Gore Vidal—or someone at least *human*—instead of this boozy old boor?

Jenny also loathed Captain Mulcahy, but she was delighted that he was there. Nothing that caused Lydia Fennessey so much discomfort could be all bad. Jenny had wormed the whole story—or at least one version of it—out of Desmond and she had been utterly captivated by it. She could laugh—she could *scream*—every time she saw that bumbling old booze hound lurching and staggering in Lydia's wake. It was really about the only amusing thing that had ever happened out here.

Desmond hated Rory Mulcahy because he was a.) Irish; b.) a bore; and c.) because Rory considered Desmond his oldest and dearest friend and clung to Desmond like a barnacle. Rory, having arrived with only the clothes on his back and the dirty socks in his brief case, had taken to borrowing clothes—and usually Desmond's, as their sizes most nearly matched. Underarm deodorants, soap, and even water seemed to be a never-never land to Rory. However, Rory did like nice things—Desmond's. When he tired of a suit, after six or seven continuous wearings, he left it in a wadded ball in the middle of Desmond's sitting-room floor and chose another. The suits were burned immediately and their duplicates ordered by telephone from London. Desmond blamed Lydia exclusively for Rory's presence in the house. He himself had picked up hundreds of people and dumped them without ceremony. One more Bushmill's and Rory would have passed out, thus giving Desmond ample opportunity to steal away. But Lydia, always the actress, always onstage, had to shoot off her big mouth in front of Justin. And now this ignorant clot was their constant companion, and especially Desmond's.

Miss Rafferty disliked anyone who came into the household, walked on the rugs, ate the food, used the toilets, soiled the towels and sheets, or strained her stringent budget by as much as one cent. This included all of the Fennesseys, whose house Cousin Briddy considered to be her own. Ideally, she would have preferred it emptied of people—save herself—

and hermetically sealed. *Then* she could show perfect miracles of domestic economy. Masochistically she took bad enough in her stride and grudgingly accepted the blood members of the Fennessey family, their spouses and—to a certain degree—their servants.

Miss O'Neil, now, she was a sweet-natured and good-humored little thing and neat as a pin. You could eat right off her floor if you had a mind to. Father Alonzo, albeit a man of God and Miss Rafferty's confessor, was a pig—and a Spanish pig at that. Mr. Earnshaw, for all his fine talk, was worse. Miss Rafferty could tell you things about the state of Mr. Earnshaw's bathroom that would curl your hair, if a lady would even mention such matters. The other Protestant, that young Mr. Smith, he was hardly any trouble at all. Tidy, for a man, although he used an ungodly lot of towels and left his window open, letting in heaven only knew what kind of dust and germs. But as for the new one, saints above! Of all the hairy, heathenish, dirty, shanty Irish bog jumpers Miss Rafferty had ever seen in all her born days—and she had seen plenty—this Rory Mulcahy was the worst!

Among the young, feelings were mixed although they did not run high. To Luis Fernando, fully conscious of being the exquisite son of a rich mother and a titled father, Captain Mulcahy existed only as a very bad smell. For many hours Luis Fernando practiced quivering his nostrils before his mirror and was inordinately proud of being able to do it whenever Rory appeared upwind of him. He was not pleased to have his sister Consuelo burst into roulades of giggles and tell him how like a rabbit he looked.

Consuelo herself was not really bright enough to have strong likes and dislikes except insofar as colors, flavors, and various performers went. Rory Mulcahy made her giggle a great deal. He enjoyed her reactions, crediting them to his native wit rather than to Consuelo's near-simple-mindedness.

Sean and Shelagh were still of an age when anything having to do with intoxication struck them as riotously funny. They burst into snorts and snickers whenever Captain Mulcahy hove unsteadily into view.

Deirdre laughed too. Not when Rory was drunk but when Rory was being serious, when he recited in ringing tones and a velvety brogue bits and snatches of what he claimed to be his work. Captain Mulcahy, notoriously insensitive about almost everything else, felt Deirdre's scorn bitterly and kept his distance. For this, Deirdre was grateful, the others envious.

Peggy O'Neil was almost as fortunate. Whenever Rory attempted to draw her into one of his interminable conversations, Peggy merely announced that she had work to do in some other part of the house and left him alone.

Rory Mulcahy made J. Winstanley Earnshaw uneasy. All men did. Stan suspected, quite correctly, that Justin Fennessey thought him vulgar; Desmond thought him a fool; Travis thought him a windbag; and that the new man, this Smith, thought him a—well, Stan wasn't quite sure what he did think, but he had the feeling that it wasn't entirely flattering. If Stan could endure them and their silent scorn, he could certainly survive Captain Mulcahy, totally unpleasant as he was. This was the plummiest job he had ever had and he had no intention of letting it go.

But it was John Wesley Smith who suffered the most with Rory Mulcahy. To begin with, they were of an age, although John Wesley's Spartan routine of what his mother called Clean Living made him look at least ten years Rory's junior. Finding Desmond Fennessey often awesome or distant or simply out, Rory selected John Wesley to show him the ropes, to lead him around the house and describe its contents and their probable values and to give him the lowdown on the various Fennesseys. While the other members of the household could conveniently disappear, Rory always knew exactly where to find John Wesley. During the daytime hours it was usually in the schoolroom that had been hastily converted from a small servant's cubicle up under the blistering eaves of the house. Whenever alone and lonely, which was often, Rory would saunter in unbidden. "Ah, is it Spanish you're talking?" he would say.

"No," John Wesley would answer over Consuelo's giggles. "Miss Mondragon is improving her French."

"French is it now? That calls to mind a story of the time that I and my buddy Morris Chevalier was in Paris together. I was temporarily out of funds and . . ." Classes would suspend. If any of the young people had shown the faintest glimmering of scholastic aptitude, John Wesley would have lodged a complaint with Justin Fennessey. As it was, they were happier snickering at Rory, and his intrusions saved John Wesley the embarrassment of trying to teach them anything. Thus of his eight daily tutoring hours, a good four to six of them were spent in the uninvited company of Captain Mulcahy.

Nor, unlike the others, could John Wesley escape to the privacy of his own bedroom, for his bathroom adjoined the quarters assigned to Rory and had to be shared. Also to be shared, John Wesley discovered, were his own razor blades, shaving soap, toothpaste, and whatever other of his modest toiletries caught Rory's fancy. Not to be shared, apparently, was the task of cleaning up after Rory's sporadic ablutions. The toilet was never flushed, except when John Wesley did it. Nor was Rory exactly William Tell when it came to perfect aim. Towels ended up as soggy gray swamps on the tile floor. Daily the wash basin was transformed into a stagnant pond of whey-gray scum peppered with the black bristles of Rory's considerable beard and with a razor blade left rusting on its banks. Rory, as had been generally noticed, rarely bathed. When he did, the tub wore as its service stripe a wide band of mouse-gray velvet and a merkin of curly black hairs clogging its exhausted drain. On one unforgettable occasion John Wesley discovered ten yellow-gray toenails glowering up at him from its white porcelain interior.

But the worst feature about their mutual bathroom was that it offered direct access to John Wesley's room. No matter how stealthily John Wesley tiptoed around in the dark, Rory always seemed to sense when he was in and would come bursting through the bathroom door. Even pretending to be asleep was useless as Rory would shake him until his teeth rattled. The purport of each visit—two, three, four a night—was never very important. "I thought I'd come in and have a smoke with you."

"I don't smoke."

"Well, just a visit then. A sort of chin, like." And the monologue would commence.

To be found by Rory at his desk and to explain that he was writing a letter—an important letter—would result only in having Rory hang over his shoulder. "What a neat handwriting you've got; tidy like. Oh, and is that how you spell 'organization' in this country? With a zed, is it? Back on the other side we write it with an ess."

The hours after midnight, when John Wesley was really asleep, were even worse. He would be wakened by Rory's retching, hawking, and spitting in the bathroom and lie there cold with apprehension for the door to open and Rory to appear in his dirty, drooping underwear. The conversation was always the same.

"Are you asleep, chum?"

"Yes."

"Then I won't be bothering you. But I don't suppose you've got a drop of the creature?"

"A what?"

"A bit of whisky, Johnny-boy. Bushmill's if you've got it handy."

"I don't have any whisky. I haven't any liquor at all."

"What a pity. It's for me teeth, mind. But now that you're up, I'll stay and have a smoke. Take me mind off the pain."

"I'm *not* up."

But by then Rory was down, sprawled out in the little chintz chair and lighting the lamps.

John Wesley had endured brief and pointless interviews with various members of the household about the agonizing Rory Mulcahy situation, but the one with Justin Fennessey was the longest, the most elaborate and the one most impossible to wriggle out of. It was held in Justin's office to which John Wesley had been summoned at the specific hour of three. John Wesley had never been in Justin Fennessey's office at the summer quarters of the foundation although he had passed it many times. Its walnut doors were lettered with Justin's name and title, just like Desmond's, and by this time John Wesley had good reason to suspect that the "office" would be nothing more or less than an elaborate bedroom suite. At exactly three o'clock he tapped on the walnut. The doors were opened by Peggy O'Neil. John Wesley walked in. The room contained a Directoire desk rather too small for a man of affairs, or for a man at all. Otherwise nothing else in the room suggested work. It was all just a bit sissy. "Sit down, Wes," Peggy said. "I'll call the Great White Father."

John Wesley sat down on a little *toile de Jouy* chair and gazed at the paintings on the walls—a David, an Ingres, a Flandrin, and a Prud'hon. He halfway expected Madame Récamier to appear on the couch opposite. But perhaps this was just some sort of anteroom adjoining a more businesslike place where the real guts of the organization throbbed and rumbled. But no. The other pair of doors opened wide and

Justin Fennessey appeared. Behind him John Wesley could see a pair of dainty beds, a chaise longue, a dressing table.

Justin entered the room, offered John Wesley a limp, white hand, sat down behind the little fruitwood desk, moved its *bouillotte* lamp an inch, and riffled through some important papers, which happened to be a wedding announcement and two invitations to cocktail parties. He treated John Wesley to a small, V-shaped Gioconda smile and allowed his lenses to gleam briefly in the general direction of the *toile de Jouy* chair. "Getting adjusted all right?" he asked.

"Adjusted to what?" John Wesley said. He was amazed at himself, but it was a sensation he rather enjoyed. Justin let the question drop.

"Children doing well at their studies?"

"No," John Wesley said.

"No-o-o-o?" Justin repeated, his pale brows shooting above the rims of his spectacles.

"No. They have no interest in learning. With the schools as overcrowded as they are, I suggest that you let them drop out as soon as it's legally possible. They'll never have to earn their livings anyhow." That would surely do it. Now Justin would fire him.

"*I* work for *my* living," Justin said. He paused. There was no reply. He rearranged the invitations on his desk and changed the subject. "And how is Consuelo doing with her French?"

"She speaks well enough. It's simply that she has nothing to say."

"Mmmm. Yes. Pity."

John Wesley was appalled. He'd never been quite so daring, quite so frank, quite so rude to anyone in his life. Yet here was this great man, this rich man, this national figure sitting there and taking it.

Justin rearranged his vital documents according to size—

wedding announcement on the bottom, red-bordered invitation next, visiting-card invitation on top. "Uh, Jack—people
do call you Jack, I believe?"

"No, Mr. Fennessey. No one does."

"I see." He moved the lamp again. "Um, about Captain
Mulcahy?" John Wesley did not reply. Justin repeated the
question in a slightly different tone. "About Captain Mulcahy?"

"Well, what about him?"

"You know him pretty well, don't you?"

"I see him every day, if that's what you mean." When, oh
when, would that welcome ax fall?

"Yes. Of course. We all do. Pity isn't it?" Justin chuckled
grimly. John Wesley supposed that it was an attempt at
witty intimacy. He remained silent and unsmiling. Justin
plowed on. "You know a great deal about drama, the theater
—that sort of thing—I believe."

"It's my field, sir."

"Well then, could I have your candid opinion of Captain
Mulcahy's talents as a playwright?"

"Never having seen or read anything he's ever written, I
can hardly give you a considered opinion." John Wesley
frankly hoped that the loudmouthed ignoramus had been
able to hoodwink the Fennesseys into believing that he was
the new wave, the white hope of the theater and that Justin
would now dismiss John Wesley immediately as being too
uninformed to tutor his children.

"Neither have I," Justin said. "I've never heard of him and
nobody *I've* ever heard of has ever heard of him either.
Frankly I believe that *Mrs.* Fennessey has made a serious
mistake in engaging him." Justin paused. The lenses gleamed
in John Wesley's direction. "You were with my wife and my,
uh, brother that evening . . . down the road. I don't suppose, uh, you could tell me exactly how, uh, Captain Mul-

cahy became . . . attached to the Fennessey Foundation."

"No, sir. I couldn't."

"I admire your, uh, loyalty."

"Loyalty has nothing to do with it, Mr. Fennessey. I simply don't know—or care—how Mr. Mulcahy got here." There, *that* should do it.

"Lydia—my wife, that is—is a great devotee of the theater. She was a most promising young actress before she decided to give up her career to become a wife and mother. Of course that was before your time. You probably didn't even know that Mrs. Fennessey was on the stage."

"She's told me all about it. Twice. I'm sorry to say that I never heard of her, either." *Now!*

"How fleeting is fame," Justin said with his shark's smile. "But then my wife is a very modest woman—and a very kindhearted one. You may have noticed."

"No, I can't say that I have."

"Well, in any event it was through Mrs. Fennessey's auspices that this Mulcahy is with us. I am frank to admit that I believe Lydia's good nature got the better of her. I even sense that she feels the same, although she's far too kind to admit her earlier error. To be perfectly honest about it, Mr. Smith, I have no belief in Captain Mulcahy's talent and even less personal fondness for the man."

Justin paused for John Wesley's response, but there was none. He would not give him the satisfaction.

"He is, to put it bluntly, uncouth."

"Granted, Mr. Fennessey, but I don't see how that concerns me—unless you'd like me to give him lessons in manners and personal cleanliness *after* my eight hours of trying to teach the children something."

"What I want you to do, Smith, is to *get rid* of this Mulcahy."

"Wouldn't that be Mr. Earnshaw's duty? Or even yours?"

Then John Wesley added bitterly, "After all, I *am* the Director of Projects."

"Right!" Justin snapped. "And your first project is to get that dirty, drunken bum out of my house!"

"And if I refuse?"

"If you *what?*" The word "refuse" seemed to be strangely foreign to Justin Fennessey.

"I said, if I refuse, which, by the way, I do."

"Listen to me, young man," Justin said with surprising passion, "you're not the only summer tutor in the world. College instructors like you come at a dime a dozen and—" Justin's diatribe was interrupted by the clink of a dime on his desk.

"Here, Mr. Fennessey," John Wesley said, rising to his feet. "Buy twelve more like me. And now if you'll excuse me, I'll start packing." He stamped across the carpet to the door and pulled it open. Peggy O'Neil almost fell into the room.

"Mr. Fennessey, I'm sorry to interrupt, but it's very important . . ." Peggy began, Rory Mulcahy on her heels.

"Aha," Rory said. The reek of whisky on his breath was enough to send a strong man reeling. "So it's you, is it? I've searched the whole place high and low to find you. I just seen a piece in the papers that reminds me of an amusing story concerning me chum Brendan Behan and I. It was back in fifty-two—no, fifty-one it was—"

"Mr. Mulcahy, *please,*" said Peggy. "Mr. Fennessey, the man from Internal Revenue, Mr. Bertram, is here to see you."

Projects

♣ ♧ ♣ ♧ ♣ ♧ ♣ ♧ ♣ ♧ ♣ ♧ ♣ ♧ ♣

Large as it was, Justin's Directoire sitting room seemed thronged. John Wesley, summoned back, occupied as un-obtrusive a spot as possible. Justin sat at the little desk, which was now piled high with papers and Manila folders that had materialized from somewhere. Stomach in, chest out, but-tocks taut, J. Winstanley Earnshaw stood in front of the fire-place. Peggy O'Neil sat in a straight chair near the desk, her shorthand pad open on her lap. The marquesa sat primly on the Récamier sofa looking rather as though Daguerre were about to come in and do a tintype of her. Desmond Fennes-sey straddled a fragile chair looking diabolical and amused. Mr. Bertram was trying to hold the center of the floor, but he had not reckoned with Lydia. She was on. Looking splen-didly Junior League in natural linen and trim pumps, Lydia paced diagonally across the Savonnerie carpet gesturing with her upstage arm. Her performance, which reminded John Wesley of every bad "society type" he had ever seen, was somewhat hampered by Gretchen. The dog held the true

center of the floor, where she lay lapping noisily at her vast
pink underside. Lydia could have happily kicked the bloody,
bleeding bitch's stump tail right up between her flopping
ears, but that would have been completely out of character
for a benefactress of mankind. "But surely neither you nor
the government can entertain, for a moment, the r-r-ridicu-
lous notion that a family as prrrrominent—as much in the
public eye—as the Fennesseys would ever dare—would even
drrream—of doing such a thing as you so darkly hint, Mr.
Bertrand."

"Bertram."

"Do forgive me. Mr. *Bertram*. As my husband and Mr.
Earnshaw have *tried* to tell you, we are all up here with our
stoff at work on a ve-ry important project. After all, Mr. Bertram, Rrrrome was not built in a day."

"I realize that, Mrs. Fennessey," Mr. Bertram said, "but the
Fennessey Foundation has been in existence a thousand days
—more—with offices in New York, Palm Beach, and here—
and no evidence that anything has been accomplished or
even started."

"Well, of course all these big projects take a little time to
get off the ground," Justin said without much conviction.

"That's just it. What projects? What ground?"

"Well, now, see here, Bertram," Stan said, very much the
commander in chief. "I suspect that I know a good deal more
about these setups than you do."

"I doubt that. This is my specialty."

"When I was called in to take charge of the Community
Fund drive of Greater—"

"Please, Stan," Lydia said from between her lovely teeth.
"As I was saying, Mr. Bertrand—Ber*tram*—the project we
are considering at the moment is one which is so important
that we have not wanted any publicity until everything is
ready to form a united whole." Lydia liked that one so well

that she tried it again, her lips puckered like a glass blower's. "Yes, a united whhhhhole."

"Mrs. Fennessey, we've all talked a long time and said nothing. Just name *one* project and I'll be perfectly satisfied."

Lydia did a quick half turn and spread her arms, charm bracelets clanking. It was a gesture she had copied from the late Constance Bennett although the final result was more reminiscent of the late Al Jolson singing "Mammy." "Well, I'm only *trying* to—" In such cramped quarters, Lydia's footing did not have its usual sureness. She trod on one of Gretchen's outstretched paws. With a yelp of wounded indignation, the dog leapt to her feet and limped hastily toward Justin's desk, tossing Lydia a reproachful glance over one shoulder.

Desmond let out a most unbusinesslike guffaw and even Jenny, in a rare moment of closeness, buried her face in Desmond's shoulder and quivered briefly with merriment.

"Justin," Lydia said, "*must* that dog be . . ."

"Awwww, Gretl, *die kleinchen,* did Mommy hurt you? Mommy didn't mean to. Did you, Mommy? You must forgive poor Gretchen, Mr. Bertram. She's in heat."

"Perfectly all right. That reminds me, there's a bill for horsemeat on the foundation budget. Go on, Mrs. Fennessey."

Lydia had had her lines killed before—someone going into an epileptic fit during the *Skylark;* that drunk throwing up into the orchestra pit at the Winter Garden; *trying* to work with Miss Bankhead. Her roles never having been large, Lydia treasured every word, every pause, every bit of business assigned to her. She did not take kindly to interference. But today, Lydia was almost grateful to that damned dog as she hadn't the faintest idea what her next speech was to be. "Do forgive me, Mr. Bertram, but I've quite lost track of what I was about to say."

"Project."

"Oh. Oh, yes." Lydia cast her eyes upward to an allegorical pastorale painted on the ceiling in the manner of Gérard and wondered just why the hell she'd got herself into this big scene when, actually, she didn't give a shit if Justin and the whole Fennessey family wound up in Leavenworth.

"The project," Mr. Bertram said.

"Uh . . ." Justin said.

"Br . . ." Stan interjected.

"Ah . . ." Lydia commenced.

Just then the *deus ex machina* stumbled, without knocking, through the door. It was Captain Mulcahy. He was in his stocking feet and wore, rakishly tied, John Wesley's dressing gown. Two recent urine spots darkened the front of it. "And so it's here that everybody's hiding? I been searching the whole house high and low and not a sign of hide nor hair of no one."

"Captain Mulcahy," Justin said, "we are in a meeting and . . ."

"Oh, a meeting is it?" Rory sat down on a delicate chair, his robe—or, rather, John Wesley's robe—flying open to offer a seductive glimpse of his hairy thighs, his yellowed stockinet underpants. "I seen this piece in the news today reminds me of a most entertaining tale about me old chum Brendan Behan and I . . ."

"Captain Mulcahy," Mr. Earnshaw barked in his best parade-ground voice, "as Mr. Fennessey has just told you—"

"Excuse me," Mr. Bertram said, "but who . . ."

Jenny giggled helplessly. Desmond rose to his feet. "How rude of us. Mr. Bertram, surely you have heard of Captain Rory Mulcahy? He is our playwright in residence."

And then everything clicked into its proper slot in Mrs. Fennessey's brain. "Of course," Lydia said, as though her performance had just been saved by a cue hissed from the prompter's desk. "Captain Mulcahy is, as yet, unknown in the United States. But he is a crrrreative wrrrriter of very, very grrrreat and unusual talent, whose work will some-day . . ."

"Why, yes, yes. Of course," Justin said.

"You mean you're putting on a play? Millions of dollars and one play?"

"Not—not so much a play, Mr. Bertram," Lydia said. Again she cast her eyes toward the painted ceiling. "It's—it's more of an *allegory*."

"Let me get this straight. Three years and now you're putting on a play."

"Captain Mulcahy has been committed," Desmond said.

"Or at least he should have been," the marquesa said.

"I've been writing some poetry, like," Rory said.

"Yes!" Lydia said briskly. "Poetry. It's a whole new art fawm."

"Art film?"

"Why, why, *yes!* Exactly, Mr. Bertram. An art film! In that way the work of the Fennessey Foundation can reach thousands—millions—more people."

"What's it about?"

"Why, ah . . . well, as I said, it's an allegory."

"Cast of thousands," Desmond said. He tossed a ludicrous wink in his sister's direction. Jenny went immediately into a choking fit and lurched out of the room.

"What's the matter with the countess?" Mr. Bertram asked.

"My sister, the marquesa, suffers from vertigo," Desmond said. "Perhaps I'd better go and see if I can help her." With that he, too, deserted the ship.

"Have you got a script I could see?" Mr. Bertram asked. John Wesley sensed that he was no pencil-pushing night-school accountant. His sympathies were all with Mr. Bertram. He wanted to blurt out that the foundation, the Fennesseys, Mr. Earnshaw, and Captain Mulcahy were all frauds, that he was ashamed to be in the same room with them and that they all belonged behind bars.

"A—a what?" Justin said.

"A manuscript."

"They're at the typist's," Peggy said smoothly. John Wesley was displeased. He admired loyalty but he hated dishonesty.

"Aren't you a typist?"

"The mimeograph," Lydia said. "Scripts are always mimeographed."

"Yes, uh, exactly," Justin said. "Mimeographed."

"And when do you plan to start work on this . . . art film?"

"Why, uh—"

"Tomorrow," Lydia said with ringing tones. *"Tomorrrrrow."*

"May I be excused?" John Wesley said.

Pleas

John Wesley had just finished packing when he heard a tap at his door. Rory? No. Rory never bothered to knock.

"Who is it?"

"Jack?" a voice said, ringing cheer and good fellowship. "It's Jus."

"*Who?*"

"Justin. Justin Fennessey."

"And Lydia," another voice said with phrenetic vivacity.

John Wesley opened his door and Mr. and Mrs. Fennessey ventured inside. "Come to check on my luggage?" John Wesley said. "I haven't taken any spoons, but feel free to examine anything you like."

"But, my dear young man," Justin said, laying a soft hand on John Wesley's sleeve, "what is all this?"

"Two suitcases, a typewriter, an attaché case. If it's all right with you, I'll leave some money with Travis to have the heavy stuff shipped."

"But surely you're not planning to leave us?"

"I thought I made that clear this afternoon, Mr. Fennessey."

Lydia cooed, "But, Mr. Smith—may I call you Wezley?—you're one of the family."

"Oh no I'm not."

"Ummm, well, I've been thinking over what you said this afternoon, uh, Smith. I've also been rereading your contract."

"Yes, I know, Mr. Fennessey. It's airtight and all in your favor. However, I don't think you're in a very good position to do much about—"

"Oh, come now. That's not what I meant. It's a question of the salary. I can't imagine, heheheh, whoever suggested such a ridiculous figure."

"You did."

"*I*? I must have been out of my mind."

"So must I. Anyhow, it's all over now. We both made a mistake. No hard feelings."

"But of course the salary will be adjusted. Doubled, in fact."

"Yes, and Justin dear, this pokey little room," Lydia said. "I had no idea that our nice Mr. Smith was tucked away back here. Don't you think the Empire room?" The word rolled out of her mouth as "Ompeer."

"Oh, by all means, my dear. The Empire room *and* the salary doubled."

"Miss O'Neil could type up a new contract right now, darling."

"Miss O'Neil is busy calling the movie-equipment companies. We can just change the salary in the margin and initial it."

"Don't you think that kind of money is a little high for a summer tutor, Mr. Fennessey?"

"As a matter of fact, I've been, uh, mulling over your opinion of the children's, uh, scholastic aptitudes and I've come to the conclusion that perhaps—in fact, most probably—you are perfectly correct."

"Yes," Lydia said. "They're much too sensitive for formal education. Especially Deirdre. I know. I was, too."

"Then there'll be no need for me to stay at all," John Wesley said.

"Oh, but there *willllll!*" Lydia cried.

"Absolutely! As you undoubtedly heard Lydia tell that man from the government, we expect to be starting our film tomorrow."

"Starting your film? *What* film?"

"Well, uh, that's just it. As you already know, Captain Mulcahy is a writer of international repute."

"World-wide fame, you might say," Lydia added.

"Yes, uh, but undisciplined."

"Oh, totally," Lydia agreed. "So many geniuses are."

"Please, Lydia. Well, as it happens, Captain Mulcahy has a manuscript of sorts with him. Some of it very interesting."

"Oh, brilliant! If *I* were a young actress starting out all over again . . ."

"*Lydia!* But it needs pulling together."

"Oh, I would say pulling together, weeding, tightening, pruning are of the essence."

"And?" John Wesley asked.

"And we feel—in fact, we *know*—that you're the one to do it."

"Oh, yes. When I think of the way you got those silly little Ponsonby girls up on the stage performing like real professionals. Deirdre—"

"I happened to be doing a play by Shaw that was written at the turn of the century and performed at least a million times since. It didn't need any pulling together, as you put it. But I wouldn't feel competent to be working on a film that would cost upward of a million dollars to produce."

Justin paled; Lydia plunged right on. "Oh, but what I mean, Wezley, is that your approach is so fresh, so new, so unspoiled. Nothing old hat or hackneyed. That's the sort of thing we *want*. Isn't it, darling?"

"Just what sort of actors were you planning for this . . . this art film?"

"Why, uh . . ." Justin started and stopped.

Then Lydia pounced. "Why, also fresh, new faces. With, of course, a few competent old pros. Dierdre, I thought . . ."

"Deirdre as what, Mrs. Fennessey?"

"Call me Lydia, please, Wezley," she said with an engaging smile. "Why, as . . . well, as sort of the ingenue."

John Wesley realized perfectly well why these two fatuous hypocrites were here in his room flattering him so outrageously when, only a couple of hours ago, they would have been happy to have seen the last of him. Now they were in trouble. They had lied their way out of one predicament and into a worse one. They needed help in the worst way and they were asking for his, not because they had any great belief in his talents—why should they have?—but because he was the nearest port in a very bad storm.

John Wesley knew that he was going to stay on. He neither liked nor respected the Fennesseys; he didn't believe their blandishments; he wasn't seduced by the doubled salary or the promise of grander quarters. But he would remain out of sheer curiosity. The bumbling *chutzpah* of these people fascinated him. For better than three years they had done nothing to satisfy their tax-free status as a nonprofit foundation save send out a few overblown press releases. Now with the government breathing down their necks, would they really dare to put together an elaborate home movie and call it Art? While his better judgment told him to have no part of this insane enterprise, he was simply too inquisitive to walk out. But first he would play with them just a little.

"Can you give me some idea as to what Rory's script is about?"

"Oh, it's brrrrilliant!" Lydia cried, gesturing as if she were Judith Anderson.

"Absolutely first-rate," Justin said.

"That's fine. But I asked what it's about."

"Wellllll . . . Really, Justin, Cousin Bridget is getting so careless." Lydia busied herself at straightening the Georgia O'Keeffe, which was already quite straight.

"I mean," John Wesley said, "is it boy-meets-girl? Is it period or contemporary? What is the locale?"

"W-w-w-w-well, it's . . . it's . . ."

"I'd say it's Irish. Wouldn't you say it's Irish, Justin?"

"Uh, yes. Rather Irish."

"Naturally," John Wesley said, "I wouldn't want to commit myself until I've read the material."

"Oh, but you know it's brrrrilliant," Lydia said, with an Ina Claire *moue.*

"No. I do not know that. Why don't we find Rory and read it?"

"Splendid idea," Justin said.

"Yes, Wezley," Lydia said. "Why don't you run down to the libr'y and have a nice script consultation with Captain Mulcahy? I must change and—"

"No," John Wesley said. "We'll *all* go."

Captain Mulcahy was in the library, as expected. As unexpected, he had shown a sudden interest in the works of Marcel Proust, thus discovering the large cache of liquor. He was well on his way through it when John Wesley and the Justin Fennesseys found him. He looked up at them through bleary, bloodshot eyes. "So it's a film you'll be making. Perhaps you could use me. I used to do a bit of extra work at the old Ealing Studios in London. Stunts and the like."

"And what kind of stunt do you call this?" John Wesley asked.

"Yes, Captain Mulcahy," Lydia said carefully. "The cocktail hour won't be until seven. Wezley, here, has shown *such* an interest in reading your manuscript. We all have. Haven't we, darling?"

"Ummm," Justin said.

"Manuscript?" Rory said dreamily.

"Yesssss," Lydia said in loud, clear, ringing tones. "Your play."

"Play?"

"Play. Film. Pageant. Whatever it is that you've been talking about."

"?"

"Where is that brief case you're forever lugging about with you?" Lydia snapped.

With a dirty, stubby forefinger, Rory pointed vaguely in the direction of the desk. Lydia marched to the desk, snatched up the brief case and opened it with a militant snap. Some sheets of grease-stained paper fell out, followed by the pair of dirty socks, the remains of liverwurst sandwich, some yellowed photographs of ladies wearing what were once known as "teddies" and which must have been considered racy to the point of pornography around the time of World War I, and, finally, a terrified cockroach. Lydia stepped back, appalled.

Peggy O'Neil came in to report. "I've telephoned the film-equipment companies. They'll all be here tomorrow morning, early. Would you like me to call an exterminator, too?" She stepped forward and ground the cockroach into the carpet.

Regaining her composure, Lydia smiled brightly at Peggy

and said, "Were you able to locate Mr. Plover, the director?"

"It wasn't easy, Mrs. Fennessey. His answering service wouldn't answer. When it finally did, the girl said that he was directing summer stock in Ogunquit, Maine. I finally got in touch with him there. He said that he has a contract through Labor Day."

"Did you tell him the salary we were offering?" Lydia said.

"I did. He'll be here tomorrow."

"Good!" Lydia said with a sigh.

"Plover? Plover?" Justin said.

"A brilliant young director, dear," Lydia said. "I've been interested in his work for some time."

"But, Lydia, my dear, how can you possibly engage a director without even having read the . . . the script?"

"Just how many directors do *you* know personally, Justin?" Lydia asked darkly. That seemed to be the end of that.

"If that will be all?" Peggy said.

"Not quite, Miss O'Neil," Lydia said. "We need *all* the help we can get. Mr. Smith has graciously consented to stay on in an advisory capacity. Haven't you, Wezley?"

"Maybe. It depends on the material."

"Yes," Justin said. "Just so. The material. May we now see your work, Captain Mulcahy?"

"Well, it isn't exactly what you'd call a work, like."

"Whatever you call it," Justin said, "may we read it? *Now.*"

Lydia snatched up the pile of crumpled papers, rattled them imperiously, and riffled through them. "I can't make head or tail of this, Rory. You don't seem to have numbered the pages."

"I . . . ah . . ."

"Mulcahy, get off that sofa and please help Mrs. Fennessey. This is important!" Justin said, desperate.

Rory struggled up off the sofa and shuffled across the room. He was still wearing John Wesley's dressing gown, which was now caught in the crease between his buttocks. For the first time John Wesley began to understand Desmond Fennessey's wicked extravagance in burning all clothing borrowed by Rory Mulcahy.

With trembling hands Rory took up the pages. "I . . . I seem to have misplaced me spectacles somewheres. I'm lost without them."

"I don't remember ever seeing you wear glasses, Captain Mulcahy," Peggy said.

"Nor I," Lydia added. "Not even when you flew Desmond's plane back from Boston."

"Well, that's just it. I don't know where I lost me spectacles and I can't see me nose in fronta me face without them."

"You seem to be able to read the print in *The New York Times*," Peggy said. "Aloud."

"And over my shoulder," John Wesley added.

"Oh, for God's sake," Justin snapped, "why don't we just—"

"Here," Lydia said. "Let *me* try." She cleared her throat, arranged her voice to its husky, onstage best and began:

> Come away, O human child!
> To the waters and the wild
> With a faery, hand in hand,
> For the world's more full of weeping than you
>   can understand.

Why, that's lovely, Rory. Wasn't that nice. Justin?"

"Very moving. What did you think, Smith?"

"I thought it was just great. Nearly as good as when William Butler Yeats wrote it."

"Really!" Lydia said.

"Do you mean that you're trying to pass off stuff written by other . . ."

"Ah, dear old Billy Yeats. A great chum of mine. He sent that to me in a letter just the other day. That must be how it got in among me papers."

"Yeats died in 1939," John Wesley said.

"Well, everyone's complaining about the postal service nowadays," Peggy said.

"Now, listen to me," Lydia said sharply, "this is serious. We have a good deal of expensive talent and equipment arriving here tomorrow to make *your* film . . ."

"Have you now?" Rory said. His tone was that of a child who had just been told that the circus was coming to town. "Perhaps there'd be something in it for me. I used to do stunts, like, at the old Ealing Studios."

"My God, Lydia, this good-for-nothing soak you and Desmond picked up can't even keep track of what we're talking about. I tell you, it's absolutely—" Justin stopped, hypnotized, as Rory tottered back to the sofa and collapsed on it. Save for a soft, sweet snoring, nothing more was heard from him.

"That does it, Lydia," Justin said. "We'll simply lend the art collection to Chicago or Cleveland or someplace like that after the summer is over. I'll telephone Mr. Bertram and tell him—"

"You will do no such thing, Justin Fennessey. Poor little Deirdre has her heart set on making this film and—"

"Poor little Deirdre isn't even here, my dear," Justin said. "She knows nothing about—"

"Be still, Justin. Wezley, would you please step over here and glance at this. It seems to be called *Cinderella Flanagan* and what little I can read of it is ra-ther good."

"Good?" John Wesley asked.

"Well, I mean it's ghastly, but the plot is foolproof and—"

"Lydia, my dear, do be realistic and—"

"Shut up, Justin, I'm reading. And this page—there's only

one, so far—seems to be quite a lot like *Last Year at Marien-bad*. And then there's a sort of Jean Cocteau bit about—"

"Drink time, everyone," Desmond said, popping his head through the doorway.

"Shut up, Desmond, and come in here. We need your help. *We need all the help we can get.*"

Action

The heat, the light, and the noise were beyond belief. Squinting and staggering, John Wesley groped his way down from the immense structure shaped like a boat and draped like a tent that was bed in the Empire room. He gasped as he saw a naked man standing in his room and then realized that it was he, reflected in a cheval glass bristling with golden helmets, spears, and fasces. His dressing gown, wadded into a ball, lay in the fireplace where he had put it early this morning just after the footman who had put Captain Mulcahy to bed brought it to him, held at arm's length like a dead rat. The dressing gown could stay there. Better to spend the money on a new one than risk catching—well, who knew what.

Searching for something to cover his nakedness, John Wesley tentatively opened one of the vast bronze-trimmed mahogany doors. A shrill whistle of appreciation from Miss Deirdre Fennessey told him that he was in the corridor. In an agony of embarrassment, John Wesley tried the other door.

It led to the sort of bathroom the cab driver who brought him here had been talking about—black onyx with a tub that looked like the sarcophagus of an emperor, golden ewers (purely ornamental) shaped like burial urns and gilt lion masks to spout water. There were also towels.

Wrapping himself in a bath sheet, John Wesley padded back into what was his new bedroom and tried to collect his thoughts. From the mantelpiece a Bréguet clock involving Mars, Minerva, the Continents, a chariot, three horses, and, just incidentally, the time of day, struck eleven. Never before had he slept so late. It made him feel wicked, as did his nudity, the satins and brocades, the wreaths and bees, the menagerie of swans, eagles, sphinxes, and griffins of this overpowering room.

But then, it occurred to him, never before had he worked the night through. The sun was shining, the birds singing, the fountains splashing, the peafowl strutting before he had mounted the dais to his bed, too exhausted to hunt out his pajamas from whatever mammoth mahogany commode they had been placed in by the newly attentive servants. Rory's writing. His mind was becoming a little clearer. Glancing across the room he saw a grubby pile of papers stacked as neatly as possible on the lower lip of a yawning *secretaire à abattant*. Making sense of the scraps of paper vomited forth from Rory's brief case had been more a problem in cryptology than in editing. With varying degrees of effort, Lydia, Justin, and Desmond Fennessey had worked on it before offering vague excuses of other duties in other parts of the house. Captain Mulcahy, himself, had been worse than useless, snoring wetly on the library couch. Peggy O'Neil had stayed the longest, excusing herself shortly after three in the morning. Captain Mulcahy had been carried away—quite literally—at five. Now his magnum opus, abridged of unpaid bills, snatches of other people's work, bus transfers, soiled tissues, a leaflet extolling a product said to be efficacious in the treatment of crab lice, and, of all things, a photograph of Shirley Temple, sat on the desk. If that was talent, John Wesley thought angrily, so was the wastebasket in any elementary-school classroom.

From the gardens outside the noise became increasingly loud, culminating in the blasting of an automobile horn, a long, low rumble, a terrible crash, and a burst of profanity more eloquent than anything John Wesley had heard since his army days. Clawing and grappling with the tangle of tassels, swags, festoons, and jabots hanging at the windows of the Empire room, John Wesley looked down upon a scene that was beyond belief. He felt that it *should* have recalled days of childhood when the traveling circus set up for twenty-four tinselly hours in his home town, but there was no glamour, no glitter in the mob scene below. If a crew had been suddenly called in to demolish the Fennessey house as quickly as possible—Fennessey Demolitions, perhaps—it would have looked more like what was going on today. In fact, John Wesley could not be entirely certain that these people didn't have exactly such an aim in mind. Great trucks were rutting the velvet lawns. A huge generator, already bogged down in a round flower bed of delicate pinks and yellows and whites, sent forth an ominous humming and even an occasional terrifying blue flash. A truckload of enormous klieg lights was dumped onto the driveway with a terrifying rumble and a frightening crash of glass. A battery of enormous cameras and mystifying sound equipment—at least John Wesley supposed that it was sound equipment—had come to a hopeless impasse at the portico. A group of people were having a voluble argument with the local taxicab driver, their luggage spilled out on the blue gravel of the driveway. Men in coveralls, brandishing sheets of paper to be signed, were grumbling and cursing.

On the outskirts of the crowd, but obviously anxious to drive right into the thick of it, a man in dark glasses, ascot, and cap sat at the wheel of a Jaguar convertible, no longer in its immaculate showroom condition, but rakish withal, blasting away on the horn. Lydia, crisp and epicene in hop-sacking slacks, caroled gaily and flapped a red chiffon handkerchief in the general direction of the Jaguar.

Miss Rafferty streaked through the crowd screaming and shaking her fist like a small, hysterical Savonarola. Sean and Shelagh, suddenly freed from their intellectual endeavors, wandered about touching things that surely must have been dangerous. Luis Fernando had already made the acquaintance of a taffy-haired young thing who looked like the kind of girl who refers to herself as an actress when caught in a vice raid. Consuelo stood at the edge of the crowd trying to stifle her giggles. Miss Deirdre Fennessey was not above curiosity as to what was going on. With Gretchen yelping at his heels, Justin Fennessey rushed about pointing out as diplomatically as possible that this truck had driven into an ancient—and priceless—boxwood hedge, that another had parked in the middle of a rose bed, that yet another was blocking the driveway. More or less covered by a silk robe, Desmond Fennessey, drink in hand, shouted irrelevant and irreverent things to them all from the balcony off his bedroom.

Peggy O'Neil, looking unusually harassed, moved from disorganized group to disorganized group trying to bring about quiet, order, and sanity. But today not even the calm and collected Peggy was making much dent on the noise, the hubbub, and the general lunacy.

The Empire room curtains and John Wesley's towel fell simultaneously as he clutched at his head. "My God, my God, my God," he said aloud. "Not just a producer and possibly a director to *talk* about their stupid movie, but the whole kit and kaboodle actually here to *shoot* it!"

There was a discreet tapping at the door and then it was flung open. It was Lydia, her arm linked through that of a middle-aged man—the driver of the not-so-new Jaguar.

"I—I'm not dressed," John Wesley said, clutching at his towel. One end of the long bath sheet trailed on the floor behind him.

"You look divine, Wezley."

"Yess," her companion said, "sso Roman. Or maybe like ssome ssort of old showgirl in the *Sscandalss.*"

Speaking of clothes, John Wesley thought irritably, these two were hardly got up for maximum anonymity. Lydia, in her sissy little slack suit, the ruffled shirt, the pompon pumps, the drifting red chiffon handkerchief, called to mind one of the more widely published photographs of Sarah Bernhardt, circa 1870. To do her justice, it was exactly the image Lydia wished to evoke. Her companion was a fat-thin, hairy-bald man nearing fifty. He wore suede loafers, suede pants, and a suede coat. "Thiss room's ssimply too kicky, Lyd. Sso *L'Aiglon.*"

"*Do* you like it, Wyn? It's one of my favorites," Lydia purred. Then the cogs of her voice box meshed as she shifted into her Gracious Lady register. "Wezley, I came pounding up here at this ungodly hour because I was so anxious to have you meet a ve-ry brrilliant director—and a ve-ry dear old friend—Wynton Plover; John Wezley Smith. Wezley is supervising our script. Aren't you, Wezley?"

"Well, I . . ." John Wesley grabbed at his towel with his left hand while Mr. Plover took his right just a bit too long and just a bit too firmly.

"It'ss going to be ssuch fun working with you," Mr. Plover said. "With *all* of you."

Lydia cast an appraising glance at Wynton Plover and did not miss the appraising glance he was casting at John Wesley. "Shall we sit down for a moment?" she asked. "Here, Wyn. Next to me," she said pointedly, patting the cushion of

the meridienne. Like the manliest of little fellows, Lydia
crossed her knees and dangled a pump from her swinging
foot. With a fleeting *moue* of disappointment, Mr. Plover sat
next to her and removed his cap—also suede. He took it off
very gently so as not to disturb his carefully, casually arranged coiffure. His hair, brushed forward in sparse bangs,
was the current salvation of the juvenile no longer young. Its
color was also noteworthy. "Charcoal Gray," it was called at
Pierrot's Salle des Hommes, where a shampoo, razor cut, tint,
and youth masque could run to a full day's pay, if not a full
day's time. Not black, not white, not blue. Charcoal Gray
was the inhospitable halfway house between youth and age,
just as the François I bangs were the meeting place between
the Kennedy swoop and the Yul Brynner polished shave.
"And it doesn't *look* dyed," Pierrot assured his more dubious
clients. It did. Even so, it was probably some improvement
on the dismal brindle Wyn Plover's hair would have been.

Lydia was conscious of her own little gasp as Wyn removed his cap and patted what he hoped was the hair on his
crown. Lydia remembered it, twenty years ago, as the most
heavenly russet color. She noticed, too, that his eyebrows
had been dyed to match. "And what else?" she wondered
grimly.

Oh, there hadn't been anything much between them,
really, although they had slept together every night for the
whole summer season in Woonsocket. Wyn had been too
much. Divine. Sex on the hoof and no doubt about it. She
had supposed that he liked boys just as well, perhaps better.
Supposed, hell! She damned well knew it, and all about that
Stock Exchange closet queen who kept Wyn in an arty little
flat on Sheridan Square—just six minutes from Wall Street.
But Lydia hadn't cared. People in the arts had to make personal sacrifices for the sake of their careers. Lydia, herself,
had crawled into Mr. Plover's bed only in the hope of being
hired for the summer. But once in it, she hadn't wanted to

leave it, even for the time necessary to sign the contract. He had been like an eel. An electric eel, considering the way he could turn Lydia on. During her years as *the* Mrs. Fennessey, Lydia had often recalled and with longing her squeals and pitchings and writhings with Wyn in that lumpy cot at Woonsocket. For almost twenty years she had kept the memory aglow while she forced herself to perform with ladylike undulations and well-timed moans beneath the torpid lard of Justin Fennessey. Now she wondered why. Wyn's career as a director had come to zero, just as had his careers as actor, dancer, and choreographer. Oh, Lydia had seen his name now and then on the drama page of the *Times.* He was forever being hired to direct those little poo-poo plays, starring absolutely nobody, that any idiot could predict—and correctly— would fold in New Haven. Or if it wasn't that it was another summer of stock, an industrial, an occasional Junior League Follies or some dreary sesquicentennial pageant in West Douche Bag, Tennessee. Wynton Plover's name had hardly become the household word that hers had. Nor, Lydia was frank to admit, had he weathered the years as well as she had. That hair! If you could dignify it by such a name. Lydia's hair was quite honestly her own as to color, body, and sheen. Not a white one yet. Lydia knew, because she searched carefully every day. It would be years before Lydia, unlike Jenny, would have to bow her head unto the dye vat to become the standard, suspect ash blonde of uncertain age—*years!* As for her figure, Lydia could still slip into the size ten she had worn on the day she became Mrs. Justin Fennessey in the Lady Chapel of St. Thomas More's. That is, if she would own anything as tatty as that little forty-nine-fifty rayon *peau de soie* rag. Lydia still seethed when she thought back to the muffled snigger issuing from the tremendous collar of the Marquesa de Mondragon's Balenciaga coat. All wrong for Jenny, to be sure, but still Balenciaga. That snigger had made Lydia eternally grateful that Mom and her sister Pearl were unable to attend the ceremony; were, indeed, entirely unaware that it was taking place. But the body that Lydia had brought to Justin Fennessey's bed, only a little the worse for wear from a season in Wynton Plover's, was still the same, thank you. And just look, would you please, at Wild Wyn today! The concave belly, the jutting hip bones, the countable ribs, the marionette thighs, the hard little bottom; where were they now? Lydia knew. Hiding beneath the suet of indifference, neglect, and middle age. Really he was just a fat old fag. Come to think of it, by sheer, odious comparison, Justin Fennessey wasn't as bad as she had thought. And something that was even better was this prim, puritanical young John Wesley Smith, sitting huddled in his towel like a virgin at the gynecologist's. Lowering lustrous lashes which were also her own, Lydia gave John Wesley an approving glance. It met with Wynton Plover's equally approving glance at the inside of John Wesley's left thigh. Lydia cleared her throat sharply.

"You've put on weight, haven't you, Wyn, dear?" she said.

"Some," Wynton Plover said, pulling in his belly.

"It becomes you," Lydia said in that special tone of voice which she knew would be taken for utter insincerity. It was.

"I ought to be getting back to the gym," Wyn said, lowering his eyes.

"Jim who?" Lydia said levelly.

"Uh, Mrs. Fennessey . . ." John Wesley began.

"Wezley, I thought we'd agreed. You're to call me Lydia."

"Uh, yes. Well, if you'd allow me to find my clothes and get dressed, then we could all—"

"Oh, don't bother, pleasse," Wyn said.

"No, Wezley, what with all hell breaking loose down below, I think that we ought to talk about Captain Mulcahy's script right away. You know Rorian Mulcahy's work, of course?" Lydia asked Wyn, knowing damned well that he couldn't possibly.

"Oh, yess. Interessting."

"But the trouble is," John Wesley said, going to the desk and taking up the meager pile of soiled high-smelling papers, "there's nothing to talk about. I've been sorting out this stuff all night. It's all here in *some* kind of order. But still it's nothing."

"Nothing?" Lydia said, arching her brows.

"Some poetry ranging from mediocre to passable. A few bits and pieces of prose. Three different scenes. Short ones. I don't even know whether any of it's original. There are a lot of things among his papers that are other people's work."

"But, Wezley, if there are *three* scenes?"

"But they're just little snatches from three different plays. Different locales, different characters. One is a sort of fairy-tale sequence written along the lines of Lady Gregory."

"Lady Gregory!" Lydia's eyes sparkled. "Ah, the Abbey Theatre. Those lovely, fanciful plays like *The Dragon* and . . . and . . ." Lydia tried to dredge up another Lady Gregory play from some faraway course in the drama. Alas, she could not. "And *The Dragon,*" she finished lamely.

"Very bad Lady Gregory. And written practically in Gaelic or Erse or whatever it is."

"Well, of course in a *film*, Deirdre could always—"

"Another snippet reminds me of John Synge's *Deirdre of the Sorrows.* It—"

"But how appropriate!" Lydia cried with the enthusiasm she used to save for a third-act curtain. "It's almost as though fate had—"

"Sorrows doesn't begin to describe it. Not only is it unplayable, it's unreadable."

"I . . . seeeeeeee," Lydia mused, implying that she did not.

"And finally there's the thing you saw last night called *Cinderella Flanagan.*"

"Ah, yes," Lydia said.

"It runs a scant ten pages and Mulcahy must have been pretty far gone when he wrote it, or copied it, or whatever. Anyhow, it's a foolproof plot. At least it always has been." John rose, tugged at the drawers of one of the Empire commodes and fished out some clothes. "Here," he said, handing over Rory's papers to Mr. Plover. "Look it over while I get dressed. This is as much as I can do with it—without a total rewrite." He went into the bathroom and closed the door.

John Wesley decided to take his own sweet time. He bathed as well as shaved, dawdling in the immense black tub, almost wishing for a flotilla of toy boats, a school of plastic fish to make his bath take longer. He'd been up all night trying to make sense of this garbage. Now let some of the Fennesseys worry with it. It was their idea in the first place.

When he emerged, refreshed and dressed, Lydia and Mr. Plover were sitting in opposite corners of the room almost, but not quite, glaring at one another. ". . . paying you the highest fee you've ever had in your life to do an easy little job that any—" Lydia was saying.

"But, Lyd, you've ssimply nothing to work *with*."

At John Wesley's appearance both Lydia and Mr. Plover put on bright though ill-fitting smiles. Of the two, Lydia's was more successful. "Wezley," she said, "I believe you mentioned something about a total rewrite?"

Conference

♣ ♧ ♣ ♧ ♣ ♧ ♣ ♧ ♣ ♧ ♣ ♧ ♣ ♧ ♣

John Wesley felt, rather than heard, his stomach rumble as he glanced down the long dining-room table. He had had no breakfast and, alas, this was not a meal but a meeting. The ashtray, the pad, the pencil at each place—it all looked so familiar. John Wesley wondered if out in the *real* world, in places that manufactured lightbulbs and pipe fittings and tractors and chewing gum for a profit, the meeting was as ubiquitous. Or was it simply an occupational hazard of nonprofit foundations and academic circles where time and wind were more abundant? Except that the room was grander and the faces changed, this was in no way different from the eternal faculty meetings and department meetings at Ponsonby. The same pompous clichés—"the question to which I address myself . . ." "Mr. Fennessey brings up an interesting point . . ." "If I may be permitted a moment of levity . . ." "may I preface my explanation with . . ." "I should like to answer that question with yet another question . . ."—set off the same rambling fatuities, all saying absolutely nothing in the maximum number of words (each of which was being dutifully taken down by the impassive Peggy O'Neil). As in all such meetings, those with the least to say said the most. As always, two-thirds of the people present had no involvement with, no knowledge of, or no interest in the problem at hand; indeed, no need to be there at all.

After great discussions of who was to sit where and much scraping of chairs, the meeting had been opened with a prayer by Father Alonzo. But as it was in Spanish—and there had been quite a lot of it—it made no difference to anyone. Justin Fennessey, quite naturally, presided. He was awfully good at presiding. If at any desperate moment it appeared that every inane question had been unsettled by an equally inane non-answer, that even the most indefatigable of orators, such as Stan Earnshaw, had run out of breath and bromides, Justin could always be counted on to toss a new and equally trivial subject into the arena to be mauled by the waiting gladiators.

Desmond Fennessey, both bored and amused, sat tilted back in a Chippendale dining chair, simpering, snickering, and even laughing aloud at some of the more ponderous statements. It was Miss Rafferty who reminded him how much each of the chairs had cost, from what stately home of England the set had come, how much time and money each would require to be repaired.

Cousin Bridget had been invited to the meeting as billeting officer, quartermaster, and caterer. What she had to say was terse and sensible but it dealt only with her one interest —the saving of money. Travis sat at her right as a sort of aide de camp, taking copious notes of the proceedings. Except for Peggy O'Neil, who had to transcribe it all, and Deirdre, who created an elaborate doodle, no one else had yet touched pad to pencil,—and the meeting was more than two hours old.

Better than half an hour had already been spent on the

housing of the considerable film company, even now visibly disporting themselves in the swimming pool after having consumed a simple al fresco luncheon, which was more than anyone sitting in the dining room could claim. Out of the corner of his eye, John Wesley caught a glimpse of one of them, a raffish blonde rather broad of beam, squealing in the clutches of a nearly naked Luis Fernando. He also noticed that Mr. Earnshaw, launching into a lengthy anecdote concerning bivouacking procedures at West Point and, therefore, having some slight bearing on the care and feeding of the film crew, caught the same glimpse.

Deirdre Fennessey had come to the conclave, John Wesley supposed, as a sort of visiting star, as it was principally for her—and, of course, the federal government—that anything was being done at all. Visiting stars, John Wesley felt, should exude a little more glamour—perhaps a smart suit and sable; mink at the very least—and a bit more condescending graciousness. Deirdre, exposing herself to the crotch, sat with her bare feet tucked beneath her, indifferent to Earnshaw's less than subtle inspections and to Cousin Briddy's pointed reminders that the fabric on the Chippendale chairs was handwoven in Lyons ("Lions, France") and cost fifty-five dollars the meter in bolt lengths. Nor had the star been terribly gracious. She had said "Bananas" once, "Balls" (softly) twice, and yawned three times. They had not been the tight, jaw-breaking, concealed yawns which John Wesley had mastered during the course of several hundred Sundays in church with his mother. No, they had been great, leonine, voluptuous yawns—arms thrust upward, breasts thrust outward, lips squared back like a proscenium arch around her white teeth. It must have been apparent to Stan Earnshaw, halted finally in mid-anecdote by the third such spectacle, that Deirdre still had her tonsils. Looking lower he might have seen what other parts she had—or didn't have.

Sucking in his stomach, tightening his buttocks, and thrusting his pelvis over the edge of the dining table, Earnshaw resumed the story. "When we used to go out on forty-mile hikes with full equipment . . ."

"Ssonny Tuftss," Wyn Plover hissed. Lydia simpered into her red chiffon handkerchief. Deirdre said "Bananas" again.

J. Winstanley Earnshaw was at his worst in the presence of any man of equivocal sexuality. His voice, rather shrill when he was not thinking about it, dropped a full octave to something between the bellow of a bull and the roar of a bear. Eyebrows meeting at the bridge of his nose, forehead corrugated, nostrils dilated, his face became as ferocious as a Dionysian mask—and about as convincing. His gestures, ordinarily inclined toward the airy, were held to the minimum— a gridiron straight-arm to drive home his most pungent points or a clenched right fist crashing into his left palm (and more often than not bruised on the West Point class ring which he had no right to wear). But at such times he most often kept his hands thrust so deeply into his pants pockets that even the most casual observer wondered if his genitals had possibly been misplaced. Whether pertinent to the subject or not, he dragged in references to his three children by his two ex-wives, the West Point football and wrestling teams (of which he had not been a member), and—in exclusively male company—pointed references to an abortion he had caused to be performed some twenty years ago and to an importunate pansy he had beaten to a pulp in a bar in Baltimore. Having been dragged in by the heels, all such references were dumped and left for dead in the middle of the conversational battlefield. Placed opposite the orchidaceous Mr. Plover, Stan's masculinity was turned on so strong that John Wesley half expected him to fling poor old Miss Rafferty onto the table and have his will with her on the bed of roses that adorned its center.

"Him Tarzsan, me Jane," Mr. Plover said to Lydia in a trained stage whisper calculated to carry to Nyack. Lydia snorted ecstatically into her red chiffon. With a guffaw, Desmond nearly went over in his chair, the shrieking of two-century-old mahogany all but causing heart failure to Cousin Briddy. "Ba-*nan*-as!" Deirdre cried. The marquesa, caught in the midst of lighting a Delicado, went into a gasping coughing fit, dropping her *pavé* sapphire cigarette case with a clatter. Since the withdrawal of family financing had ended Chuchu's career as a nightclub entertainer, Jenny felt it only proper to consider anyone connected with the performing arts beneath the notice of the nobility, but as Stan Earnshaw ranked even lower, she threw back her golden head and permitted herself a golden peal of aristocratic laughter, her lower lip drawn in like a marsupial pouch to camouflage equally golden inlays.

Mr. Earnshaw, crimson with anger, said, "I wasn't aware that I had said anything funny."

"I wasn't aware that you had said *anything*," the marquesa snapped, "and that's exactly what you've been saying for the past hour."

"Jenny!" Justin said from the head of the table.

"And don't call me Jenny!" The marquesa gathered up her cigarette case, her lighter, and her sunglasses and dumped them into her purse. "Sorry, but I have a *really* important appointment," she said. Indeed she had. That clever little Hungarian with the electric needle had done so well with Consuelo's mustache that Jenny had invested a bit more into having the girl's beetle brows shaped into two arcs of worldly inquiry. *That* had gone so nicely that both bristling armpits had been denuded. Today Consuelo's shaggy shins would be exposed to frontal attack. Jenny felt so elated by the whole process of deforestation that she didn't know *where* she'd eventually stop. (True, it hurt Consuelo quite a lot. "*Pero, Mamá, no soy un acerico.*" "Don't pincushion *me*, Consuelo. You want to be beautiful, don't you?" Deep in her bones Jenny felt that Consuelo didn't really care. Well, whether she did or not, she was going to be.) "And so if you'll all excuse me . . ." the marquesa said, rising.

Lydia was in unaccustomed accord with her sister-in-law. "Yes, Genevieve," she said, according the purest French pronunciation to Jenny's name, "you're perfectly right." It occurred to Lydia, just vaguely, that perhaps she was getting more than she had asked for and that just now it would do her no harm to have as many allies—both likely and unlikely —as possible. "Mr. Earnshaw, I think that we have discussed housing of the film crew and the actors more than enough, thank you. In the long run Cousin Briddy and Travis will know exactly what to do with them. Cousin Briddy does these things so perfectly," she added, casting Miss Rafferty, whom she loathed, a bewitching smile of confidence.

"If it was *my* say, I'd have the lot of them at the bottom of the Hudson River," Miss Rafferty said.

"Well, it *isn't* your say, you mick bitch," Lydia muttered under her breath. Wynton Plover, ever mindful of his coiffure, tossed his head carefully to the right and the left and guffawed theatrically. Stan Earnshaw glared at him from across the table, wondering what that big fruit had said about him this time.

Wyn jammed a cigarette into his holder, lit it, and blew a cloud of smoke across the table at Mr. Earnshaw. Then just for the sake of mischief, he lowered his eyes and smiled at him. Further—and just to be on the safe side—he gave Lydia's slim thigh an affectionate squeeze beneath the table. "Oh-oh," Lydia thought, "there'll be none of *that*, thank you. Not this year—or next, either."

"Ahem, then it's decided that the—uh—film people will be put into the Cozy Courts. Is that agreed?" Justin asked.

"Well, not *quite*, darling," Lydia said. "I do think that Mr.

Plover, as our director and someone to be in constant consultation over the—uh—script, would be better off here in the house. And more comfortable, too." On the strength of a twenty-year *tendresse*, Lydia had arranged to have Wyn placed in the Charles X room with its wonderful *bateau* bed; infinitely masculine, soundproof and exactly ten paces from her own bedroom. But a glimpse of him after a hiatus of two decades had made none of these advantages seem worthwhile. The room was again under its dust sheets. "I thought that Wyn—Mr. Plover—could have Wezley's old room—if he doesn't mind sharing the bahth with Captain Mulcahy . . ." Mr. Plover went pale. "*Or*," Lydia added with bright malice, "Mr. Earnshaw has a lovely big room with twin beds. If he wouldn't mind sharing?" Now Stan paled.

"I think, in the long run, Lyd ssweetie, I'd be better off down in the motel with the kidss," Mr. Plover said.

Perfect! "Well, Wyn, whatever you say. Now, if we could get to the next point. I'm starving and I know everyone else is, too."

"You don't think it's way past lunchtime?" Miss Rafferty asked. She had been brooding about what could be done with the uneaten luncheon. The jellied madrilene would last indefinitely; the salad could be recrisped for this evening; the *vitello tonnato* (there had been a special on veal) could keep until tomorrow when it made its farewell appearance as *oiseaux de veau*. That would be a saving of . . .

Lydia knew exactly what Miss Rafferty was thinking. "You're so right, Cousin Briddy. How silly of me."

Miss Rafferty permitted herself a chilly smile of victory.

"*Instead*," Lydia said, "let's just have a little picnic. Travis, please ask Cook to open up some simple things—caviar, *pâté*, smoked sturgeon, a nice little Westphalian ham, some Camembert, and lots of bread and rolls. We'll all make our own sandwiches right here. Just pig it." There, that would knock the old cunt's budget into next November. "*Now*, I think we

should work out some definite sort of shooting schedule—
union laws permitting—for Captain Mulcahy's film."

For the first time since his unheeded request for a drink
two hours before, Captain Mulcahy came to life and spoke.
"Is it a picture you're making? I—"

"Oh, Jesus," Mr. Earnshaw moaned, cradling his head in
his hands.

Never one to hold back with a monologue twice as long
and twice as pointless as any of Mr. Earnshaw's, Rory, it was
only fair to say, had sat at his place glassy-eyed and zombie-
like without a word of interruption. Now he felt honor-
bound to show just a little interest. "A film, is it, yer all talking about?"

Lydia's long left hand came down on the dining table with
a crash, her ring digging into its glossy surface. "Yes, for
shit's sake, you bumbling lush. *Yes!*"

"Lydia!" Justin gasped, horrified. John Wesley was even
more horrified, but assured himself that he had heard Mrs.
Fennessey incorrectly. Her next statement disabused him of
such a fantasy.

"Shut up, Justin," Lydia said. Then she turned with blaz-
ing eyes to Captain Mulcahy. "Yes, you stinking stumble-
bum, it's a film we're talking about. *Your* film, if you can call
that crap that fell out of your grouch bag fit for anything but
the city dump. And last night while you were so fucking
drunk you couldn't hit your own ass with both hands, the
rest of us were working *our* asses off trying to make a little
sense out of that crock of shit you've been calling a masterpiece."

Rory's jaw hung ajar. It was a reaction shared by everyone
else at the conference table. Lydia felt simply marvelous.
She hadn't had such a good time in years—not since she let
fly at the stage manager of the Winter Garden on the night
she was leaving the show to become Mrs. Justin Fennessey.
Elated, Lydia plunged on. Except that the lines were earth-

ier, this was the best thing she'd done since she'd understudied the role of Nora in *A Doll's House*. "And furthermore, you free-loading, drunken no-talent, Wes, here, says that there isn't one mothering word in the whole rotten mess that . . ."

Justin's energetic pounding with his gavel on the mellow patina of the table eventually drowned out Lydia's big scene. Flushed, she fell back into her chair, too spent to go on.

"Lydia! There can be no provocation to justify such—"

"Oh, up yours, Justin!"

"Ca-*ray*-zy," Deirdre said. "Man, Ma, can you ever blow your cool!"

Miss Rafferty crossed herself three times. Father Alonzo, alert at last, bubbled and hissed as to what la Señora Hoosteen could possibly have been saying. Desmond roared with laughter and applauded heartily. Captain Mulcahy, frozen, stared goggle-eyed at Lydia, his jaw still slack exposing an interesting openwork pattern of missing teeth. Peggy O'Neil looked up intently from her notes. "Excuse me, Mrs. Fennessey," she said, "but do you prefer the word 'ass' spelled with a double ess or in the British fashion with an—"

"Miss O'Neil!" Justin gasped.

"I merely wanted to have accurate notes for the—"

"You will please remove *all* of Mrs. Fennessey's most recent statements from the record."

Inspired by Lydia's glorious outburst, John Wesley rose and spoke for the first time. "I don't like to repeat myself and waste a lot of time, but as that doesn't seem to be much of a consideration around here, may I say once more that you're going at this movie thing all backwards."

"Putting the cart before the horse? Letting the tail wag the dog? First things first?"

"Desmond! Don't be flippant!" Justin said. "This is a matter of vital importance to the foun—"

"You're right, Desmond," John Wesley said, using his

Christian name for the first time. Although his contempt for the Fennesseys was not new, his feeling of superiority to them was. Their enormous wealth, their smug sense of complete security, their glorious possessions, their pretensions to culture, refinement, class no longer impressed him. He saw them as what they were: a group of bumbling, shallow, frightened people caught in a series of traps of their own making. "You've had the gall to think that you can hoodwink the whole country by putting on some little amateur charade and calling it Art and a Public Service . . ."

"Mis-ter Smith!" Justin said, banging with his gravel.

"The table, Justin," Miss Bridget said.

"Don't interrupt me," John Wesley said. "I've sat here for three hours and listened to your nonsense. Now you can listen to some sense for a change."

"Bravo!" Desmond said.

"Coooool," Deirdre cooed.

"By using your money, but not your brains, you've got the whole place overrun with directors and cameramen and actors and baskets of costumes. Directors to direct what? Cameramen to film what? Actors to act what? Costumes for what scenes? What you haven't got is the first thing you need—a script. And from what Lydia describes as the 'crock of shit' sitting on the desk in my room, you never will have. So why don't you just pay your taxes, like everybody else does, and forget the whole stupid thing?" Conscious of one of Rory's decayed eyeteeth exposed in a snarl of hatred, John Wesley sat down. There was a profound silence.

Lydia colored and touched her throat. She could happily have ripped her tongue out by the roots. True, her outburst had served as a powerful purge, a glorious emetic, the panacea for nineteen years among the Fennesseys and to nineteen years before them as the scared, unsuccessful little actress being charming to just everybody because a girl never knew.

In a way, it had made up for her thwarted ambitions
—the career that might have been; the dreariness of Justin;
the long pregnancies and disgusting deliveries; giving up the
excitement of town for the boredom of the country; the dogs;
the children; the Fennesseys themselves. But in one minute
of rage she had destroyed the work of years, the step-by-step
development of her greatest character portrayal, Mrs. Justin
Fennessey. She was grateful that Jenny had left the room,
but not very. Desmond, she knew, would repeat the scene,
word for word, to his delighted bitch of a sister, and any particular line he could not remember verbatim would surely be
improved upon. Adjusting her voice to its customary great-
lady timbre, she began to speak but her heart just wasn't in
it. "But, Wezley, doing a film is ra-ther different from doing a
stage play. I mean we can do one bit now and an earlier bit
later and—"

"Not if you don't have any bits worth filming, Lydia," John
Wesley said.

"You mean jusst ssort of make it up as we go along—like
the old Esssanay Sstudioss?" Wyn asked cattily. Mr. Earnshaw growled audibly from across the table. "Oh, sstop it,
Ssuperman! Your virtue's ssafe with me," said Wyn.

"Ah! Yes! Impromptu. Ra-ther like the—uh—old *comme-
dia del' arte*," Lydia said with some trace of her old fire.
"After all, it *is* an art film."

"If you want to go on wasting more time and money I suppose you could do that. But I wish you wouldn't toss the
word 'art' around quite so loosely," John Wesley said.

"From what the tax chap had to say yesterday," Desmond
offered, "I get the impression that the important thing is to
have something in the can—if you'll pardon the expression.
It doesn't really matter how good it is."

"Hmmmm," Justin mused.

"But, Desmond," Lydia said, "it *does* matter. This film will

also serve to introduce Deirdre as an *actress*." Deirdre
sighed. "Unless you would rather I simply launched her on
an empty life as a social butterfly. Something like *Jenny*
wants for Consuelo."

"It would be cheaper," Desmond said.

"That's true, Lydia," Justin said.

"Yes," Lydia said, "but it's not too easy to turn a girl into a
leader of smart society when she has to visit her father—*and*
her uncle—in prison every week. So let's stop this shilly-
shallying and get on with the film."

"Hear! Hear!" Desmond shouted with mock enthusiasm.

"Quite so, Lydia, my dear," Justin said, running a trembling finger around the inside of his damp collar.

Still standing at the far end of the table, John Wesley
leaned forward and rested his weight on his palms. It was
one of his favorite classroom stances. Truly, these people
were as silly and empty-headed as the girls of Ponsonby.
"Lydia," he said, "you are still talking about the film as
though it were something already accomplished. The film is
a triumph. Deirdre's a star. The Fennessey Foundation
smells like a rose—a real benefactor to American arts and
letters. But before you choose your dress for the world premiere, will you answer one question: who is going to supply
the basic ingredient—the story?"

"Why, that's easy, Wezley. *You* are!"

Defeated, John Wesley sank back into his chair. Truly,
these stupid, selfish rich were *worse* than the girls at Ponsonby. They were like the children he had counseled at summer camps getting ready for a picnic. As though to prove it, a
small procession of footmen marched through the pantry
door bearing the *fête champêtre* of the tax-exempt Bourbons.

Story Time

♣ ⚜ ♣ ⚜ ♣ ⚜ ♣ ⚜ ♣ ⚜ ♣ ⚜ ♣ ⚜ ♣

Along with the Empire room and its Roman bath, the library had also become John Wesley's exclusive domain. It was reverently—and quite seriously—referred to as the Story Department. The slave had become the master. The Fennesseys now deferred to John Wesley. Was he comfortable? Had he plenty of light? Did he need a secretary? Was the air conditioning cool enough? Too cool? The slightest complaint—and John Wesley went to some trouble to invent at least one per day—was taken care of immediately. Despite the rigid principles of his Methodist upbringing, John Wesley could not help but enjoy his new position as a power among powers. He took an almost sadistic delight in pricking Lydia's beautiful dream-bubbles of fame and fortune for her daughter. As far as Lydia was concerned, Deirdre was even now accepting the Academy Award. With infinite pleasure John Wesley would wait until her fantasy was built, furnished, and ready to move into, then he would painstakingly tick off the long list of promising young actresses—especially *society* actresses—whose careers had come to naught, and even worse, while watching Lydia's beatific smile harden like concrete in the July sunshine.

Justin was even easier, quicker, and more fun to dispatch. His only interest in the film was as a means to get out of serious trouble as quickly and as cheaply as possible. Deirdre disturbed him, mystified him, and frightened him quite enough as she was. The thought of her as a symbol, an electric sign, a legend in her own time was too terrifying to contemplate. His own unvoiced hope for his elder daughter was marriage to some nice, steady, Catholic boy like Cornelius Slattery's son at Fordham Law School. A big wedding at the cathedral (St. Thomas More's was nicer—lesser Kennedys tended to marry there—but not nearly large enough to hold the Fennessey social and the Slattery political connections), a house in Stanford or Greenwich to fill, at regular intervals, with children and then peace.

Besides, there was the Fennessey name and position to consider. All very well for Gloria Vanderbilt and Princess Radziwill to bumble about 'way off Broadway. The Vanderbilts and the Bouviers had been established a lot longer than the Fennesseys. Although he pooh-poohed and vilified the book as arcane and archaic, democratic Justin quite liked being listed in the *Social Register*. It was within his memory that the Fennessey family had made the grade and it had taken some doing: the pressures of his gentle mother's genteel family plus the clandestine burning of a mortgage the Fifth Avenue Fennesseys held on a branch of the Stuyvesant Square Stuyvesants. Even more than the full column he commanded in *Who's Who*, Justin enjoyed the scant inch which he, his wife, and children occupied on page 275 of that ill-printed little black and orange book. Precious few actresses and no film star whom Justin could recall had ever been allowed in. Getting Lydia admitted had not been a lead-pipe cinch, and no one, least of all Justin, had ever considered Lydia really an actress. Even Don Jesús, as a foreign, unknown, and, fortunately, unseen entity had been easier. Oh no, Deirdre just couldn't undo the work of generations—well, two generations—by indulging Lydia in this maniacal whim. Secretly Justin wanted Deirdre and the art film to fail and with as little expenditure of time, money and effort as possible.

Sensing this, John Wesley delighted in taking the opposite tack with Justin. The film was going to be solid boffo—Radio City Music Hall material. Deirdre was a natural, the sole successor to Marilyn Monroe. So good that it was a crime to operate on this little nickel-and-dime budget when something along the lines of two or three million dollars was so obviously indicated.

Wynton Plover, who had never been paid so handsomely for so little work and who was not entirely above minor prostitution to further his career, made a noble ally. "Oh, Jusstin, she's splendid. Absolutely ssenssational! We should sstart all over again in *color!*"

Sorry that he had inquired at all, Justin would smile feebly and retreat, aghast, from the Story Department.

John Wesley was in his way a perfectionist, even though he realized it would make little difference whether the film was good, and he was firm about work. It began punctually at nine. Grimly, Rory Mulcahy, who rarely rose before eleven, and Wyn Plover, who never got up before noon, appeared in the library grumpy, disheveled and gummy-eyed, cowering before his eager up-and-at-'em-ness. John Wesley supposed that all the people involved hated him. He hoped so. He hated all of them, too. He knew that he was smarter than Rory Mulcahy and sensed that he was at least *as* bright as Lydia's Mr. Plover, although Wyn's glib usage of terminology such as "fade-out," "fade-in," "whip-pan shot," "dolly in," and "dolly back" was helpful in lending the material a more professional air than it actually possessed.

From a hopelessly scratched and scarred print of *The Cabinet of Dr. Caligari* through what seemed to have been the forty-eighth hour of *Last Year at Marienbad,* John Wesley was all too well acquainted with the art film. During his days as a boy in high school his mother had inaugurated a course "The Motion Picture as an Art Form" in the church basement. His attendance had been mandatory. *Greed, Intolerance,* the best of Garbo (which had been none too good), *all* of *Les Enfants du Paradis,* Charlie Chaplin, *The Man of Aran,* the complete works of Jean Cocteau and Hecht and MacArthur had flickered and danced before his eyes one afternoon a week for longer than he cared to remember. Only a scholarship to an out-of-state college had saved him from *Gate of Hell* and a long series of grunting, snorting Japanese pictures. Just once had he dared to hint that he found them something of a bore; comical when they should have been moving, dreary when they should have been comical. He should have known better. Mrs. Smith, who was nowhere if not in the intellectual vanguard, had let him have it for fair. Who was he, a provincial adolescent, to fly in the face of the greatest critics of all time with his own uninformed opinions of an Ingmar Bergman trilogy? Next week *Orphans of the Storm.*

As in all things, Mrs. Smith had, of course, been absolutely right and John Wesley absolutely wrong. If he now found such films pretentious or dull, oversimplified or overcomplicated, he told himself that it was because *he* was pretentious or dull or too simple or too complicated. Stoically, silently recognizing a lack within himself, he had sent his classes packing off to the auditorium of the Museum of Modern Art or to grimy West Side grind houses, where culture, crabs, and a proposition were all available for the price of a single admission, to yawn and fidget through the uncut works of David Wark Griffith, Erich Von Stroheim and the newer Poles, Czechs, Italians, and Swedes, while he resigned himself to lifeguard duty at the Ponsonby pool to mourn the loss of whatever vital ingredient was missing from his own intellectual make-up.

Now, having kept his hopelessly bourgeois tastes as dark a secret as a suspected malignancy, John Wesley found himself captain of the team that was to create the art film of all time. In the actual work of writing, Rory Mulcahy, the author, was more hindrance than help. Loudly expansive about his work when it had lain like a fetus in the warm, dark womb of his brief case, he was sullenly defensive of it now that the defective child had been seen by all. It might not be perfect now but, never fear, it would turn into a thing of beauty. No comma could be changed without argument and arbitration. Even when Rory had been shown that his best lines—in fact, his only good ones—had been used before by other writers there was no graceful surrender; only dark mutterings about suing long-dead playwrights for plagiarism. The slightest hint of criticism over the most minor point—no matter how delicately broached—met head on with Rory's noisiest indignation. John Wesley and Wyn, jealous of Rory's talent, his fame, his popularity, his manhood, his position in the Fennessey household, were all too obviously out to sabotage a work of art which had been acclaimed by Noël Howard, J. Alfred Rank and Truman Capone. (Although wonderfully resourceful with the names he dropped, Rory was less than meticulous about their accuracy.) But there was a way of dealing with Rory. It lay in—or, rather, behind—the works of Marcel Proust, where the library supply of liquor was kept. Rory mellow, Rory incoherent, Rory unconscious proved a far better collaborator than Rory sober.

Mr. Plover—"Call me Wyn, Wes," pat, squeeze, pinch—

was more facile than creative. His running patter, delivered through clouds of cigarette smoke from the library chimney-piece, before which he spread-eagled himself like a limp Jesus, was the standard pansy repartee of the late thirties. Its humorous impact depended upon the audience's familiarity with fashionable New York shops, restaurants, decorators, dressmakers, and actresses of the period. Being just half Mr. Plover's age, John Wesley was not always able to appreciate glib references to Pringle, 1-2-3, Ruby Ross Wood, Herbert Tappé, or Jane Cowl—all having passed their zenith some years before his birth. Although at that time Wyn himself was dressing at Klein's, dining at Child's, and decorating the cold-water flat he shared with another chorus boy from *Knickerbocker Holiday* at the Goodwill Industries, he thought it very square of John Wesley not to bubble convulsively at the immediate recognition of these ultrasmart names.

In addition, Wyn was a long-time movie buff. Although only fifty, his filmgoing career seemed to have commenced with *The Great Train Robbery* and to have continued without interruption until the present moment. As with the world of chichi New York, Wyn's golden age of moviegoing had taken place some years before John Wesley's birth. It was just a trifle ghoulish. Clara Bow, Nancy Carroll, Carole Lombard, Jeanette MacDonald, Jean Harlow, Ann Sheridan, Margaret Sullavan, all dead and buried, seemed to have been the flames of Wyn's younger days. (John Wesley, quite naturally, had no inkling of the brief but passionate walk-on Lydia Fennessey had played in Mr. Plover's rather steamy career. Nor, considering Wyn's behavior, would he be likely to suspect any interlude quite so normal.) Wyn remembered all of the long-gone leading men, principals, character actors, and bit players as though they were members of his family. The superannuated Sirs and Dames who had spent their declining years comfortably contracted to major Hollywood studios were a specialty with Wyn. As mother images, he had Marie Dressler, May Robson, Laura Hope Crews, Edna May Oliver, Minnie Dupree, Ethel Barrymore, Pauline Lord, Maria Ouspenskaya, Sara Allgood, Flora Finch, Alice Brady, Alison Skipworth, and as many more whose total ages would surely have passed the million mark. Further, Wyn could and would tell you whether Adrian, Travis Banton, Omar Kiam, or yet some other dead designer had dressed them. Directors, dance directors, art directors, who did the make-up, the hair, the background music—fascinating facts such as these tripped off Wyn's tongue. He also had total recall as to where and when and with whom he had seen each picture; even what the organist had played on the mighty Wurlitzer in whichever defunct Roxy or Orpheum or Rivoli or Tivoli the film had been shown. Sometimes he could even tell you what the picture had been about. The only thing he forgot— or at least never mentioned—was his single real screen experience—a stag movie, in which he had appeared (a much younger man) in the select company of two longshoremen, a Cuban whore, and a donkey.

Wyn's recollections were occasionally helpful but, more often than not, a time-wasting nuisance. John Wesley, taking full advantage of his knack for sudden deafness, went on with the script over Rory's soft, liquid snores and Wyn's running commentary on the history of the motion picture.

". . . Joan Crawford wearing a ssequin sheath . . . Antonio Moreno . . . dresssed by Oliver Messsel . . . Ssir C. Aubrey Ssmith . . . Dame May Whitty . . . then Lilyan Tashman turnss to Kay Franciss and ssayss . . . Thelma Todd . . . no, excuse me, it was *Dorothy* Gish, not her ssisster . . . Gloria Sswansson trying to ssing; too campy . . . Don Ameche . . ."

"Excuse me, Wyn, but would you mind reading this scene?"

"Hmmm. Yess. Ve-ry good. I can make it work. But, Wess,

there was one ve-ry much like it in *Peg O' My Heart*. Marion Daviess sslinkss down the sstairss and ssayss to . . ."

"Wasn't that Laurette Taylor?"

"On the sstage, my dear. I ssaw the movie at the Balaban & Katz Granada. There was thiss sscene where Marion confrontss Mississs Chichesster and . . ."

In spite of everything, *Cinderella Flanagan* got written. Art film or no, it even had a plot and what John Wesley hoped would be a few flashes of humor. As any attempt at a brogue broke Miss Fennessey up, speech was cut to a bare minimum. Visual effects, Mr. Plover assured the Fennesseys, would be everything. Mr. Plover had some very definite ideas as to what he wanted—shots of roses floating in a toilet bowl, nude men photographed through gauze, an interesting study of the eye of a fly, a rat gnawing at Cinderella's pumpkin. An evil priest had been quietly vetoed by Justin. Likewise, Mr. Plover's suggestion that he and a female impersonator of his acquaintance—"Ssuch a camp, ssweetie!"—play Cinderella's ugly sisters had been censored by Lydia. "I don't care how Cocteau it is," Lydia snarled, "this is an art film, not a drag show." More publically Mrs. Fennessey went on record as saying that she found transvestitism in ra-ther questionable taste.

The Fennessey house was considered suitably palatial to serve as the palace, with the lower gallery to be used as a multimillion-dollar ballroom setting. Justin felt that in that way the Fennessey Collection would be exposed to quite a number of people without undue wear and tear on the carpets. Similarly, various other rooms in the Fennessey house, their lamps and ashtrays replaced by candelabra and snuffboxes, would do very nicely for period interiors. One river looking very much like another, the Hudson could pass as the Liffey, and, if it would ever rain, the hills and knolls of the Hudson Valley could probably pass for Ireland's green.

In the interests of economy and keeping as many as possible of the expensive film employees occupied and at least halfway earning their keep, considerable footage of trees, rocks, meadows, grazing livestock, and just one dew-specked spider web had already been taken and processed. The disused stable yard had been economically transformed into Cinderella's village without and some very rustic interiors for Cinderella Flanagan and her family within. An elaborate horse-drawn hearse had been found decomposing in a barn in Garrison. With only minor changes, it would pass muster as the heroine's coach. Not including salaries, only a bit more than a hundred thousand dollars had been spent in less than a week. Mr. Plover was very proud of that. Mr. Fennessey was aghast.

The actors whom Wyn had brought out with him presented something of a problem. There were six of them—five unemployed friends of Wyn's and a fast-fading juvenile who, without quite realizing it, was approaching the last night of an extremely limited engagement as the eminent director's protégé. As Lydia, whose critical facilities became sharper by the hour, observed, few, if any, of them were Right.

"But, Lyd, ssweetie," Mr. Plover pointed out with some justification, "it'ss not eassy to casst a sstory you've never even read. I jusst got together some sstock characterss who happened to be at liberty."

"Stock is right," Lydia said. "Now let's see how fast we can get them back to liberty."

The blonde with the big behind was the first to go. The marquesa, who had noticed Luis Fernando's attachment to the girl with more than a little displeasure, had suggested her dismissal. "Not at all an Irish type," Jenny said. (The girl had changed her name from Mary Murphy to Mona Moore.) "*Much* too pretty to be either of the stepsisters and too young to do for the fairy godmother, the stepmother, or the queen." Wyn Plover, who had reluctantly stopped entertaining any notions concerning John Wesley, and who had also noticed Luis Fernando, agreed. Mr. Earnshaw, who had spent upward of fifty dollars on the girl at the Slipper Inn and felt certain that ten dollars more would surely get him over the threshold of her room at the Cozy Courts, voiced the first of his theatrical opinions. "I'd thought she'd be perfect as the fairy godmother."

"And I thought *you* would," Wyn said.

It was not Mr. Earnshaw's day. His growled invitation to Mr. Plover to step outside was drowned out by the laughter of Lydia, Jenny, and Desmond, and when he went stalking indignantly off to her cabin at the Cozy Courts, he found the girl in bed with the bartender from the Slipper Inn.

Wyn's protégé was the next to topple, much to Wyn's relief. In less than a month the boy had changed from the grinning, eager-to-please hopeful at auditions into a waspish, greedy Antinoüs to Wyn's Hadrian—damned expensive and disrespectful enough even to suggest that Wyn was a lesser director than, say, Max Reinhardt. High time he was let go and a perfect excuse for getting rid of him. But the dismissal had not been easy. There had been tears, a scene—several, in fact—and a rather nebulous attempt at blackmail. Eventually the boy was granted a screen test. That did it. Wyn didn't even bother to misdirect him. On the other hand, he made no effort to deter him from putting on too much make-up, to see that he was well lighted, or that the sound was correctly mixed. Nor did Deirdre Fennessey do much to make his screen test a resounding success. She broke up three times: first upon his entrance, dressed and painted like a principal boy in pantomime; second over his big speech; and finally at the climax of their love scene, when she had doubled over slapping her knee and howling with mirth. No need, Wyn said, to reshoot. The test was shown to an audi-

ence of Fennesseys the following evening. Save for Mr. Earnshaw's growls of outrage, it was greeted by a shocked silence
until Desmond said, "But which one is supposed to be Cinderella?" The protégé returned to New York on the next train
leaving Wyn to suggest that perhaps Luis Fernando might
be interested in playing the prince.

"Oh, Mr. Plover, I *hardly* think so," Jenny said. "After all,
Luis Fernando will inherit the title and Don Jesús' family is
so strict about . . . well, I really don't think so."

"Visually he'ss ssimply perfect."

Jenny cast him a long glance. "Irish, Mr. Plover? Oh, I'd
never say that Luis Fernando looked Irish. Anyhow, Luis
Fernando has a perceptible Spanish accent when he speaks."

"I could cure that in two or three ssessionss," Mr. Plover
said.

That was exactly what Jenny was afraid of. "I tru-ly think
not. Luis Fernando is still a minor and it would require the
permission of both parents. Uhhhh. *No*, Mr. Plover."

"I think you're absolutely right, Genevieve," Lydia said
with the sympathetic smile of one mother to another. "The
thea-tah is no place for a young man of Luis Fernando's . . .
uh . . . temperament."

"Thank you, dear," Jenny said, wondering what the old
chorus girl was getting at.

Lydia was getting at plenty. This was to be *her* daughter's
film and not some little family stunt to be shared with those
spik Mondragons. Although it was on the tip of Lydia's
tongue to suggest Jenny for the mean stepmother and Consuelo for the stupider of the two ugly stepsisters, she re-
frained admirably. "But I do think it might be fun for your
two—for all of us, in fact—to do little walk-ons. The ball
scene, courtiers, villagers. That sort of thing."

"Yes, darling, that *would* be fun," Jenny said. The mention
of a ball scene reminded her that she had been able to get

absolutely nowhere with Justin on the subject of a dance here at the house to launch Consuelo on her conquest of North America. Lydia was a mother, too—God alone knew why—and she had managed to bring Deirdre out in the white heat of Justin's most democratic phase. A word from Lydia would go a long way to help. Arms about one another's waists, the two sisters-in-law strolled affectionately down the gallery. Really, Jenny thought, she's skin and bones. You don't suppose she's got something . . . fatal? Aha, Lydia told herself, giving Jenny a loving squeeze, that is a roll of fat over her girdle!

One by one Mr. Plover's little troupe was sent packing with sun tans, full stomachs, and a month's severance pay for doing nothing all week. Naturally, being actors, they were voluble in their complaints. Each of them, it appeared, had sacrificed a starring role in the new Tennessee Williams play, a guaranteed thirty-nine-week contract—with residuals—on television, or a three-picture package at Universal just to come out here and sit around.

Although Mr. Plover generously volunteered to fly out to Hollywood for a couple of weeks to cast the picture, Justin was unusually firm in his refusal. And it amazed almost everyone to see how many perfectly established actors were ready, willing, and able to appear at a moment's notice and only minutes' haggling over such mundane details as salary and billing. The major casting amounted to an even dozen telephone calls. Two shrill comediennes who, but three years ago, were the hottest things on television arrived to play the ugly stepsisters. In their wake came a grotesque old character woman, some decades ago the winner of an Academy Award as the best supporting actress, for the evil stepmother. A beautiful young man whose annual income as part-time actor and full-time model amounted to five times Wynton Plover's stepped off the noon train looking more like Prince

Charming than possible. Mr. Plover was enchanted until he learned that the beautiful young man's wife and three children would be arriving later and that the b. y. m.'s sole topics of conversation were a.) diaper rash; b.) the joys of giving the kids a month in the country; c.) his wife's present pregnancy; d.) his actual years—"Yep, thirty-five in September and that's the beginning of middle age, Mr. Plover. Gotta put something by for the kids and Midge in the lean years"— and e.) his investments. Sagging with disappointment, Wyn limped away to allow himself a quick reappraisal of the second footman.

The other actors were recruited from local summer theaters to arrive like day laborers at seven every morning, yawning and moaning and perfectly delighted to be working for scale. Through the law offices of Cornelius Slattery it was discovered that servants, locals, and even the Fennesseys themselves could appear as extras just this once without the trouble and expense of joining a lot of nosey unions. After all, the whole thing was being done on an open-end art grant, so it was charitable work of sorts and not subject to *all* the restraints applied to commerce.

"Ssixx dayss of sslavery and ssuddenly it'ss all done," exclaimed Wyn, suddenly and expansively the Cecil B. de Mille of the Hudson River Valley. "Shooting sstartss tomorrow." Over his brandy balloon he treated the assembled Fennesseys to a patronizing smile. "Sstory, sscript, shooting sschedule, cassting, ssetss, cosstumess. It'ss all in knowing how."

"How divine, Wyn," Lydia purred. She could see it now— Deirdre in her diaphanous ball gown on the cover of *Life*. No, *Time*. No, *Life*. No, *both!* "A real contribution to the dismal cultural life of—*Costumes? What* costumes?"

If the drawing room were on fire the Fennesseys could not have left it faster. Tripping over one another, they raced to the loggia where a long rank of trunks, hampers, shucks, and portable wardrobes stood against the wall.

Lydia tore open the top of the first hamper. There was a whinny of ancient wicker and a centurian's helmet fell to the terrazzo floor with a clank. It was followed by a dented metal lorica, scuffed leather shield, and lank canton flannel toga. An indignant moth flew out of the hamper and circled the bronze overhead lantern hysterically.

"What the hell *is* this stuff?" Lydia screamed, prying open a standing wardrobe. Some bedraggled Elizabethan court costumes, reeking of sweat and grease paint, tumbled out.

"Oh, my God," Jenny said, holding a tasseled G-string at arm's length. "Strippers!"

"*Mamá! Mira!*" Consuelo squealed, spinning around with a beaded and bustled creation of the 1880's. "*El polizón! Que drolático!*"

"Oh, shut up, you simpering idiot!" Lydia snapped.

"How dare you speak to my daugh—" The huge carton Jenny had been struggling with burst open, inundating her with its load of molting feather boas.

"Now, pussykins," Justin said, walking about dazedly with a medieval mantle of stained corduroy and yellowed rabbit.

"Don't pussykins me, God damn it!" Lydia roared. "Wyn, just what the hell do you think you're putting on here? One of your high school frolics? What is all this crap?"

"But, Lyd, ssweetie, you never ssaid what period. There was thiss cosstume housse on Wesst Forty-sseventh that was sselling out their entire sstock for sseventy thoussand dollars and . . ."

"How much did you say?" Justin whispered.

John Wesley tiptoed quietly up to the Empire room and began writing letters of application for a teaching job.

Shooting

♣ ♧ ♣ ♧ ♣ ♧ ♣ ♧ ♣ ♧ ♣ ♧ ♣ ♧ ♣

Shooting—at least that was what it was called—began at seven the following morning. By the time the clock in the stable block struck its four high notes and its low seven notes there were more than a hundred people trampling the front lawn. Save for John Wesley, the beautiful young man who was to play Prince Charming, and the camera crew, they were all people from the nearby village who had arrived either to watch the fun or to apply for jobs as extras. Word had leaked out that the Fennesseys were producing a multi-million-dollar movie; that the Fennesseys were filming a television spectacular; that the Redgrave sisters and/or Elizabeth Taylor and Richard Burton were to star; that it was religious; that it was all about sex; that the Beatles were to be in it; that the fabulously generous Justin Fennessey was paying one hundred dollars a day just for walk-ons.

Quite without vanity, the beautiful young man was scrutinizing his face in a magnifying mirror. "Not much time left for the old pan," he said.

"I beg your pardon?" John Wesley said.

"Thirty-five in September. Beginning of the end. Middle age. Might stretch it another five years if I get peeled."

"Wh-what?"

"Face peeling. Hurts like hell but it's worth it. Face comes out smooth as a baby's ass. Acid. That and a tuck."

"A tuck?"

"Yeah. Lift the eye bags," (he had none) "tighten the uppers, pull up the chops. Costs about a thou and a month before you can face a camera again. But I might get another ten years off the old map." He spoke of his face as impersonally as though it were a bit of old real estate that might or might not profit from remodeling. Actually he looked about twenty years old and it seemed to John Wesley that he had seen him for almost that many years grinning out of the pages of magazines in expensive shirts, cheap underwear, bathing suits, and raincoats. He was the cute boy-daddy showing the wife and kiddies a whale of a time in Bermuda; the rapt young man treating his porcelain girl friend to a belt of imported brandy; the rising executive, prop spectacles and all, in a wash-and-wear suit; the happy husband whose insurance problems had all been solved.

"Quite a lot of very successful actors are much older than thirty-five," John Wesley said kindly.

"Shit, I'm no actor. Hate it anyway. Up all night. Never see Midge or the kids. It's okay if I don't have to learn a lot of lines. Good build, big basket, sing a little, do a time step. That's all they care about. Pizza stands."

"I'm sorry?"

"Pizza stands. Buy a franchise. Good location. Regular gold mine. Half my dough goes into pizza stands. The other half into growth stocks. Midge is a great little manager. Acts as my agent and the kids', too."

"Midge?"

Right on cue, the beautiful young man's wife appeared, trailing three cherubic children. She was as plain as her husband was exquisite, and enormously pregnant. "Hi, honey! Hi, kids!" the beautiful young man shouted. A touching family scene, reminiscent of many of his full-color advertisements, was enacted.

"Did you find out?" Midge asked. "Do they need child extras or don't they? I gave Debra Ann a Toni just in case."

"I don't know, honey. Nobody else is around yet."

"Damn fools," Midge said. "I'd hate to think where we'd be if you showed up late for every sitting. Time is money, you know. Say, can you get the *Wall Street Journal* out here?"

"The Fennesseys subscribe," John Wesley said. "It ought to be in the library right now."

"Hmm. I don't suppose you know what Xerox is doing?"

"I'm afraid not."

"We bought it when it was Haloid—at four," the beautiful young man said.

"New shopping center going up out here," Midge said. "Noticed it driving out. Big Macy's and a lotta boutiques. You think a pizza stand? Or maybe frozen custard?"

"But Howard Johnson's is there, honey."

"You're right for a change. Pizza, then. Debra Ann, stop fooling with your bridge! Sixty bucks just for that pivot tooth. But at least she can still smile on camera. Did you check on the kids' mutual funds like I told you to?"

John Wesley sidled away. He now recognized the beautiful young man's children, too. He had seen their faces a hundred times beaming over phosphate fruit drinks, instant puddings, and cavity-proof toothpaste. He could even remember the three of them singing a particularly offensive commercial on television—something about "Mummy gimme yummy something something for my tummy." He wondered if Midge had her unborn child already signed to a long-term contract.

Yet they seemed perfectly happy and healthy and were probably having a more amusing and profitable childhood at NBC than he himself had had with the YPG.

He caught sight of Peggy O'Neil coming out of the house and hurried to her side. He had scarcely seen her in the past week except to hand her chunks of manuscript for typing, retyping, and stenciling, or at Fennessey meetings or Fennessey meals.

"Can you believe it's really happening—the Fennessey Foundation actually doing something?"

"I can believe it, but I'm not sure that I want to," Peggy said.

"How did things end up last night? I stole away."

"I know you did. I hated you for it. Not well. There was a big brouhaha with Mr. Plover over the costumes. At the moment every little sewing woman in Putnam, Dutchess, and Orange counties is in the small sitting room making over that collective ragbag into a reasonable facsimile of the eighteenth century. Nothing like doing things right. Mrs. Fennessey's own couturier will be out to run up a few suitable rigs for Cinderella. Luckily she spends most of the picture in sackcloth and ashes."

"And what can they do with the Roman costumes? The Egyptian ones? The Indian suits?"

"Dream sequences."

"*Dream sequences?* Over my dead body! Of all the stupid, boring, old-fashioned . . ."

"Speak to the Stage Mother about it, not to me. She thought it was a great idea—and so original. Gives Deirdre all sorts of opportunities to do her stuff. It also puts all the costumes to work—if they hold up that long. Well, here comes my boss. I've also been appointed script girl—'production assistant' they call it."

Wyn Plover, aghast at the earliness of the hour, groped his

way across the lawn with Lydia haranguing him like a comic-strip mother-in-law. Lydia had driven to the Cozy Courts and yanked Wyn bodily from his bed. He looked it, bleary-eyed and unshaven, the helmet of carefully arranged charcoal-gray hair standing about his head like a fright wig.

Confusion was everywhere. John Wesley had never seen a film being made before and now he was fairly certain that Wyn Plover hadn't either. Anyone with a modicum of experience in handling crowds—even a pack of girls in a classroom at Ponsonby—could have done better.

"If you'll all pleasse be sstill and jusst lissten for a ssecond . . ." Wyn cried petulantly. His command drew several lewd whistles but no appreciable silence. Suddenly there was an earsplitting whistle and Peggy could be seen standing precariously on a canvas chair, her fingers between her teeth. "Quiet! Right now. That means everybody." The crowd was still. "Now what was it you wanted to say, Mr. Plover?"

"Oh, yess. Extrass. We need ssome extrass. Not more than ssixty. I want Irish villagerss, arisstocratss for the ball sscene, sservantss, and musscle men ssix feet or more. Now, firsst . . ."

John Wesley wasn't sure what Wyn wanted with muscle men, but he was afraid that he could guess. Knowing that it would be a long, long time before he was needed on the set, he went into the house, closed the library door, and lay down on the sofa.

At nine o'clock he was awakened by Lydia's voice outside the window. "The idea! No *real* star *ever* oversleeps, *ever* shows up late. Lynn Fontanne, Mary Martin, Rosalind Russell . . ."

"Oh, balls, Ma. Who cares?"

"Deirdre! The sacrifices I'm making."

"Name one."

At ten he was awakened again. This time by Wyn's voice,

hoarsely shrill, echoing over the waters of the swimming pool. "No, you. The one in the jockey shortss." Propping himself on an elbow, John Wesley watched twenty gangling youths shuffling around the edge of the pool in their underwear while Wyn, like a sultan's eunuch, picked the twelve most likely to succeed.

At eleven Captain Mulcahy stumbled into the room and made it almost to the works of Marcel Proust before he noticed John Wesley. "A fine thing you're doing. Sleeping while all the rest of us are at work on me film." Indignantly, he staggered out of the room.

At twelve there was a major *crise* in the small sitting room where a dozen seamstresses toiled. It was Lydia once again. As with the script, her critical talents were far sharper than her creative ones. She didn't know exactly what was wrong with any of the costumes. They simply weren't right.

At one, Miss Rafferty furiously announced that box lunches were ready to be served. They were skimpy beyond John Wesley's wildest fears.

At one-thirty the heavens opened. Everyone rushed into the house for shelter, tracking mud, bread crusts, and banana peels over the Aubussons of the gallery. The extras were paid for a day's work and sent home. Not an inch of film had been exposed on the first day of shooting.

"I'm starving," John Wesley said to Peggy.

"So am I. A dry cheese sandwich and a banana isn't my idea of a working girl's lunch."

"Let's get into your car and sneak off for a square meal."

"In all this rain?"

"In all this rain."

"Where? The Slipper Inn?"

"No. Far away. Have you ever heard of a place in Garrison called the Bird and Bottle?"

"Who hasn't? How are you fixed for cash?"

"Fine. After all, you forget that I'm Director of Projects for a billion-dollar foundation."

"So I did. Just let me fix my face and I'll be right with you."

Sex

It was barely light when John Wesley opened his eyes. In the grayness he could make out an unfamiliar room—small, pretty, and rather prim. He closed his eyes and tried to think. He could not. This, he knew, was a real, genuine hangover. He felt terrible.

He was conscious of being quite naked between cool sheets and of a feminine smell—more pleasant than otherwise—emanating from the vacant pillow next to his. Across the room he could see his clothes neatly hung on a ruffly slipper chair.

Pressing the palms of his hands to his burning eyes, he tried to reconstruct the series of weird events that had brought him to this strange room. In patches and flashes the day before came back to him. Not so weird, really—at least not at the beginning.

He and Peggy had set out through the rain in her little red bug of a car for the pretty and expensive inn at Garrison. Except for a table of bibulous Westchester ladies bickering amiably about the advisability of ordering another round of grasshoppers, the place was empty. Damp and chilly, they had taken a table in front of the crackling fire and immediately ordered drinks, then more and then still more. It was after five when John Wesley had called for and paid an immense luncheon check.

Full of firm resolve to return to the Fennessey Foundation, they had, instead, driven to Cold Spring to a place called Something-by-the-Sea which was actually on the banks of the Hudson. They had had a lot more to drink and eventually, John Wesley believed, something to eat.

And after that? After that? John Wesley beat against the sides of his head with the heels of his hands. Other than hurting quite a lot, the gesture proved ineffectual. He took a deep breath. Yes. The rain had stopped for a little while and he and Peggy had strolled hand in hand through the deserted streets of Cold Spring singing. Singing! And a nice old Methodist hymn of all things!

It had gone:

> Holy, holy, holy,
> Fennesseys almighty . . .

Their lyrics had been so witty—at least at the time—that they had made up special words for each of the Fennesseys and were about to attempt scanning a name like Mondragon y Alonzo into the Greater Doxology when a klaxon-voiced woman shrieked invective at them from an upper window.

"Aw shut up," a man's voice bellowed from across the street, "you're makin' more noise than those poor drunks ever could."

"Don't you give me none of that, you dirty womanizer. If this town knew about the fancy hoors you got comin' and goin' . . ."

From still another house yet another voice joined in. Then another then another. A full-fledged riot seemed to have been started. John Wesley and Peggy had run for the car.

And then? Ah, yes. Then they had gone . . . Well, just where had they gone? No, they hadn't gone anywhere for a while. They had just sat in the car clinging to one another—for quite a long time. But *then,* after Peggy had shaken her head to clear it and said that they'd really have to be getting home before they did something they'd regret . . . well, they still hadn't driven straight home. No. They'd stopped off at . . . At? Well, John Wesley didn't actually know where. He remembered only that the place was dark and deserted and that he and Peggy had sat huddled together at a banquette table kissing and kissing and kissing until— "Oh, my God," John Wesley groaned. Until they'd been thrown out! Yes! Asked to leave an anonymous little corner saloon at the crossroads of nowhere. John Wesley felt his face burning with shame—or possibly fever. Oh, how terrible he felt!

He heard the familiar chiming of the stable-block clock. Quarter of six. He was in the Fennessey house, but where? Gradually achieving consciousness, he heard the sound of water. Not the swimming pool; not the fountains; but a real deluge. Could it still be raining? He stepped gingerly from the bed, nearly collapsing when his bare feet and unsteady legs were forced to support his weight. Lurching across to the window, he peered through the blinds. No rain. The sky was clear and there was a bit of pink in the east. Still the sound of water. Aha! It was the shower in the adjoining bathroom. But who? Not Rory Mulcahy, who rarely bathed and never showered. Had they changed his room again? If so, he liked this one with its four-poster bed and forthright colonial furniture much better. He staggered again and caught his balance on the edge of a dressing table. In the dimness he could see a couple of small bottles. He lifted one and sniffed at it. The same odor he had smelled on the pillow

—feminine but at the same time fresh and rather crisp. As he put the bottle back, his hand brushed against something soft and woolly. Knitting.

"My God," he said again. "Peggy!" Now it came back to him. They had come home and made it up the horseshoe staircase—just. He had seen her to her door and kissed her for a long, long time. Then she had opened the door and drawn him in with her. After that . . . after that he couldn't remember.

Although not quite a virgin, John Wesley could count his sexual experiences on his fingers and a couple of toes. Commencing with a girl in the choir back home and continuing, most sporadically, with the doxies operating in college towns and on the fringes of army posts until his most recent encounter with a dollar-a-minute Times Square hooker the night before he had come to the Fennessey Foundation. Without exception, he had found the experiences uncomfortable or sordid or shaming or expensive, but as essential as they had been joyless. For some years now, John Wesley had had reason to believe himself highly sexed and dangerously so. Was it, perhaps, a distressing family trait inherited from his ne'er-do-well father? He could never bring himself to discuss the matter with his mother. Nor did it seem advisable to take it up with his clergyman whose daughter, in fact, had been his first conquest. Instead John Wesley had tried to depend on prayer, higher thinking, cold showers, and violent exercise to quell the carnal desires that simmered within him.

But now! John Wesley took a furtive step toward his clothes. Too late. The bathroom door opened and there stood Peggy O'Neil swathed in a bath sheet.

"Feeling better?" she said.

"Please. I'm not dressed."

"So I see. But then neither am I."

John Wesley's hand lunged out for at least something to

cover his shame. In the darkness he came up with a wholly inadequate necktie.

"Don't bother," Peggy said. "I've seen everything there is by now. It's all very attractive. In fact, I'm the one who undressed you."

"Do you mean . . . that we . . ."

"I do. And we did. And it was perfectly lovely."

"Peggy, I'm—I'm sorry."

"Well, I'm not."

"Peggy, do you do this sort of thing with everybody?"

"Everybody? Please, Wes, you might credit me with a little discrimination. If you mean anyone around here, anyone you know, the answer is no. But it has been known to happen —and rather too infrequently, I'm sorry to say."

"Peggy!"

"Please don't try to tell me that this was *your* first time."

"N-no."

"All right then, we're even. I'm a normal, healthy human being with normal, healthy appetites. And from your performance of an hour ago I perceive, somehow, that you're exactly the same."

"Peggy, you could have a baby."

"Not without dragging the name of a well-known pharmaceutical company through the mud. Anyhow, I might even like one—if it turned out anything like you."

"Peggy, I had an awful lot to drink."

"You certainly did. I promised myself about twelve hours ago that if I had to slip you wood alcohol, knockout drops, and aphrodisiacs I'd land you right here between the Irish linens. Never underestimate the power of a woman. You're not sorry, are you?"

Chivalry forbade him to say that he could hardly regret something he didn't even recall. Instead he changed the subject. "I've got to get out of here."

"Try. Just try. The door's locked and I won't tell you where the key is until I'm damned good and ready."

More steadily John Wesley made his way to the door and turned the knob. The door refused to budge.

"You see?" Peggy said. "I never lie. It's a sin. Anyhow, you'd look awfully funny wandering among the Bermans and Légers in the buff, even if you are a damned fine figure of a man."

"We could be caught."

"Not unless you decide to scream. Why are you anxious to get out of here when plenty of men asleep right under this roof have been pawing the earth to get in—Stan Earnshaw, Mondragon *fils*, even our Founder once hesitantly suggested it. So far you're the only one who's made it across the threshold. Except for Gramps, of course."

"*Old* Mr. Fennessey?" John Wesley was horrified.

"For entirely different reasons."

"Peggy, my conscience . . ."

"I know all about that delicate Protestant conscience of yours. Don't worry. You're in the clear. This was all my doing and since it isn't bothering me . . ."

"Peggy," John Wesley said, taking a step in her direction, "I think you're . . ."

"A brazen, wanton daughter of Rome?"

"Peggy, I think you're wonderful. I—I love you." He took her in his arms and, for the first time, realized how actually wonderful she was—firm and yet soft, warm and yet cool.

"Now that's more like it."

The stable clock struck six.

"Peggy, we've only got a few more minutes."

"Then let's make the most of them," she said, moving toward the bed.

Troupers

"Wyn, darling," Lydia said from beneath the flattering shade of her golf umbrella, "this is just a suggestion, but *don't* you think the scene might be more effective if Deirdre were on camera alone? I mean, *without* the little dog."

Refraining from remarking that the dog was the better actor, Wyn replied, "Perhapss, Lydia, but the impression we're sstriving for is one of lonelinesss, not ssimple-mindednesss." He no longer bothered to smile when he spoke to Lydia. He had dealt with stage mothers before; every one of them a frustrated ham; every one of them a thoroughgoing bitch; every one of them willing to commit arson in order to grab an extra line, another bit of business for her own brat. "I mean she can't ssit there and talk to hersself, can she?" he asked.

Consuelo giggled immoderately, almost overturning her canvas chair.

"Genevieve," Lydia said to her sister-in-law, "could you use your Spanish to say whatever is necessary to your daughter to achieve a little quiet on the set when I'm conferring with the director?"

"*Calla te!*" Luis Fernando said to his sister.

"Why do I have to blast at all?" Deirdre asked from her humble hearthside. "The lines are strictly grubsville and—"

"Deirdre," Lydia said, "the true function of an actress is to *interpret* the lines of a playwright and not to criticize or attempt to rewrite them."

Rory Mulcahy, who had been only semiconscious during the creation of that particular scene, applauded sloppily and reached for the thermos of what he said was tea. He nearly went over in his canvas chair, too.

Oi, Mr. Plover thought. It was a long time ago, but he could still remember Lydia as the dewy-eyed little apprentice full of eager ideas for enlarging and improving her own part, no matter what the playwright had written. "But don't you think when Sally comes on she ought to wave. . . . But has he made it clear in the speech what the maid really means? Shouldn't she add. . . . Wouldn't it have more impact if I came downstage and faced the audience. . . ." And now here she was, the dowager duchess, spouting all this crap about fidelity to the written word.

Importunate had been the word for Lydia twenty years ago. Good God, she'd nearly worn poor Wyn to the bone, mentally and physically. No amount of vitamins, brewer's yeast, or phosphorized oil could help any man to keep up with her demands. Time after time, night after night for thirteen exhausting weeks in Woonsocket. And was that brave little good-by at the station *really* the end? Indeed it was not! Somehow she'd found out his unlisted telephone number and taken to calling while he was spending his nights with more useful acquaintances. Today there were *two* words for Lydia: importunate *and* imperious. Sitting on a billion bucks,

Lydia had become Aphra Behn, Sarah Siddons, Irene Selz-
nick, and Mrs. Astor rolled into one soignée ball.

Missss Fennessey! My dear, would you believe it? Lyd
now even had Deirdre's own cousins calling her "Miss Fennessey" because Deirdre was now a *sssstar!* Wyn could remember Lydia's kowtowing to visiting stars—yes, Mr. Cook
. . . no, Mr. Rathbone . . . thank you, Miss Cornell—
when for two cents she'd have cut their throats or leapt into
their beds, whichever seemed more efficacious. And now this
nothing-actress was having people refer to her daughter as
though Deirdre were Ethel Barrymore. It would have been
better for Deirdre and for the film if her role had been written as a mute. And he, Wynton Plover, a famous director,
had to sit there and take it. Why couldn't *he* have found a
Justin Fennessey?

"Wezley," Lydia repeated a little louder, "what do you
think?"

"Huh? Excuse me. I was thinking."

"Exactly, Wezley. And now may we have those thoughts?"
Really, Lydia said to herself, all these so-called professionals
around here and *I* have to do everything.

If you had my thoughts, Lydia-stupidia, you'd faint dead
away. I was thinking about Peggy and how wonderful it was
in the pool house last night and again at sunrise in your
stuffy husband's stuffy study; and what it was like all weekend long at the Bear Mountain Inn (Oh, the puns we made
about the name of that place!) when you thought that Peggy
was visiting a cousin in Croton and I was at a film festival
(Matter of fact, we couldn't even make it as far as the dining
room, Lydia!); and how great it was in that old hearse you
call Cinderella's coach; and what we plan for tonight—
weather permitting.

In the last week John Wesley had spent every free moment
with Peggy. He couldn't take his eyes or his hands off her. In
seven nights he had nearly compensated for as many years of

slipshod celibacy. With John Wesley, sex was still in the ex-perimental stage and each experiment turned out to be more successful than the one before it. And afterward, when they lay together whispering and laughing, they wondered whether any two people before in history had ever felt the same way.

"Oh," John Wesley said vaguely, "I was thinking about a big love scene." His eyes sought Peggy's. Elaborately impas-sive, she was seated next to the director and pretending to study the script. John Wesley wanted only to cross the semi-circle of canvas chairs, take Peggy by the hand, and run with her into the neatly manicured forest. But that had been planned for tonight.

"But about *this* scene," Lydia said edgily, "do you think it should be played *with* or *without* the *dog?*"

"Why don't you try it both ways and use the one that works best?" John Wesley said.

"Why, what a splendid idea! Brrrilliant!" Lydia said. She couldn't have admired John Wesley's thinking more if the idea had been her own. Actually, she had come to admire him more and more and more since the day Wyn had re-turned, dissolute and disappointing, into her life. This boy had a brain and, from what she'd seen, brawn. Lydia won-dered what he did with his nights. Twice now, after Justin was sleeping, she had armed herself with a copy of the script, put on a crisp, tailored robe and just enough make-up, and tapped at the door of the Empire room. Either John Wesley slept more soundly even than Justin or else he was out. Lydia would have to speak to Justin about imposing some sort of curfew. After all, it was dangerous just having people wan-dering about the house all night long. "Wyn, Wezley sug-gests . . ."

While several dozen people were dispatched to round up the small white mongrel who had been bought to play Cin-derella's dog (in the interests of both paternal pride and economy, Justin had offered Gretchen but she had been found wanting), John Wesley shut off his hearing and resumed his thinking. Had he slept at all the night before? Yes. About two hours, cradled in Peggy's arms on an air mattress in the pool house. And he felt wonderful—both ten years older and ten years younger. Young enough to turn cartwheels down a hundred-yard slope of lawn, as he'd done in the moonlight last night just to show Peggy what a juvenile delinquent he was. But older, too—masterful, protective, and very, very male. He wondered if the change in him showed. But of course it did. It must. He put on his dark glasses to disguise the hungry glint in his eye and, unobserved, to stare at Peggy.

Peggy sat in what she called the Dress Circle—the half ring of canvas chairs reserved for the director, his staff, the writers, the principal players, and, of course, the Fennesseys. She felt marvelous, too, and she hated herself for it. Like a mother superior, she scolded, chastised, flagellated herself. You must be mighty proud of what you've gone and done, Peggy told herself. The poor innocent baby! Oh, but aren't you just the *femme fatale* of County Clare! Circe O'Sullivan, Aphrodite Macaffrey, Delilah Delahanty, Cleopatra Clancy. Just couldn't leave well enough alone, could you? And now that you've got him, by using every low Irish trick you knew and a few you just made up on the spur of the moment—now that you've got him, what are you going to do with him? And even more to the point, O, Serpent of the Shannon, now that *he's* got *you*, what are his plans? Marriage? Never! He's just sweet enough—sap enough—to ask you. And you're just decent enough—*just*—to say no. At least I hope you'd say no. Oh, can't you just see it, in glorious Vistavision—that cornfed Methodist Eagle Scout from South Minnebraska, or wherever it is, and Mary Margaret Mother Machree O'Neil, Belle of the Bricklayers' Ball. It's a long way to Tipperary, but it's even farther from Flatbush Avenue to Main Street, Middletown. And it's—

"Misss O'Neil! I wass sspeaking to *you*."

"Yes, Mr. Plover?"

"I ssaid, Misss Fennessey sseemss to have forgotten her next line—her *only* line in thiss sscene."

"I'm sorry. It goes, 'Faith, I'm so lonely with all the others gone to the ball at Kilkenny House.'"

"Um, I wonder," Justin said. "Would you mind very much just changing the name of that house. Something, uh, more euphonious."

"Cat House?" Desmond suggested.

"Couldn't I just say 'gone to the ball,' Dad? It's not so much to memorize."

"If you prefer to ssay that, Misss Fennessey, I ssee no objection. Now, could we take it again? Thank you ssso much, Misss O'Neil." Wyn did not care for these sharp, pretty young things who somehow gave the impression that they had heard what he was saying before and knew what he was going to say next. Peggy O'Neil fell into that category.

Peggy resumed her seizure of self-castigation. He only wanted to take me to lunch, she told herself. His only motive was hunger. I did all the rest. Oh, my God, I don't care how much older he is, he still makes me feel like his mother. Well, not his *real* mother, God forbid. No. I started it and I'll break it off clean. He'll hate me for it, but not as much as he would if I let things go on this way—get too serious. Too *serious!*

On the other hand, Peggy thought, I did make a reservation at the Motel on the Mountain for this weekend and even sent my own check as a deposit. And another thing—what am I doing with a man who's so square that he doesn't think there's anything funny about signing John Smith to a hotel register? But still, he's so nice. He *smells* so good—soap and water and decency. And as for the rest of it—well, I don't know what they teach the boys at John Knox U. but he must have been *summa cum laude*. That solemn choirboy knows tricks that would put Porfirio Rubirosa to— Oh, what am I talking about? He doesn't belong in this place. He knows it. So do the Fennesseys. He'll be out of here in September and that'll be the end of that. A snowy Christmas card in December and in June a chaste announcement to tell me that he's married a nice home economics teacher. Damn him!

"Lydia," Wyn called across the Dress Circle, "we're *both* right. Thiss sscene workss much better without the dog. Alsso without Miss Fennessey sspeaking any lines."

"But, Wyn. Cinderella *must* communicate to the audience her—"

"Yesss, dear, and the besst way to do that is a ssimple closse-up of her expresssive little face."

"Bananas!" Deirdre said. Consuelo giggled. But Lydia seemed placated.

"Yessssss," Lydia said. "I *quite* see what you mean. Don't you agree, Wezley?"

"Wh-what?"

"We can work on that later. Now may we ssee the fairy godmother?"

The woman who had been engaged to play the fairy godmother spoke when spoken to, pleasantly and articulately, but nothing more. Mostly she sat in her canvas chair doing crossword puzzles, double-crostics, and cryptograms. Not many people remembered that twenty-five years ago she had been a white hope among young leading ladies—an ethereal blonde of the Julie Haydon-Julie Harris-Julie Christie school. Lydia remembered. And Lydia, who had not been important enough to know her, also hated her for her rocket-like rise to the top. Her descent had been nearly as rapid. Now Mrs. Justin Fennessey could look at her with a sigh of pity and satisfaction. Those fragile blondes just didn't hold up—portly and puckered as a prune and surely not *much* more than forty, poor thing.

The fairy godmother rose and strode confidently to the set.

Very pulled together, Lydia had to admit. Lydia had hoped that she drank or took drugs.

"Would you like to run over your lines, dear?" Wyn asked.

"Not unless you'd like me to."

"Well, I think Misss Fennessey might be a little ssafer if—"

"Whatever you say, Mr. Plover."

"Thankss, dear. Now, ssweetie, do you think you can manage to come down the chimney without breaking your neck? Real Ssanta Claus sstuff."

"I think so, Mr. Plover. I've taken a lot of dives before."

"Will I ever forget your divine sswoon down that flight of sstairs in *Ssilent Sstars!*"

"Why, thank you. Your memory goes back a long way. Just up that ladder and down the chimney? As simple as that?"

"Yess, dear. She'ss a real trouper," Wyn announced to the Dress Circle when the fairy godmother disappeared behind the set. Lydia covered a delicate sneer with her handkerchief.

"We'll jusst run through it once and then try a take. Ready?"

"Ready," the fairy godmother's voice came hollowly from the upper reaches of the chimney.

"All right, Miss Fennessey, if you'll jusst ssit back a little. There. All right, fairy godmother. We're waiting."

With infinite grace the fairy godmother shot down the chimney—and then she kept right on going. From the disused manure pit below came a dull thud and a short, rather startled moan.

"Good grief," Deirdre said, "who put the fireplace right over that old trap door?"

From below, the fairy godmother called calmly, "Sorry, Mr. Plover, but I'm afraid my leg's broken."

"Miss O'Neil!" Justin said. "Call my lawyers! Call Slattery!"

"Don't you think it would be nice if we called a doctor first?" Peggy said.

A major casting change was made over lunch, which had gotten bigger and better now that Justin had democratically decided to join the cast and crew, thus putting an end to any pleasure they might have had. The fairy godmother had been safely dispatched to the Butterfield Hospital and Justin had assigned Peggy to collecting a quarter apiece from everyone involved on the film to send her a bouquet and a crossword-puzzle book. "Show her what a great little trouper she is and how much we all care."

"That poor, poor thing," the marquesa said over a stuffed egg. "And such a good actress. A real pro. Lydia, don't you remember her in—"

"I wasn't old enough to have seen her," Lydia said more sharply than she had intended. "But now the problem is where to get another fairy godmother on short notice. And, if possible, someone a little more . . . well, I've always thought of the fairy godmother as chic and ra-ther worldly. And if the dream sequences are to be Freudian . . ."

"Well, Lydia," the marquesa said, "there's always you— unless you've let your Equity membership lapse."

"Why, yessss," Wyn said.

"Oh, I couldn't," Lydia said, going all coy. "I simply couldn't."

"I don't see why not, darling," the marquesa said. "It's exactly your type of thing."

Lydia did not care for the word "type," but she let it pass. "Oh, no."

Like an old war horsse ssmelling ssmoke, Wyn told himself. Aloud he said, "I do wish you'd conssider it, Lyd. You could be ssuch a help to Misss Fennessey."

"Hmm, that's true," Lydia said.

"Lydia, I really don't think—uh—people in our—uh—position . . ." Justin said. And then to demonstrate his democracy, he shouted, "How're things goin,' Stretch?" to the tallest of the muscle men. "Uh, no."

"Oh, nonsense, Justin. Look at Mrs. Belmont, Mrs. Blodget, Mrs. Ward. . . . That's Eleanor Robson, Cornelia Otis Skinner, and Jane Wyatt," she explained to Wyn, re-establishing the distance she had traveled from that lean-to in Woonsocket.

"Yesss, I know," Wyn, who hadn't, said.

"I thought the other woman—what's her name?—was *awfully* good. But *I* would have played her as a sort of well-bred matron . . ."

The way she's played every part from Lyssisstrata to Ssadie Thompsson, Wyn thought.

"You mean like Billie Burke?" the marquesa asked.

"No, *Jenny*, much younger. Here, let me show you."

"Lydia," Justin said, with more than his usual force, "I repeat: people in our position . . ."

"But, *darling*," Lydia cried, "what mother wouldn't make every sacrifice possible?"

And so now there were two stars to cope with—mother and daughter. As a despot, Mrs. Justin Fennessey made Mrs. Patrick Campbell, Mrs. Leslie Carter, and Mrs. Fiske—long-gone ladies notorious for their waspish dispositions—look like weak sisters. Line by line, word by word, the fairy godmother's role was enlarged and enhanced. Under Lydia's editorship, the character became an eccentric duchess interested in the occult, who was to be glimpsed, far more often than absolutely necessary, gazing into a crystal ball to see

how things were going at the palace, in the village, and at
Cinderella's fireside. Little by little the character, attended
by two blackamoors, was injected into the village streets
("But, naturally, the duchess would want to do a bit of shopping, Wyn. That's only realistic."), into the ball scene ("But,
of course, a *duchess* would be invited. And, anyhow, she'd
want to keep an eye on her protégée, wouldn't she?"), and
into every pointless dream sequence, to draft wordlessly, but
beautifully gowned, through the moth-eaten overstock of
costumes. Eventually—inevitably—a prologue and an epilogue were written, more or less at Lydia's direction. Their
meaning was rather obscure.

Lydia's dressmaker was summoned again to run up a few
simple costumes—not just two, as he had done for Cinderella, but a round dozen with furs to match. Lydia's recently
developed allergy to theatrical cosmetics required the presence of her personal make-up man, and Lydia's own hairdresser appeared daily to create adaptations of eighteenth-
century hair styles.

Once having crouched like a mother lioness on the side
lines checking Deirdre's every close-up and camera angle,
Lydia now was far more interested in her own. Deirdre, it
appeared, could be eliminated from whole scenes, which
would be far more effective if the fairy godmother simply
explained to the audience what had been going on. And
Deirdre, who heretofore had been apathetic and indifferent,
began to develop some claws of her own.

"Why don't you just play *both* parts, and let me wig out of
this freak show?" Deirdre suggested.

"Dar-ling," Lydia said in the Madeleine Carroll voice she
had developed for the godmother role, "Mother is only trying
to help you get the *feel* of acting professionally. If only *I* had
had a mature, experienced actress to help me when I was
starting out. Someone to show me the ropes."

"I can tell you what you should have done with that rope," Deirdre snapped.

John Wesley was horrified. That is, he felt that he *should* have been horrified at a girl talking to her mother that way. Actually, his sympathies were all with Deirdre. Of the two, the daughter was the more cooperative, the more relaxed, and the more talented by far. An amateur, indifferent as to whether she was on the threshold of a great career or not, Deirdre was a natural—when she could remember her lines. And natural was a word that could never be applied to Lydia's acting.

"Two sstarss, two directorss, and two sscript editorss— that'ss what we've got to contend with," Mr. Plover hissed. "I've never sseen it fail. Every time I've gone out to the sstickss to direct ssome amateur production there'ss alwayss ssome broken-down ssemiprofessional like Lydia who'ss done a sseasson of sstock or ssung on the Ted Mack hour and thinkss she'ss Misss Show Biz. And, my dear, she'ss usually worsse than the worsst beginner. That'ss our Lydia."

Having once considered John Wesley Smith and Wynton Plover vital to the project, Lydia now began to deprecate the very talents she had admired so extravagantly, pointing out long, dull patches in the script (those in which the fairy god-mother could not possibly be inserted), the paltriness of Mr. Plover's past assignments, and the golden opportunities he was missing on this one (chances to add another close-up, another scene for the fairy godmother).

John Wesley did not care. He found all of *Cinderella Flanagan* a pretentious bore and wicked waste of time, money, and talent. He wanted only to fulfill the few remaining weeks of his contract and get out of this madhouse, taking Peggy with him.

Wyn was almost as philosophical. "Conssider the ssource," he said.

Captain Rory Mulcahy, however, took more and more of a

proprietary interest in the film. It was odd, considering that not a thousand words of the story were his or that he had been barely more than comatose during the patching together of his script. True, he was still more drunk than sober during every hour of the filming, but with each hour he grew more and more possessive of what he called his masterpiece. Nonetheless, he did serve certain purposes. Once, when teetering on the brink of unconsciousness, he had been cajoled into a drooping eighteenth-century costume and, in the role of the village sot, had managed to stagger and lurch for a dozen paces before falling flat onto the cobblestones. John Wesley considered it the most brilliant moment of the film so far.

"One-take Mulcahy," Desmond had said admiringly. It was fortunate that it had worked out so well, as the performer was in no shape to offer an encore.

But with Lydia's intrusion into the film, Rory had become mean and watchful, fighting her every suggestion, purposely belching loudly in the background during her scenes or bursting noisily into song. Lydia held her temper, excused herself, and summoned Justin. Less than half an hour later Rory was called into the library and ten minutes after that he came crashing out of the house shouting that no amount of money could buy him off. Rory stayed on.

Peggy, ever rapid with pencil and paper, figured out that Rory could have bought just over two hundred cases of Bushmill's with the pay-off money—more money than he had ever seen in his life or would probably ever see again. John Wesley wondered at his drunken obstinacy. Still Rory stayed on. At Lydia's insistence there had been more than a few nattering telephone calls to the law offices of Cornelius Slattery regarding Rory's legal status. The law regarding rights of actors, writers, directors, and such being as specialized as it is, Mr. Slattery was frank to admit that he wasn't entirely sure of Rory's exact position but that he had a suspicion that Rory held an ace or two and to be patient while he checked with the Wharton office, the Feitleston office or *someplace* that specialized in that never-never land of the theater. And still Rory stayed on.

But the big surprise was yet to come. *Old* Mr. Fennessey appeared on the set and stayed and stayed and stayed. The old man had not been heard from very much since work on the film began. The parade of doctors and nurses and barbers and masseurs had not halted but, owing to experiments with a new drug said to be miraculous, the old gentleman had lain quiet in his quarters embarrassing none of the Fennesseys for weeks. But what no one had expected was that the drug, having been absorbed molecule by molecule, had had its originally intended effect. The old man rose up in his bed like the Eiffel Tower, saw from his window the commotion going on in the stable block, put on his stateliest dressing gown, and pounded down the stairs to join in the fun, with his nurses— two Jamaican women whom he called the Black and Tans— shrieking after him. (The male nurse, Mr. Nelson, had finally departed with his needlework after suffering a final gross indignity from Gramps.) In the brilliant sunlight with his white hair rising like a cockatoo's crest, his visual impact had been overpowering.

"But Ly-dia," Wyn cried, "why didn't you tell me about . . . about *old* Mr. Fennessey? Jusst *look* at him!"

"And just look at yourself, missy," the old man said. "What kind of getup do you call that leather outfit?"

Wyn smiled wanly and continued. "And his hair! Why, it'ss ssimply . . ."

"I wouldn't be talkin' about nobody's hair if I had that painted muck glued around me head like you have, missy. Peggy, darlin'!" With a firm step old Mr. Fennessey went round to Peggy and embraced her.

"Gramps! Darling, do you really think you should be up?"

"And why not? Do you know what it is they've been

squirtin' inta me? Cow's piss. Would you fancy! And I'd hate to tell you what it costs. Why, when I was a boy on the other side we had rivers of it free."

Wyn tripped quickly over to the cameraman and whispered frantic instructions.

"Wyn, no!" Lydia said. "Mr. Fennessey is a ve-ry old gentleman. He shouldn't be up."

"But would you *look* at him! *Lissten* to him. Hiss sspeech. The lilt."

"And would you listen to yerself, missy? Who ever taught you to talk, the Sisters of the Sacred Heart?"

The Fennesseys, who all preferred their grandfather out of sight, clustered around the old man, wheedling, cajoling, urging him back to his bed. He would have none of it.

"But we've ssimply *got* to use him," Wyn said. "He's abssolutely perfect."

"Not in my film we won't," Rory growled.

Old Mr. Fennessey regarded Rory briefly. "Small potatoes and few in the hill," he said calmly. Stunned, Rory settled back into his chair.

Justin pulled himself together. "I'm, uh, afraid, Mr. Plover, that your suggestion is impossible. Our grandfather is a very, very old man and very, very weak."

In reply the old gentleman fetched Justin a backhand blow to the solar plexis that left him doubled up and gasping for breath. "Soft, Justin. That's the trouble. Ye're soft. Now, missy, what is it you want of me?"

"But can't you ssee it! The presss! Ninety-year-old billionaire makes sscreen debut."

Justin could see it. Exactly. "Mr. Plover, something like this could kill our grandfather."

"Good!" Lydia muttered.

"And don't fergit, Justin Fennessey, that your grandfather could kill *you*. Now, what is it exactly ye want me to do?"

From that point on, *Cinderella Flanagan* had three stars.

Movies

And so the film went—painfully, slowly, unsurely.

A character dubbed Squire McGafferty was quickly written in to suit old Mr. Fennessey. With the Black and Tans in shrill attendance, he was on the set punctually at seven each morning. He eschewed a canvas chair of his own, preferring (when not on camera) to sit in Peggy's with her perched on his knee. His lines were unimportant, as the old man either could not or would not learn them. Instead, he did just about as he damned well pleased and he was perfect, wandering through the film making his own devastating observations— some of them even printable. "He's the biggesst sscene sstealer ssince Will Rogerss," Wyn announced, weak with admiration.

"This is going to kill poor Grandpa," Justin kept saying almost longingly. Science did not agree. The limousine-borne doctor who had been attending Fennessey aches and pains, accouchements and crotchets for years at astronomical fees was spending the month in Bar Harbor, leaving behind a dedicated young assistant whose function was to keep old

Mr. Fennessey alive, but little more. The assistant had far exceeded his mission. "It's amazing," the young doctor kept saying. "Absolutely amazing. With these injections and a new interest in life he's like a man of thirty. His heart, his pulse, his blood pressure. Even sexually . . ."

"Really?" Justin said. The thought of a newborn uncle or aunt was not appetizing.

"He tells me he'd like to go back to work again and I think it's a keen idea. You see, Mr. Fennessey, I specialize in geriatrics and there are entirely new theories . . ."

"Hmmm. Perhaps a sedentary post on the foundation?"

"No. Not the foundation. Old Mr. Fennessey said he'd like to be back in the brewery—right on the floor with the men."

Justin winced. Why, oh *why*, hadn't they sold out to Ballantine's when that perfectly good offer was made two years ago?

"And old Mr. Fennessey has also shown great interest in taking a trip back to Ireland on his ninety-fifth birthday. Just imagine!"

Justin could. "Oh, never. Ireland? Never!"

"No reason why he shouldn't, Mr. Fennessey, with a competent attendant to look after him. You see, Mr. Fennessey, in revitalizing certain tissues . . ."

Justin silently prayed for an unusually inclement autumn in County Kilkenny and, while the young doctor described old Mr. Fennessey's tissues, wondered just how large a grant would be required to send this bumptious, meddling kid well to the north of Kashmir to study the Hunzas, who *really* lived for a long time and would be far less likely to disturb Justin's placid existence.

"Yes, Mr. Fennessey," the young doctor continued, not realizing that his own days as aide de camp to a prosperous Park Avenue general practitioner were numbered to something under ten, "with any luck at all, there is no reason why your grandfather can't go on for years."

Nor did there seem to be. Old Mr. Fennessey had found a new life and he was loving it. He relished his days on the set, showing off to the young, insulting Wyn and Rory, and doing a running impersonation of Lydia. Growling and snarling, he was led away for his nap only to rise again for dinner (washed down prodigious quantities of Fennessey's Kilkenny Ale) and depose his grandson Justin from the head of the table.

Gone at last were the transparent slices of veal and chicken, the Lilliputian dabs of crab and aspic. Over Miss Rafferty's woebegone sighs and silent sobs, great bleeding sides of beef, rosy hams, and barons of lamb were passed once, twice, three times.

"One of nature's true gentlemen," Mr. Earnshaw said and quite correctly. He had never paid the vaguest attention to old Mr. Fennessey before but, sensitive as always to any sea change, Mr. Earnshaw surmised—and just as correctly—that Gramps found him a fool and that it would do no harm to get on the good side of the old codger. Anyhow, John Francis Xavier Fennessey, ninety-four going on ninety-five and worth millions, was the best name for dropping purposes he would ever come across.

After dinner, rushes of the previous day's work were shown in the small sitting room. It was old Mr. Fennessey's favorite time. He loved watching the takes, the accidents, the fluffs. He adored seeing himself on the screen and he roared with helpless laughter through all of Lydia's scenes.

John Wesley had thought—at least had *hoped*—that when Lydia saw herself on the screen, she would realize how terrible she was and alter her performance. Lydia did just that. Sharply critical of everyone else in the film, she was merciless with herself. "Oh, how could I have? Oh, Wyn, why didn't you stop me? Oh, dear! We're going to have to shoot that all over again tomorrow."

Reshoot they would, and in every scene Lydia's performance was broader, bolder, hammier than it had been the day before. It seemed to John Wesley, sitting in the rear of the darkened room with Peggy, that if she got any more monstrous, she would burst out of the screen and devour her audience.

Later in the upstairs gallery he told Peggy, "I don't think I can take much more of this woman and her lousing up everything. You know, parts of that movie—the parts that Lydia is out of—are almost good. Deirdre, the old man, Prince Charming, the stepsisters. Not great, but adequate. And then Lydia comes roaring on and . . ."

"Do you really care, darling?"

"Well, no. But then again, yes. I mean I didn't originally come here to make a film, but as long as I'm involved in it, I'd like it to be as good as possible. Now with Lydia sticking her nose into everything, including the camera lens . . ."

"Come to bed, darling," Peggy said.

The suggestion was more than enough to make John Wesley forget about *Cinderella Flanagan* and start thinking about better things. "Where can we go? Not my room."

"No. It makes me feel like Pauline Borghese."

"I didn't mean that. It's just that Lydia comes around there at nights some times. She slips notes under the door. I can't imagine what she wants."

"I can."

"Something to do with her part, I suppose."

"More likely something to do with yours."

"And your room is out, now that Gramps is up and around and likes to come visiting."

"Never mind. We'll find a place. I'll meet you downstairs in a minute."

"Sooner?"

"Even sooner," Peggy said, kissing the cowlick that spun around on the crown of his head. "But let's go separately.

The whole household is downstairs wrangling over Mrs. Justin Fennessey's interpretation of Goneril. It might be better if they didn't see us going off hand in hand into the night."

"I'll get there first."

"Do you want to bet?"

John Wesley should have accepted the wager. Running down the horseshoe stairs, he stopped at the landing to blow a kiss to Peggy ringing for the elevator above and then in the half-light hurried downward. He felt his foot strike something. He heard the startled yelp of Gretchen. He heard the long, low rumbling of his body plummeting down the carpeted staircase. He heard a loud snap and then another. He heard Peggy cry "Wes!" And then he heard no more.

Part Three

♣ ⚬ ♣ ⚬ ♣ ⚬ ♣ ⚬ ♣ ⚬ ♣ ⚬ ♣ ⚬ ♣ ⚬ ♣

Sick Bay

♣ ♧ ♣ ♧ ♣ ♧ ♣ ♧ ♣ ♧ ♣ ♧ ♣ ♧ ♣

"Peggy?" John Wesley croaked. There was no reply. "Peggy?" he gasped again. His throat was parched. Painfully he opened his eyes. Above his head he saw the dim glimmer of a large, square steel frame. His right arm, encased in plaster, was held above his head in a Fascist salute. A pair of sandbags swung listlessly and obscenely in his line of vision. Beyond them he saw a mound of white plaster. Five toes—his own—protruded from it. He tried to wriggle them. He could not.

He felt a sudden draft and tried to close his eyes from the pain of a shaft of light. "You can go in now, Miss O'Neil. Your friend's coming around."

"Thank you."

John Wesley heard the click of heels on the floor. Vaguely he recognized their staccato tapping as Peggy's but right now, right here, her every step hurt his head. In a moment her face was bent down over his. "Feeling better?" she said.

"Better than what? Where am I?"

"You're in the hospital, darling."

"But what have I got?"

"A broken right shoulder, a broken left ankle—two places
—two black eyes, and a slight concussion. Otherwise you're
just fine. Are you comfortable, Wes?"

"Not outstandingly."

"Poor baby. You've been waking up in some awfully odd
places since you've known me."

"Would you mind telling me just how I got here?"

"Don't you remember?"

"Would I bother to ask if I did?" Oh, he felt foul!

"That effing Gretchen, to quote Mrs. Justin Fennessey."

"Gretchen?"

"Gretchen the Weimaraner. You were running down the
horseshoe stairs. Gretchen was lying on the landing, licking
herself, as usual. You tripped over her and landed on the
floor of the lower gallery. Gretchen is unhurt. I thought
you'd like to know that."

"I wish she were dead. I wish I were, too."

"Hush, darling. The Fennesseys are terribly upset."

"I'm so sorry."

"Lydia fainted. (On the sofa, needless to say.) Deirdre
spoke one whole declarative sentence in basic English. Father Alonzo was all set to give you extreme unction—in
Spanish. Consuelo nearly split her leotards giggling. Our Mr.
Earnshaw delivered a learned lecture on first aid as rendered
on the field of battle. Jenny kicked Gretchen and slapped
Justin. Even Luis Fernando got off his *hacienda* long enough
to help Desmond pick you up off the floor—but only when
Gramps took over and gave the orders. Gramps was wonderful."

"How was I?"

"Out cold. Now you're here in your own little hospital-
green hospital room. Justin felt that you'd be less lonely in a
public ward, but Gramps vetoed that."

"How did I get here?"

"In a great big beautiful ambulance—horns whooping, sirens screeching, red lights twirling. I came with you—my first trip in an ambulance."

"Mine, too."

"Justin thought that the gardener's pickup truck would be faster—and certainly cheaper. But you traveled first class all the way."

"That's a great comfort."

"Wes, dear, you mustn't talk any more. You must feel terrible."

"Right. I do. What time is it?"

"Nearly six, darling."

"Night or morning?"

"Morning."

"And how long am I going to be here?"

"That all depends on how fast your bones knit. Not very, I shouldn't think. The doctor who put you back together said he'd never seen such a healthy animal. Neither have I. But then I'm prejudiced."

"Nymphomaniac!" He tried to reach out for Peggy's hand. He could not.

"Wes, hush. You're not supposed to talk until your poor head is better. Does it hurt?"

"Naturally."

"My poor, poor darling."

Again he felt the draft, the piercing shaft of light across his eyes. "Miss O'Neil, I'll have to ask you to leave the patient now. He needs all the rest he can get."

"Yes. Yes, of course. Good-by, darling. I'll be back later."

John Wesley winced at the clatter of Peggy's heels, the boom of the door as it was gently closed. Then he shut his eyes and drifted off again.

John Wesley awoke much later in the day. His room was

crammed with the famous Fennessey flowers—the lilies, the orchids, the faintly naughty blooms he had grown so accustomed to during his stay at the foundation. A nurse bustled in with an asymmetric arrangement of birds of paradise. "Oh! You're awake. Good. Feeling better? I've never seen so many lovely flowers—and all arranged so we girls don't have to drop everything and hunt up vases. Gorgeous!" John Wesley didn't answer. He didn't need to. While the nurse went on talking, he wondered how much money Justin Fennessey had collected from the company of *Cinderella Flanagan* to have so many flowers cut and arranged in the Fennessey Foundation's greenhouses.

"Once we had Mrs. Whitney staying here. Mrs. Wilmerding W. Whitney. Of course you know who *she* is." John Wesley didn't. "She got beautiful flowers, too. But nothing like these. Say, are you some kinda celebrity? Super and I were wondering when all these flowers came. What's your name, anyways?"

"Smith. John Smith."

"Oh, come on, dearie. Don't try to kid me. Although we get a lotta women here call themselves *Mrs.* Smith." She giggled conspiratorially. "I betcher some kinda TV star. Without those shiners you sure could be. Comfy? Once we had this other big TV actor—you'd know his name if I could remember it. Hemorrhoids. He got lovely fl—"

Another nurse darted into the door and whispered something to John Wesley's tormentor. Her eyes opened wide. "*Well!* Say, I guess you *are* somebody. You got a visitor. Mr. Justin Fennessey! Show him right in, honey." She stood aside just far enough to show deference to the Great Man, and yet close enough to touch the hem of his garment.

Justin entered, followed by another man and, at a respectful distance, by Peggy. Behind their backs, she kissed the air in John Wesley's direction, sat down, took her shorthand pad and a pencil from her purse. Justin stared at John Wesley as though he might have been some hideously deformed fetus in a jar of formaldehyde, cleared his throat, and shouted, "Well, how yuh feelin', fellah?" As there was no reply, he pushed his companion forward. He was a tall, thin, pale man who looked younger than Justin. John Wesley was conscious first of his eyes, big and blue with bright pink rims. "This is an old friend of mine—Cornelius Slattery. Neilie, this is our invaluable Mr. Smith."

John Wesley remembered that Slattery was the Fennessey lawyer.

"We were in school together," Justin added.

John Wesley recalled that Justin had gone to law school.

"How do you feel, fellah?"

"How do I look?" John Wesley asked.

"We were all terribly worried about you."

"That was nice of you."

"Gretchen's sorry, too."

"Sorry doesn't begin to describe her."

"Heheheheh. But you *are* feeling all right?"

"As well as can be expected; I believe that's the accepted hospital term."

"Mm-hmmm. Well, that's good."

"It's just swell, thanks. Ginger-peachy."

"Uh, Wes, Neilie and I were wondering if you'd mind signing this paper we ran up between us."

"Signing it? With *what?* My—"

"Uh, Jus," Mr. Slattery said with a certain edge to his voice. "It may be a little *early* to talk with Mr. Smith."

"Yes, uh, heheheheh. But you know, Wes, there are so many people around nowadays looking for, uh, free money. I mean the people themselves are decent enough, but they get into the hands of some shyster lawyer and—"

"Justin," Mr. Slattery said darkly.

"Yes, Justin?" John Wesley said.

"Well, heheheheh, you know the old saying, 'It's better to dive in front of a Rolls than a Ford.' Heheheheh."

"Justin, Mr. Smith must be pretty tired after his tumble and—"

"Well, Wes, you know; a lot of people take a spill on the ice in front of a big town house and the next thing you know they've decided that there's a lot of money there and—"

"Justin, are you suggesting that I'm going to sue you?" John Wesley said.

"Oh, heheheheh, *no!* I, uh, merely—uh—uh . . ."

"If we could just have a simple statement, Mr. Smith?"

"Yes, uh, Wes. I mean didn't you have quite a lot to drink before dinner last night?"

"Nothing, as a matter of fact. I was in my room writing a new scene for Lydia. You know that. Travis had to come up and tell me that dinner was on the table."

"Oh, yes. Yes. I'd forgotten."

"But I can give you a simple statement. Ready with your pad, Miss O'Neil?"

"Ready, Mr. Smith."

"Very well. I was coming down the horseshoe stairs. They were inadequately lighted. They always are. God knows why, as the public foots the electric bill—"

"Now, Wes."

"We had just eaten a delicious dinner through the courtesy of the U.S. taxpayer and so, presumably, had your Weimaraner bitch, Gretchen. She was lying on the landing at the top of the horseshoe. I stumbled over her in the darkness and here I am. All smashed up. End of statement. Got that, Miss O'Neil?"

"Yes, Wes."

"Wesley, that is a ve-ry dog-in-the-manger-ish attitude to take."

"Justin," Mr. Slattery said, "Mr. Smith isn't feeling himself today . . ."

"I have precious little left to feel myself *with,* Mr. Slattery."

"Heheheheh, Wes. You and your little jokes."

"Now listen, Justin, and get this straight. I don't intend to make my fortune out of falling over your goddam dog. In a way it was my fault as much as the dog's."

"Did you get that, Miss O'Neil?"

"*Justin!*" Cornelius Slattery bellowed.

"But I do expect my salary to continue while I'm lying here. And I expect my expenses to be paid by your insurance company or by the Fennessey Foundation or by you, yourself. I'm not signing anything. Wouldn't if I could. It was nice of you to put me in a private room, Justin. But as long as it *is* private . . ."

"Yes, Justin," Mr. Slattery said. "Mr. Smith must be feeling pretty rocky and I've got to be getting—"

"He isn't himself," Justin whimpered. "We'll be back later, Wes. Come, Miss O'Neil."

"No, Justin. You won't be back later. Miss O'Neil will join you in a few minutes. Good-by, Mr. Slattery."

From the corridor outside his room, John Wesley could hear Slattery saying, "Damn it, Justin, you need a lawyer."

The days crept slowly by. John Wesley eventually grew accustomed to perpetual discomfort, to icy bedpans and urinals thrust beneath him, to a constant stickiness from inadequate rinsing after bed baths; to alcohol scalding the crevices of his body after slapdash massages; to hit-or-miss shaves with the hospital's electric razor; to the pallid meals, poked in by his left hand; to the mandarin length which his nails, unnoticed by the overworked hospital staff, had grown.

Peggy came to see him every evening and as often during

the days as she could. So did other representatives of the Fennessey Foundation—most of them wanting something.

Lydia was the first. The floor supervisor was so impressed by the appearance of Mrs. Justin Fennessey, social leader, great beauty, and latter-day saint, that she announced the apparition herself. Lydia's getup was not quite Gray Lady, not quite nun, and not quite madonna, but a bit of all three. She hesitated, framed in the doorway, for a count of three beats so that John Wesley could take in her costume. She wore a gray cape, demurely buttoned down the front, her long, pale hands thrust through its slits like the limp fronds of a weeping willow. Her hair had been drawn back—but not *too* severely—into a classic coil aided and abetted by a chignon of false curls brushed into a shining figure eight. Over it she had flung a length of blue chiffon, which John Wesley recognized as one of her more irritating hand props from one of her most unnecessary scenes in *Cinderella Flanagan*. Nacreously pale, her personal make-up man had obviously spent hours on her face.

"Wezley!" Lydia said in low, thrilling voice. Graciously dismissing the supervisor, who was not at all anxious to leave, with a "Thenk yew," she floated to John Wesley's bed and placed both of her hands into his left one. He realized from their touch that they had been made up, too.

"Wezley, forgive the way I look. I simply threw this old thing over—well, over nothing—and hurried here during the luncheon break. I—I'm a sight, I know. I haven't slept a wink since your terrible, terrible accident."

"You look fine, Lydia."

"Thank you. You *are* sweet. Oh, those dogs of Justin's! I've begged him to get rid of them. And I'm afraid they're vicious as well."

Lydia Fennessey's calling any other living thing vicious caused John Wesley to smile.

"Ah, you *are* feeling better, Wezley. I'm *so* glad."

"Sit down, Lydia."

"Thank you, Wezley." Allowing her chiffon veil to float floorward, Lydia sank into a chair and crossed her ankles, displaying her buckled gray pilgrim slippers. "Poor Wezley, it must be so dull for you here—not to mention your discomfort, poor darling. Oh! I brought some things for you—a lobster mousse, some rolls, a cold chicken, a few bunches of grapes, Liebfraumilch, and an awfully good Brie. I *know* what hospital food can be." Lydia lowered her eyes, inferring by her silence a long and grave illness once nobly endured. John Wesley was more impressed by the subtlety of the paint job on her lids—pale blue-violet and white. Difficult as he was, that make-up man of hers was a true genius. "The chauffeur is having them put in the refrigerator."

"Th-that's awfully nice of you, Lydia. Thanks."

"And I've also brought you some things to read. Something worthy of your intelligence. Those hospital funny-funny books can be so deadly."

The chauffeur appeared at John Wesley's door with a stack of abstruse journals. "Thank you, Adamson," Lydia said. "Just put them next to Mr. Smith's bed—close enough so that he can reach them." John Wesley glanced at the titles—*Ciné, Cinematic Arts, Film Quarterly, Film Culture, Films in Review, Art Film Monthly, Motion Picture International, The American Journal of Motion Picture Arts and Techniques.* God, what a stack! He had never heard of any of them before. He looked rather wistfully for a good, trashy fan magazine—something along the lines of *Photoplay* or *Silver Screen*—but he was disappointed.

"Now that the picture is so close to being finished—we're winding up the ball scene this afternoon to get rid of all the extras—we'll be wanting to get these truly influential authorities"—she waved a hand toward the magazines—"in to see the first screening. Naturally the other critics—"

"But, Lydia, don't these look kind of high and inside?" The

idea of *Cinderella Flanagan* being treated seriously by learned journals did not come easily.

"This is everything, Wezley. The cream of the field. But I thought for our next—"

"Next? Next what?"

"Why, our next film."

"What next film? Do you mean that Deirdre—"

"Oh, not for Deirdre. Wezley, I may as well admit it. I was wrong. Oh, at first I had the usual mother's hopes and ambitions for her child. But now—seeing Deirdre work, working with her—I can admit that I was wrong. She's just a prettier-than-average average girl. She hasn't the flame, not even the spark, necessary to carry a young actress forward."

"Don't underrate her. She's pretty good."

"Pretty and pretty good, Wezley. Thanks. That was loyal of you. But prettiness and mediocrity aren't enough. *Quick-silver!* That's what an actress needs. Deirdre hasn't got it."

"Well, then that makes any question of another film sort of . . ."

"This wouldn't be a film for Deirdre. This would be a film for me."

John Wesley was thankful for the traction. It was all that kept him from falling out of bed.

"What does Justin think?" he asked evenly.

"Justin doesn't know about it yet. Leave him to me. But, Wezley—the maddest thing! We even own a *studio!* Yes! A jiggery-pokery old place out on Long Island where they used to make those darling old nickelodeon things. The Fennessey Trust has had it for so long that everyone forgot all about it. It took *me* to discover it. It's sweet, really. Smallish. But with a few hundred thousand dollars to do over the dressing rooms, bring in some equipment . . . I could take a small place in town so as to be—"

"And Wyn? What does he say?"

"Oh, Wezley. Please don't joke. Wynton Plover? *Wyn*-ton *Plo*-ver? Wyn is a darling—one of my dearest and oldest friends. And Wyn *is* clever and resourceful. Amusing. But Wezley, let's face it, Wyn's been around for a long, long time. (He's a good deal older than he looks, poor thing.) And he simply hasn't made it. Oh, he works on and off. Yes. But for a really big project I would feel safe only in the hands of a really big director. George Cukor. He's marvelous with women. Ford, Huston. Possibly some of the younger men— Mike Nichols or one of the Italians—Fellini, or that madcap who did *Blow-Up*—or even the English. You see, I have this idea for a picture. It's about a more mature woman—not old, you understand, but, say, thirty. She's a famous designer and . . ."

God deliver us, John Wesley thought as he lay there help-less against the force of Lydia's enthusiasm. All finesse laid aside, Lydia, with burning eyes, was describing the sort of picture that had thrilled shopgirls and Wynton Plover thirty years ago, and using the names of directors she'd recently discovered in *Film Quarterly!* From late night television, John Wesley could almost see Joan Crawford, Norma Shearer, Claudette Colbert in the endless fashion parade that used to pass for a plot. Her story was even titled *Designing Lady*. Surely *that* had been used at least a dozen times.

John Wesley could read into her every sentence all of the terrible things that have ever been said of actors in general— of their stupidity buttressed by narcissism. Even worse, this handsome, power-driven, untalented woman had all of the money, all of the power necessary to make her schoolgirl dreams come true. He had heard of women who, on the strength of a few voice lessons and rich, subservient hus-bands, had been able to hire Carnegie Hall and force tickets upon their more masochistic friends for pathetic recitals of

Debussy and Schumann. But with a billion dollars at her command, where would this maniac stop?

"Are you going to sing the 'Liebeslieder Walzer'?" John Wesley asked.

"Sing?" Lydia asked sharply, a little annoyed at being interrupted. "Oh, I might tear off a quick little song. I was the lead in a big musical when I quit to marry Justin." She almost spat out the name. "But about my leading men: I thought for the rich, society playboy . . ."

Lydia raced on and on and on until, all thought spent, her head fell back—chignon be damned—with a sibilant little hiss against the plastic cushion of her chair. The light slanting through the blinds made her lids look very unusual, very blue, very white, very painted.

"Uh, well, that sounds challenging, Lydia," John Wesley said. "I certainly hope to see your, uh, picture—once it's finished."

"See it? But, Wezley, you're going to write it. You and I. Together."

John Wesley was saved only by the arrival of the girl from the laboratory with her tray of glass bottles, rubber tubes, corks, and needles.

"Sorry to interrupt," she said, "but doctor wants a routine run-down on you this afternoon."

"Th-that's perfectly all right," John Wesley murmured.

"Oh, Wezley," Lydia moaned, her voice now in its bad Beatrice Straight three-octave range, "look at the time! I've far overstayed my welcome. Do forgive me." A ballerina's curtsey and her veil flew into the air and fluttered above her lovely head in the finest old Doris Humphrey tradition. A less fortunate performer would have been enveloped to the waist in clouds of floating chiffon. On lucky Lydia it made a perfect landing. She swept the ends of it around her throat and resumed her Lady with a Lamp role with a vengeance.

"Wezley, darling," she moaned in the mightiest diapason the organ of her voice would allow. "Good-by. Good-by. I must get back to the set. No rest for the weary. Good-by, Miss . . . uh . . . yes. Good-by." And then she bent down to kiss her supine victim. The reek of her professional paint job! It made John Wesley long for Peggy.

"Say, who was that, anyway?" the laboratory girl asked. "Some kind of actress?"

"Y-yes," John Wesley said. "Some kind of actress."

"Hey! You're trembling all over. This won't hurt. You know it. You'll just feel a little prick and—"

"Hehehehehe," John Wesley laughed lewdly. It was a weak, futile attempt at bawdiness.

"Okay, let's have the middle finger. Just like always." She jabbed it expertly with her needle. "*He-ey!*"

John Wesley burst into tears, helpless, ridiculous, maudlin tears. Unable to control himself, he lay there sobbing until the bed quivered with his loud, wet self-pity.

The floor nurse bustled in. "Well, whaddaya know? Best patient we ever had an' lookatum now!" A hypodermic appeared. The shock of it silenced his sobs. He felt one thousand years old. Above the noise of his own breathing he could hear the floor nurse and the laboratory girl discussing him *sotto voce.*

"But I must of stuck him a thousand times before . . ."

"Honey, don't you know who that lady was?"

"Some kinda actress. Gorgeous!"

"But, honey, that was *Mrs. Justin Fennessey.* Mad about her. Oh, she's got a dozen on the string."

"Gawan! A lady like her?"

"They're the worst kind, honey. He was trying to kill himself on account of her. That's common knowledge."

"*No!*"

"Surest thing you know, honey. Oh, I seen all kinds here

and those society ones are the worst. We yoosta have Mrs. Whitney, Mrs. Wilmerding Whitney, and she . . ."

And then John Wesley drifted off to sleep.

Wynton Plover's visit followed later that afternoon. If Wyn's rakish old Jaguar convertible didn't create much of a stir with the hospital staff, his black leather suit, leather boots, and beret did. He brought John Wesley a book entitled *Mr. Madam,* describing it as a "sscream." It was not. John Wesley, helpless, endured a more ardent than usual series of pats and squeezes and then, recreation period over, Wyn drew the armchair up to the bedside and got down to the business at hand.

"You've ssimply got to help me, Wesss," he began.

"Help you what?"

"With that sstinking picture. We wrapped it up today—except for ssome ssilly little retakes."

"Just how do you think I could help anyone do anything, lying here in this contraption. I can't even . . ."

"It'ss Lydia. Wesss, I promisse you that she's gone sstark, sstaring mad. In the firsst place, she couldn't act her way out of a paper ssack, but do you think *she* can ssee that? Not even when she ssees how ridiculouss her whole performance is in the rough cutss every night. She jusst inssisstss on doing the whole thing over—*worsse!*"

"Nothing new about that, Wyn. And there isn't much that I can do."

"But, Wesss. You could *talk* to her. She resspectss you. That and a bit more—if you don't mind your old mother telling you a few bassic factss of life."

"Sorry, Wyn. It's pretty much out of my hands by now."

"*And mine.* Everything'ss done. The only hope we have now is the editor. I found a brilliant one. A Greek. Sso far he's been doing nudiess. Did you ever ssee *Ssinerama?*"

"No."

"Made millionss. Or *Ssweet Ssexteen?* or *Ssadie-Mae?*"

"Afraid not."

"Well, they're all ssimply appalling. A lot of broken-down old sstrippers sswinging their titss around for the Forty-ssecond Sstreet trade—sstrictly no-talent sscript, acting, photography, direction. The workss. But conssidering the terrible sstuff he had to work with, Bassil did a brilliant job."

"Basil?"

"The editor. The one who did the cutting. Anyhow, he's going to *try* to do ssomething with thiss mess. If only Lydia sstayss away. Actually everybody elsse is pretty good. The girl'ss adequate and the old man—Grampss—is ssenssational. As for the sscript, well, even that seemss to make ssome ssensse—believe it or not. You've done yeoman sservice, Wesss."

"Thanks, Wyn. It wasn't easy."

"And that bringss me to the real purposse of my vissit."

"Oh?"

"Wesss, you've got a real flair for sscreenplayss. You ssee thingss in the people. Character. Little quirkss. Teamed up with me and ssomeone like Bassil who really knowss his editing, we could do ssome ve-ry interessting thingss."

"Using what for money?"

"Well, that'ss what I wanted to talk to you about."

"Don't waste your breath. I haven't got any."

"No, not you perssonally. But what about the Fennesseys?"

"Justin? Never."

"No, Wesss. Not Jusstin. But what about Desmond?"

"Desmond? Desmond Fennessey?"

"Yess. Why not? He's got lotss of money. I know. Lydia told me how much. He's ssmarter than all the resst of them put together. He's had a sscrumptiouss time jusst ssitting around watching uss make thiss abortion. My dear, you should have sseen him as the court chamberlain in the ball sscene. The puresst camp! He likes you. That'ss obviouss. He likes ssitting in on the shooting. He's got tonss of money and nothing to sspend it on. You could talk him around if you really tried. I know you could." Wyn gave John Wesley a conspiratorial wink.

"Well, Wyn, thanks for thinking of me. I—I'll have to let you know later. I'm not really sure of my own plans yet."

"Well, don't ssay no without giving it ssome thought, ssweetie. Heavens! Would you look at the time. I ssaid I'd meet Bassil at the sstation. The firsst sstation of his crosss, you might ssay. Sso long, Wess."

"So long, Wyn. And thanks for the book."

"Oh, you'll ssplit your ssides. It'ss the ssissssiesst thing! Well, sstay well." As Wyn fled the room, the floor nurse cast John Wesley a glance of darkest suspicion from the corridor.

John Wesley was *the* celebrity patient of the small, exurban hospital. If there had ever been the slightest doubt about it, the arrival of Desmond Fennessey quite put John Wesley over the top. Desmond alighted from his splendid car wearing hunting pinks. His sickroom gift was a portable bar, its bottles filled and beautifully fitted into a pigskin case. "Just set this up on that chest of drawers and bring some ice, would you please?" Desmond said to the slack-jawed floor nurse.

"Y-yes, Mr. Fennessey," she stammered, and scuttled away.

"Wes, dear boy!" Desmond said, thwacking a glistering boot with his riding crop.

"Desmond! I didn't know you rode."

"I don't. At least I haven't for years. I just found this in my dressing room and put it on. It kills a lot of time. And I'm sick of my other clothes. How *are* you, anyhow?" He dumped his gloves and crop into his inverted hard hat and straddled a straight chair. The whole effect was pure Regency rake. It was not wasted on the floor nurse who reappeared goggle-eyed with a bowl of ice cubes.

"Thank you, my dear," Desmond said. "By the way, do you know how to make a vodka martini?"

"W-why, ye-yes . . . sir."

"Splendid. Make three. One for yourself, of course."

"Oh, I couldn't, Mr. Fennessey. Not on duty, that is." She treated Desmond to what she considered a winning smile, implying drunken orgies after seven o'clock.

"Pity. Then just make two, would you? Chill the glasses, please."

"*Yes*, Mr. Fennessey!"

"Cheers," Desmond said, raising his glass after the floor nurse, casting a come-hither glance over her shoulder, had left the room. "How do you feel, anyhow?"

"Bored. That's about all. No pain."

"*You're* bored? Wes, I almost envy you. How pleasant to be in a nice quiet hospital with plenty to drink and no having to listen to those horses asses Justin and Stan Earnshaw. No Lydia and no Jenny bitching at each other. No Deirdre saying 'Bananas' and no Consuelo giggling. No having to pretend that I don't know what Father Alonzo is saying. (I speak Spanish, by the way. French, Italian, and German, too.) Not that he has anything interesting to say. It's just *cursi*. (That's Spanish for vulgar, dear boy.)"

"Yes. I know."

"No having Travis breathing down my neck. I swear that the old fart listens at doors. Although what he expects to hear of any interest is beyond me. No more listening to my grandfather's stories . . ."

"I think some of your grandfather's stories are very interesting."

"Perhaps. *Now*. But don't forget, I've been hearing them

for more than forty years. No more watching Luis Fernando trying to seduce the maids or Lydia's Mr. Plover trying to seduce Luis Fernando. You're well off where you are."

"I don't think you'd really like to trade places."

"Well, dear boy, I'd like to be *some*where else. If it weren't for my curiosity about Lyd's home movies, I'd clear out and go to . . . well, I don't know where. *Cinderella Flanagan* is the only faintly amusing thing that's happened since Mummy and Daddy put up that place. Oh, if you could have seen it in the old days—gaggles of nuns and priests coming for lunch and Justin being a perfect prick in his little blue serge suit. Mummy making her perpetual novenas, Daddy making money, Jenny making the stableboys, and Grandpa making fun of all of us. Nothing's changed—really—except that Jenny's no fun and Mummy and Daddy are dead. Justin's still a prick and Grandpa still sees through us like glass. . . . Ready for another?" Without waiting for John Wesley's answer, Desmond spun out two more martinis.

"I suppose you think I'm a wicked, profligate wastrel."

"I never said any such thing, Desmond."

"You didn't need to. I was able to read your message. Whenever I can't get away fast enough Father Alonzo is always chewing me out for my wasted life—not that *he* does much more than eat and sleep. If I'd been a priest after all . . ."

John Wesley's hand twitched so violently that half his drink splashed onto the coverlet. "If you'd been a *what?*"

"You mean you didn't know? I was slated to be the sacrificial lamb. It was my poor mother's dearest wish. Justin was supposed to watch over the money as head of the Fennessey family. Jenny was to be our social leader and Baby Desmond was to be the bishop of Birmingham or some such godforsaken place. By the time I came along the family could afford an intellectual. I was it."

John Wesley couldn't trust himself to speak. It wasn't necessary. Staring deep into his martini, Desmond went on. "I wasn't always the black sheep of the family, you know. That crown was once worn by my sister Genevieve until marriage, motherhood, and that store-bought title gave her a certain nebulous respectability—if you don't look *too* closely. I picked up the torch just after she and Chuchu picked up that cut-rate papal marquisate. Until then I was the brightest boy in the seminary. Little black suit, little black tie, gassing away with a lot of seminarians about virgin birth and bodily ascension. Oh, I was a sketch!"

Considering vain, worldly Desmond Fennessey sitting there in his musical-comedy hunt attire, John Wesley wanted to laugh until he saw that Desmond was actually moved. "What happened?"

"Nothing. That's the trouble. Nothing happened. Everything was up here"—Desmond touched his beautifully combed hair—"nothing here." John Wesley could hear the faint clank of a gold cigarette case as Desmond tapped his heart. "I was in my last year at the seminary when I finally faced up to it."

"What did you do?"

"Well, when I was finally able to confess it to myself I thought I'd better confess it to somebody else."

"Father Alonzo?"

"That old nincompoop? Certainly not! No. I went to the head of the seminary and told him. Oh, there was pluperfect hell to pay. Such moaning and groaning and praying as you can't imagine. Not only were they losing their brightest boy —they were losing the Fennessey dime. At least my share of it."

"I think the Catholic Church could get along without it."

"Probably. Anyhow, they said to take a year out in the cold, cruel world and think it over."

"Then what?"

"So I went out into the cold, cruel world."

"And?"

"And here I am. It's been twenty years now."

"But did you think?"

"Dear boy, I never think. Puts furrows into the forehead. Another?"

"No thanks."

"Well, much as I hate to drink alone . . ." Desmond mixed himself another martini and sprawled in the easy chair.

"Desmond, if you don't mind my asking, have you ever done anything useful? I mean like work?"

"Work? Please don't use those filthy four-letter words in the presence of an unordained priest." He laughed dryly. "Oh, when I was a kid I used to go out and do noble things with the underprivileged in a settlement house. You know— basketball and sweaty conversations about what a hell of a swell fellow Jesus was."

"Did you like it?"

"Not really. It wouldn't have mattered anyhow. Daddy found out about it and made me quit."

"But why?"

"He never quite said. I think the *real* reason may have been because the place was right across from the tenement where he was born. It wasn't chic to be democratic in those days. You should have known Justin before he came down with that fatal attack of Ummurricun-itis. He was better as a snob than a slob—but not much. Jenny sticks to her guns more or less. If it weren't for an advanced case of hot pants she might have been able to buy a genuine English duke instead of a broken-down old bullfighter like Chuchu."

"Don Jesús? A bullfighter?"

"Hard to believe, but true. He was also a nightclub singer. In his prime he was a sort of rough-trade Luis Fernando. The husband before him was a beery old Notre Dame fullback.

Jenny was always more at home in the locker room than the drawing room, but with the passing years she's had time to cool down."

"The marquesa?" John Wesley was truly shocked.

"Yes. I think she regrets her girlish ardor now. I'm not sure. She's always been very good at deluding herself. But perhaps when she looks at Chuchu and thinks back to Tom Muldoon she wishes there'd been a healthy dose of saltpeter in the communion wafers. A bit more self-control and she might have become a genuine English peeress with, ideally, a virile gamekeeper tucked away in the lodge. As it is, she has to be grand enough for two and she can't quite stand the strain. Lydia puts on a much better show. Dramatic training, I suppose. Mind if I have another half drink? It's your vodka."

"I don't mind, Desmond. But do you really think you ought to?"

"Probably not, but it does help to kill the afternoon."

"Desmond, don't you ever think of doing anything with yourself?"

"Well, yes, old boy. I do. It's one of the reasons for my visit. You know, I'm bloody bored. And I suspect that you are, too, having to put up with Justin and this Fennessey Foundation nonsense. You won't last, you know. Only a professional nest builder like Stan could."

"I don't want to last. The work isn't exactly what I thought it was going to be."

"Then why don't you clear out?"

"When my contract is fulfilled—that's less than a month from now—I will. By mutual consent, I'm sure."

"Perfect! Then why don't you come to work for me? Whatever Justin pays you—and it can't be much—"

"Doing what, Desmond?"

"Well, I don't like to use the word secretary because that

isn't quite it. I never write letters anyhow. And the word companion—well, that isn't it, either. I'm not lonely. Really I'm not. You'd be sort of a paid pal. Someone to talk intelligently when I feel like talking. Someone who's good company to travel with. I mean, there's this safari I'm interested in going on. Can you shoot?"

"A little. Yes."

"Or it might be fun to go down to Rio for carnival and then there's a trip on the Amazon—bare breasts, shrunken heads, and all the rest of it. Tell me, Wes, have you ever been in the East?"

"Yes. Quite recently."

"Is that fun?"

"No."

"Pity. But I thought to bash about on a houseboat in Kashmir—places like Bali, Samoa, Tahiti. Well, what do you think?"

"It's . . . it's very kind of you, Desmond. But it . . . well, it just isn't what I want to do with my life."

"You mean to say that you *know* what you want to do with your life?"

"Not exactly, but I know what I *don't* want to do with my life. I just wouldn't be very good as 'paid pal.' I don't know quite why, but I wouldn't."

"The Protestant ethic or something like that, I suppose?"

"I guess so."

"Well," Desmond said, rising, "I just thought I'd ask."

"Desmond, don't go away mad. I'm flattered. I really am. Nobody ever wanted the pleasure of my company before— let alone offered to pay for it. I'm a very dull companion. I know it. But there must be millions of people who'd jump at the chance. You're a very good egg, Desmond, and with your money—"

"There it goes again! The goddam money! I wish I'd never had it."

"But, Desmond, you do have it. It doesn't have to be a curse. It can be a blessing, too. You—"

"May I quote you for *Our Sunday Visitor?*"

"Desmond, I merely . . ."

"Sorry, old boy, but I'm late for my massage. Get well soon."

"Desmond—" Too late. Desmond Fennessey was gone. Through the window, John Wesley saw him cross the parking lot a moment later, the splendid scarlet of his hunting jacket attracting stares. But his outlandish costume had about it, somehow, the bedraggled quality of fancy dress at the end of a masquerade ball. Desmond drooped. As he got into his car he looked old and very, very lonely.

Unaccustomed as it was to titled visitors, the hospital staff found the appearance of the Marquesa de Mondragon y Alonzo something of an anticlimax. Sweltering in sables, a slouch hat, and an antelope suit (September was was not far off), she looked rich, all right, but not exactly regal.

Her call was purely social, or so it seemed at first. "We're so anxious to know if you'll be able to come to Consuelo's little party, Mr. Smith. Not her actual debut; that's for later. Just a few of her young American friends."

Fewer, alas, than Jenny had hoped for. Cheap jet travel, early marriage, and compulsory military service had scattered the marquesa's roster of really eligible young men to the four winds. Even the canned list of boys rented from a social secretary—names one had never heard of—was proving unfruitful. Nor had Lydia been much help in claiming that the list of guests for Deirdre's party the season before had been irretrievably mislaid. In revising her plans downward, Jenny did not find fifteen too young or fifty too old to dance attendance upon her daughter.

"We're having scads of Consuelo's beaux brought out on a chartered bus," Jenny said with her bright V-shaped smile.

"As parties go, hers will be unique. Instead of just a little run-of-the-mill dance, it's to be the world premiere—private, of course—of the film and *then* dancing. So much more original, don't you think?"

Jenny nearly choked on her own words. If there was anything she did want for her daughter, it was a little run-of-the-mill dance. If there was anything she did *not* want, it was having to sit through a long, dreadful movie with Lydia Fennessey and Deirdre cavorting before the eyes of young men who should be thinking only of Consuelo. Justin had been impossible about Consuelo's summer party. Debuts, he said, were undemocratic and damned expensive. Why not just ask some nice girls in for tea? Finally they had compromised. Consuelo could have her party on the night of the first showing of *Cinderella Flanagan* (Lydia had been most definite; it would be a grand opening for selected press) if Jenny would pay for the orchestra, the marquee, and split the cost of food and drink. Jenny was furious. You'd think that Justin was spending his own money! A more doting uncle would have been delighted to launch so lovely a niece. Desmond had even volunteered to spring for a whole dinner dance in November with the strict understanding that he need not attend it. Well, that was the difference between them.

"It sounds very nice," John Wesley said with less than a little enthusiasm. "But I don't know whether I'll be mobile by then. I hope so."

"Oh, and so do I!" Jenny said. At least John Wesley Smith was presentable and somewhere near the right age. Jenny cast an icy-blue glance at the traction frame, at the plaster cast on John Wesley's leg. "I suppose that even if you were released from that—that contraption, dancing would be out of the question?"

"Pretty much out of the question, I guess. I'm not much of a dancer, anyhow."

"Neither is Consuelo," Jenny said. "On the other hand, Luis Fernando dances divinely. You do have a—how-you-say —*smoking?*"

"A tux? Yes."

"Exactly. A dinner jacket. Very well then," Jenny said, drawing her gloves on over her rings. They left large, arthritic-looking lumps beneath the suede. "I mustn't tire you. But we *are* counting on you for Consuelo's little party. Tata."

Captain Mulcahy's visit occurred late during John Wesley's stay in the hospital but it was equally purposeful. He wore a magnificent blue suit that could only have been Desmond's. He did not wear it well. He showered dandruff on the shoulders. His diaphragm strained against the buttons. Neither in nor out, the pocket flaps rose like the ears of a jackass. John Wesley recognized one of his own neckties and earmarked it as another item in his modest wardrobe destined for the funeral pyre.

It took Rory some time to settle. With his usual aimless curiosity, he drifted around the room, fingering the weights and pulleys on the traction frame, ringing the bell push that summoned the floor nurse, poking into empty dresser drawers, reading the temperature chart. He was gratified to discover Desmond's portable bar and, unbidden, helped himself liberally before sitting down and coming to the point.

"Well, *Cinderella Flanagan's* near done," Rory said. "Plover's got that Greek fellah kind of rearranging it, like."

"I'm sure it could do with a lot of rearranging."

"You know, don't you, that it's the first film I've ever written? And if I do say so myself, it's a little gem."

"I'll just bet it is."

"Yes, Johnny-boy, a tiny, shinin' diamond." Rory rose and refilled his glass. Over the rim of it, he cast John Wesley a quizzical, bleary glance and sat down again. "I'm expecting great things from it."

"Well, I wouldn't hold out too much hope."

"An old chum of mine telephoned me from California last night. Maybe you know him—Cyril B. de Mille."

"No, but I read about his funeral some years ago."

"Ah, yes. A grand film. One of his greatest."

John Wesley gave up.

"A lot of me old chums seem to have got wind of this. 'Rory,' they tell me, 'you could make your fortune writing for the cinema.' And so I could."

"That's nice for you," John Wesley said. He hoped desperately that a nurse with a bedpan, the girl from the laboratory, the garrulous Gray Lady with the book cart would come in. Then he realized, just as desperately, that Rory could outsit any one of them.

"But you know, Johnny-boy, I'm having a little trouble with the American language."

"Really? I thought it was more or less the same."

Not listening, as usual, Rory went on. "And so I thought that if I could team up with a smart assistant, like, to smooth over the rough spots. Well, what do you say, Johnny-boy?"

"What do I say about what?"

"About teaming up with me and writing for the cinema, We'd use my name, of course, but I'd give you ten per cent."

"For doing ninety per cent of the work? No thanks."

"So what do you say, Johnny-boy?"

"I just said it, Rory. No."

"No?" Hearing him for the first time, Rory was shocked.

"No. I'm not interested in writing for the movies. And I don't think you should, either. But if that's what you want to do, go to it."

And then John Wesley was saved. His doctor, a nononsense, businesslike sort of man charged into the room accompanied by two assistants. "Well, Mr. Smith, I think we'll be taking the plaster off today. And so, if we could have the room cleared . . ."

Peggy's visits were the best. She came only to see John Wesley, not because she wanted anything for herself. She brought the gossip of the day—frank and impartial—books and magazines (Lydia's highfalutin screen journals had been plentiful but unreadable) and John Wesley's sparse personal mail. She remembered to bring nail clippers and emory boards, soothing lotions and cool colognes, and she used them gently and expertly. She found a dry shampoo and administered it with loving fingertips twice a week. It was Peggy who gave him an only slightly disastrous haircut with her embroidery scissors. How he loved her! And it was Peggy who brought Gramps, so full, as he put it, of "piss and vinegar" from all those injections that he pinched the floor nurse and quaffed three of the dozen bottles of Fennessey's Kilkenny Ale which he had brought John Wesley.

After the cast came off, Peggy's visits were better still. They had even tried to make love one evening—a project doomed by telephone calls from Lydia and Deirdre, by the appearance of the floor nurse to ask whether John Wesley wanted ice, and by a visit from the hearty, pipe-smoking chaplain. So much for sex. But at least he could take a shower and go to the bathroom all by himself. Physiotherapy had worked wonders.

And then suddenly, miraculously, it was all over. "Yes, you can go," the doctor told him. "Most doctors would insist on your staying here at least another week. I don't agree. I think the sooner you resume your normal life, the better. It means taking it easy, using your cane and also your common sense. But I'm ready to discharge you as of right now."

With a leap he regretted immediately, John Wesley bounded off his bed and was half dressed by the time the doctor had signed the papers for his release.

Homecoming

♣ ❦ ♣ ❦ ♣ ❦ ♣ ❦ ♣ ❦ ♣ ❦ ♣ ❦ ♣

The driveway of the Fennessey Foundation was once again jammed with cars and trucks as the taxi jogged through the gates. An enormous pink-and-white striped marquee was being erected. While the driver was saying something about a big revival meeting and a Catholic plot against the Hudson River Valley, John Wesley paid the enormous fare and limped up to the portico.

As Travis opened the door to him John Wesley realized for the first time how weak he really was. He felt lightheaded and dizzy and was forced to rest his weight on his aluminum cane.

"Why, Mr. Smith!" Travis said. "We never expected you back so soon. If only you'd telephoned we could have sent a car."

"What's going on?" John Wesley asked, hobbling into the rotunda. The place smelled damp and green, ladders were everywhere, and florists' men were festooning the cornice and the malachite columns with garlands of white camellias.

"Why, Mr. Smith, had you forgotten? This is the night of the premiere of Mrs. Fennessey's film and also Miss Consuelo's party."

"Oh, Lord. I should have stayed in the hospital another day!" He lurched forward and grabbed a table for support.

"Oh, Mr. Smith!" Travis said, grasping him by the shoulders. The pain of his gesture was excruciating. "You should go right to bed. You're ever so pale. Much thinner, too."

"Thanks, Travis. I guess maybe I will. Is Miss O'Neil here, by the way?" He tried to sound very casual.

"She's in New York, sir. At the hairdresser's. All the ladies are. Even Miss Rafferty and Miss Shelagh. Now let me help you up to bed."

John Wesley slumped in a chair while Travis bustled about the Empire room drawing curtains, turning down coverlets, and plumping pillows. He had never imagined that he would feel so weak and helpless.

"A nice, hot tub first, sir?"

"No thanks, Travis. I think I'll just climb into bed." He staggered to his feet, writhed painfully out of his jacket and fumbled with his necktie.

"Here, let me help you, Mr. Smith. Mustn't overdo all at once."

There was something about Travis' touch, about his very nearness that John Wesley disliked. Travis was the first real, live butler John Wesley had ever met. At first he had been in awe of the man's overpowering grandeur. Later he had simply taken Travis for granted as though he might have been the wallpaper. This was the first time John Wesley had ever been alone with him, the first time they had ever exchanged more than a couple of sentences. Now he sensed that there was something inhuman—or, rather, ex-human—about the man; the slightly taxidermic touch as the servant deftly unknotted his necktie, undid the buttons of his shirt; the odorless odor of a thing long laid away. But most of all, he hated the air of embalmed mateyness which Travis now assumed. So lively for one so dead.

"A shame, I call it, that the doctors let you out so soon. But of course you'd want to be back for the big doings tonight, wouldn't you now? Mrs. Fennessey's heart would be broken not to have *you* at her gala premiere?"

Now just what did he mean by that?

"Miss O'Neil, too, I'll wager." John Wesley made no comment. "Here's your pajamas, sir. Would you like a nice, warm robe, as well? Mr. Desmond has masses of them."

"No, thank you."

"Yes, it's to be a very grand affair this evening. And expensive! Chartered buses to bring out all the film critics. And then Miss Consuelo's friends as well. It's not my place to say, of course, but I don't see how Mr. Fennessey can justify all of this at government expense, do you?"

If it isn't his place to say, why is he saying anything? John Wesley wondered. "I really don't know anything about it, I only work here."

"Yes, I guess that's it, sir. The haves and the have-nots. Of course I don't know much about the government of the United States, but it does seem to me that—"

"I don't know anything about it either, Travis. Now, if you'll excuse me, I think I'll crawl into bed." John Wesley had never imagined that he would be defending the Fennessey Foundation against anyone, but there was something detestable about this man.

"A nice cup of tea, sir?"

"No, thank you, Travis."

"Or perhaps something stronger?"

"No, thank you."

"An extra blanket?"

"No, thanks."

"The windows open?"

"No."

"Goodness," Travis said, gazing out of the window, "here comes the champagne for tonight. Three truckloads! Some people just have money to burn. I don't suppose you could give me some inkling as to how much this film has cost, could you?"

"No, Travis. I couldn't. But shouldn't you be down there supervising?"

"No rest for the weary, eh?"

"Well, I'm weary and I'm going to sleep. Thank you, Travis. Nothing more."

John Wesley did not know how long he slept. When he opened his eyes again the lamps were lighted and he saw Peggy's face bent over his.

"Wes! How wonderful! Why didn't you tell me you were coming home?"

"Peggy," he said, throwing his arms around her.

"Mind my hairdo, *if* you please. Seven hours portal to portal. Oh, Wes, I'm so happy that you're back." Heedless of her elaborate coiffure, Peggy lay down on the bed beside Wes. Once again he felt perfectly fine.

Debut

There had been two different sets of invitations engraved for this night of nights: the first a large document stating that the Board of Directors of the Fennessey Foundation for the Furtherance of the Arts and Sciences requested the honor of one's presence at the world premiere of an experimental film *Cinderella Flanagan;* the second, a neat bristol card, proclaimed beneath the blind-embossed Mondragon y Alonzo crest that Marqués y Marquesa Don Juan de Jesús María José Ildefonso Santiago Mondragon y Alonzo and their daughter Srta. María Antonieta Consuelo Concepción Alicia Guadalupe Mondragon y Alonzo y Fennessey were At Home and there would be Dancing. (Actually, of course, the marqués was safely stashed in Mexico.) Both invitations were for eight o'clock and punctuality was stressed.

At eight o'clock only the orchestra had arrived. A moment after eight, the young people from the village began to appear to Jenny's seething annoyance. Justin had allowed democracy to overrule economy and insisted that all of the ex-

tras be invited to the screening of their film. Lydia, delighted
to be spiking Jenny's social guns, backed her husband up
thoroughly and further suggested that the stagehands and
their wives be invited as well. "Just think, darling, of the
publicity value."

"Say, pussykins, that's a great idea. Gr-reat!"

Speechless with rage, the marquesa retired from the fray,
telling Travis privately that the locals were to be served only
domestic champagne.

To John Wesley's eye, the vanguard of the guests looked
exactly like the merrymakers at a high school prom back
home. And an hour later, when the *jeunesse dorée* began to
appear in its sports cars, its station wagons, its chartered
buses, he was unable to distinguish between the classes and
the masses, except that the village kids were somewhat better dressed and considerably better behaved.

From the turnout, John Wesley wondered why Peggy had
said that Jenny was worried about a sufficiency of young
men. What was even more amazing was the throng of film
critics, columnists, and "names" in the arts. Desmond, impec-
cable in a bottle-green brocade dinner jacket, had said, "Old
boy, the way to get celebrities to come to your parties is to
invite them. People will go anyplace for free food and drink."
Lydia had done her job well. John Wesley was amazed at
the magnitude of some of the names as they were announced.
Not the least of her strokes of genius was the installation of
a bar in the critics' chartered bus. Some of the gentlemen of
the press had to be helped down and assisted into the rotunda where a small but formidable reception committee
waited.

As there were two parties, there were two hostesses.
Lydia, serene in black lace and emeralds, glanced at her
counterpart, Jenny, on the opposite side of the rotunda.
"Really," Lydia sighed to Justin, "how *can* your sister get

herself up that way?" Gamboge chiffon, sequins—sequins in *August!*—canary diamonds and a bobbing topknot of corn-colored false curls. Jaundice time!

"I think Jenny looks very pretty, pussykins. Young."

"*Pretty? Young?* She looks like a retired call girl, thank you."

"Now, pussykins."

"Be still, Justin. Here's Haskins from *Art Film Monthly*. Mis-ter Haskins, how very good of you to come to our little celebration. *Do* you know my husband and Mr. Plover, our director?"

"*Will* you stop that fidgeting, Consuelo, and stand up straight," Jenny hissed at her daughter. "Don't giggle, and *stop* fiddling with your bouquet." For eighteen years Jenny had looked forward to this night as the first of a brilliant series of evenings when her debutante daughter would conquer New York as she, herself, had almost managed to do. Now she wondered why she had ever bothered. Consuelo was simply impossible. Equally fluent in Spanish and English, both languages seemed to desert her when some really attractive boy whose parents were somebody appeared. But with the stagehands and the little nothing extras the silly girl jibbered away like a Trappist suddenly released from the vow of silence. And her dress! Mainbocher and it looked like Main Street. Why was it that Consuelo could never put on anything right?

"Mummy, there's something wrong with one of my lenses. Everything looks all spidery."

Jenny observed her daughter. "Oh, my God!" Three hours at the Institut des Beaux Yeux and already a strip of artificial eyelashes hanging like Spanish moss! "Go upstairs, Consuelo, and take off your eyelashes."

"*Pero, Mamá, mis pestañas artificiales—*"

"Do as I say this instant. And hurry back. There are some

boys I want you to meet." Jenny glanced across the rotunda
and cast a brilliant smile at her sister-in-law. Lydia was talking to a famous society columnist and putting on the dog as
Mrs. Justin Fennessey. Hamming it up. Lydia—or, rather,
Lena—that little slut from No-place, Michigan, swanking
around in dead-crow black lace and the Fennessey emeralds
as though she were the Duchess of Marlborough. Wasn't she
ever going to let the society columnist loose, damn her?
Jenny certainly didn't want to talk to any of those Jewish
movie critics of Lydia's. Couldn't Lydia play fair just once in
her life? Jenny hadn't loused up Deirdre's coming-out party.
She hadn't even bothered to go to it. Jenny shot another radiant smile across the room. At last Lydia got the message. And
now Jenny could hear Lydia's beautiful contralto. "I do want
you meet my little Mexican niece." *Mexican!*

Jenny was conscious of Consuelo once more standing at
her side, her eyelids red and puckered, glistening with irides-
cent flecks of dried glue. Lydia swept across the porphyry
floor in a flurry of skirts. "Consuelo, dear, I'd like you to meet
—But what's the matter with your eyes, darling? Been crying again?"

The bitch! The dirty, vicious, evil bitch! Jenny sucked in
her stomach, extended a long, white kid glove, beamed. "So
glad you could come."

Leaning on his cane, John Wesley kept to the edges of the
crowd, sitting down wherever and whenever he could. He
longed for Peggy, but Peggy was very much on duty, seeing
that Lydia's famous critics and columnists got more than
enough to drink, that everyone met everyone else, that no
one got stuck.

John Wesley noticed the beautiful young man who played
Prince Charming moving across the lawn in an almost visible
aura of handsomeness. So dazzling was he in his summer dinner clothes that the crowds parted at his approach. Less ex-

quisite, but equally awe-inspiring, his wife followed with waddling tread, mountainous in a flowered maternity evening dress.

"Hi!" he said to John Wesley. "Feeling better?"

"Much better, thanks. And you?"

"Oh, busy as usual. I'm doing a full-color series for Mac-Gregor Sportswear, some formal stuff for After Six and a cigarette commercial for TV. The residuals alone—"

"There's an agent here from the William Morris office," his wife snapped, "and I've saved seats right next to his, so come on. He says maybe—"

"Sure thing, Midge honey, but—"

"Don't argue. If I could get you into movies—and maybe the kids, too—we wouldn't have to . . ." Her voice drifted off as they moved into the crowd—beauty and the beast.

Another star of the evening was Captain Mulcahy. Reeling about the garden in one of Desmond's older dinner suits, the studs of his finely pleated shirt popped open to reveal his hairy sack of guts, he had reached just that point of inebriation where someone who had never met him before might find him picturesque, even if barely coherent. Champagne, John Wesley observed, worked a little more slowly on Rory than Irish whisky.

It was after ten o'clock when the guests were finally herded under the pink-and-white striped marquee to see the screening of *Cinderella Flanagan*. A morbid curiosity led John Wesley onward. The orchestra was playing vividly undistinguished music loosely based on "The Minstrel Boy," "I'll Take You Home Again, Kathleen," and some hackneyed Irish reels and jigs when he limped in. A friend of Wyn Plover's had composed it as background music for the film. So that he might make his getaway quickly and secretly, he chose a seat in the last row of little gilt chairs and then noticed that Lydia's assemblage of famous critics had done exactly the same thing. Every critic held a glass in each hand, the elaborate souvenir program lying unread on his lap.

Gazing around the marquee, John Wesley saw Justin Fennessey in eager conversation with Cornelius Slattery. Deirdre was fighting off a flock of admirers. Consuelo, ignoring her mother's frenzied signals, was squealing hysterically at something Rory Mulcahy was saying. Rory, too, had a glass in each hand. His shirt had worked out between his cummerbund and the top of his trousers. His butterfly tie had crawled over toward one ear. Entranced, Consuelo stared at him with glazed eyes while the marquesa made frantic but vain gestures toward more attractive men.

Mr. Earnshaw, gray of eye, gray of hair, and wearing a gray dinner jacket that looked as much like a West Point dolman as possible, had cornered for himself a village girl of undistinguished prettiness and just old enough to be his daughter. Over the music and the roar of voices, John Wesley could hear him saying, "My great friends, General and Mrs. Eisenhower . . ."

"Wasn't he some kind of politician?" the girl asked.

Poor little thing, John Wesley thought, she must have still been playing with dolls when the Eisenhowers left the White House.

With a final, syncopated blast, the music came to a halt. There was a roll of drums. The lights went out. The white beam of a film projector jiggled across a pink satin curtain. The curtain opened with a little series of jerks, and there was Mrs. Justin Fennessey—upside down. The audience was in hysterics.

The lights came on again and with a fluttering of black lace, Mrs. Fennessey herself whirled to the front. John Wesley could see that she was furious. But her poise, her self-assurance, her rather schoolgirlish reticence were admirable. Maybe she wasn't quite as rotten an actress as he thought.

"Friends," Lydia said throatily, "you must forgive us. *Cinderella Flanagan* is meant to be shown right-side-up. Truly it is. But we're all just the rankest amateurs trying to do our very little bit. And so if you'll just be patient . . ." The waiters circulated with more champagne. The critics once again took two glasses apiece.

In a remarkably short time the film was set to rights, the lights went out and there was Lydia again, a hundred times bigger than life, beautifully made-up, exquisitely lighted. John Wesley moaned softly, settled back in his chair, closed his eyes, and waited for the worst.

It was not long in coming. A burst of laughter and he opened his eyes again. There was Lydia once more being carried through the village street (the stable yard) in a sedan chair. Her pair of blackamoors (two colored waiters from the local golf club) belied the fiction that all Negroes had a natural sense of rhythm. They were woefully out of step. The sedan chair rocked and pitched like a canoe on the high seas, while Lydia, a beatific smile frozen on her face, lurched from port to starboard inside it. John Wesley found himself laughing with the rest of the audience. But it wasn't meant to be funny.

The scene on the village street looked like the opening of a high school operetta, the villagers, recruited from the vicinity, as gauche and self-conscious as the people on an audience-participation television show. Fortunately, it was slightly—and inadvertently—out of focus, which gave it a fashionably unreal quality. The total effect was rather like a parody. The extras themselves murmured in appreciation. John Wesley heard one of the critics sitting nearby saying, "It's a camp." Rory's drunken tumble brought a laugh, but then that hadn't been acting. Old Mr. Fennessey, as Squire McGafferty, was genuinely good. His first appearance brought a round of applause.

In their opening scene, the cruel stepmother and the ugly sisters, who were at least tried-and-true professionals, switched around in stays and petticoats, preening and primping in front of the mirror, and causing no laughter at all. It was meant to be funny. However, the scene was so dark (Justin had been concerned about the electric bill) that it had a chiaroscuro effect, and the actors could barely be distinguished at all, which helped.

Deirdre in clean but threadbare cotton, dabbing ineffectually at the firedogs, brought an indulgent chuckle. Everyone in the audience knew, of course, that one of the greatest fortunes in the world lay behind the poor little drudge on the screen. But when Deirdre spoke, the walls of the marquee billowed with unsuppressed laughter. Her accent was pure Ponsonby—a nasal "society" whine totally incongruous with the poor little waif's scrubbing floors and emptying slops. John Wesley had never seen rushes with the sound, but he realized that Deirdre's voice, perfectly pleasant in real life, simply did not come over mechanically. He was thankful that her lines had been cut to a minimum.

"It's a real pants-wetter," a hysterical critic in front of him roared to his neighbor.

But the ubiquitous fairy godmother, that eccentric duchess, got most of the laughs. Lydia's dramatic scope ran from a simpering girlishness, all but bobbing her sausage curls, through the honey-voiced sort of woman who reads aloud to the infantile and the senile, to a parody of a seductress. As low comedy went, her performance lacked only a strategically placed banana peel or a well-aimed custard pie. But even without these time-tested devices, the audience was ecstatic, the laughter so loud that most of the lines (dictated by Lydia herself) were inaudible. Just as well.

Gradually John Wesley realized what the matter was with whatever Lydia said or did: she was just slightly off. Like a soprano singing one quarter tone higher than the music, her performance was a shade off-key. Looking more beautiful than anyone else in the film, she went just a trifle too far with every speech and every movement. No other performer could have managed it without obviously overacting. With Lydia it was natural, unavoidable, and the final effect was devastatingly funny.

John Wesley looked for something good about the picture, aside from the unintended. Not Rory's lines, and certainly not his own. They were trite and dreadful. Not Cinderella herself, nor the ugly sisters and the mean stepmother. Try as they would, they could not rise above their material. Not Prince Charming. The beautiful young man photographed magnificently. From every angle he was handsome of face, broad of shoulder, slim of waist, and small of bottom. But, as he had pointed out, he was no actor. Even if he had been, the silliness of his lines, the fatuity of the role itself were insurmountable. His very beauty turned the character into a minor laugh-riot. The costumes, with the exception of those designed for Lydia, had the slightly bedraggled air of moth-eaten old duds hired out to a hundred church pageants, which had been precisely their history. The scenery? Well, that was good but it had all been there—the magnificent house, the stable block, the lush lawns, the formal gardens, the authentic period rooms, the Fennessey Collection itself. Anything that had been specially constructed for the picture had a haphazard, home-made look to it. Cinderella's fireplace positively jiggled when Lydia appeared down the chimney in a puff of smoke. It was good for a laugh, but not for much else. The music was perfectly blah—ersatz Eric Korngold and so corny that the audience giggled whenever the unseen philharmonic orchestra, about one-third the size that it should have been, burst into symphonic variations of "The Rose of Tralee." John Wesley finally settled on the editing as the best thing in the whole film. Considering what he had to work with, Wyn's Greek friend had done as good a job as— And then, to his horror, John Wesley saw a jet flying across the horizon of eighteenth-century Ireland. The rest of the audience roared.

Trying not to see any more of the debacle than possible, John Wesley studied the people connected with *Cinderella Flanagan*. He could hear old Mr. Fennessey's delighted chuckles and Consuelo's maniacal giggle, which was never silent. The marquesa had obviously never enjoyed anything so much in all of her life. John Wesley could hear her quasi-aristocratic laugh, see her golden head thrown back, her cluster of ringlets rocking ominously. Even Father Alonzo, in his rather glum Hispanic fashion, was laughing. Deirdre, whose dramatic ambitions were pallid to say the least, could be heard saying, "It's a groove!" "Bananas, man!" "Kicky!" and once but unmistakably, "Balls!" And then John Wesley saw the back of Lydia's head, erect on her rigid neck as she sat between Justin and Wyn Plover. Was it only his imagination, or did her Psyche knot and her dangling diamond-and-emerald earrings seem to quiver? John Wesley wondered what she could be thinking. He was not long in finding out.

She writhed through a couple of sepia dream sequences, which seethed with obvious symbolism and were inserted into the film only to give her more opportunities to make a fool of herself and to utilize the superfluous costumes. Then the unforgettable dream sequence of all time flashed onto the screen. John Wesley had never seen it; it had been written and filmed during his stay in the hospital. Through billowing sheer curtains, he recognized the Fennesseys' classical swimming pool. Around its rim stood Wyn's twelve muscular village boys in the dented helmets and tarnished armor of Roman centurians. Nymphs and dryads in diaphanous veilings wallowed at the water's edge. Flowers bobbed in the pool, blossoms drifted downward. Through clouds of vapor, Lydia appeared, trailing miles of chiffon behind her. After hogging the camera for just a moment too long, she floated to a golden statue, discreetly draped in lamé, standing on a golden column. John Wesley saw that it was the beautiful young man gilded. Lydia raised her wand and touched the statue. The eyes opened, the arms began to move, the drapery to flutter. The audience gasped sharply, then burst into a fit of low, snorting snickers. Above the noise, the voice of the beautiful young man's wife rose clear as a trumpet. "Damn it, I toldja to wear a jock strap!"

"But, Midge, honey . . ."

Nothing further could be heard. The audience was in an uproar.

With a rushing of lace, Lydia charged up the aisle, Wyn Plover behind her.

"Lydia, ssweetie. You can't!"

"Don't speak to me, you no-talent faggot!" With that Lydia burst out of the marquee, Wyn still in pursuit. John Wesley grabbed up his cane and followed—anything to get out of this place.

"Champagne, Mr. Smith, sir?" It was Travis.

"No. Scotch. A whole bottle of it. And I'm taking it upstairs with me."

"Yes sir. I'll have one of the men take it up to room imeejuttely. From what I can hear, the audience does seem to be enjoying Mrs. Fennessey's film. Not staying till the end, sir?"

"This *is* the end."

John Wesley limped up to his room, lay down on the enormous bed, and got gloriously, maudlinly, tearfully drunk.

Hangover

♣ ♧ ♣ ♧ ♣ ♧ ♣ ♧ ♣ ♧ ♣ ♧ ♣ ♧ ♣

When John Wesley was finally able to open his eyes, he regretted it. He lay fully dressed on the big bed in the Empire room, his dinner clothes creased and crumpled. On the table beside him sat one-third of a bottle of Scotch, a sticky, half-filled glass, and a slushy bowl of what had once been ice cubes. The lamps were still burning and the room, the bed, his clothes, his breath reeked of whisky. The sun blazed in through the windows, hot and blinding. Struggling up to a sitting position he wondered idly what hurt most—his ankle, his shoulder or his head. Drinking was bad enough, but solitary drinking! The Fennesseys, he could honestly tell himself, had finally driven him to this.

He struggled across the room to open the windows, to clear the room of some of this distillery stench. Quite naturally one of the windows jammed and he pinched his finger. He said a word he had never said before—never considered himself capable of saying—and finally managed to get the window open. It was hot outside. Hot and noisy.

The lawn was a shambles, littered with cigarette butts, burnt-out matches, and broken champagne glasses. A noisy rabble of starlings fought and bickered over the crusts of canapés, the bits of party droppings. The gay pink-and-white striped marquee lay collapsed on the lawn in a tangle of cables and rigging, like some unspeakably grotesque monster dredged up from the sea. The maple dance floor, the fluted band shell, the crates of dirty plates and glasses were being loaded onto trucks. Last night's beauty was simply today's garbage. The party was definitely over.

He felt fierce. Worse than he ever had before in his life. His head throbbed, his eyes burned, his tongue was like steel wool. The idea of eating anything nearly made him retch, and yet he knew that he should. Think of breakfast as medicine, he told himself, and rang the bell. Then, so that no servant could see him and his room in such condition, he quickly scrambled out of his evening clothes, struggled into pajamas, poured the contents of his glass, the whisky bottle, and the ice bowl into the toilet and hid all evidence of his debauchery in the laundry hamper. He had just finished brushing his teeth and dunking his face into cold water when he heard a discreet, servile tapping on his door.

To John Wesley's surprise, it was Travis himself, instead of one of the footmen, who arrived with coffee, toast, and a tall glass of peppery tomato juice.

"Good morning, sir," Travis said. "I took the liberty of bringing this up to you myself. The men are all busy below-stairs. I thought you might want the tomato juice—especially after last night."

Wondering what he meant by that, John Wesley said only "Thank you, Travis," and remained on his feet, waiting for the man to go.

"Oh, dear!" Travis cried, springing to the bedside table. "Would you look at the rings on this lovely old nightstand!

The men will get what-for from me. I can promise you that."

"It's my fault, Travis. I set a glass down on it last night."

"Oh, well, in that case, I expect we can manage. A bit of Reviva, some toothpowder, some cigar ash. I've suggested to Mrs. Fennessey time and time again—and so has Miss Rafferty—that the table tops be liquor-proofed. But she wants all of the antique pieces kept in their mint condition. It's not easy. Not with so much entertaining going on in the house."

John Wesley said nothing.

"May I pour the coffee for you, sir?"

"No, thanks. I can manage." John Wesley was not at all sure that he could—not even with both hands. But he wanted to be rid of Travis. He sat down and took a shuddering sip of the tomato juice. Seething with Worcestershire and Tabasco sauces, with lemon juice and great, coarse bits of peppercorn, he could feel it clawing its way down his throat. He gagged slightly and hoped that he wouldn't be sick on the rug.

"Quite some party last night, eh, sir?"

"I don't know, really. I went to bed early."

"Pity. So did Mrs. Fennessey. One of her migraine headaches, I expect. The sun was nearly up before the last car drove out of here. Mercy, what a mess! And what a lot they all had to drink. I thought we could lay down a few dozen bottles but—"

"Have you seen Miss O'Neil?"

"Oh, not likely, sir. Everyone's still abed. Even Miss Rafferty. I expect you could call the whole evening a grand success."

"Could you?" Even though John Wesley had managed, finally, to drink himself into oblivion, he had not been able to wipe from his memory the disaster that had been *Cinderella Flanagan.*

"Most definitely so, sir. The film especially. Some of the critical gentlemen had to be helped from the marquee when it was over. From laughing, I mean. A lot of the young people were begging for it to be run again but Mr. Fennessey put the kibosh on that."

"I'll bet he did."

"All in all, I'd say that the party went ever so well. As debs go, Miss Consuelo isn't a patch on what Miss Deirdre was last year. Pity. But she seemed to be having a good time—especially with Captain Mulcahy." Travis paused, waiting for John Wesley's comment. None was forthcoming. "I wonder how they arrange the paying for such an affair."

"I think the Fennesseys can afford to give a party every now and then."

"Yes, sir. But I mean, part of it being professional, like, for the film people and the other part being purely social for Miss Consuelo."

"I really don't know."

"I mean, do you suppose the marquesa pays half and the Fennessey Foun—"

"Travis, there must be an awful lot of work downstairs after the party last night."

"Work! Oh, Mr. Smith, you should see it. Caterer's chairs going out, the Fennessey furniture coming back in. Cigarette ends everywhere. Ladies' gloves left on the—"

"Well, please don't let me keep you. Thank you for bringing breakfast."

That got rid of Travis. John Wesley wondered if it was the hangover that made him so imperiously rude to Travis, and realized ruefully that it was not. He hated himself for hating Travis, for treating him like—well, like a servant. It wasn't right. The man had done nothing to him that wasn't helpful and friendly. Yet John Wesley couldn't stand him.

He finished a pot of coffee, forced down some toast and the

rest of the tomato juice. Now that he was properly dressed for it, he wondered if he ought not go back to bed. No, that would be weak and sybaritic. A swim, he decided, would either kill him or be beneficial. The therapist had said something about mild exercise. So John Wesley gathered up his trunks and made for pool.

The chill of the water, the warmth of the sun made John Wesley feel a *little* better. At least he told himself that. He was longing for the sight of Peggy when he heard the clatter of heels on the marble stairs leading down to the pool. It was Deirdre in one of her most indecent bathing suits. That was a surprise. Of all the Fennesseys, Deirdre could and would sleep the latest. She dived into the pool, swam across it, climbed out, and sat down. "Hi," she said cheerily.

"Good morning."

"Some blast, *la nuit dernière*."

"You—you mean you didn't mind?"

"I've been to so many parties I wouldn't care if I never saw another one. But as those things go . . ."

"I don't mean about the party. I mean *Cinderella Flanagan*."

"I thought I'd bomb right there in the tent. It was the kickiest thing since pot."

"You mean you didn't mind?"

"*Mind?* Man, I all but wet. Fun-nee! As though Ma wasn't put-on enough, didja dig old Golden Boy flashing his works under that lamé drag? What a groove! They almost had to carry me out."

"Your mother got out under her own power pretty well."

"*Et comment!* Poor Ma. She sure blew her cool."

"Is she resting now?"

"Resting? Balls! She's up there sweating it like mad. But officially we call it a migraine. Like when she gets the vodka bottle stuck in her mouth."

"Do you mean that your mother, uh, drinks?"

"That's what I mean, man. And after that Mickey Mouse piece last night . . ."

"But, Deirdre, aren't you a little disappointed? I mean I'd always understood that you might be interested in acting as a career."

"Me? In wigsville? No, it was all Ma's idea and so she finks out. No one to blame but herself."

"Deirdre, if you don't mind my asking, just what do you intend to do with you life?"

"Huh?"

"Your life. You know, a career, marriage, that sort of thing."

"How should I know? Play it by ear, see what happens. But one thing sure, I'm splitting this scene. No more Ponsonby and no more Fennesseys. I think I'll go get a pad in Frisco. Blow a little grass."

"Blow grass?"

"Smoke pot, baby."

It was not easy to picture the immaculate Deirdre Fennessey unwashed and soaked in drugs. On the other hand, it was no easier to imagine her as a young mother in the suburbs, as a graduate student, as an earnest secretary or a conscientious salesgirl or working at any of the other careers open to a girl of her age. She was at least honest, and beneath her monumental silliness she had some sort of common sense that would see her through.

"Well, I'm for a swim before I split this banana farm for Amagansett from now through Labor Day. I've got to get out of here, especially with Ma wigging out all over the place. *Formidable!*"

"Is your mother angry at me, as well?"

"Ma's mad at everybody—except herself." Deirdre plunged into the pool, swam expertly across it, stepped into her mules, and clattered away.

Stretched out on a mat in the sunshine, John Wesley began to feel a lot better. He heard the twins pass by.

"Is he asleep?" Shelagh asked softly.

"I hope so."

"Good, then let's leave him alone. In the mood Ma's in, she'll have us back in the schoolroom with him."

"But I want to go swimming," Sean said.

"Later. Anyhow, here comes Aunt Jenny."

"Oh, her! Let's go."

The marquesa was of many moods this morning, which was unusual. She was generally just cross. Today her emotions were mixed. She had, in the first place, just the tiniest twinge of alcoholic acidity, yet she had to admit that the party had gone well. Consuelo was not and never would be— oh, a mother might as well face it—a menace in the ballroom. That was bad. On the other hand, she hadn't been a total disaster. That was good. Furthermore, Jenny had read about two organizations that might be of considerable help: one, a sort of charm school that taught girls very quickly how to walk, talk, and sit; two, a place in the East Sixties that implanted eyelashes, hair by hair, on a more or less permanent basis. That was hopeful. She had made note of both addresses. There might be time for a last-ditch attempt with Consuelo before the social activity *really* started in October. If only Luis Fernando had been a daughter! But last night's party had been a success.

And it should have been, considering the size of the bill from Justin which she had found slipped beneath her bedroom door this morning! Really, Justin was cheap. There was no other word for it. Jenny's six hundred guests had been figured down to the last sip of champagne, the last forkful of lobster Newburg, the last fading flower, the last bleat of the Lester Lanin band. There had even been a list of the young people who had attended, typed up by that efficient Miss O'Neil, in case of arguments. And Jenny would have argued

—plenty—over the size of the tab if it hadn't been for *Cinderella Flanagan*. Oh, dear God, that movie! It had made Consuelo's little party unique in the annals of debutante history. Jenny, in her salad days, had attended parties with fireworks, with popular singing stars, with famous stand-up comedians, with circus motifs including ponies and trained elephants (Jenny's own debut had even featured the scrub team from the Ballet Russe de Monte Carlo as entertainment) but nothing anywhere could ever hope to match *Cinderella Flanagan* for sheer, belly laughs. Jenny herself had laughed till she ached, until her chignon had toppled and her body stocking split. It had taken the better part of half an hour to repair the damages caused to face, figure, and hair by *Cinderella Flanagan*.

Lydia! That Lydia! For twenty years—ever since the night Justin had first proudly pointed her out coming down the stairs at the Winter Garden—Jenny had waited for a chance to do something really good to that tacky bitch. And now, without Jenny's even having to lift a finger, Lydia—*Lena*, yes, from now on the marquesa would call her sister-in-law nothing but Lena—had done it *to* herself and *by* herself. It was too perfect! Even the few young people with manners enough to say good night to the hostess and thank her for a lovely evening had all said that it was the funniest movie they had ever seen. And Jenny had said thank you and promised that she would deliver the message to her sister-in-law, confined, alas, to her room with a sick headache. And Jenny most certainly would! At daybreak, late as it was, tired as she was, Jenny had gone to Desmond's sitting room and the two of them had collapsed in silent, helpless, quaking laughter. Then she had tottered, shoulders heaving, off to her own bed and laughed there until the tears had dampened her *crêpe de chine* pillow cases. Right now she loved the whole wide world—even that cheap penny-pinching Justin. Hell, she'd be happy to pay for the whole party and for all of *Cinderella Flanagan* as well just for the pleasure of sitting next to Lydia for one more screening. "Good morning, Mr. Smith!" she caroled. "A lovely, *lovely* morning!"

Mr. Earnshaw felt perfectly rotten. He usually did in the mornings. Today he felt even worse. Dragging the razor across his jowls, his hand shook so violently that he nicked himself. He almost wished that he had cut his throat, once and for all. Then he decided that things weren't all that bad. Not quite, just almost. He sensed from Lydia's violent departure of the evening before, from Justin's grim-jawed expression, from the marquesa's hoots of triumph that there was going to be all hell to pay. He would have liked to stagger back to bed, fix himself a nice glassful of equal parts of Scotch and milk, and stay there for the next twenty-four hours. But something told him that today it would be smart to look damned busy.

In his many years with charitable institutions and non-profit foundations, J. Winstanley Earnshaw had ridden out a lot of black days. There had been, for example, that mysterious disappearance of thirty thousand dollars from the Milk Fund Ball in a suburb of St. Louis; that embarrassing mix-up with the petty-cash box in Grosse Pointe; that damned girl in the Junior League of Atlanta screaming rape when she'd all but broken down the door of his hotel room to get in. Yes, he had overcome all of those minor crisis, but at least he had had some inkling of what they were about. Today he smelled trouble—Big Trouble—and for once he knew himself to be innocent. *He* hadn't wanted to produce an art film, not Stan Earnshaw. Except for war pictures and stag films, Stan didn't even *like* movies—and least of all *Cinderella Flanagan*. Dressing himself hastily in his best conservative gray, he picked up a sheaf of fly-blown papers, crammed them into

his attaché case and, shoulders back, buttocks taut, and diaphragm in, marched down the stairs.

"Will that be all, Mr. Fennessey?" Peggy asked. Would
that be *all?* Here it was going on for noon and Peggy was still
wearing her evening dress from the night before. White it
was—or at least it had been until some society punk invited
by the marquesa had overturned a whole plate of food onto
it. It was the most expensive dress she had ever owned. She
had bought it only with Wes in mind and now she never
wanted to see it again.

"Hmm?" Justin murmured dangerously. He was standing
at the window, knotting an ascot at his throat and glaring
down at the people gathered around the swimming pool.
How dared they laugh, smile, even speak on a day like this?

It had been quite a night. And, for Justin, a night that still
had not ended. What Lydia had put him through was more
than any mortal should have borne. He had suspected the
worst from the moment his wife had sailed out of the marquee. Telling himself that it was his duty as a host to stay
downstairs until the last sodden critic had been loaded onto
a chartered bus, he had postponed coming up to his bedroom until the latest possible moment, hoping that Lydia
would at last be asleep. And just for protection, he had
brought Miss O'Neil with him.

Asleep? Lydia had been stalking the rooms of their suite
like a tigress, her lace evening dress crumpled into a tattered
ball on the floor of the dressing room, the Fennessey emeralds lying in a glistening heap on the carpet. Wordlessly, Justin had bent down to pick up the necklace and, just as wordlessly, Lydia had hauled off and kicked him squarely in the
rump. With as much dignity as possible, Justin had picked
himself and the Fennessey emeralds up from beneath the Directoire desk.

"Pussykins!"

"Don't pussykins me, you slob. Making me a laughingstock in front of every important critic in the industry just so your crooked foundation can bilk the government out of—"

"Pussykins, Miss O'Neil—"

"Screw Miss O'Neil! And screw you, too, Justin Fennessey. I'm sick and tired of this. The sacrifices I've made for you and what happens? Forced to make a fool of myself in your little amateur movie. Rory Mulcahy and John Wesley Smith! Nobody ever heard of either of them. Thrown like an old bone to a no-talent fag director like Wyn Plover just so your daughter can play at being an actress and your rotten foundation can come up out of the sewer smelling like a rose. Well, I'm sick of being bullied and pushed around and made a fool of by the Fennessey family!"

Lydia had been indefatigable, for a woman who was usually too tired for more than a good-night kiss. She had stamped and screamed until the sun was high. She had run her full dramatic gamut and then some. There had been screaming rages, dewy tears, haughty denunciations, and sullen silences. It had been during one of these silences that Justin had thought to bill his sister for her share of the party. It had been a dreadful mistake, bringing on one of Lydia's loudest and most athletic tirades. A lot of *gorge-de-pigeon* opaline glass and the *bouillotte* lamp had been sacrificed on the altar of Lydia's rage. The lamp, Justin reflected, could probably be repaired. The glass never.

Stealing a surreptitious glance at his wristwatch, Justin figured that his wife had now been rampaging for exactly twelve hours. Was she trying to set some sort of record? Thank God she finally charged into her bathroom, slamming the door with a cannon report that set the chandelier to swaying. There was a dreadful crash. That would be the collection of lalique glass which Justin's Paris agent had picked up cheap when it was out of fashion. It had appreciated about ten times since. Oh, well.

Justin finished tying his ascot. He did not do a very good job of it, but he knew that now was the time to get out, to get away from the Fury that was Lydia, to seek the company of other people and to stick to them like glue. He regarded Peggy, standing patiently in her ruined evening dress. "Well?"

"I said, Mr. Fennessey, will that be all?"

"All? Yes. Isn't it enough? Or would you like the house to be struck by lightning as well?"

It seemed a splendid idea to Peggy. "That's a thought," she said.

Justin glared. "Did you bill the marquesa as I told you to do?"

"Yes, Mr. Fennessey. I put it under her door at seven."

"Well, then, there's nothing else."

Peggy went to bed and stayed there.

Fireworks

♣ ⚘ ♣ ⚘ ♣ ⚘ ♣ ⚘ ♣ ⚘ ♣ ⚘ ♣ ⚘ ♣

There had been fireworks at the party the night before. In his stupor, John Wesley had been vaguely conscious of rockets, Catherine wheels, and aerial bombs going off outside his window. But they were nothing compared to the pyrotechnics Mrs. Justin Fennessey had planned for this evening.

Lydia was pacing the rotunda when John Wesley came in from a long walk. She was dressed in a trim suit with a frothy jabot, her hair pulled back into a peruke. Her aim had been toward a crisp, efficient—though pretty—woman of affairs. To John Wesley she looked like a faintly sissy Lafayette. "Mr. Smith, where have you been?" she asked.

"Hello, Lydia. Out."

"Please bear in mind that as long as you are under contract to the Fennessey Foundation, you will observe the daily hours."

"Well, I won't be much longer, will I? But what hours are those?"

"No, indeed you will not be. But when I wish to speak to

you on important matters I would like at least to know where
to contact you."

"Never use contact as a verb, Lydia. What is it now—algebra, conversational French, diving lessons for Sean?"

"I wish to speak to you and to the others involved in last
night's—uh—fiasco. In the library and right now."

The group in the library was smaller than Lydia usually
liked to have as an audience, although John Wesley wondered why she would want any audience at all after *Cinderella Flanagan*. Sitting solemnly around the room, as though
they might be waiting their turns for full extractions, were
Justin, Desmond, Stan Earnshaw, Rory, Wyn Plover, and the
marquesa. Of the lot, only Jenny wore the sweet, saintly smile
of a Christian Scientist coming down with a bad cold.

"Everyone who is concerned is here now, Justin," Lydia
said. Casting her sister-in-law a malevolent look, she added,
"And even one who isn't concerned. Would you mind terribly
getting out of here, Jenny?"

"Yes, I would mind, Lena." There! She'd said it.

"May I remind you that this is not a social occasion, but
business dealing with the Fennessey Foundation. And as
head of this house—"

"And may I remind *you* that not only was I born in this
house, but I also sit on the board of the Fennessey Foundation. Whatever you have to say is going to be of the greatest
interest to me, Lena."

"Pussykins," Justin said miserably, "if Jenny wants to
stay . . ."

And Jenny did want to stay. Wild horses couldn't have
dragged her from the room. Lydia was, if anything, more displeased than ever. She was furious. But short of grabbing a
hank of the marquesa's bleached hair and physically wrestling her out of the library . . . Oh, no. Never. Lydia was
playing it for dignity. Not exactly a Rosalind Russell career
girl and not exactly a Judith Anderson queen, but a sort of

combination of the two—say the first woman president of the United States confronted by a carefully planned Communist coup, once-trusted traitors to be suddenly unmasked in the Oval Room.

"You must all be very, very proud of yourselves," she began.

Captain Mulcahy smiled. He had only the dimmest recollection of *Cinderella Flanagan's* gala showing of the night before, but he could recall that everyone laughed a lot and that people—quite important people whose names he did not remember—had wrung his hand and congratulated him. That was good. It probably meant that he could stay on in this fine, big, comfortable place for a bit longer. He opened his mouth to speak. Only a quiet little belch emerged. In the long run he was glad that he had said nothing.

Lydia continued. "Yes, very proud. Grown men—or at least you may call yourselves men—taking advantage of one lone woman whose only wish was to make a contribution, however small, to the arts."

"It was small all right," Desmond said.

"Do not be facetious, Desmond," Justin said.

"I'm not being. Anyhow, I enjoyed the picture immensely."

"And so did I, Lena," Jenny said.

Lydia decided to ignore them. "Calling yourselves professionals, you circled this house like vultures waiting to swoop down on some weak, willing thing . . ." Abandoning metaphor, Lydia continued. "To begin at the beginning, you, Captain Mulcahy, came to us with a script in your hand, claiming to be a famous Irish playwright."

"Me?" Rory gulped.

"Not quite correct, Lyd," Desmond said. "You and I got potted in a bar in Boston and picked him up—principally to fly the plane home."

"Yes, Desmond," Lydia said, snatching at the only available straw, "another of your barroom pickups for us to shelter, feed, pay, *and endure.*" There, she'd turned that into a minor victory.

Desmond only smiled. What was the point of arguing with this virago, or even trying to set straight her vast flights of fancy? And what was the point of the Fennessey Foundation? Something about tax avoidance. Desmond had never quite understood. He really cared very little about money. He had so much of it in his own right—Daddy and Gramps and Cornelius Slattery's father had seen to it that, short of flinging it out of the window, he would never be able to get rid of all of it. And so why this silly and faintly fishy foundation in the first place?

"You, Wezley, came here as an expert in the drama."

"That's not true and you know it, Lydia. I was hornswoggled into this house as a summer tutor with the trumped-up title of Director of Projects."

"Aha! Yesssss! And that was a great project you directed for us last night. How you must be laughing up your sleeve."

"I didn't direct it. I only tried to make as much as possible out of hopeless material at a time when you had the law breathing—"

"Oh, and what you made of it! That prologue! 'Children of all ages!' What tripe! What trash! What utter drivel you forced me to speak!"

"But I didn't do that, Lydia. There never was a prologue *or* an epilogue until you got into the picture. You added those scenes yourself. I have them up in my room in your own handwriting if you'd like to see them."

"What Wesss ssays is true, ssweetie." Wyn Plover spoke for the first time. He should not have.

Lydia wheeled on him, pointing her famous upstage accusatory finger. "And as for you, Iago, I blame you most of all. I took you out of some nothing job, paid you a small fortune, gave you an opportunity to be a big director, and what thanks did I get for it?"

Over Lydia's roar and Wyn's sibilants, John Wesley considered, for what he hoped would be the last time, this incredible woman. It was Lydia and only Lydia who was responsible for this ridiculous film. She had started the whole thing, first as therapy for a daughter who didn't care and then as a vehicle for herself. Nearly everything that was wrong with *Cinderella Flanagan* could be traced directly to Lydia, from the staff of incompetents she had chosen to surround herself with to her own dreadful performance. And now she was trying to blame everyone else. What was worse, she obviously believed every word she was saying.

John Wesley wondered idly just where Lydia—Lena—would be today without Justin Fennessey. At worst, a blowsy, aging, jobless actress telling tall tales of her past triumphs over chilling cups of coffee in Walgreen's; at best, the pillar of culture in some hick town producing *The Trojan Women* in bed sheets and aluminum foil at the local little theater. In either case Lydia would be ludicrous: a bitchy, power-driven, egocentric, unfulfilled woman. She was still ludicrous, still bitchy, power-driven, egocentric, and unfulfilled, but she was all of those things in a dress that had cost easily John Wesley's monthly income in a paneled Georgian room of museum quality. Costumes and scenery were all that saved Lydia's present production from slapstick comedy. Money. It was the only answer.

"And now," the Tragic Muse concluded, with as little regard for truth as for syntax, "that you have foisted off your shabby little schemes on my husband and I, picked our bones clean, made the Fennessey Foundation *and* me objects of ridicule, I hope that you are satisfied. But before you leave my house—which I fervently hope will occur before midnight—there is one final scene I should like you all to witness and then the comedy is ended."

With three long, leggy, showgirl paces, Lydia strode to the needle-point bell pull and gave it a forceful yank. Too soon, almost as though he had been waiting in the wings for his cue, Travis entered. He carried a silver tray. On it was a writhing mass of what looked like black serpents. It was *Cinderella Flanagan,* its ten reels carefully removed from their metal spools. "Thenk yew, Travis," Lydia said. She grabbed up the coils of celluloid and carried them to the carefully laid grate.

"Pussykins! The government . . ."

"May I have a match?" Lydia said. It occurred to John Wesley that the prop man should have supplied her with one before the scene began.

"Sorry, I don't smoke," John Wesley said.

"I do. Here, Lena, take my lighter," Jenny said.

"Mr. Fennessey, I thought you might be interested in these." It was Peggy. "The afternoon New York *Post* and the early editions of tomorrow's *Times* and *News.*"

"You may add them to the pyre, Miss O'Neil," Lydia said. "I do not wish to read them."

"As you like, Mrs. Fennessey, but I think you may be rather pleased and surprised with what they have to say. The entire women's page of the *Times* is devoted to you. The entertainment page is pretty well filled up with *Cinderella.* As for the society page—"

"Here, don't throw those newspapers out," the marquesa said. "What do they say about Consuelo?"

Fame

♣ ♧ ♣ ♧ ♣ ♧ ♣ ♧ ♣ ♧ ♣ ♧ ♣ ♧ ♣

"Well, pussykins," Justin said, "*Time* magazine just telephoned. It's not going to take as long to do a cover story as I feared. They want to write a little on Desmond and Jenny and quite a lot on you, pussykins."

"Do they, darling?" Lydia said from the chaise longue. "What a bore. I'm simply worn out from talking to people. And now that *huge* press conference this afternoon. But do listen to this." Lydia deftly snatched a newspaper from the stack of periodicals at her side. It opened, as though by magic, to the proper page and Lydia began to read: " 'In even the most proficient hands, the experimental film may be interesting, moving, or disturbing. Rarely is it gay. A delicious exception to this rule is *Cinderella Flanagan,* the frothy romp produced with funds granted by the Fennessey Foundation. If the term "high farce" describes anything nowadays, it surely applies to famed Irish poet Rorian Mulcahy's lighthearted and irreverent spoof. Nothing is sacred

Schmaltzy folklore, murky Freudian symbols, hackneyed plots, "arty" camera angles and every cliché of the motion picture are raked over the coals in this—' Ouch! you bitch," Lydia snapped at her hairdresser.

"What was that last, pussykins?"

"Oh, just a lot of adjectives and then it tells what the story's about. We all know that, Justin. But, precious, listen to this. '. . . all are delightful.' Blah, blah, blah. Oh, yes. Here it is. 'But the one who walks off with all honors is the fairy godmother, played by Lydia Fennessey parenthesis socialite wife of philanthropist Justin Fennessey parenthesis a completely unknown amateur.' Well, I'm not so sure I care for *that*. After all, I *was* on the stage in—"

"Read on, please, pussykins."

"Oh, yes. Here. 'Few great comediennes of the past and almost none of the present day can hold a candle to Mrs. Fennessey. She combines the beauty of Carole Lombard with the timing of Josephine Hull, the gloriously bogus grandeur of Margaret Dumont with the *fablunget* quality of Beatrice Lillie. Her—' "

"What was that word, pussykins?"

"*Fablunget*. It's Yiddish. It means disorganized. Incompetent."

"Really, Lydia, I've always considered you extremely competent."

"Well, yes, Justin, thank you. But when I'm trying to portray a rather helter-skelter character, I—"

Peggy stood in the door of the Fennesseys' bedroom. "Mrs. Fennessey, someone from the *Tonight* show is on the telephone. They wonder if you'd be interested in appearing."

"Oh, Miss O'Neil, dear, will people *ever* leave me in peace?"

"Shall I say that you're out?"

"Oh, no! I think I should appear. If only for the good of

the foundation. . . . I think a softening wave just here, please," Lydia said to the hairdresser, "will be the best for the press conference."

"I still can't believe it," John Wesley said, reading once again through the stack of newspapers and magazines. "Just listen to this. 'The beautiful and witty Mrs. Justin Fennessey concluded the interview by saying, "I am first and foremost a wife and mother. My home, my husband, my children, my dogs are all I truly crave. But how selfish that would be! We must do more, more. We must—"'"

"Please, Wes, I'm going to be sick if you don't stop reading those interviews," Peggy said.

"But, Peggy, how can they fall for it? They all think that rotten little picture is the laugh riot of the century."

"Well, you've got to admit that it was pretty funny."

"But it wasn't *supposed* to be. The Fennesseys have fooled them all. And now they're all busy fooling themselves. Especially Lydia. She's convinced that she's a clown—the biggest thing since Fanny Brice. Forty-eight hours ago she was mad as Medusa and ready to set fire to the master print."

"A good thing she didn't. There's talk about running it in the Music Hall at Christmas with, of course, certain deletions. Our star is even now scheduling her television appearances—the *Today Show*, *Tonight*, the *Ed Sullivan Show*, and a spectacular starring—"

"But she'll fall flat on her face. She's terrible."

"And she's not the only one with plans. Speaking of falling flat on faces, Captain Mulcahy is mulling over offers to write a witty Irish musical comedy based on *Finnegans Wake*, a witty Irish film based on *Riders to the Sea*, and a witty Irish television series based on *The Goldbergs*. He's having lunch with his new agent at '21' right now."

"But he couldn't write a postcard."

"But they won't discover that immediately. Our Mr. Plover is also very much in demand. He, too, is in town turning down scripts as fast as he can read them. He is what you call hot."

"Wyn might just squeak through. He's not good, but at least he's conscientious."

"Even Gramps has a couple of offers, and Prince Charming has been signed to a three-picture contract (in pants) begining right after Midge's accouchement. And our Mr. Earnshaw has graciously been granting interviews pointing out the true aims of the Fennessey Foundation. I heard him saying something about the likelihood of a Nobel Prize for Justin Fennessey but I don't put much stock in it."

"Peggy, this is terrible. It's disgusting. Nauseating. Has the whole world gone mad?"

"Temporarily."

"But, Peggy, the film *was* lousy."

"If it had been only mediocre everyone would have said too bad and forgotten it. Thanks to Lydia, it was so bad that no one can really believe that it wasn't on purpose. (Of course the champagne helped, too.) Now she's upstairs preparing herself to wow the working press."

"Good God, she was a flop! I'm a flop. And *Cinderella Flanagan* is a flop! Partly because of me. But we're both flops and I know it."

"Do you like it?"

"No, but at least I admit it. I don't take advantage of a fluke to kid myself into thinking I'm great."

"You could, you know."

"I could what?"

"You could jump on the bandwagon with all the rest of them. You're the only intelligent one involved in the whole picture. You know it and they all know it, too. Forgive me for seeming to pry, but I believe that Lydia and Wyn and Rory, too, have all put out little feelers for the pleasure of your company in their future projects—even before they *had* any future projects."

"No, thanks. These people make me feel—I don't know exactly how to say it—somehow soiled."

"Oh, do they indeed? And just what kind of people do you think populate the world—nice Methodist young men who think about truth and beauty and honor, like you; or the Stan Earnshaws, the Wyn Plovers, the Justins and Lydias who go out and get what they want?"

"Peggy—"

"You're a nice boy, Wes. Too nice a boy."

"Too nice for the Fennesseys, at least."

"And too nice for me, too. You've got brains and you've got taste. This is your big opportunity to show the world what you can do—to make something of yourself."

"You mean to falsify myself."

"No, I mean to get going—to do something on your own. Or do you plan always to be an assistant instructor in a nothing-school like Ponsonby—a little schoolteacher droning away to people who aren't even listening?"

"Peggy!"

"I mean it, Wes. Your high moral tone may wow 'em at the Epworth League, but I've been reading it all of my life in *Our Sunday Visitor*. And I'm sick of it. I'm sick of being poor and a nobody of a secretary to an idiot like Justin Fennessey. By fair means or foul, the Fennesseys have pulled off a master coup. Without you they never could have. And now you want to go all Rover Boy and duck out, just when you have a chance to be somebody. From now on the Fennessey Foundation is going to be big. Really big. It has to be. You could be big with it and I'm going to be, too. So just go back to your Sunday school class and think about how saintly you are.

Take your integrity to bed every night and just see how
—Yes, Travis?"

"Begging your pardon, Miss O'Neil, but the men are setting up the picture gallery for Mrs. Fennessey's press conference. How many chairs did you say?"

Meet the

Press

♣ ♧ ♣ ♧ ♣ ♧ ♣ ♧ ♣ ♧ ♣ ♧ ♣ ♧ ♣

"Snippy minx!" Travis muttered at Miss O'Neil's retreating back. Travis had been setting up parties and buffets since before that little fly-up-the-creek had been born and now she'd practically snapped his head off. The bar was to be placed in the rotunda, the speakers' table here instead of there, and the buffet for nearly five hundred reporters moved out to the pool terrace. And the whole time she'd been blowing her nose and dabbing at her eyes.

Well, she'd been crying a lot harder when Mr. Bertram got out of Mr. Justin's study. He and two of his cronies had been in there for nearly half an hour and Travis was not budging from the picture gallery until they came out. Evidence. That's what Travis had. Evidence that would prove that the whole Fennessey Foundation was a fraud. It was right up in his room just waiting to be handed over to Mr. Bertram and the Department of Internal Revenue. Travis' fingers actually itched. He could almost feel that big, embossed check from the government . . .

"Mr. Travis," one of the footmen said, "are the little gold chairs to be placed in rows of fifteen or—"

"I don't give a bloody damn *where* you put 'em, my boy. After today there isn't going to be any more Fennessey—"

The door to Justin's study opened. Mr. Earnshaw, standing at attention, blocked almost the entire opening. Beside him, Travis could see part of Justin Fennessey. They almost look like they were standing in front of a bloody firing squad, Travis thought.

"Travis!" Mr. Earnshaw barked. It was hardly the voice of a beaten man, but then Earnshaw always had been a great bluffer.

"Yes?" Travis said. He did not bother to add the "sir." After what he had to show Mr. Bertram, such niceties would hardly be necessary.

"Mr. Bertram and these two gentlemen would like a word with you."

"And *I'd* certainly like a word with *them*," Travis said in what he liked to believe was a debonair, offhand manner.

"And then, Travis," Justin said, sounding like a saint forgiving his tormentors, "then you may leave."

The study door closed and Travis hurried up to Mr. Bertram and the two men—government men they must be.

"I've got it for you, Mr. Bertram—everything you need. Evidence. Heaps of it. Bills, receipts, letters—"

"I don't understand it," Mr. Bertram said to nobody in particular. "I don't understand it. We run into all kinds of nuts in this business—cranks, people with grudges—but I just don't understand this."

"Ah, but you will, Mr. Bertram. Especially when you see the evidence. Now if you'll just excuse me for a second . . ."

The two men with Mr. Bertram stepped forward effectively blocking Travis' way.

"Mr. Travis. Elbert J. Travis, you are under arrest."

"What?"

"When is the last time you filed an income tax return?"

"Why, I—"

"The department has uncovered thirty-six savings accounts in your name paying total annual compound interest of—"

"Mr. Bertram, I . . ."

"This is a very serious matter, Mr. Travis. Bad enough for a citizen, but even worse for an alien."

"Mr. Bertram, I tell you—I've already told you—those Fennesseys—the whole family—they're no better than common criminals. They—"

"The matter of your flagrant evasion of income taxes on what amounts to a fortune falls under the jurisdiction of my department, Mr. Travis," Mr. Bertram said. "But the question of illegal entry into the United States is a matter for these two gentlemen to deal with. Men, I turn him over to you."

One of Mr. Bertram's companions stepped forward brandishing an official-looking sheet of paper. "Elbert J. Travis?" he said. "I have a warrant for your arrest."

"Can't understand it," Travis heard Mr. Bertram saying, as Travis was being led down the picture gallery, ". . . fine job with a fine organization like the Fennessey Foundation and this is the kind of loyalty he shows. Gotta have a screw loose somewhere. It just doesn't make sense."

Miss Bridget Rafferty was in ecstasy. She had never had so much to complain about; all of these hundreds of newspaper people trampling the rugs with their dirty feet; cases and cases of twelve-year-old Scotch and vintage champagne costing the Good Lord only knew how much; television lights —already the fuses had blown twice—and cameras being dragged over her porphyry floors; Desmond's plane sent especially to Maine to pick up a fortune in fresh lobsters, as through the chicken and roast beef and *pâté* and hothouse asparagus on the buffet table weren't enough. (Oh, the Fennesseys would pay for this spread; except for Ember Days, they would be eating chipped beef and top round for the rest of the year, or her name wasn't Bridget Rafferty!) And to top it all off, the perfidy of that stiff-necked English butler! Travis had been led off like the common criminal he was. "The will of the Good Lord in Heaven and that's a fact," Miss Rafferty grumbled. "But couldn't He have waited till *after* this dirty crowd of newspaper people clear out of me nice clean house?"

"Bridget!" Justin barked. "Get an extra man on the rotunda bar and have another bar set up on the lawn. The reporters are beginning to come." And then, with Gretchen loping along at his side, he turned on his most genial, his most democratic, his most man-of-the-people grin and charged forward, hairless hand outstretched. "Hi, fellahs! I'm Jus Fennessey. C'mon in and bend an elbow."

Even with the air conditioning turned on full blast, the picture gallery was stifling. The television lights, the heat from hundreds of bodies, the smoke from thousands of cigarettes made the atmosphere unendurable. The rows of gilt ballroom chairs had been filled for half an hour and still the press kept coming, leaning against the walls, sitting on the floor, perched on the bar, dragging chairs and sofas in from the other rooms.

The speakers' table stretched across the picture gallery at the foot of the horseshoe stairs. It, too, was filled—or very nearly. There were eleven places set up at the table. When Justin rapped for order and, with a great deal of droning and crackling, adjusted the microphone set before him, eight of the seats were taken. J. Winstanley Earnshaw, as Executive Director of the Fennessey Foundation, occupied a prominent place near the center. Gramps, as red, white, and blue as the flag, had entered to thunderous applause and been seated at the table. As members of the Fennessey family and officers of the foundation, Desmond Fennessey and the Marquesa de Mondragon y Alonzo were placed side by side. Demurely, Jenny patted her damp brow and sighed something about the formidable heat of the room. She reached forward to the water pitcher and poured herself an icy glassful. Conscious of the cameras focused on her, she lifted the glass to her lips and took a dainty sip. There was a violent gagging and Jenny spewed forth a fine spray of hundred-proof vodka.

"Desmond," she croaked, "what in the—"

"Sorry old thing," Desmond said, "but I had *this* pitcher filled with gibsons."

Wynton Plover, melting within a Pierre Cardin suit of midnight blue antelope, was feeling very full of himself. "Yess," he told whatever members of the press who might be listening, "I have jusst about ssigned with the Metropolitan Opera to direct an all-Negro production of *Falsstaff.*"

Father Alonzo, who had been hastily summoned to do a prayer for the benefit of the correspondents from *Il Osservatore Romano,* the Brooklyn *Tablet,* and the *Irish Echo,* dozed at a far end of the table.

The place next to Father Alonzo's, marked for Captain Mulcahy, was empty.

"Drunk again," Desmond said, filling his glass from the pitcher of gibsons.

Peggy O'Neil was there with her notebook. John Wesley sat down angrily beside her. "Peggy, I—"

Whatever it was that John Wesley was going to say was drowned out by Justin Fennessey. With a screech of static that sent a small tempera Pietà plummeting down from the wall, Justin began his short speech of welcome. "Hi, folks! I guess I better start off introducing myself and my family. I'm Jus Fennessey . . ."

Poised at the head of the horseshoe stairs, Lydia waited impatiently, one ear cocked for her entrance cue. She had waited twenty long years for this descent and here it was—television cameras from three networks, correspondents from every major publication and syndicate, writers from *Vogue, Harper's Bazaar, Figaro, Elle, Claudia*—every great women's magazine—on hand just to see what she would be wearing. There was the world, literally, at Lydia's feet. Now if Justin would just shut his fatuous mouth and say the words they had rehearsed so carefully not two hours ago . . . Ah, here they were! The public address spluttered again—really, was Justin suffering from gas or was he just too chintzy to hire a decent p.a. man?—and Lydia heard her cue: ". . . but none of the works of our little foundation—nothing—could have been accomplished without the help, the guidance, the inspiration of my beloved wife and partner, Lydia Fennessey."

"Get your big, black ass out of the way," Lydia muttered, kicking out at Gretchen's recumbent form, as she began her slow, stately trip down the horseshoe stairs. Twenty mothering years she had waited and—yes—it had all been worth it. The television lights, the flash bulbs, the deafening applause!

Lydia reached the bottom of the stairs in a frothy flurry of skirts—tailored but feminine, that's what she was today, in blue the color of the Virgin's robe. She made a semiobeisance to Father Alonzo, blew kisses to those at the speakers' table —even Jenny. Then she bent down and kissed the top of Gramps's white head.

"Bitch!" he muttered. Lydia was sure that no one had heard the old maniac. The applause was still ringing throughout the room. Next she was in Justin's arms for a sedate but affectionate husband-and-wifely kiss that had been inspired by photographs of General Eisenhower's return from the wars. And then she sank into her chair, graciously awaiting the questions from the floor.

John Wesley groaned. "Peggy," he whispered.

". . . our girl Peggy," Justin boomed out simultaneously. Peggy rose and bowed to the press, to the cameras.

"Peggy," John Wesley began again.

"Be still and get up. They're talking about you."

John Wesley was glad that he had been told. Otherwise he would never have recognized himself from Justin's overblown description.

". . . talented young genius who pulled together the many, many components of our little project, Mr. John Wesley Smith."

John Wesley sat down again to the clatter of applause. "Peggy—"

"Shhhhh. I'm trying to take notes."

John Wesley groaned.

An hour later he groaned again. He had sat, stricken, through three prepared statements to the press which had been read out first by J. Winstanley Earnshaw, then by Justin Fennessey and finally—and at the greatest length—by Lydia. For the first time John Wesley saw that Stan Earnshaw had his uses. Stan had written all three speeches, of that there could be no doubt. They were as windy, as dull, and as pompous as Stan himself. But only a great artist could dig up so many platitudes, so many clichés, so many truisms —". . . Air of cautious optimism . . ." ". . . working side by side in tandem . . ." ". . . cultural contribution to the world at large . . ."—and stretch them out so neatly end to end on paper. Like the dozens of Independence Day and commencement orations John Wesley had half-listened to during his life, these statements to the press were the purest hot air. They said nothing. But, ah, how beautifully they said it! The Fennesseys had triumphed, had truly fallen into a sewer and come out smelling like roses.

There was a scuffling of feet, coughing, a slight shifting of chairs. John Wesley could see even more cigarettes being lighted in the audience. So, presumably, could Lydia. She raised her hand daintily for attention. "You've all been so very gracious, so very patient to listen to the many plans and aims of our little foundation. And I promise you a little lunch —just a snack to keep us all from fainting from hunger, hahahah—immediately . . ." John Wesley had seen the buffet table that ran the length of the swimming pool. A snack like that would guarantee rave notices from *Pravda* itself. "But first, are there any questions from the floor?"

"*Questions?*" John Wesley groaned. "There ought to be a Congressional investigation. Peggy—"

"Hush! Can't you see I'm busy?"

"Too busy for me?"

Hands shot up around the picture gallery. More importunate members of the press leapt to their feet, right arms upraised in Fascist salutes.

"Mrs. Fennessey—"

"Mr. Fennessey—"

"Mr. Earnshaw—"

"Mrs. Fennessey—"

"Please, *please*," Lydia cooed. "One at a time. Let the ones with questions raise their hands and I'll call on you. I'll try not to miss a single question, I promise."

"My God, she's really taking over," John Wesley said. "She *is* the Fennessey Foundation."

"Shut up," Peggy said, her pencil dancing across the pages of her shorthand book.

"Are you really taking down all this hogwash?"

"Ah," Lydia said. "You there. The one in the front row in that divine brown suit."

"Renée Green from *Women's Wear Daily*. Is that dress you're wearing from one of the French collections?"

"That's sweet of you, my dear," Lydia cooed. "No. I still

find time to design and make a good many of my own clothes. *This* dress is from the Lydia Fennessey collection."

Jenny gasped audibly. She reached out for Desmond's pitcher in front of her and filled her glass to the brim.

"Mrs. Fennessey. Katy Walch from *Variety*. Any truth in the rumors that you're considering offers from some of the major studios?"

"*Me?*" Lydia simpered. "Miss Walch, I would never consider *any* offer that took me away from my home, my husband"—a little pat on Justin's shoulder—"my children. But if a suitable film—a really *interesting* project—were to be presented, I *might* be able to find the time. Next?"

"Mrs. Fennessey, we've met everyone connected with *Cinderella Flanagan* except this—this Rorian Mulcahy, the author. Is he available for comment or could you tell us something about him?"

"Hahahahaha! Of course you're speaking of our own, dear leprechaun, Rory," Lydia said. She was thinking fast. "Well, I'm afraid that Captain Mulcahy found it impossible to be with us today. He's frightfully shy and—"

Jenny nudged Desmond under the table. "She's really got her tail in a crack with this one," Jenny muttered. "Where is Rory indeed!" Jenny scowled down into the audience at Luis Fernando, sitting with his hand on the knee of a shapely researcher from *Time*. Like father, like son. Luis Fernando had been something of a disappointment this summer. Maybe Jenny should be a little nicer to Lena—*Lydia*. It wouldn't hurt to have her on hand at some of Consuelo's parties this season. No doubt about it, Lydia was In, damn her!

Jenny was roused from her reverie by Miss Rafferty tapping her on the shoulder and thrusting a scrap of paper into her hand. "Jenny, this was in yer room," Miss Rafferty hissed.

"Thank you, Cousin Briddy," the marquesa said in a loud, gracious tone. (Lydia wasn't going to hog up all the attention.) Between clenched teeth she added, "And don't call me Jenny."

The note was in Spanish. Jenny was at a loss to understand more than a few words.

"Desmond darling," Jenny said, "I seem to have left my lorgnette upstairs. Would you be a dear and read this for me?"

Desmond glanced at the note, threw back his head, and roared.

"Something amusing, darling?"

"Amusing? It's going to kill you."

"Well, what does it *say*?"

"All of it or just the gist of it?"

"Desmond, what does it say?"

"It says that your daughter Consuelo has just run off with Rory Mulcahy. Consuelo asks for your blessing."

Jenny picked up the brimming glass of vodka and tossed it down in a single gulp. "That spik nymphomaniac!" Then she reached out for Desmond's pitcher of vodka and filled her glass again.

John Wesley heard a question addressed to Gramps. "Mr. Fennessey, senior, please. As a man who has lived for nearly a century, what is your opinion of the work of the Fennessey Foundation?"

"Sonny, if I was to tell you and you was to write it down, you'd be excommunicated. But since you're askin' me—"

"Next question!" Lydia roared. Then, with the soft, sweet smile of a madonna, she said in a lulling voice that echoed through the gallery, "You must forgive darling Grandpa. He's not very well today."

The poor old man seemed to shrink in his chair, almost to fade before John Wesley's eyes. He looked defeated at last. Lydia was too tough even for him. Peggy glanced up from her notes and sighed.

"How much more of this can I take?" John Wesley muttered. "For God's sake, Peggy, how much more can *you* take?"

"Shut u-u-up, damn you."

"A quaistion for Mrs. Fennessey, pliz. I om Vladimir Rubienkov of the *Soviet Cinematic Review*. Whot, if annything, is the social significance of *Cinderella Flanagan?*"

"Uh, why, uh . . . well . . . well, I think that your question could be better answered by my husband. He's the political thinker in *our* family. Hahaha." Lydia sank to her chair.

"Uh, well, uh. Well, I'm glad you asked that question Mr. —uh—*yes*. Yes, *glad!*" Eyes bulging, Justin remembered to arrange his features into a mask of friendly good-fellowship. "Why, I think that the social significance behind *Cinderella* is that—uh—all men are created free and equal and—uh— that in a great democracy like ours the little guy has got just as good a chance to get ahead as— Well, yes. Does that answer your question?"

"No."

"Next question, please," Stan Earnshaw barked.

"Mr. Fennessey, have you any political aspirations?"

Justin colored. He'd never before even thought of it, but now . . . but *now* . . . Well, why not? Possibly the governor of New York. Other rich men had made it. Look at Franklin Roosevelt, Nelson Rockefeller. And from the governorship of New York it was said to be just a hop, a skip, and a jump to the White House. Too late, Justin reflected that for tax reasons he was no longer a resident of New York but, technically, of Connecticut. Damn Cornelius Slattery and his shady practices! But maybe he could cook up something to make Justin a New Yorker once again. "Well, uh, I, uh . . . I have no political ambitions of my own. But if my fellow Americans felt that they wanted me—*needed* me—I could only bow to the will of . . ."

While Justin rambled on, Lydia considered her own future. Rapidly erasing the picture of her name in lights twinkling over Broadway, a new Lydia began to emerge in her imagination. There she was, standing in the East Room at Justin's side—no, Justin would be upstairs in Lincoln's bed, *sick*. Yes, Lydia would do it all alone, the First Lady, complete with tiara and feather fan, steering the ship of state and—

"I said *Mrs.* Fennessey . . ."

Lydia snapped to rapt attention, all smiles and eager eyes. "Yes?" Through the smoke she could vaguely make out a figure standing in the rear of the room and Lydia didn't much like what she saw—a tall, rawboned woman with a Garbo slouch hat and a voice like Feodor Chaliapin's. "Jess Fulton from *Art Film Monthly*. Are you planning another film project?"

Lydia was planning plenty, but not necessarily another pokey little amateur production with Justin watching her every move. "Why, yes. Yes, of course," Lydia twittered.

Justin sighed piteously. It now occurred to him, for the first time, that having made such a splash, the Fennessey Foundation would *have* to go on doing things—*spending money!* Was there no justice in this world?

"Tell us something about it," Miss Fulton growled.

"Wellll, of course our plans aren't definite just now." Lydia said.

"I don't expect definite plans, just a general idea."

Really would this bull dike ever sit down and shut up and stop tormenting her? Lydia didn't go to the movies very often nowadays. She really didn't understand—or *like*—the new films. Lydia preferred the pictures from her girlhood—sweet, simple stories with Joan Crawford or Norma Shearer, dressed by Gilbert Adrian, drifting through white drawing rooms. And that was just the sort of story she had intended *Cinderella Flanagan* to be; just the sort of story she had discussed with John Wesley when she visited him in the hospital. Lydia didn't know—didn't *want* to know—anything about "cinematic statements" or the *auteur* theory (something about tension between actor and director, although there had been plenty of tension between Lydia and Wyn, God knows); psychedelic lights made Lydia dizzy; surrealism was something she connected with a terribly overpriced Salvador Dali painting Justin had once been talked into buying; and "grainy" film made Lydia wince—Lydia liked a porcelain glaze on everything, especially herself. Just who the hell was this Nouvelle Vague anyhow? Damned foreigners!

It wasn't Lydia's fault that *Cinderella* had turned into a farce, a satire with all sorts of wobbly camera effects. But Lydia had been given—and had gladly taken—full credit for the fluke success of *Cinderella Flanagan*. It was bigger than she was and now she was expected to stand up here in front of all these reporters and exchange arty chitchat with this impossible female impersonator.

"Well, our new project is, uh, well, it's going to be something entirely different." Lydia thought fast, but not fast enough. "We thought we'd get one of the new foreign directors"—there, that would put Wyn Plover in his place, wherever that was—"that big Italian, uh—"

"Which big Italian?" Miss Fulton asked.

"Oh, he's terribly famous his name is, uh . . . Isn't that maddening! It's right on the tip of my tongue! Wyn, dear, what *is* the name of that Italian director?"

"I really couldn't ssay, ssweetie," Wyn said. There! Wyn actually did have a couple of offers. He'd never need Lydia again. Just let the imperious bitch stew in her own juice.

"Justin, darling, we were talking about him only the other evening."

"Uh, *I* don't know, pussykins. The artistic department is all yours."

"Fellini?" Miss Fulton suggested ominously from the back of the room. "Antonioni?"

"Genevieve," Lydia said, considerately giving the name its French pronunciation, "*you* remember?"

The marquesa considered her sister-in-law with glazed eyes and then her head went slowly forward, downward until it hit the speakers' table with a resounding thud. The topknot of curls bounced off and sat, like a golden bird's nest, next to the empty pitcher. Flash bulbs popped.

"Wezley!" Lydia gibbered. "John Wezley! Wezley, *do* tell all of these nice people about the project."

"What project?" John Wesley said.

"Why, you know, dear. The new project. *My* project."

"I don't know anything about your project, Lydia, but *my* project is to get out of this place just as fast as I can."

With that, John Wesley rose to his feet and began to walk the length of the picture gallery. He was conscious of a terrible uproar, of men shouting, women squealing, Gretchen barking, flash bulbs exploding all around him—and of Lydia's chiffon handkerchief waving like the flag over Fort McHenry—tattered but not down. Her voice, its rich, aristocratic timbre amplified to a bull's bellow, filled the gallery: "And now shall we all have lunch?"

Departure

♣ ♧ ♣ ♧ ♣ ♧ ♣ ♧ ♣ ♧ ♣ ♧ ♣ ♧ ♣

It was a horrible taxicab. Was it a Kaiser? A Frazer? A Tucker? John Wesley did not care. It had been waiting in the driveway and it was taking him to the station.

The taxi stalled. "Motherin' heap!" the driver growled. With a phthisic wheezing and retching the car was coaxed back to life.

"Big doings at the Fennessey Foundation, eh, Jack?" the driver said.

"Too big for me, Mack."

"Fine folks, the Fennesseys. Makin' a big contribution to culture and like that. I seen about it in the paper.

"Say, don't I recall that you got some connection with the Fennessey Foundation, Jack?"

"I had."

"Well, just lemme ask ya: I got this daughter, Sandra Lee, six years old. She's takin' toe dancing and you should see that sweet little kid dance. Like a regular perfessional. A real little doll. So I says to the missus, 'Maybe we could get some money from the Fennessey Foundation to send little Sandra Lee and the missus and I to Europe to study.' And I was wondering if you could use your influence with the Fennesseys to—"

The cab screeched to a halt. John Wesley was thrown from his seat.

"Goddam women drivers. Oughta be put off the roads every last one of 'em. That dame cut right in ahead . . ."

John Wesley picked himself up from the floor. The taxi was partly in a ditch, partly out. Stopped an inch in front of it was Peggy's little red car.

"How much will that be?" John Wesley asked.

"Cantcha signal when you wanta pass, you dizzy . . ." the driver was screaming.

John Wesley opened the door and stepped out of the cab. He got into Peggy's car and silently the two of them drove off.